ZOMBIE PULP

TIM CURRAN

"Bring me the Zombies!"

—Bela Lugosi, Voodoo Man (1944)

CONTENTS

SHELTER

Doc told us to kill the electric lights because he didn't want us running the generators anymore than necessary, so we were sitting around in the shelter by candlelight, drinking and playing cards, listening to the wind howling out in the blackness. That's when Earl and Sonny came in. They'd been out sweeping the perimeter and they'd found something that turned their faces the color of old cheese, made their eyes swim in their sockets.

"What is it?" I said.

Sonny swallowed maybe three or four times, said, "It's time. It's time again."

For a second there, I didn't know what the hell he was talking about or maybe I was just pretending that I didn't. Earl had a sheet of paper in his hand. It had been tacked up to the back door of the shelter like a political flyer. In a scraggly, almost childish scrawl was written:

FRIENDS,
AUGUST 13 DELIVER THE SIX
IF YOU DO NOT WE WILL COME FOR ALL
WE WILL SKIN YOUR CHILDREN AND WEAR THEIR
ENTRAILS
D.

"What the hell is that? A joke?" Shipman asked.

The rest of us looked at each other, our eyes hooded and blank. It was no joke and we knew it. What would come to pass now would be dark and ugly.

"Who's this D-person?" Shipman asked.

"Dragna," Sonny said, but would say no more.

Shipman just didn't get it. He was one of the newbies, came in that beat-up shitheap Jesus bus out of Scranton with his ragtag bunch of survivors the week before. He seemed like an all right guy. Lonely. Scared. Just like the rest of us. Just glad to have made contact with other human beings. But Murph, of course, started feeding the poor bastard from his private stash of Jim Beam. Some people can handle the sauce and some can't. The more Shipman drank, the louder he got. He went from this mild-mannered wallflower in a bad suit to a two-fisted drinker looking for a good fight. He started telling dirty jokes, claiming that him and liquor were old friends. Said he didn't have a drinking problem—he drank, he got drunk, he threw up on himself. No problem. Murph thought that was funny. So funny he decided Shipman was all right, his kind of people. He even stopped calling him "Shitman" and referred to him by the infinitely more chummy "Shippy."

And now this. Now this.

"This ain't funny," Shipman said. "Which one of you fuckheads think this is funny?"

"Settle down," I told him.

"Fuck you," he said, just plain as day. A couple hours before the guy had to work up the nerve to ask where the can was and now he was ready to punch my head off my shoulders. His eyes were bulging, pupils glassy and black like those a mad dog. He had bared his teeth and there was a foam of white saliva on his lower lip. "You better just shut the hell up, friend, and tell me what the fuck this is about."

"Easy," Murph told him. "What you need is a taste of the Jimmy."

"The thirteenth is the day after tomorrow," Maria said, her huge dark eyes mirroring the vast abyss where her soul had once been.

Maria and Shacks looked at me and I looked at Sonny. "You better get Doc," I said.

Sonny took off down the corridor like he was simply glad to get away. I suppose he was. But Shipman was far from being pacified, Jimmy or no Jimmy. "Who the hell is this Dragna?" he demanded.

"He's the Devil," Shacks said.

2

In the air, the tension held. Heavy. Electric.

Shipman kept looking at us in turn, wanting answers but our throats were so dry we could have spit sand. Even Murph wasn't saying anything. No off-color jokes or pessimistic remarks. No wild, gamy tales about waking up in a cellar in Wichita with a half-dozen flyblown Girl Scouts dry humping him.

Shipman slammed his drink down and spilled it all over himself. "Hell is going on here? Somebody better tell me! Somebody better tell me right now!"

Murph lit a cigarette with a shaking hand. "Every now and again Wormboys demand fresh stuff. We give it to 'em, they leave us alone. That's all there is to it."

"Fresh stuff?"

"Yeah," Shacks said. "That's what they eat."

Shipman was shaking his head from side to side. "But they eat people, they goddamn well eat people."

Murph blew out a cloud of smoke and smiled at him with yellow teeth. "That's right. We offer up six of 'em. Now it's just a matter of deciding who stays and who goes."

Shipman looked horrified. The way, I suppose, we all looked when we first learned about Doc's rules of survival and what we had to pay Dragna and his army of the living dead so they'd leave us alone.

"Lottery," Earl said. "We play a lottery. All of us."

Shacks nodded. "It's the only fair way."

I shivered, thinking about the Wormboys out there trolling for meat.

My guts were knotting themselves into figure eights. Just the idea of what would come next made my blood run cold and the sap of my soul run lukewarm and rancid. *Lottery*. The idea of sacrificing our own to those things out there made me feel less than human, something that should've crawled through the slime on its belly.

We were all so wrapped up in ourselves and the possibility of "winning" the lottery, that we weren't paying attention to Shipman. I should have seen it coming. I was in the

Army once…I'd seen guys crack plenty of times towards the end. But I, like the others, had been too busy feeling sorry for myself. So nobody noticed that the blood had ran out of Shipman, left him white as ivory, that the muscles of his face were constricted and corded like a man who was on the verge of a massive coronary. And nobody noticed that mad-dog gleam or how he was pumping his fists until they were red as juicy tomatoes.

"Lottery," he said under his breath. "Lottery, my ass."

Then he moved.

And for a guy that was pissed-up and sassy and soft in the middle, he moved damned fast. He jumped up, knee catching the table and spilling drinks and cards and overturning the ashtray. Shacks made a grab for him. So did Maria. I hooked his arm and got a fist to the jaw for my trouble. Murph just started laughing. Earl didn't even flinch. Shipman bolted from the room, jogged down the corridor and threw the locks on the main door and out he went.

Into the night.

And whatever waited out there.

I went after him. God knows why I did it. I pulled my ass off the floor where he had knocked me, found my feet and sprinted after him without so much as a jack knife in my pocket to defend myself with. As I made the door, I heard Murph laughing out loud. "Two for dinner," he said.

Outside.

The parking lot was hung with shadows, they flowed and flapped like sheets on a line. The wind was blowing, hot and moist, the stillborn breath of August dog-days. It smelled like it had blown up out of a drainage ditch filled with green, rotting things. I looked this way, then that. Then I caught sight of Shipman. He was making for the Jesus bus he'd stolen from a Baptist school in Scranton. Silly bastard. Drunk, confused, still bitching and moaning under his breath about the lottery. I was younger than him, in better shape. I knew that if I turned on the juice, I could catch him before he made the bus.

That's when the lights came on.

I was about twenty feet from him and somebody, probably Maria or Earl, threw the breakers and flooded the lot with light. It was like being simultaneously slapped in the face and kicked in the ass. Just that blackness in an unbroken weave, then the light razoring it open. I couldn't see for a moment. I stumbled, dizzy, went down on one knee. When I got up, the flesh was crawling at the back of my neck because I was smelling something dirty, low, and mean. The stink of walking carrion.

A shadow stepped out of a pocket of blackness hugging the shelter itself.

A girl. A girl of maybe seven or eight in a white burial dress gone gray and ragged. She smiled at me with a flat, inhuman evil. Rats or maybe dogs had chewed the meat away from the left side of her face. There was nothing there now but sculpted gray muscle and ligament shrouding gleaming white bone. The wind blew her hair around in a wild halo. She looked up at me with a single eye that was yellow and glossy like an unfertilized egg. "Hey, mister," she said in a scraping voice. "You wanna fuck?" Then she lifted her dress, exposing a hairless corpse-white vulva of ghost-flesh that was puckering with maggots.

I think I might have screamed.

Or maybe it was Shipman doing the screaming. The Wormboys and Wormgirls had found him, ringed him like starving dogs. They came from every direction and out there in the parking lot, Shippy looked like a lone swimmer in a moonlit choppy sea surrounded by sharks. He started this way, then that, finally fell to his knees and started praying in a high, whining voice.

The dead.

It wasn't enough to wander the gutted landscape anymore searching for meat. In the two years since they'd started rising, they'd gotten clever, imaginative, and tribal. Their faces were scarred from ritualistic cutting and carving so they resembled fetish masks. Noses had rotted into hollows or been sliced clean, flesh gouged in half-moons or jagged triangles, tongues slit so they were forked, lips peeled free so gums and teeth jutted obscenely. Many had shaved heads, some peeled right down to the raw bone beneath, and others wore dangling scalp-locks greased with human fat and braided with the tiny bones of children.

Every Wormboy tribe had its own look, you might say.

The little girl was ready to leap at me and I can't say that I would've gotten clear of her. Luckily, Earl stepped out with his sawed-off twelve-gauge pump. "Smile for the camera, honey," he said.

The girl bared her teeth like a wolf moving in for the kill.

Saliva hung from her shriveled graying lips.

Earl gave her a round that splashed what was left of her face off the skull beneath. Brains, meat, and bloody mucilage splattered against the wall of the shelter and she went down in loose-limbed heap.

"C'mon!" he called to me.

The Wormboys had Shipman and he was howling like an animal being put to death. They weren't eating him or even chopping him into shanks with their machetes, they were just *biting* him. One after the other, biting and nipping, sinking in their teeth and making him suffer.

A dead woman stepped out and smiled at me.

At least, I think she was smiling.

Her face was a writhing mass of larval action, worms roiling in her eye sockets. She was naked except for a purse that she carried for some reason, and her skin was throbbing and undulant from what was feeding upon it. She held a hand out to me that was knotty and scabrous, the nails black and thorny like those of a beast. She would have gutted me cleanly with them, gutted me and stuffed herself with my entrails while I was still alive if Earl hadn't put her down.

"How's about you and me and baby makes three?" she said in a hollow voice.

The dead often say such nonsensical things, re-spooled, replayed bits of their lives, I suppose. I once had a Wormgirl dressed in the filthy cerements of a Burger King uniform ask me if I wanted cheese on my Whopper right before she tried to take my head off with an axe.

Earl killed the woman, grabbed me by the arm and dragged me into the shelter. I was shaking. I was nauseous. I was disappointed in myself because I'd frozen up out there. Mostly, I suppose, I was in shock. I stumbled blindly back to the table and Murph giggled as Maria poured bourbon into me and Shacks put a cigarette in my mouth even though I hadn't smoked in years.

"Nice going, soldier boy," Murph said.

I ignored him. It was easy. "Thanks," I said to Earl.

He grunted. "Need you for the lottery, don't we?"

Then Doc was standing there, smiling thinly down at me and shaking his head with the quiet, patient shame a man feels for a son who has brought disgrace upon him once again. "Now that wasn't a very good idea, was it, Tommy?" he said.

"I...I tried to stop him. I tried to save him."

"Fucking moron," Murph tittered.

"Shut the hell up!" Maria shouted at him. Maria came from Puerto Rico when she was a child and when her Latin temper got boiling, one look from those smoldering dark eyes of hers could peel paint from a door.

"Mr. Shipman was a loose cannon," Doc said. "He simply couldn't adapt. I was expecting him to do something like this. But I was expecting better from you, Tommy. You were a soldier. You know better than to go out alone and unarmed at night."

And he was right: I did.

The Wormboys were active day or night, true, but at night they were just a little deadlier, a little more insidious. They became crafty, wicked, using the shadows as camouflage. I'm not sure if they were technically nocturnal, but they were nasty by daylight and absolute hell after dark. I remember a guy once told me that when they reanimated, most retained a rudimentary intellect while some were unnaturally cunning, but all were driven by predatory instinctual drives. And like any beast of prey, they made the darkness their own.

I sat there wilting under Doc's gaze, but I wasn't going to give in. Maybe my tactics weren't so good, but my heart was in the right place. "I couldn't let him just...I mean, I couldn't let those things slaughter him."

Doc shook his head. "Tommy, Tommy, Tommy. You haven't been with us long enough. It takes time. Sacrifice is simply a way of life here."

"The lottery," I said.

"Yes, that's part of it."

I had been in the shelter for two months. I had never played the lottery before or marched the "winners" out into the killing fields to be trussed up for sacrifice. The idea of that sickened me.

"You can't do it, Doc. You can't hand your own people over to those fucking monsters."

"I have to."

I slammed a hand on the table. "It's sick! It's cold blooded! You can't do it! You just can't do it!"

"It has to be done, Tommy."

Maria was holding my hand and Shacks was patting my back, making me part of them, I guess. But I didn't want to be part of...of *that*. "Goddammit, Doc. We can fight. We have guns. We can fight."

"Thirty-seven of us against thousands of them?" He shook his head again. "No, it would be a massacre. It would be the Little Big Horn all over again. We must survive by any means necessary. At whatever cost. It is our only reason for existing now."

Thousands of them. I didn't doubt that...but how could an offering of six every so many months keep thousands full and happy? I put that to Doc.

"It's a symbolic offering, Tommy. That's all. Dragna lets us live as long as we choose who dies. It's simple as that."

"Dragna's a fucking monster," was all I could say. "And so are you."

Doc just smiled and left the room, calmly as ever, and I sat there, something running hot inside me. "He's a fucking animal," I said, not really meaning it, but meaning it all the same. "How can he do it? How can he?"

"He does what he has to do," Shacks said.

Murph chuckled. "That's life in the big city, Tommy. Get used to it. Get used to watching your friends die."

I just shook my head, trying to clear the stink of that Wormgirl from my mind. "But Doc...he's so...so *cold* about it."

"Do you think so?" Maria said. "Well, he doesn't ask anything of us he doesn't ask of himself."

"Really?" I said, the sarcasm so thick in my voice you could have caulked a window with it.

She nodded. "Yes. Tomorrow it might be you or me, Tommy, but last year, last year before you arrived...it was his wife. She won the lottery."

"And he marched her out?"

"Damn straight he did," Shacks said, his eyes shiny and wet. "I was there. I saw it. He marched her out and tied her to the post. And when they came to take her, he pretended he couldn't hear her screaming."

3

It was Doc who set up the shelter.

And like scattered metal filings drawn to a magnet, we came from every direction and he took us in like a crazy old lady collecting stray cats. See, Doc was an extremely practical man. He'd worked for the CDC years before the world shit its pants

8

and the dead started rising. He knew sooner or later one of those nasty bugs the CDC field teams were always studying in remote places like Ghana and Zaire was going metastasize and become an infectious plague of biblical proportions.

So he took precautions.

He bought up an abandoned Air Guard weather station in Carbon County, PA. It dated from the Cold War and had a control center made out of reinforced concrete and steel with a bomb shelter below that could hold sixty people. Using his own money and financial support from a few wealthy friends with like minds, he updated the structure, put in dorms and a dining hall, generators, an air filtration system and a water purification plant. He supplied it with freeze-dried foods and military MREs, medical equipment, survival gear, you name it.

And then it happened.

A mutant virus appeared out of nowhere and mimicked the symptomology of pneumonic plague. Spread by a variety of vectors including the wind, the water, insect bites, and human contact, it ravaged the world. Within sixteen weeks, the world population was reduced nearly two-thirds by all estimates and then with the resulting collapse of the ruling political, industrial, and military infrastructure, there was only chaos. People got sick, they died, the world fell apart...and then the most incredible thing happened: the dead came out of their graves.

And they were hungry.

Nobody knew where the virus came from, not really, but there were lots of theories. Most claimed it had more than a little to do with the BIOCOM-13 satellite which had been sampling the upper atmosphere for alien microbes, was cored by a meteorite, and crashed outside Clovis, New Mexico. Clovis was the first city in the world to become a graveyard. But after that, they all went.

As it turned out, a great many people were immune to the virus. And one by one they began showing up in Carbon County. Doc and his boys gathered up as many as they could. Maria came from Pittsburgh and Shacks from Philly; Sonny came from Newark and Murph drifted in from Delaware. Earl had been one of the first and he was still there. Me, I barely escaped Buffalo. And they kept coming: New England, the Midwest, even the deep South. Some died, some were killed, some went by disease, and others were taken by the Wormboys.

And still others won the lottery and were culled. But more always came. Always.

There were nearly forty people in the shelter now...what was six to save the lot?

What was six?

Yeah, that Doc was really something.

He gathered his flock, he tended them, fed and fattened them, kept them safe and sound. Then somewhere along the way he made a deal with the Devil and the Devil's name was Dragna. Nobody seemed to know shit about Dragna other than the fact that he or *it* had wielded together dozens and dozens of zombie tribes into a single cohesive unit that was about as close to an army as you were going to get this side of the global holocaust. He was to the Wormboys and Wormgirls what Dracula was to bloodsuckers, more or less.

Somehow, someway, Doc had struck a bargain of sorts with this monster.

So every few months, Dragna demanded his payment, his protection money, like a good little extortionist from hell. And as long as Doc and his people played ball, there was safety. But the day we didn't, Dragna would send his troops in by the thousands.

Yeah, Doc. Good old Doc. Father, therapist, priest, general, saint and prophet to those of us in the shelter. He was essentially good, essentially kind. He took care of everything from keeping his people busy to feeding and clothing them and delivering their babies and even presiding over makeshift weddings now and again. Everyone looked up to him. Everyone loved him. Everyone respected him. They did what he said and obeyed his rules and he kept them alive and somewhat sane.

With the good he did it was easy to forget he also created the lottery.

And in my mind that made him flawed, less than human. He was the farmer and we were the livestock. He raised us like pigs and brought us to slaughter come season.

And because of that, I hated him as much as I loved him.

4

That night—the night before the lottery—I came out of a very thin, nightmare-haunted sleep to the sound of a crash and a blaring car horn. Two minutes later, still dragging on my clothes, my mind fuzzy with some dream of absolute darkness

10

and absolute death, I found Sonny up in the tower watching the action out in the parking lot through the observation port. The tower rose up thirty feet above the lot and it was the only part of the shelter that still had a window—shatter-proof and bullet-proof—but still a window.

"Hell's going on?" I said.

"See for yourself."

Sonny had the parking lot lit but I almost wished he hadn't bothered. Apparently, a few more had decided to make a run for the shelter. This time it looked to be four people in a little minivan. What the circumstances were, I didn't know, but they must have panicked when they saw all the Wormboys and Wormgirls hanging around the perimeter in drooling wolf packs. That must've been what made them drive at the shelter itself. Unfortunately for them and very fortunately for us, Doc with his infinite foresight had had a series of concrete barriers erected around the shelter so no one could ever breach it in such a way.

That minivan slammed right into one of them and it must have been putting out some speed when it did because the front end was smashed-in, the hood crumpled into a V. I could see spiderwebbed sheets of glass and spilled fluids on the pavement. As it was, the minivan looked like a cracked open egg and what had crawled out were four people. A saw a guy with shattered legs crawling towards the shelter, leaving a trail of something dark behind him. A woman was screaming nearby, holding her face in her hands. She was reaching out towards a cluster of the walking dead as if there was mercy in those cold, reptilian brains. One of them, a woman in a pink dress, took her down. Even from the tower I could see the clouds of flies rising from her.

"We have to do something," I said.

Sonny pulled off his cigarette. "Doc and Earl are at the front door. Any of 'em make it that far they'll bring 'em in."

"Yeah, but—"

"No, Tommy. Use your fucking head for once. Wormboys are everywhere. Anybody that goes out there is meat, nothing but meat."

He was right, of course. I knew he was right but even at that point I simply was not as hard and cold as Sonny and the rest of them. God knows I should have been after some of the awful shit I had seen, but even through it all there was hope and humanity and pity still flowering in me like sweet green shoots rising from the cracked, blackened soil of a graveyard.

I ran downstairs and found Doc and Earl waiting for survivors to make the door, but none had. They just looked at me, said nothing. They knew what I was thinking and Earl had his shotgun up. If I tried to throw the deadbolts and locks he would have killed me without a second thought.

I knew it.

He knew it.

Doc knew it.

I looked out the gunport slit and I could see the action just fine. The Wormboys were coming from every direction, waxy faces like melting goat curds or rippling papier-mache. A hot steam of rot rose from them in a sickening, churning mist. Some of them were walking, but others had crawled from ditches and pockets of shadow and many of them were missing limbs. I saw headless trunks. Severed hands. What looked like a rolling head. A woman whose flesh looked like it had been boiled saw me watching her and turned, shambling over towards the door. Her eyes were slimy rotten eggs bulging from raw red sockets, her face a worm carnival. She thrust her backside at me and lifted the ragged remains of her dress. Something like a gushing stream of rice pissed out from between her legs.

I turned away, barely able to keep my stomach down.

"You don't need to be here, Tommy," Doc said. "Why don't you go back to your room?"

"Those people need help."

"Yes, they do. And if it's at all possible, we'll help them."

"Mister Bleeding fucking Heart," Earl said.

I ignored him. Out there the zombies were feeding on the injured, but one guy was still pretty spry. He must have slipped out of the van after the crash but ran off in the wrong direction. Now he was coming back. He came vaulting across the lot. Two Wormboys made a grab for him but they weren't fast enough. He darted past another and jumped over a couple crawlers.

In my mind I was with him, pumped with excitement at the idea that he would make it. It was like the good old days, watching Earl Campbell charging into the flak, flattening defenders, jumping, spinning, ducking, whirling around, but never, ever losing his consistent forward momentum.

He was no more than twenty feet from the door when three Wormboys got in his way and he broke to the right, tripped over a crawling husk, and went down. They converged on him from every side, literally covering him in their numbers. I heard him scream with a brilliant, piercing cry of absolute defilement.

But it wasn't him at all.

It was the woman. The Wormboys had her and they were killing her a bit at a time, tearing out handfuls of flesh, biting into her, nibbling and nipping. I saw her face before it sank away in that carrion ocean. The pain, the horror...it had driven her mad. She clawed her eyes out with bloody fingers.

I turned away and got up real close and personal with Doc. "We could have saved that guy. We could have charged out there and dropped some of them, cut him a path to the door."

"Not without endangering our community," Doc said.

I glared at him. "You're a fucking asshole," I said and then went back to my room, helpless, hopeless, desperate. I was filled with a black concrete weight that was sinking me day by day.

5

The lottery.

Doc gathered us up in the dining hall because it was the only place big enough to hold us all. Everyone was there, of course. All of us except the children. There were fourteen kids in the shelter ranging from teenagers to infants. But thank God Doc left them out of this sordid mess. This was a party for adults and you should have seen them—eyes staring, faces sweating, hands trembling. Some chain-smoking until the air fumed over in a blue haze and others mumbling prayers over and over again until you wanted to kick their teeth out. Jesus. What a scene.

Then Doc showed up, smiling that plastic smile of his that made me bleed inside. "This isn't anything we enjoy," he said. "But it's something we have to do and I think we all know that."

Nobody agreed or disagreed with that and I couldn't even look at that prim, proper, fatherly butcher because the sight of him made my skin crawl. Maria and I sat side by side, holding hands. Shacks was with us. Sonny, too. Murph was there...only he was scared white and he couldn't even muster a pale shiteating grin or a nasty remark.

Doc held out a cigar box. "There are twenty-three slips of paper in here, folded. One for each adult here in the shelter. Six of these papers have an 'X' on them and you all know what those mean. Now, one by one—"

"Yeah, yeah, yeah, Doc," some guy named Corey said. "We know the drill. Just get to it already. I'm about to have fucking kittens here."

A woman next to him who'd come in with Shipman made a sound that was somewhere between laughter and sobbing, a brittle sort of sound like something had just shattered in her throat.

"Well, then," Doc said. "Well."

Earl and two other guys—Jerome Conroy, an ex-cop, and Ape, an ex-biker—stood by the exit with shotguns. Both of them had seen their share of violence before the dead started rising and plenty since. But neither liked the job Doc had given them: security. It was human nature to bolt and run when you were handed a death sentence and they were there to see that no one did.

Doc, smiling like a tentshow preacher, all teeth and gums, walked around with his cigar box. He took out his slip of paper first. Then one by one we all dipped into that Pandora's Box. The paper was heavy vellum and you couldn't see through it. Couldn't know until you unfolded it.

Corey was the first to say, "I'm staying! You hear that? I'm fucking staying!"

He was joined by three others, including Shacks, who could make the same boast. The woman who was sitting by Corey unfolded hers and stood straight up like something hot had just been jabbed up her ass. She held out her paper and there was an X on it. She was trembling so badly she nearly fell over.

She was chosen.

Corey and the others moved away from her like she had something catchy.

Only Doc went to her, put an arm around her, said, "I'm so sorry, Mrs. Pearson." She fell limp into his arms.

Then everybody was unfolding their papers and looking at them. Some, like Sonny, jumped up and danced for joy. "Knew it wouldn't be me. Shit, yes." Others cried out. One guy fainted dead away. And another guy shook his paper in the air, saying, "Praise the Lord, I have been chosen. Praise the lord." Then he fell to his knees and began sobbing uncontrollably. It was a nightmare. People dancing. People hugging and kissing, others on the floor, moaning and whimpering. People came and went at the shelter and I did not know all of them that well. But I knew what all of them thought every day: *if I can just get through the lottery one more time, I'll make plans to get out. I won't flirt with death twice.* Yes, that's what they told themselves because I told myself something very similar. If I can just get through it this one time, then I'll get out. I won't do it again. This was my first one. But many of them had played this sick game several times. People like Murph and Earl and Doc himself. And human optimism being as deluding as it is, they all told themselves that this would be their last time, that they would get through it and leave.

But very few of them did.

What took place in that room during the next fifteen minutes was more horrible than anything I had ever witnessed up to that point and I'd seen plenty. For the zombies are monsters, ghouls, predatory things like starving dogs that will use every ounce of instinct, subterfuge, and animal cunning to get the flesh they need to fill their empty bellies. They have an excuse for their savagery. We, however, did not. We were normal, uninfected, rational human beings and yet we were willing to play that perverse game, to sacrifice our own, anything to get a few more weeks of life.

The lottery was the greatest evil I had ever known.

Five sacrifices had been chosen.

One more.

Sighing, I unfolded my paper and as I did so some fatalistic urge within me hoped there would be an X on it so this nightmare would end and I wouldn't have to live with myself, with the guilt that would come unfettered and sharp-toothed when I knew I had lived at the expense of others. Because it *would* come for me. There was no doubt of that. Like an unquiet ghost it would visit me in the dead of night, wrap its icy hands around my throat and throttle me awake, sweating and shaking, and there in the darkness I would have to face myself: all the evils I had done coming home to brood in my soul there in the midnight hour.

My slip of paper was blank.

I didn't jump for joy. I felt...neutral, not happy and not sad, just...*nothing*. I felt like an empty can, to tell you the truth. A vessel, I guess, that every drop had been poured from. There was nothing left in me.

At that moment, as I tried to get a grip on what I was feeling, Murph rose up from his seat like he had suddenly been inflated. He did not stand up, he *rose* like a column of hot air. We all turned and looked at him and we all knew, of course. "I got picked," he said in a flat voice. "You hear me, you assholes? I got picked. *Me.*"

He fumbled a pack of cigarettes from his shirt pocket, tearing at the cellophane with clawing, fumbling, apelike fingers. He dropped two cigarettes, then a third, got the fourth between his lips and lit it. His face was oval like a moon, speckled in sweat, his eyes darting wildly in their sockets. He started laughing and he couldn't seem to stop. Smoke drifted from his mouth and nostrils in a halo that enveloped his perspiring, bright red face and made him look like a cartoon devil.

"AHH-HA-HA-HA," he went at the top of his voice. "AH-HA-HA-HA-HAAAAAH!"

"Murph," Doc said, coming over to him, wanting to smother him in empathy and goodwill, give him the speech about sacrificing for the good of all. He even reached out his arms right before Murph—not laughing now, his face hooked in a snarl of animal hate—bunched his fist into a ball and gave old Doc a shot right in the belly that folded him up to the floor.

Doc's goons, Sonny and Earl and Conroy and that monkey-grinning slab of shit Ape, charged in and beat Murph to the ground and he took it. He did not even try to fend off the blows that came for him. He accepted them like they were his inheritance. He lay there on the floor, sobbing and trembling, curled up in the fetal position. The goons had to drag him out the door and by then nobody was saying a goddamn thing. You should have seen the self-satisfied, greedy fuck-you-I got-mine looks in their eyes like fat-bellied rats that had found another crumb to gnaw on that would keep them safe one more day.

This is what it had come to.

The germ had taken the good people and many of them were wandering around outside the shelter looking for food. What remained behind were the people in that room—writhing human worms squirming in the smelly dungball of the world.

They made me sick.

And the sad part was, I was *one* of them.

6

Doc's sacrifices—his selections of juicy pink meat for the Wormboys—were set to be marched out the next night. They were separated from the general population...*put in isolation,* as Doc called it. Why? I don't know. Did they pose a threat to us? Did we pose a threat to them? Or was Doc just afraid that if we had to look on them and see what was in their eyes, that depthless pain and desperation, that we might start acting like human beings again? That we might feel some intrusive, obstructive things like pity and remorse and remember that culture, true culture, was built upon morality, ethics, and *compassion?*

In order for civilization to function, you see, people must act *civilized.*

Doc was nothing if not a student of human psychology by that point. He was probably worried that the whole cloth of his little disenfranchised community might start to unravel thread by thread once we stopped worrying about our own skins and realized exactly what we were doing to those poor people.

I had it out with him as he knew I would, being the bleeding heart goody two-shoes that I am. Basically, I argued that if we were condemning those people to a horrible death, the least we could do is let them *be* human beings with all that entails for the last day or so of their lives.

"Tommy, Tommy, Tommy," he said, as if he were addressing a particularly stupid child. "Do you have any idea the trouble that would cause?"

"No, but I'm sure you're going to tell me."

He smiled thinly at that: paternal, patient, a just and loving god. "Tommy, these people need to face this together. I feel as you do for them, but misguided pity at this point will only make it harder on them and us. Nobody forced them to play the lottery. They did it of their own free will."

"They did it out of fear," I said. "Fear that you'd throw them out to the living dead if they didn't."

"We have to have rules or we have no society."

"This isn't a society," I said, "it's a fucking zoo."

Doc just smiled patiently at me. "No, it's a community, Tommy. We survive by working towards a common goal and thinking as one. When we lose that, it's all over. Now...this isn't a prison or a cult. If you're unhappy, feel free to leave. We'll give you a rifle, food, you can even take one of the vehicles out there." Then he leaned in close so I could see that beyond the fatherly warmth in his eyes there was something fierce and steel-gray as a gathering storm. "But if you walk out of here, Tommy, don't ever think you can come back. You won't be welcome."

I just sat there, filled with too many emotions.

"Well?"

I stayed.

7

It was about eight that night when I heard a high trebly scream cut through the compound. I was in bed with Maria and I jumped up and nearly threw her to the floor. All I could hear was that pitiful cry and then I was pulling on my pants and shirt and boots and stumbling down the corridor, my heart pounding in my throat.

I heard the scream again and then I saw Earl stumbling in my direction, near the main entrance, and Ape was backing away from him like he had the plague.

Earl let loose with another shriek of pitiful wailing and I saw he was clasping his stomach and that his hands were red and glistening. "Help me...I'm cut...oh god...I'm *fucking cut...*"

He went down to his knees, moaning and sobbing, the entire front of his shirt like a blossom of blood. By then, dozens of feet were running in our direction, people shouting out to know what was happening, if the Wormboys had breeched the shelter.

It was about then that Murph came vaulting towards us, loping out of the shadows like a big monkey. His face was huge and shiny like a new moon, his teeth gleaming ice. He had a knife in his hand and there was blood right up to his elbow.

Ape watched him run by.

He had a shotgun in his hands, but he'd apparently forgotten how to use it as Murph threw the locks on the door and pulled it open, frantic and enraged and filled with the need to flee like an animal fresh from a cage. "FREEDOM!" he cried into the darkness out there. "FREEDOM! AH-HA-HA-HA-HA! FREE AT LAST! FREE AT LAST!"

He dashed out into the night, fading into the shadows while we all stood around gape-jawed and wide-eyed with our thumbs most surely shoved up our asses. I don't know how far he got, but I heard a grunting sound out there and something splatter over the pavement and then the hysterical, screeching of the undead as they began to feed with sucking and chewing sounds.

"CLOSE THAT DOOR!" Doc cried out, stumbling up the corridor. "FOR THE LOVE OF GOD—"

You would have thought it would be our first reaction, but it wasn't. We were still wired in place with shock and bewilderment and surprise. I was one of the first to even attempt it and as I moved towards that rectangle of darkness and those positively hideous sounds of slobbering mouths beyond, I caught sight of Maria's face. It was twitching with horror.

I heard a sound like the buzzing of malarial larvae and felt a dank envelope of rot come blowing in from outside. When I turned, *she* was standing there; one of the Wormgirls was in the doorway bringing the cool, putrescent stink of the night in with her.

Somebody screamed.

Earl made a gurgling sound as his mouth filled with blood.

Just about everyone made a quick and hasty retreat but Maria, myself, Doc and Ape. And Earl, of course, because he wasn't going anywhere that didn't feature harps and pearly gates.

The Wormgirl took two lumbering steps in my direction and her feet made slow, oozing, squishing noises like sponges saturated with syrup. She was a large woman, distended with gas to the point that it looked like she was nine months along. Her face was crawling green pulp and there were so many flies on her you could see very little else beyond one glistening red suckered hole for an eye. I think what we all saw—and wished to God we hadn't—was that her genitals were swollen blue with decay, the labia puffed out and drooping like the udders of a cow. She reached out a hand towards me. It wasn't a violent seizing motion like most of them would do...it was almost gentle and caressing and maybe I might even have accepted it as such if her hand wasn't a writhing larval mass, massive nodules and blisters popping with yellow gas.

I fell away from her and Maria pulled me back.

There was a moist smacking sound and a hole opened in her face that must have been a mouth, strings of tissue webbing the lips together. Her tongue was a bloated flap of maggots. When she spoke it sounded like her mouth was full of warm gruel. But as bad as that was, what she said was somehow worse: *"Going...to the chapel...and I'm...going to get...marrrieeeeed."* And that barely even left her mouth in her slopping, regurgitive voice when Ape opened up on her with his twelve-gauge pump, firing not only out of fear but pure, unreasoning disgust.

He blew holes in her big enough to pass your arm through. Flesh that had the consistency of gelatin blew off her, revealing rungs of rib, a pelvic wing, a ladder of spinal vertebrae. He kept pumping and shooting and she made a sort of globby, mewling sound as she came apart in a cyclone of meat and black blood, gray ooze and suppurating tissue like rice pudding, leaking piss and shit and yolky egg-like masses of tangled red graveworms. Before she went down into a seething mass of carrion and plumes of corpse-gas, something fell from between her legs and splashed to the floor.

I saw it.

We all did.

A rubbery doll-like form...a cross between a human infant and a bloated white coffin-worm. It squirmed free of the slime and ichor. It looked up at me with a face like a glistening grub, reaching out with yellow-green gelid fingers.

That's what I saw right before Ape blew it in half and then in thirds and then I could not be certain I wasn't looking at a colony of undulant maggots.

The woman hit the floor in a splattering of meat and fluid and a flyblown, acrid stink that nearly reamed my nose out.

But we were hardly done.

The above nightmare probably only lasted a minute or two, but the entire time the door was open to the night and what waited out there. They were crowded outside the door by then: graying, gibbering ghost faces—dozens of them—that looked less like dead humans than the carven ritualistic masks of Chinese festival demons. Another sect of the undead with their own look: I saw bald, mottled heads, viscid yellow-silver eyes sitting in carved, up-tilted pits, noses fallen into skullish hollows, faces elaborately cut and scarified into braided, convoluting patterns, the corners of mouths slit up to cheekbones...all of it creating the gruesome effect of grinning death fetishes.

These were Wormgirl's boyfriends, her suitors and lovers, maybe.

Then Ape kicked the door shut and without even thinking, I was throwing locks and muttering nonsensical prayers under my breath.

Then we stood around in the remains of Wormgirl and her progeny, seeped to the skin in a noisome membrane of rot. We had averted disaster...but just barely.

8

Once we had shoveled out the remains of our visitor and incinerated them, scrubbed down the entry with caustic antiseptics, and disposed of Earl's corpse, we were faced with a new problem. Murph had been number six in the lottery and that meant we had to play again. We had to go through that insanity again scarcely a day later. Usually, there was a month and sometimes three, I was told, but here we were again, gearing up to play Doc's sadistic little game and learn all about the creepy-crawly things that lived inside each other's heads.

There was nothing quite like the lottery to bring them slithering out.

Maria and Shacks were probably the only two that were on my side, ready to mount an armed insurrection at my say so. But I wasn't saying so. What I didn't want here was some violent purge that would not only destroy Doc's half-assed utopian society but leave a trail of bodies. These people had to simply refuse to play. I was pretty sure that Ape and Sonny and Conroy, Doc's would-be goons, would stand with us if it came to that. They were not evil men any more than the rest of us. They were scared, is all. They were following Doc because Doc had a plan and they had spent their lives as good little soldiers doing what they were told. None of them were particularly well-practiced in the smarts department.

But like I said, I didn't want bloodshed.

And if I swung them my way...what then? I had no plan other than a half-baked possibly suicidal idea of us loading up in the trucks and buses outside and making a run up for Canada. I had a feeling the Wormboys and Wormgirls and all the wriggling, drooling Wormkids wouldn't do real well in sub-zero temperatures when their limbs started locking up.

I was your basic anarchist in that I wanted to destroy the government but once everything lay in ruin I had no idea what to do next.

So lacking a cohesive plan we went about business as usual.

We played the lottery.

21

Again, the same scene: a group of shifty-eyed, borderline neurotic people packed into the dining hall, whispering, praying, chain-smoking, or just staring into space with a steely silence that spoke volumes. You could smell the stale sweat, the feverish anxiety, a fear that was bright and hot coming off every one of them and I had to wonder if that's what it smelled like in those packed cattle cars bound for places like Treblinka and Sobibor during World War II. There was very little talking. Now and then a peal of almost hysterical laughter that was sharp as a pin would break out amongst the condemned.

Because we *were* condemned, you know.

Each and every one of us who stayed and played that awful fucking game were most definitely condemned. It was only a matter of when sentence would be passed.

Before we filed in there, Shacks pulled me aside and said, "I keep thinking about the things you're saying, Tommy...I mean, *really* thinking about them. Maybe I never did before. Maybe I never wanted to. But...but to be tied up out there, *alive*, while those things feed on you...Jesus."

And that's exactly what needed to happen: every one these goddamn scared rabbits in Doc's personal warren needed to do some thinking. Some real thinking. They just couldn't go on like this, hiding behind a crumbling wall of denial that it would never happen to them while their odds dwindled and dwindled.

I sat by Maria and stared at Doc. "Well, let's get going, Doc. Let's find out whose ass is raw meat."

"Tommy—"

"Why don't you shut up?" Sonny said.

"You think they start with your throat or your balls?" I asked him. "Which do they bite into first?"

Ape glared at me with full menace and I smiled at him. "You better cold-cock me, asshole, because I won't shut up. But don't damage me...Dragna likes his cold cuts fresh and chewy."

An elderly woman named Peggy began to sob and her husband made a low wailing sound that put chills up everyone's spine: it was the sound of bitter, broken finality, of life accepting death and it was eerie.

"Please everyone," Doc said. He cast me a look that tried unbelievably hard to be tolerant and sage, but it was wearing thin and Doc was getting very fucking sick of me and my mouth. I think as far as he was concerned, I was guilty of treason and sedition. He was probably hoping that I'd draw the X and he'd be rid of me.

The cigar box made the rounds.

People either tore them open with a mad, suicidal glee or held them out in trembling fingers like they were poisonous spiders.

"Hallelujah!" Sonny cried out in the giddy voice of a nine year old on Christmas morning, born again on the spot. "It's not me! It's not me!"

"Me either!"

"My skin is saved! Ha! I'm staying!"

I can't say that they were all as piggish, crude, and insensitive. Many just took the verdict quietly and calmly with a modicum of self-respect. But others jumped for joy, pigs wallowing in the full glory of their filth.

One by one by one, people held out empty pieces of paper. There were only two that had not had been checked and those belonged to Maria and I. The knowledge of that nearly suffocated me. I felt sweat break open on my face, the neurons of my brain ready to overload and burn out.

All eyes were on us...there was pity in them and guilt. But in some there was a twisted, vicious euphoria. It wasn't *them* so now it was a game to see who went on the spit, high drama and nail-biting suspense.

Maria and I looked at each other and the others pressed in, *all of them now*, eyes wide and shining, licking their lips, some of them nearly drooling. They were eager for it, I tell you. *Hungry* for it. Like crazed villagers filled with manic glee at the idea of burning one of their own as a witch. I saw the innate brutality and bestiality of the human race at that moment.

And I hated.

God, how I hated.

I swore to myself then and there that I would kill each and everyone of them if I got the chance. I prayed it would be me. I really did. But even before I opened my slip I knew it would be blank. And it was. Maria opened hers, smiled thinly, held up her slip with the X on it. "It's me," she said quite calmly. "I'm the one. I'm chosen."

Everyone sighed...that unbroken circuit of tension died.

They were all safe and the fun was over.

But, without knowing it, they had just signed their own death warrants.

Doc decided to soften the rules.

Maybe after the Murph thing he saw that he had to and I guess I looked on him a little more compassionately because he did so. He did not cull Maria off. He did not lock her in a cell or put her into isolation. He let her and the other five have twenty-four hours in which to come to terms with themselves and their maker. Nobody guarded the doors during that time. If you were chosen and you decided to run, take your chances with the hordes of Wormboys, nobody would stop you. Dragna would have his six either way. But the most amazing and frightening thing of all was how many *didn't*. How many just accepted it and walked willingly out into the killing fields.

I guess that says something about the human condition I don't even want to contemplate.

Later, I was alone with Maria in her room. I don't think she was ever lovelier than that night...her long black hair, her big dark eyes, her smooth olive skin. I told her we would run together. We would fight our way out and make a life for ourselves somewhere, somehow.

But she simply shook her head. "No, Tommy. What is done is done."

I wanted to slap her, to beat her unconscious and steal away with her while there was still time. But mostly I wanted to hold her and never let go. The tears came. I hadn't cried in a long time, but I did then.

Maria looked at me and owned me with her eyes. "You can do one thing for me, Tommy," she said, as strong and persevering as only those of Latin blood can possibly be.

"Anything," I said, still trying hard not to sob and failing miserably.

She touched my cheek, tracing the track of a tear from my eye to the corner of my lips with one long finger. "You can spend the night with me. You can make me feel like a real woman one last time, like a human being."

She fell into my arms and I melted into her as quick.

The next morning I found Doc in his little office. He looked surprised to see me. He knew I had something to say and he kept quiet, waited until I worked it out and laid it at his feet.

"I want to be part of it," I said.

"Part of what, Tommy?"

"You know. The lottery."

"You were."

I shook my head. "You don't understand. I want to go with Sonny and Conroy and Ape when they march them out tonight. I want to be part of that."

"Tommy—"

"No, listen, Doc. Maria is my friend. I love her. I think she loves me. I don't want her going out there alone without a friend. She needs me to be there. To...to see her off. She needs it. So do I. I don't think I can ever be part of this unless you let me."

He sighed. "Tommy, I don't think it's a good idea."

Before he spent twenty minutes trying to steer me around to his way of thinking, I said, "I know I've been a pain in the ass, Doc. I know I've been nothing but trouble...but this isn't easy. You gotta understand how hard all this is for me. For all of us. Just let me do this. This is something I need."

Doc just stared at me for a time like he was trying to read what was in my mind, but I had it locked up tight as a vault. He was not getting in there. I emoted sincerity mixed with pain and confusion, grief and loss. But certainly nothing rebellious.

Doc started to shake his head, then he just sighed. "Are you sure, Tommy? Are you sure this is what you want?"

I nodded. "More than anything."

Poor Doc. He was such a fucking fool. Always in charge. Always having to deal with it all. I almost felt sorry for him at that moment. "Okay, Tommy. If it's what you want. Go ahead."

"Thanks, Doc. This means a lot to me."

He smiled and patted my hand like a favored uncle and I left his office. In the corridor I started grinning. None of them knew it, but I was about to bring hell down on each and every one of them.

12

We marched the six out exactly one hour after dark that night.

Sonny, Conroy, Ape, and me. We were all armed with pump shotguns and .9mm sidearms. Ape had an Army-issue flamethrower strapped to his back that he had looted from an armory. We were ready to defend ourselves if need be, but it wouldn't come to that. The lottery didn't work that way. We were the meat-bringers, so to speak, and you don't kill the steward that sets your table.

Ape and Sonny led the way out to the killing fields, Conroy and me in the back, the chosen ones sandwiched in-between. Maria was there, of course. Mrs. Pearson, a young woman named Sylvia whose husband was in the shelter. Three men—Johnson, Hill, and Keeson. They all had the same dead-eyed look of manic desperation in their eyes and to look into them was to know the depths of hell and how hot it burned.

I wasn't naïve.

I knew that Doc did not trust me anymore than I really trusted him or any of the others. That's why Conroy was stationed behind me. If I caused trouble, I wouldn't be coming back.

The killing fields are an easy city block out past the shelter and the parking lot. Like the name implies, just a field. Nothing but grass and a number of wooden poles speared into the ground. I'm not sure what their use was back in the good old days of the weather station, but now they had been put to an extremely dark purpose. As we walked into the grass, a ghost of moon began to rise. And as it did, there came a rumbling, a pounding, a rhythmic hammering from somewhere out in the hills that surrounded us. It was a jarring, discordant sound that echoed around inside your skull. It was like those voodoo drums in old movies, but much more primitive.

"Hell's that?" I said.

"Wormboys," Sonny said. "Tonight's the night and they know it. They're getting excited. They're celebrating and beating their drums."

They weren't drums, of course. The Wormboys were pounding on garbage cans and twenty-five gallon drums, crates and barrels, anything handy. Just the sound of it made my guts crawl up the back of my throat.

"Doesn't it ever stop?" I said.

"Sure...later," he told me. "Keep walking."

Ten minutes later, we were at the killing fields. The shadows had grown long and we had to use our flashlights to do what had to be done. The poles sat atop a low hill, splintered and cracked, leaning this way and that. There were eight of them, but we only needed the six. I couldn't get the image out of my head that this was like some kind of pagan sacrificial altar or sacred Druidic grove for secret offerings to primordial, hungry gods. Maybe that's what it was.

When we got the chosen up there, Mrs. Pearson fell to the ground and began crying and wailing, begging for her life. Anything, anything, she said. She would give us anything if we would only spare her. Sonny tried to explain to her that it wasn't us, but them, the Wormboys. I've never seen anything so pathetic, so pitiful in my life, as that poor woman on her hands and knees in the pale moonlight. I was already angry, but this cinched it.

"Chain 'em up," Conroy said.

I chained up Johnson like a good little Nazi and that seemed to relax Conroy a bit. The others, at this final moment, began to fight and Ape and Sonny and Conroy had their hands full trying to chain them up. I led Maria over to the farthest pole while the others fought and cried out.

"Get her chained!" Conroy called to me over his shoulder. "Fuck you waiting for?"

Maria looked at me with such serenity it squeezed tears from my eyes. She did not fight. She waited for me, the guy who loved her, to murder her. Because that's what I was doing and nobody could tell me different. Oh, she had talked herself into some half-assed Christian martyrdom like some fool saint dying for the good of all. But what she failed to realize is that her god had died with civilization.

"Chain's broke," I said.

"Dammit," Ape said.

Maria looked at me, shook her head, but I lashed out and shoved her to the ground. "You're not going anywhere," I told her like I meant it. Sonny came over, having finally gotten Keeson secured. All I could hear were those makeshift drums pounding in the distance and the rattling of those chains like something from a medieval dungeon. Conroy and Ape were still having a hell of a time with Sylvia and Hill who fought with everything they had and Mrs. Pearson who'd gone limp as a rag.

I heard Sonny's boots crunching through the summer straw grass. The night had come and it seemed impossibly clean and cool, the moon brooding above ghostly white like the eye of a corpse, frosting everything in wan phosphorescence. I heard crickets chirping, nightbirds screeching in the sky. It was a surreal scene. My throat was dry as wood shavings, my eyes wide, an electric sort of alertness thrumming in my veins. I felt something rise in me, something dark and ancient and unbelievably certain of itself. It filled my brain with reaching shadows, eclipsed things like reason and morality.

"What's the problem?" Sonny wanted to know.

"Right here," I said and brought my .9mm up and stuck it right in his face. His eyes rolled in their sockets, stark and mad. I squeezed the trigger and popped three rounds right into him. He jerked back like he had been kicked and landed in the grass, blood that was almost black bubbling from the ruin of his face.

"Tommy!" Maria shouted and I knocked her clear.

Conroy brought up his shotgun and I fell to the ground and popped off a couple wild rounds that weren't so wild because one of them shattered his left kneecap and he folded up like a lawn chair, dropping his shotgun and screaming in pain. Ape brought up his flamethrower, but maybe seeing how close I was to Sonny, he didn't use it. He was a big man, but extremely fast and extremely lethal. He had a bead on me, it seemed, before I could even aim in his direction. He yelled at me and would have torched me, but Sylvia rushed him, hit him like a train. She couldn't have been more than 110 pounds, but she hit him hard. Hard enough to throw him off balance. He squeezed the trigger and a gout of flame lit up the field.

He missed.

I didn't.

I cored him twice in the belly and when he went down, Sylvia and Hill and Mrs. Pearson went at him like animals. As pumped and blood-maddened as I was, it even made me take a step back. Gut-shot and pissing blood into the grass and in considerable agony, Ape couldn't fight back and they rushed in, kicking and kicking him. Maria cried out for them to stop but they did not stop. There was only the grunting, growling sounds they made and the sound of their boots thudding into him.

When they backed away, I went over and stripped the flamethrower from him. He was unconscious, probably brain-damaged from the way they'd been booting his head around.

That's when Maria screamed.

The dead had arrived.

They came rushing out of the shadows, skeletal things like ghastly marionettes with carved faces, rotting faces, faces hanging off the bone like rags, hair matted and teeth sharp in the moonlight. They screeched and squealed and howled like mad dogs as they came gliding forward, saliva hanging from their puckered mouths in ribbons. They came on their feet, on their hands and knees, creeping and crawling and shambling en masse like insects on the march.

They took Maria.

I saw it happen. One minute she was rushing to my side and the next she went down, dropped like a tree, and there were a dozen on her feeding, chewing and tearing, burying their teeth in her throat, her belly, between her legs. I killed three with my shotgun, but there were too many. As I ran frantically through grass glistening with gore, I could hear them chewing on entrails and sucking marrow from bones. Conroy let out one long and pitiful wail before a woman jumped on him and tore his tongue out by the roots with her teeth.

Then I was running dead out, stumbling, trying to get away...but every direction I started in the dead were coming, massing in ranks, swarming through the grass like locusts. I remembered when we'd gotten the note from Dragna, how I suggested we fight and Doc said it would be a massacre. Oh, how right he'd been. You can't possibly imagine what *thousands* of zombies look like until they're pressing in on you and your stomach pulls up into your chest, already feeling the blackened teeth that will bite into it.

Good God.

In the moonlight...out across the fields and hills...it looked like an outdoor festival in Hell...as far as I could see, nothing but Wormboys and Wormgirls and Wormkids. This was the tide of the undead that Dragna kept at bay via six sacrifices.

They moved in for the kill slowly because they had all the time in the world and knew it. They carried machetes and pipes, axes and bones and hammers and knives. Their faces were carved fright masks like the Wormboys the night before, but more elaborately decorated. They had pounded nails into their skulls in intricate patterns, replaced their fingernails with shards of glass, their teeth with surgical needles, slid shiny silver pins through their lips and braided fine chains and filigrees of copper electrical wire through them. Moonlight found all that metal and glass, made it blaze with a cold reflective fire.

I fired every round in my shotgun and roasted dozens with the flamethrower, but still they kept coming. Sylvia was at my side shooting, as was Hill...at least until they took him down. I saw what they did to him in the glow cast from burning corpses. He screamed and then as I turned, a scarlet mist of blood broke against my face and I had to blink it away. Six or seven Wormboys and one solitary Wormkid were on him, biting into him, killing him slowly and making it last and milking every last drop of agony from the poor guy. Sylvia and I shot through them, but it did little good by that point there were so many.

Hill looked like he had been fed into a wood chipper.

The zombies went after him in a frantic, starving feeding frenzy like piranhas in a meat tank, reducing him to a grisly gore storm: Gouts of blood fountaining in the air as arteries were laid open, bones sucked dry like candy straws and mashed to a fine meal, tissue and gut and organ reduced to a fragmented flying spew of human debris. He was opened, emptied, gnawed down to his basal anatomy then bisected, trisected, halved and quartered and ultimately ground down to a great, globby, wet stain on the earth as the Wormboys and Wormgirls and hollow-cheeked Wormkid waifs fought over the scraps, the stronger ones engaging in darkly comic tugs-of-war with the cherry-red hoses of his entrails.

I burned them.

I burned them all down.

I saw what they did to Hill and I fucking torched them. About thirty of them, I'm figuring. I lit them up like Fourth of July sparklers and Guy Fawkes dummies and true to the latter, they stumbled about blazing like hay-stuffed scarecrows, burning pieces and sections falling off them. One by one, they hit the yellow, straw-arid grass and lit it up and before long that whole goddamn summer-dry field was burning. Dozens of them were caught out in it as the flames came at them from every direction, encircling them, then claiming them and roasting them down to blackened, twitching, crumbling things.

But by then we were on the run, Sylvia and I.

My empty shotgun had been used to split the skull of an inquisitive Wormboy. Sylvia had a few rounds left in her .9mm. Mine was gone. We had fire...we had the will to survive...we had hot terror leaping in our bellies...but that's all we had. The dead kept coming like we were some wondrous new tourist attraction they had heard of and they just had to get a peek...or a stray nibble.

I cooked about a dozen more of them, trying to cut us a path to the front door but it was no go. Maybe the walking dead will never understand quantum physics or write a truly great sonnet, but they are not entirely stupid. They knew we'd be making for that door and there had to be hundreds crowded in the parking lot waiting for us.

It was hopeless.

Taking Sylvia by the hand, we circled around back, clinging to the shadows thrown by the outbuildings, the generating station, and the water tanks. The action was lighter back there. We found a shadowy crevice between a couple tanks and we waited.

"There's too many of them," Sylvia whispered in my ear. "We can't make it."

"You got a better idea?"

But she didn't.

I had this crazy idea that if we could wait until daylight, we might have a chance. The Wormboys were more sluggish in direct sunlight.

That was my plan, anyway.

13

I don't know if they could see in the dark or just smell prey, but about five of them showed within minutes and they knew right where we were like they were being guided by some unseen intelligence. I had no choice but to toast them. And in the light of those shambling human corpse-fat candles, I saw there were at least a dozen others closing the gap. I saw a face that was infested with crawling red beetles. They skittered out of holes and tunnels in the cheeks and forehead, nipping and chewing, carrying bits of tissue back into their nests in the skull like cartoon ants stealing away with picnic goodies.

More faces came into the field of light.

Many of them were clustered with feeding insects, but many others had no eyes. They'd been sewn shut and these ones were hunting by sound alone. Sylvia pressed her .9mm into my hand without me asking for it. It was so greasy from her sweaty palm that I nearly dropped it.

The lead Wormboy—I don't know what else to call him— was this massive naked man who'd apparently lost his own skin at some point because he was wearing what at first looked like a rippling pale poncho but soon revealed itself to be a patchwork of human skins sewed into a single garment and then tacked to the muscle and tissue beneath. It fluttered in the wind. I saw a section that was tattooed joined to another with a single flaccid breast which itself was stitched to another with a puckering navel. His face was a creeping mass of fungal rot, green and dripping, moving with slow, greasy undulations over the jutting skull beneath.

I shot him point blank in the face and then put another through the side of his head and he crashed drunkenly to the ground, his hastily-sewn garment/pelt/skin bursting open. The others fell on him right away, stripping him like carrion birds. He was torn open, his wormy guts ripped free, rib bones snapped off and gnawed, skull crushed and the gray slime within sucked up by anxious mouths.

Then I saw something that turned even my stomach.

By that point, I assumed it impossible to be sickened.

But I was wrong. The zombies that were busy feeding on him suddenly reared away, stumbling, crawling, tearing at their throats and making hissing/gobbling sounds and then I watched as they began to regurgitate what they had just eaten in clotty globs of worms, inky fluid, and rancid meat.

Maybe there was something after all they couldn't abide.

Sylvia and I ran. I don't know where we thought we were going, but we were determined to get there. Then something smashed into us...a couple big Wormboys and I heard Sylvia scream as she was pulled away into the night. A Wormgirl came at me and I forgot the gun tucked in my pants and went at her with absolute rage. I don't think she was prepared for it. I launched myself at her, breaking her face open with my fists, then clawing her skull clean of flesh until she fell to her knees and I cleaved her head open with one good punt.

I was alone.

But they were coming for me.

14

I ran for the parking lot, thinking that if I couldn't make the front door there always the vehicles parked just off the tarmac. If worse came to worse, I'd find one with keys in it and take off into the night, circle around until dawn. But to my surprise, the parking lot was nearly deserted. I used up the last of the fuel in the flamethrower to toast a few stragglers and then I was beating my fists against the flaking green steel door, screaming for help.

Doc opened the door for me and said, "What in God's name have you done?"

I whipped out Sylvia's .9mm and put the last round through his left eye socket. Then I threw him outside to the wolves. And as I did so, I saw thousands of the dead massing for a concerted attack.

I slammed the door, locked it, then the siege began.

The shelter was not intended to withstand the barrage it took.

The doors did not come off their hinges, they *blew* off them. The children were all locked down in the bomb shelter beneath, but everyone else was on the main floor. There was no time to set up any defenses. There was no time for anything.

The dead rushed in.

Wormboys and Wormgirls came in with axes and machetes and knives and cleavers and sharpened broomsticks. They brandished decapitated heads on poles, chewed and worried things spattered with old blood. Some were naked, others dressed in shrouds and rags and shapeless ponchos that looked to be sewn together out of tanned human hides. Naked bodies were painted with arcane symbols. Some were bald, others without scalps, still others had their hair greased into mohawks and scalp locks with corpse fat. They were adorned in necklaces of human scalps and loops of dried entrails. Some wore death masks. Most had the carved, slit, and beaded faces of warriors. A few had gotten truly creative and inserted needles into their faces, spikes, shards of broken glass. They had removed hands and replaced them with blades and cleavers.

They didn't waste any time.

They mowed down the survivors. The air was cacophonous with shrieking and screaming, people begging for mercy, praying to gods that would not listen...and the gnawing, tearing, and grinding sounds of the living dead as they fed. Blood sprayed the walls, pooled on the floor. Limbs were broken, chewed, tossed aside. People were disemboweled while they were still alive. Sylvia's husband was eviscerated with a butcher knife and when he screamed, flopping on the floor, his own entrails were stuffed down his throat.

It was a slaughterhouse.

They must have got poor old Shacks, too, but I never saw it.

I fired every round from every gun I could find. I fought and killed and maimed, but it was hopeless. Entirely hopeless. The dining hall lived up to its name because that's where everyone was ritually devoured. Everything was red and dripping, feeding sounds echoing out, bodies quartered and skinned and peeled and then quartered again.

I should have felt an awful, eating guilt knowing that I had brought it all into being, that I was the stillborn breath of life that animated the entire nightmare. But I felt no guilt. Not then. Death was coming from every direction, empty-bellied, gape-toothed, diabolical and gluttonous...higher realms of self-loathing were denied me. There was only survival or, in the case of those in the shelter, lack of it.

I fought my way free of the dining hall and dorms with only one thought in my mind: the children. They were locked away downstairs and I had to keep them safe. The blood of those self-centered, egocentric assholes who were dying in numbers— the adults—meant very little to me by that point. It was the kids I thought of. The kids I lived for. The kids I fought for.

I darted down an interconnecting series of corridors knowing I had to get to the lower level before the undead did. I had only a bloody machete in my hand that I had taken from a Wormboy. There was no one or nothing in the hallways leading to the stairway door that went below. I felt a weird exhilaration of good luck, but it did not last.

There was a sudden stench in the air that cut through the usual stink of putrescence that had now flooded the compound. This was stronger...dank like subterranean pipes clogged with ancient filth, like backed-up sewage, the gurgling ammonia odor of urine.

I turned and there was Dragna.

I had thought—I suppose we all assumed—that Dragna, the zombie master, the lord of the ravenous dead, would be a man, but it was no man. It was female...but I wouldn't call what I saw a woman exactly. It held my eyes, made them feel varnished into sockets of flypaper, frozen, sticky with salt-tears and immobile, unable to look away from the hideous mass of corruption that was wallowing in its own juicy foulness.

At first, I thought what I saw was two naked women and then three, perhaps four that had been melted into a running, pliable human clay and then fused together under great, damaging pressure. But no...it was a single woman or something that had once been a woman...a huge, lolling slab of a woman with swollen balloon-like, blue-veined tits, seven or eight of them, bouncing against a green-gray, fungus-threaded, ulcerated flab. And not one but several enormous corpse-glutted, pendulous bellies slopping from side to side like feed bags stuffed with mush, a trickle of fluid black as ink leaking from puckered navels that looked like blow holes.

In one bloated hand she held a spear and impaled upon it, a squirming infant blown up with gas...blackened, tiny face smeared with blood, its mouth a pulsing hole ringed by sharp milk teeth.

And she was coming for me, coming to drown me in oceans of flaccid rot.

I should have screamed.

I should have ran.

But I just stood there as she came forward, filling the corridor with a black, fetid stench of corpse-gas and decomposition. From her greasy, mucid bulk I saw faces, dozens of agonized faces erupting like blood blisters, rising like bubbles of dough, each of them eyeless and the color of gray sausage, mouths opening and closing and spraying a mist of sputum. She was looking at me, not hating exactly...but almost amused beyond her voracious charnel appetites that I dared stand against her. Her face was a bulbous and liquefying clot of fleshy gruel-like white pulp riddled with graveworms and carrion beetles nesting in the hollow of her nose. Each time she exhaled out came a cloud of black, buzzing flies. Loops of greased, matted hair hung in her face and seemed to coil like flatworms.

She smiled at me with a crooked, saw-toothed pumpkin grin of gnarled teeth.

But it was her eyes that held me.

They were huge gloss-white yolks, veined with blood and oozing a clear fluid. They had no pupils...yet she was seeing me with a gyroscopic intensity, looking not just at me but into me and filling my brain with graveyard imagery...demons and corpseworms with the faces of mewling infants, babies cooked in fat-bubbling pots and oil-skinned women who offered me vaginas sluicing with steaming larvae.

She came closer, her breasts pulsating, throbbing with sloshing milk, lactating freely with a grayish bile that ran down her flab and squirted through the air.

Opening her mildew-specked thighs, she gave me a glimpse of the corkscrewing darkness between her legs that dripped with slime like a slobbering mouth, teaming with parasites...insects and hookworms and green suckering planaria.

And it was with that second mouth, I knew, that she would eat me...after she made me suckle the fleshbags of her tits.

Maybe I should have run like I said, but I was all that stood between her and the children. Such was her arrogance and appetite, she had come to feed on the children alone, to stuff herself with sweetmeats and kidflesh, selecting the most succulent cuts and rarest treats for her own discerning palate before turning her hordes loose on what was left.

She probably expected me to cry and cower and shiver, terrified and overwhelmed, struck mad by her horror as others had been...but she didn't get that. Machete held high, I attacked with a mindless ferocity and she reached out for me, her tongue like a thorny rose stem flaking into petals...and we collided there in the corridor. All those faces began to scream and maggots began to fountain from her mouth and eyes, her breasts and cunt, the ulcers in her hide...they came out in a slimy pink flood to drown me.

And as she took hold of me, I brought down the machete again and again as I gagged on her mortuary perfume, snotty tangles of blood and foam and slime gushing from her. Carrion paste blew from her mouth and the channel of her nose as I slashed her open and beat her down. Then she fell apart...bursting into a pink river of tissue and worms and rot and sticky ova. I fell away as it flooded the corridor, rushing past me in hot rivers of decay. I saw a dozen malformed, grotesque fetuses drowning in that outpouring, crying out with mewling voices that echoed into nothingness.

The revolting waste of Dragna went to a boiling steam that was hot and suffocating. In the end, I sat there, shocked and mindless as she evaporated around me.

15

It's been two weeks now since I destroyed her.

Two weeks since the adults of the shelter were exterminated.

Two weeks since I cleaned out the compound and burned the remains in a huge funeral pyre in the parking lot and two weeks since I gathered the children together and told them we are a family and we must look after one another and care for another and only this way can we survive. It sounded like one of Doc's speeches and I felt an eerie sense of déjà vu while I gave them the spiel. But I believed it. And I think they did, too.

I feel no guilt over what I did. But every day I miss Maria and I dream about her every night. I know she would be ashamed of my petty revenge on Doc and the others and that hurts. But, likewise, I know she would respect how I care and teach the children.

Following Dragna's destruction, I noticed something very peculiar with the Wormboys out there. They had devolved into your average b-movie zombies. Shambling deadheads, wandering around, bumping into one another, picking at scraps. No organization whatsoever. Dragna had been their brain and without her, they were really just mindless walking corpses. Creatures of opportunity.

It gave me hope.

I started planning out how we would escape the shelter. Go somewhere and find other people. Maybe an armory or a military base somewhere. But the more I thought about it the more I began to picture us wondering the wastelands, finding empty city after empty city, nothing but the dead haunting the cemetery sprawl of the brave new world.

Soon enough, I pictured us becoming little better than animals. Maybe living in caves, huddled around fires, drawing crude pictures on the walls of Wormboys sacking civilization until we reached the point in our crowded, primitive brains where we could no longer remember what civilization was.

Hope sometimes dies a cruel death in the face of reason.

I don't dare go out at night, but during the day—if I'm armed—I can handle the dead as long as they don't cluster or put on a united front. The scary thing is, lately they've been organizing again into small bands. They've been watching the shelter like they used to. Just standing out there, staring, infinitely patient and infinitely frightening.

This morning I found out why.

I found a note stuck to the door. Here's what it said:

TOMMY,

OCTOBER 13 DELIVER THE SIX
IF YOU DO NOT WE WILL COME FOR ALL
WE WILL SKIN YOUR CHILDREN AND WEAR THEIR
ENTRAILS
M.

In the back of my mind I suspected something like this for a long time and I think it was the inspiration behind me wanting to gather up the kids and get out. But we're not going anywhere. That's the terrifying reality of it. And the most disturbing thing, of course, is the note itself. You see, I recognize the handwriting: it's Maria's. They've found their new Dragna as somehow I supposed they would.

So I'm going to gather the kids together in the dining hall tonight and this is what I'm going to say to their innocent, trusting little faces: "Kids, we're going to play a new game. It's called a lottery and only six of you can win..."

Or lose.

CORPS CADAVRE

Midnight.

The prison mortuary.

The building was squat and cold, cut from blocks of gray stone stacked in a grim heap like a cairn made of interlocking skulls. The windows were barred and the doors were narrow, clustered with shadows. Sullen and utilitarian, it sat well away from the other prison buildings, connected only by a ribbon of winding dirt road. It flanked the potter's field cemetery, rising above and lording over the weedy fields of the dead—the wooden crosses riding the hills and hollows, marking the graves of the unknown, the unwanted, and the undesirable.

Inside, Johnny Walsh sat at his little desk, feet up, fingers drumming nervously against his legs. Not yet forty, Johnny had already done ten years in that hardtime joint on a double-homicide. His world before maximum security was a tight working class existence and after the murders, one of rage, anger, and oppression. A world just as dark as the skin on his face, a world where poor shanty blacks and white trash busted heads to break the boredom, where black drug gangs and the white Aryan Brotherhood shanked each other over donuts.

But that was doing life.

Johnny would taste freedom roughly about the time of the Second Coming. Breathe in, you smell the despair; breathe out, you smell your life winding out in crowded, steel silence.

Johnny was humping the night shift with the stiffs because of the riot.

Four days before, the small, seething Hispanic population decided to kill every black in the joint. They squirreled away shivs and pipes and razors. At a prearranged moment, they rose up, set on the blacks like rabid dogs. When it was over, the National Guard had been called in and seventy inmates were dead, the infirmary packed with twice that many.

And now the mortuary was full.

The freezers held more cold meat than a butcher's display case. Full drawers, gurneys and slabs packed with rigid, white-sheeted figures. You could barely walk in there now, dead heaped like firewood.

The warden decided that someone had to keep watch over all those bodies. There being so many and all, it made the old man nervous. Word had it more than one body had turned-up missing there in the past and what with the state and their impending investigation, warden didn't want no fuck-ups this time around.

So Johnny, who had a good record and was a trustee, pulled the duty. Pulled it mainly because he was in good with LaReau, the sergeant hack. LaReau was a big, mean intolerant prick the cons called "Ironhead" because he enjoyed head-butting anyone that gave him shit and when he did, he piledrived convict-ass big and small right to the mat.

But Johnny was okay with him—yes boss, no boss, how was your day, boss, and can I wash your car come Wednesday, boss? Make the peckerwood feel like he was something special and he would be easy on you.

So the mortuary wasn't a bad gig, all things considered.

Johnny kept the doors locked—warden's orders—and did a lot of reading, but mostly a lot of shivering. Because it was cold in there. Johnny had a little woodstove in the corner, but it didn't help much. The mortuary had held so many corpses in its belly through the years that the stone had sucked in all that tomb cold, let it out at night, exhaling the breath of graves.

The clock on the wall was ticking and Johnny kept hearing little sounds—poppings and crackings—but it was just the old building settling and he would not let himself think it was anything else.

Lighting a cigarette, Johnny went to the window over the little sink, started a bit at his reflection in the glass, smiled, and stared out through those rusting black bars.

A moonless, black night.

The world was caught in-between chill autumn and the promise of bitter winter, pelted by blowing leaves and a freezing, relentless rain. It turned the roads to slop and the fields to mud, sluicing and oozing and pooling in black puddles that were frosted with a scum of ice. December or not, it was miserable by the standards of northeastern Louisiana, just a stone's throw from the borders of Arkansas and Mississippi.

Johnny turned away, didn't like the night and certainly didn't like that face and those eyes and what they were saying to him. Because, yes sir, he'd made mistakes and now it was all done and he was all used-up. No more fresh air and freedom, no more t-bones and certainly no more pussy. You could get both if you had the money, guards would bring in anything for a price. But for poor trash like Johnny Walsh his days of pussy were history, for guys like him there were only the queens and Johnny preferred to do without. In fact, he—

Thump.

Johnny heard it. Felt something wither and die in his guts, curl-up and tremble. That sound. Couldn't be no sound like that here, not here. His heart pounding, that cigarette welded to his lower lip, Johnny just stood there as cold as shrimp in an ice bucket.

Thump, thump.

Johnny's heart almost blew out of his chest on that one.

He looked around, saw his reflection again. Saw the sink and the desk and the file cabinets. Saw the waste paper basket, the girly calendar on the wall showing him a fine set of Asian tits...but right then his business was shriveled-up like a breakfast link.

Licking his lips, he made himself walk first this way, then that.

The gray cement-block walls were sweating an icy moisture. He saw those walls and figured suddenly that this was no easy bit, it was the worst cage of all. There were two doors in that room. One led into an entry and out into the world, the other led into a corridor that led to the freezers and the garage where all the cheap pine caskets were stored.

Thump.

Johnny knew then that the sound was coming from the corridor...or, and more precisely, from one of the rooms back there. A wild, freezing terror flooded through him and he could feel it right down to the balls of his feet. Insane. That's what.

Because, because there could *not* be sounds back there. Sounds meant something was alive or at least in motion and nothing back there was capable of either.

He thought: Don't go on like this, don't mean nothing, just the foundation contracting or some such shit, it don't mean...it don't mean that—

Thump, thump, thump.

Johnny let out a little involuntary cry, pressing himself up against that concrete wall that was just as cold as graveyard marble. His fingers were pressed flat, drawn taut like the rest of his body, some hot blue electricity arcing through his bones now. His eyes were wide and refused to blink.

Something in his brain reminded him of those bodies that had disappeared at the mortuary. It couldn't be, it wasn't possible what he was thinking. The dead were dead and nobody since Lazarus had ever gotten up and walked afterwards.

But those sounds, Jesus, what was making those sounds?

*

The guy who ran the mortuary was named Riker.

He was a large, heavy man with arms like railroad ties all painted-up with jailhouse tattoos. His neck was thick as a pine stump and the head it supported looked like something you hammered iron on. He'd already put in twenty-five years of a lifetime sentence and before this joint, he'd done six years at Angola for armed robbery. He was a rough customer, but years of permanent confinement with no hope for parole had sanded off the rough edges, planed him just as smooth and even as a caged violent offender can be.

He was a trustee like Johnny, but he was the senior man in the trustee system and could have had any job he wanted in the prison industries. He could've stamped plates and gears in the metal shop or pushed a book cart in the library or even supervised the road gangs, but he liked the mortuary.

"The dead ones are okay with me," he often said. "You never have to push 'em on account they never push you."

When he found out that LaReau was putting a con on the night shift, he didn't like it much. He started swearing and spitting, saying the dead don't need no watching, it was the living ones you had to keep an eye on. But the warden wanted it that way, so that's how it was going to be.

42

When he got a look at Johnny, he just grimaced, shook his head, mumbled something. But then Johnny—using that brain his mama said was never worth a shit—offered Riker a cigarette and that warmed the old guy fine.

Riker took a drag and smiled thinly. "You up to this, boy?"

And Johnny didn't like being called "boy", but he got used to it. Riker was a Southerner and they called everybody "boy". You couldn't take offense to it like you might on the streets. And besides, even though Riker was pushing seventy, those fists still looked very capable of breaking skulls.

"I can do it fine," Johnny said.

"Just saying, boy, ya'll don't look real comfortable around them dead ones. Like maybe they make you uncomfortable or some such."

But Johnny gave him the line, telling him he liked the stiffs just fine, they were okay with him. You didn't have to watch your back with stiffs and that was something, all right. In this place, that was really something.

"What you in for, boy?" Riker finally asked him.

"Stupidity, boss, plain and simple," Johnny told him, none too proudly. Pride, like hope, died a quick death behind those walls. "Let me tell you about it. There I was working me a job at the foundry, sweating and straining and a-busting my ass, but pulling down a living. And feeling good, you know? Good like you can only feel after putting in your shift, working for a living. Anyhow, had me a cute little lady name of Tamara, was crazy about her. She'd been a runner up in that Miss Louisiana thing and was just as pretty as they come. So I'm working at the foundry stamping out manhole covers and she got herself a receptionist job for this white cat owned hisself an insurance company—"

"I can see where this is going, boy."

Johnny just nodded, dragged off his cigarette. "Surely. I come home one night, twisted my ankle and had to take a few days off, and what do I see? Right there in my bedroom? Just that white ass planted in Tamara's saddle, humping and pounding and slamming away and Tamara moaning and squealing and saying, gimme it, gimme it, oh you fucking me fine. Bitch never did nothing but lay there for me. Shit and shit. So I stabbed old whitey forty times, they said, and Tamara...something like thirty, give or take." Johnny started laughing then, seeing his

43

wasted life play out in his mind like some sort of cheap, unpleasant situation comedy. "Yes sir, you can just go on ahead and forget that business about going black and not going back, because—at the trial—well, I found out my Tamara was going back again and again, setting the cause back a hundred years."

"What cause is that, boy?"

"Freedom for my people, mister, what else?"

Riker thought that was hilarious. "Freedom? What fucking freedom, boy? You a convict, case you didn't notice. We all work for massah here. We all just trash society put out to the curb."

Johnny told him that was certainly true.

And then Riker admitted he was doing life for multiple homicide. Had waltzed into a bank, planning to rob it. Guard saw him and went for his piece, so Riker drilled him and then, feeling funny that day, he killed four more people so they wouldn't be able to identify him.

"My head was full of kitty litter back then, boy," Riker told him, "and I ain't so sure they's not a few turds still stuck between my ears even now."

Stories told, Riker gave him the grand tour.

Took him down that grim concrete block corridor that smelled like wet steel, tears, and pesticide, showed him the freezers. Behind iron doors, bodies crowded under stained white sheets, arms hanging out all gray and blotched from lividity. Riker showed him the cold cuts, how bad it had all been. Here a couple blacks with slit throats, there a Hispanic that had been kicked to death so that his jaw was planted by his left ear now, and here some dumb white guy who'd decided to intervene and had his head split clean open. The dumb and the dumber. In the drawers, no better. Eyes punched out and faces erased and bones sticking through dirty canvas skins like broomsticks.

Then Riker showed him the garage out back where all the caskets were piled up—cheap pine things hammered together in the carpentry shop.

"They two kinds of dead here, boy. Them what get claimed by their kin and them what end up out in potter's field. Most of these boys will end up out there on account they families is ashamed of 'em."

Back in the office, Riker parked Johnny at the desk, gave him some fuck books and a few paperback westerns, told him to just pass the time, keep the doors locked. That was it.

Then he gave him a Thermos of whiskey.

"Drink your fill, boy," he said. "A little taste is one of the benefits of sorting out the dead ones and they troubles."

*

But now Johnny was alone.

Riker said he wouldn't be back before first light.

Thump, thump.

No foundation settling or walls groaning, this was something else. Something bad. Something big and angry that did not care to be ignored. Johnny kept telling himself that there was a very good reason for what he was hearing. Maybe some con had gotten himself bagged up alive or such...but he didn't believe that.

Sucking in a sharp breath and wiping cold sweat from his forehead, he went to the door that opened into the corridor. He touched it with his hand. Cold, damn cold was how it felt. He could feel that cold seeping in through his pores, locking down everything within him in a blanket of ice. He could hear that damn clock ticking and the blood rushing in his ears.

He heard the sound again and his heart hitched painfully in his chest.

Something, something alive back there.

His face was tight as cellophane against the skull beneath, the flesh prickling unpleasantly at the back of his neck. Sweat ran into his eyes and he shivered and breathed and licked his lips slowly, slowly, feeling a sudden rushing weight settle into him and knowing it was madness. That insanity had a physical, ominous presence. His eyes studied the door, bulging and white and unblinking.

All right, then, all right.

His hand found the doorknob, eased it open. A well of shifting, damp blackness billowed out at him, fell over him, got up his nostrils and down his throat, tasted like wormy coffin silk on his tongue and stank of wet, dripping crypts. He turned on the light switch before that blackness suffocated him, drained him dry, whisked him off into the freezer like a chop put up for next Sunday's cookout.

There was a single light bulb and it created crawling shadows, made things even worse.

Outside the freezer room, staring at that riveted iron door painted the color of old blood and thinking it was like the door to some old vault, Johnny listened, brought his fingers to the latch.

Sound in there...not that thumping, but a whispering sound.

Johnny's breath clogged in his throat like grave dirt.

Open it, open it for chrissake.

The latch sounded like thunder in the corridor, clanking and groaning. The door opened soundlessly. Johnny's fingers—twisting whitely now like worms dying in the sunlight—found the old-fashioned switch and brought light into the world.

Nothing.

The drawers were all closed, the slabs still occupied, the gurneys still squeezed in-between and all available floor space was thronged with shrouded figures waiting for burial.

Johnny's fingers put a cigarette in his mouth, lit it.

He took a deep, long pull, knowing what he needed here was some strength, some balls and not those playground marbles that had sucked up into his body cavity.

The freezer room was green-tiled, stank of dirty backwaters and quarry slime, vomit and frozen meat. Johnny went in there, stepping over and around the ones on the floor, pausing—for reasons he was even unsure of—before a slab.

His heart thudded dully in his chest.

He took hold of the sheet like the page of a book, pulled it back carefully, a chilly earthen smell coming off the body. Most of the flesh was missing from the face, what was left an ashen gray speckled with dirt and dried blood. A bullet had gotten this one and a high-caliber by the looks of it. Tower guard. Gums were shriveled away from teeth, the left eye blown clear away with its attendant orbit of bone. The right eye was open and staring, glazed over.

There was something nestled on the chest.

Johnny thought at first it was some big spider...but no. Just a little figure molded from black mud and sticks. Like a little doll. How in Christ did that get there? Johnny dropped the sheet, checked two more bodies. No dolls. But a third had one and so did a fourth.

What the hell were they? What was going on here—

Thump, thump, thump.

From the drawers then. Like something in there was trying desperately to get out, hammering and pounding. Johnny went cold, went hot, felt his skin crawl and a tornado of white noise whip through his brain.

Something was happening now. There was a cool, crackling electricity, a sharp smell, a motion, a sentience, a heavy thrumming awareness. Johnny's mouth went dry as sawdust, he could not open his lips—they had been sewn shut.

He stumbled back, fell over a body, his hand brushed a fleshy arm that felt like thawing beef. He sat there on his ass, unsure, unknowing, unable to do much but shake and gasp and wonder. He could not move, could not breathe. The drawers— many of them now—thumping and banging and rattling in their housings. Their metal faces were bulging, dented out from the inside.

Then all around him, as if stirred by some secret malefic wind, sheets began to tremble and rustle and shift with motion beneath them. Arms slid out, fingers clutching madly in the air like snakes.

Johnny heard a voice whisper, another grunt, another make something like a dry barking sound. He sat there, suppressing a demented desire to start giggling. The bodies were sitting up now, sheets sliding from gray, bloodless faces and bodies like sloughed skins. Shadows crawled up from the corners, twisted like thick serpents, hissing and slithering.

A voice as brittle as crunching straw said: "*Watch out, George...that sumbitch got a big knife he...*"

But the others were talking now, too, speaking in those dry voices that were merely snarling, guttural noises that made Johnny want to scream. They were like cold steel at his spine, the flats of knife blades dragged along his belly and groin. Echoes. Just echoes. That's what they were. The worn spools of those decayed brains repeating and repeating their final living thoughts until the room was alive with a ghastly murmuring.

They had risen up all around him now.

Grinning, frowning, smirking. Those faces were hideous moons with ragged, black impact craters for eyes. A dozen morgue drawers burst open, slid out on squeaking casters, sheeted forms rising, fingers twisting and tearing at their shrouds. Oh and dear God, those eyes—blanched and discolored, staring and hollow and so utterly empty.

The dead were on their feet now, stumbling and staggering and shambling. Some were naked, others clothed in bloody prison issue or filthy hospital gowns.

Johnny crawled on hands and knees out the doorway and they followed, a ragged, grisly throng of chattering teeth and wiggling fingers and whispering voices. Ligaments popped like rusty hinges. Muscles snapped and bones splintered. They stank of tombs and drainage ditches and body pits. One of them looked at Johnny, tried to speak, but a flood of black bile oozed from his lips, hung from his jawline like ribbons of mucus. His voice became a bubbling, gargling sound.

Screaming, Johnny found his feet, scrambling madly not towards the office, but to the garage and the outside door. His fingers had gone stupid and numb and rubbery and he could barely work the lock, barely throw himself into the black wet night before they were on him. Shouting and hollering, he fell out into the rain, coming to rest in a muddy pool. Thunder rumbled in the sky and lightening flashed, painting the landscape in lunar brilliance.

They had not followed him.

Johnny sat there in the muck, rain pounding down on him. The air was cold, but the mud around him was warm and sluicing like blood. He looked frantically off towards the prison itself, could see the high towers, the buildings, the wall...but not much else.

The whispering throng was coming out now.

They paid no attention to Johnny.

Balanced atop their shoulders, they carried caskets. Single file, they pushed through the muck and rain with their coffins, a funereal parade of contusions and slit throats, stab wounds and shattered skulls. A collection of stiffly animate rag dolls trailing stuffing from snipped stitches, bearing torn limbs and dangling shoebutton eyes. And making, yes, making for potter's field. At least thirty of them, keeping an almost military cadence.

Johnny sat there for awhile, drenched and dirty and shaking.

The rain fell and the susurration of the ghouls faded into the distance and although Johnny wanted to run and run, he could not. He got to his feet, brushing mud from his arms. Then he followed them, knowing deep down he had to see this.

Through the swampy, sunken landscape he went until he caught sight of them gathered at the far side of the cemetery. In the flashing lightening, he could see they were working. Yes, they had shovels now. Dead men digging their own graves and not slowly, mindlessly, but with great effort and concentration.

Johnny could see there was someone with them.

Someone with a flashlight barking out orders.

Johnny came forward and soon enough saw Riker there, yelling at the dead men, kicking dirt at them, drumming them on the heads with the barrel of his flashlight. "Dig, you bastards!" he was screaming at them. "Dig, dig, dig! Dig 'em down deep, you know what you have to do! You know the way!"

Johnny, wordlessly, stood by the mortuary boss for some time, watching the gray rain-swept figures digging and widening and squaring off their holes. When they were done, they lowered their caskets down...and climbed into them. Within a half-hour, all the graves were dug and the last of the lids slammed shut with a brutal finality.

Then there was only silence. The sound of rain, distant thunder.

Riker, his face wet with rain, said, "See, boy, how it works is, the guards, oh they love me, on account I handle the mortuary so they don't have to. I see that the dead are registered, the graves dug and filled and I do it all by myself. I do it with *them*."

"Dead men," Johnny managed, his mind drawn into a soundless vacuum now. "Living dead men."

Riker clapped him on the shoulder. "That's it, boy! That's it exactly! See, years ago, when I started at the mortuary they was this Haitian fellow ran it, a drug dealer. He taught me about the walking dead. *Corps Cadavre*, he called 'em. He showed me how it was done. How to make the powder, the dolls, to make with the mumbo-jumbo ju ju talk—"

"Zombies," Johnny found himself saying incredulously. Because that's what they were. Dead men summoned up to dig their own graves. Just like the dead men you heard about, worked those cane fields in Haiti and Guadeloupe and those places.

Riker gave him a shovel and for the next hour or so, they filled in the graves, marking them with simple wooden crosses. Then it was done and they both stood there in that dank cold, in that brown sloppy soup of mud.

"Boy, you'd drank that whiskey like I told you," Riker said, "you'd have slept right through all this, see? I put enough seconal in there to put you into dreamland for six, eight hours."

Sure. That's why he didn't want anyone in the mortuary that night, things had been all set. The cadavers that hadn't been claimed were given that powder and the little dolls, told when they were to open their eyes and get to work. It was almost funny...if it hadn't been so damn depraved, so horrible and, yes, disgusting.

Zombies, Johnny's brain thought, *zombies*.

Empty as a tin can, he turned away from Riker and that was a mistake.

Riker hit him with a shovel, opening his head. Johnny sank into the mud like a drowning man. Fingers of gray slop ran from the open crown of his head.

"Sorry, boy," Riker said, "but I can't have you telling what you saw."

Taking Johnny by the feet, he dragged him back towards the mortuary, wondering what sort of story he might concoct. Figured it would be a good one.

*

Two nights later.

The prison mortuary.

A morgue drawer.

Tagged and bagged, Johnny Walsh lay in his berth in that cool, easy darkness. His hands were folded over his chest, the fingers carefully interlocked. He had no family, no one to claim him. Just more refuse of the state that the taxpayers would no longer be burdened with.

There was a little mud and stick doll stuck between his knees.

Johnny's eyes snapped open.

He began to speak about zombies in a dead voice, spinning out the last things his brain remembered. He clawed at his sheet, kicked his feet at the door. The drawer slid open then, Riker standing there.

"C'mon, boy," he said somberly. "Nobody's claimed you. Time to prepare your place..."

EMILY

When Emily came out of the grave, Mother was waiting there for her. She saw little Emily and began to immediately shake and sob. A broken cry came from her throat as the immensity of her daughter's resurrection hit her. She went down to her knees in the sluicing muck, gasping and staring, her mouth unable to form words.

Emily just stood there, her white burial dress dripping wet and dark with graveyard soil that fell in clots. Even in the wan moonlight, her face was pale as tombstone marble, her eyes huge and black and empty.

"Emily?" Mother said, caught in some sucking, manic whirlpool of utter joy and utter horror. *"Emily?"*

Emily just watched her, completely indifferent to the scene. Raindrops rolled down her pallid face like tears. Finally, she grinned because it was what Mother wanted. She grinned and Mother recoiled like she had been slapped. Emily had not grinned in awhile and it came out a bit too crooked, a bit too toothy. "Mother," she said, her voice dry and scraping like a shovel dragged over a concrete tomb lid.

Mother came forward, uncertain at first, but that endless week of mourning had drained everything from her and she could no longer see how this was wrong, how this was unnatural and insane. So she stumbled forward and collected Emily in her arms, squeezing her in the rain, paying no mind to the fetid stench that came off her daughter.

"I prayed for this, baby! I prayed and I wished and I hoped and I never, ever, ever lost my faith!" Mother said. "I knew you would come back! I knew you would come back to me! I knew you weren't really dead!"

Emily did not hug her back.

In fact, the warmth of Mother's flesh slightly repelled her...even though the smell of it was appetizing. She felt Mother's arms around her, but it did not move her. Emily came out of the grave with certain things, certain needs and desires, but love and affection were not among them.

But Mother did not see any of this and mainly because she did not want to. Grief had shattered her and mourning had laid her bare. The madness that comes with losing a child is a special madness, stark and numbing, seamless and all-encompassing. So Mother simply accepted. There was nothing more. Just acceptance.

Mother rambled on and on about how she had prayed and wished for Emily's resurrection, how she had sat in her bedroom grim night after night after night, staring into the flame of a single candle and wishing her little girl alive again. And how last night she had dreamed that Emily had opened her eyes in the cloying darkness of her little pearl-white casket and that's how she had known to come tonight with a shovel to set her baby free.

"But you weren't dead, baby!" Mother said again and again. "I told them at the wake and I told them at the funeral and they wouldn't believe me! They wouldn't believe that my little girl wasn't dead! But I knew! I knew! I knew you weren't dead!"

"Yes, I was, Mother," Emily said.

But Mother didn't hear that either.

There were only her delusions now which were a high, sturdy brick wall that things like reason and decency could not hope to break through. She had her Emily back and that's all that mattered, that's really all that mattered. Emily was back...or something that *looked* like her was.

"Help me, baby," Mother said, on her hands and knees, pushing wet earth back into the grave. "We have to cover this up so people don't ask questions. You know how they ask questions. But I won't let them take you away from me again."

But Emily did not help.

She just stood there, still grinning, watching Mother fill in the grave, watching her cry and sob and make funny, high-pitched sounds deep in her throat. Emily did not honestly see the point of filling in the grave. She had not been among the walking dead long enough to understand that there was a need to be careful, a need for secrecy in all things relating to her rising.

But that would come with experience.

As all things did.

Emily's memory was intact and she was sly and cunning. She would learn. For essentially she was still a child and had a child's love of play and make-believe. So she figured it wouldn't be too hard to pretend she was a harmless little girl.

As Mother labored, Emily looked around the cemetery, at the crypts and monuments and stones, enjoying this place and thinking she would like to come here often. But not too often. If she did that, sooner or later she would be seen and that would give the game up. People expected dead little girls to stay in their coffins, they did not like them wandering around cemeteries by night.

Even Emily knew that.

Mother finished the grave, filthy from head to foot, only her eyes and teeth white and shining like an old time vaudeville performer in blackface. It all added to the necessary absurdity of the entire situation. She came right over to Emily and hugged her, wrinkled her nose at the smell, but kept hugging all the same. A fat, twisting earthworm fell from Emily's matted hair and Mother cried out. But even this, she ultimately ignored.

"Let's go home, baby," she said. "Let's get you out of this awful place."

Emily allowed herself to be led away by the hand amongst the leaning stones and vaults covered in creepers. She did not want to leave. She wanted to run through this place and sing and dance, hide behind stones and leap out in the cold moonlight. The smell of rank earth and rotting boxes, crumbling flesh and yellowed bones intrigued her, made her stomach growl. She wanted to dig down far below with her bare hands and chew on things. Nibble them.

But Mother would not have that.

They went through the gates and a church bell in the distance gonged out the hour of midnight. It was a perfect time for a resurrection and Emily knew it. And knowing it, she giggled. Then they were in the car and Emily remembered that she hadn't been in the car since the night her appendix burst and the infection set in. She couldn't remember much of that, just the fever and the pain and the sound of Mother crying at her bedside.

"Everything's going to be okay now, baby," Mother said. "You'll see. Mother will make everything right."

Emily just kept grinning, feeling the hollow in her belly and wanting to get her teeth in some meat. She thought of crunching bones and chewing graying meat and the image of these things made her stomach growl. If it wasn't for the heat in the car that Mother insisted on blasting, things would have been perfect. Emily sat there as they drove into town, remembering things from before but associating no warmth with any of it.

She knew only hunger.

"Talk to Mother, baby, please talk to me."

So Emily did. "I'm hungry," she said.

*

At home, Mother told her they had to be quiet. Very quiet because George was sleeping upstairs and they didn't want to wake him. Not yet. Not before Mother had time to explain certain things. But Emily understood. When you came out of the grave, certain things had to be explained. She remembered George just fine. George was her step-father, Mother's husband. Not Emily's real dad because he was dead a long time. George had liked Emily when she was alive. He took her to the zoo and the circus, he took her shopping and bought her things and helped her with her homework. George had been very nice. But like everything else, there was no fondness associated with George now. Emily had liked him before and maybe she would even like him now...once he was cold.

"The first thing we have to do is clean you up," Mother said.

Mother cleaned herself up first and made Emily wait in her old bedroom. Emily looked at the posters on the pink walls, the princess bed and frilly pillows, the books and CDs and dolls lined up on the shelf. It meant nothing to her. Just things that she had collected up and coveted once, but no longer. She did not see how they would get her meat so they had no practical value. The bed felt soft and spongy. Emily did not like it, nor the clean stink of detergents on the Beauty and the Beast coverlet.

What she *did* like was the mirror.

She could remember how she liked to put on dress-up clothes and look at herself in it. She looked at herself in it now. She looked...*changed*. She was very thin and her skin was very white, gray shadows under her eyes, her lips almost black. Still grinning, her teeth looked long and narrow and yellow, black stuff wedged between them. Her gums were gray and her lips were shriveled back from them.

Emily liked how she looked.

She liked the patch of fungus at her throat, the soil that clung to her white lace burial dress. The beetle that crawled over her brow and the larva squirming in her cheek. She especially liked her eyes which were large and black and never seemed to blink. They stared and stared, wide and cataleptic. She held up her hands and her fingers were bony, the skin gray and seamed, dirty and damp.

She had a smell to her that was all her own.

It was fetid.

And absolutely delicious.

Mother took her into the bathroom and scrubbed her under a hot spray of water. The heat was sweltering and it made Emily nearly sick to her stomach. Mother shampooed her hair and scrubbed her with pink soap, scrubbing and scrubbing, cleaning the grave dirt off her and the patches of green mildew that had grown up her cheeks and down her arms. Emily did not like being washed. The soap smelled of berries and lilacs and the shampoo smelled of coconut and she found it nauseating. She liked her other smell. The smell of wormy earth and embalming fluid, putrescence and casket satin.

But Mother would not have that either.

She dressed Emily in lavender pajamas, the ones with prancing cutesy unicorns on them. Emily remembered that she had loved unicorns before, but now things were different. She did not understand unicorns any more. She only understood burial. And meat.

In the kitchen, Emily's other smell beginning to make itself known, seeping through the perfume of soaps and shampoos, Mother made her some food. First toast and Cocoa Pebbles. Then waffles and Ore-Ida French fries in the oven. But Emily did not want these things. She did not want presweetened cereal or bread, pizza or Hostess pies. She wanted other things.

"You have to eat something," Mother said. "You're...you're so thin."

"I'm hungry," Emily said.

So Mother went through the cupboards and refrigerator, trying to find something Emily might want. Emily was sickened by the smell of everything Mother made. But there was another odor, one that was intriguing. When Mother's back was turned, Emily followed it to its source: the garbage can under the sink. In there, amongst egg shells and old lettuce leaves and discarded tissues there were a few scraps of raw hamburger clinging to a foam carton. They were discolored and rank-smelling. Emily began to lick them free, the juices in her mouth running at the wonderful taste, the wonderfully rotten smell.

"*Emily!*" Mother said, slapping the carton from her cold white hands. "You can't eat that! It's yucky! It's full of germs!"

"I'm hungry," Emily said.

And then she heard footsteps coming down the stairs and knew it was George. She could smell his cologne and it was disgusting. But there was a good, yummy odor there as well. Some reeking juice, perhaps, from thawing meat he had dripped on his sock. Just a speck, no doubt, but Emily could smell it and it made her mouth water.

Mother heard George's approach, but too late to do much about it. Her eyes wide and frightened, she looked over at Emily. "Hide!" she whispered. "Get in the pantry."

So Emily did.

George entered the kitchen. "Christ, Liz, where have you been? You had me worried sick."

"There was some shopping to do," Mother said.

"At this hour?"

Emily could sense Mother's apprehension. She could smell the sweat that ran down the back of her neck, hear the steady tom-tom beat of her heart. "Some places are open twenty-four hours," Mother said, thinking quickly.

Like cemeteries, Emily thought.

George grumbled a bit. "What's that smell in here?" he asked. "Smells like something died."

Emily giggled under her breath.

"It's...it's the garbage," Mother said. "I was just going to take it out."

Oh, Mother's juices were running hot now, her nerves jangling with electricity. Her palms were sweaty and her lips quivering. George had her very upset. Emily thought it was funny. It was a game Mother was playing, a gag she was playing on George.

George did not seem to like it.

He stepped farther into the kitchen. Emily could see him from the darkness of the pantry, hidden there as she was amongst the shelves of canned goods and dried pasta, the bags of potatoes and onions that smelled very sharp, though not unpleasant.

"Are you all right, Liz? You don't look so good. Do you feel all right? You know what the doctor said. You've been through an awful lot, you need your rest."

"I'm fine," Mother told him. "Why wouldn't I be just fine?"

Emily grinned from her hiding place. Though the pantry was pungent with the odors of dried food and vegetables, she was smelling that drop of juice on George's sock. It was intoxicating.

"Liz...c'mon, honey, let's talk, okay? Tell me what's on your mind. Is it Emily? Let's talk about it."

"I don't want to talk about that," Mother told him, her voice growing cross.

George went over to her. "Honey, please. She's gone. We have to accept that, we have to get on with—"

"*She's not gone!*" Mother said, her eyes filled with tears, her head shaking from side to side. "She's not gone at all!"

"Liz..."

Mother was right and George was wrong, but he didn't understand. He couldn't understand any of it because it was part of the game. Emily decided it was time to teach him the game, so then he, too, would know. She stepped out of the pantry, her eyes huge and her pale mouth grinning. "Peekaboo!" she said.

George literally jumped and swung his head around. He looked and his eyes widened and his mouth opened and his head began to thrash violently back and forth. His ruddy complexion bleached to the color of new bone. In the split second that realization settled in, he began to breathe very fast, in and out, as if he could get no air. *"Oh no, oh no, oh no! Oh, dear God, no! It can't be! IT CANNOT FUCKING BE! IT CAN'T—"*

He was scared and Emily knew it.

Just scared out of his mind, his heart racing and his lungs rasping, a sharp and foul odor of fear-sweat coming off him. Something Emily could smell just as a wild animal can. She did not know, though, if he was really afraid or just pretending like they did with their yearly Halloween games.

So she jumped out at him and hissed, baring her teeth and making her fingers into claws.

George screamed and fell into Mother who kept trying to explain it all, crying and choking, her voice wavering and completely mad. *This is what they'd both wanted, wasn't it? This is what they'd both needed...Emily back with them. And now she was. And wasn't that wonderful? Wasn't that an absolute miracle? WELL, WASN'T IT?* These were the things Mother kept saying...or trying to...but George was not hearing her. He was only trying to get away as Mother held onto him, shouting louder and louder about what a miracle it all was. And then they were fighting. George was out of his mind and Mother was trying to hold him and he was hitting her, calling her names and she was crying and shaking and it was an ugly scene. *"This isn't normal! This isn't natural! Look at that fucking thing! That's not your daughter! That's not Emily! It's a thing from a fucking grave!"*

They fell to the floor fighting and Emily did not like their fighting. George was going to be trouble. So Emily pulled a metal tenderizing mallet from the cupboard and brought it down on his head, loving the pulpy sound his skull made. She brought it down again and again and again, blood spattering against her face and standing out in sharp contrast against her white, seamed skin.

"No, Emily!" Mother cried out. *"No, no, no! Stop that! Stop it!"*

So Emily stopped and George's body just lay there, very still and quiet. Emily stared down at it, liking him better this way. Now he wasn't causing trouble. Now he was happy. Emily looked at the end of the mallet. There was blood dripping from it, brain globs, strands of hair. She brought it to her mouth and pressed her tongue against it. It tasted good, so she began licking the stuff off and spitting out the hairs. It was tasty...though much too warm to be truly delicious.

"Emily! Emily! Emily!" Mother cried, afraid again. Angry, maybe, and unhappy. "Don't do that! Don't do that! *Do you hear me?*"

Emily heard her. "But I like to," she said.

That made something snap inside of Mother.

She pressed herself up against the refrigerator, sobbing and trembling and a funny look came over her. She began to talk to herself, staring but not blinking at all. Laughing sometimes so Emily knew things were all right. Mother was just going crazy again like she had when Emily had first come out of the grave. Poor Mother. If Emily had been capable of compassion, she might have felt sorry for her. Mother just sat there, that terrible look on her face like part of her mind, probably an important part, had been sucked down into some black, bottomless gulf.

"Watch me," Emily told her and went on her knees next to George's corpse.

George's head was open and things were leaking out, clear things and red things and gray things and clumping things. Emily dipped her fingers into his open skull like it was a fondue pot, the kind they'd had at her seventh birthday party last year. She dipped her fingers and licked them off. Everything was tasty. Her hunger was so severe that finger-licking was not enough. She gripped George's skull and broke it apart with her fingers, licking at the sweet red jelly inside, sucking up strands of tissue and the buttery soft folds of gray matter.

Mother just stared off into space, her mouth moving but no words coming out.

Emily cleaned out the skull until she was full. Inside, it was clean and sparkling and white like a freshly-washed pot. There was more good stuff, but Emily was full. For now.

Her bloodless face smeared with gore, Emily just stood over Mother, smiling at her.

Finally, Mother's eyes began to focus. "Oh, Emily," she said, her teeth chattering. "You can't...you can't *eat the dead.*"

"Yes, I can," Emily told her. "I like the taste."

*

Mother did not like to do what she did next, but she did it because she had to. She had to protect Emily and she would do whatever that took. She loved Emily so much and she kept telling her that. But it was lost on Emily, because whenever she thought of people like Mother, there was only coldness inside her, ice crystals and graveyard earth, nothing more...except hunger.

"George did not understand, Emily," Mother said as she dragged the body to the back door. "I wanted him to understand, but he wouldn't. He just wouldn't understand how wonderful this all is. And we'll miss him, but we can't have him causing trouble, now can we?"

Emily shook her head. Already she understood that she did not like people who caused trouble.

Mother took care of everything.

She dragged George's body out into the backyard and dug a deep hole in the flower garden and then put him in it. It was a nice hole, Emily thought, there in the rich black soil beneath the spreading limbs of the old oak tree where Emily's tree swing still hung. She wanted to lie down in there with George, be buried with him. All that dirt would be nice, but Mother said no.

Then Mother locked Emily in her room and went to her own.

Emily sat on the floor, thinking of cold things, marble stones and wilting funeral sprays, dead leaves blown through churchyards and secret buried boxes filled with good things to eat. Other than that, she just looked around her room in the darkness. Mother needed lights and Emily used to, but now she saw very good in the dark. Just like a cat. She looked at her toys and her games and none of those things interested her anymore. She had other interests now.

It took Mother a long time to fall asleep that night and Emily could hear her crying and talking to herself. While Emily waited she looked at some of her books in the moonlight coming through the rain-spattered windowpane. She had lots of picture books. Princesses and cuddly animals and little girls running and playing. She liked the pictures of the little girls. They made her hungry.

When Mother was asleep, Emily slipped out her window and went out into garden. The air was chilly and moist and she liked it. On her hands and knees, she dug George up and he was nice and cold. And very yummy. Especially the meat of his throat and all the stuff inside his belly. When she was done, Emily covered him back up because she understood that certain things—like lunch and supper and breakfast—had to be kept secret.

Emily liked secrets.

She knew lots of things other people didn't.

But she would never tell.

*

The next few days, Emily and Mother settled into their new life together. It was not exactly like it was before. But Emily did not mind. She liked to watch Mother and her craziness. The way she talked when there was no one in the room and the way she sometimes cried. Her eyes were very red and her hands shook. Sometimes she would look at Emily like she was disgusted and other times she would look at her like she was afraid of her. Emily did not mind, because Mother kept telling her that she loved her and Emily believed her.

Mother took a lot of pills and drank from one of George's bottles of whiskey. She had quit smoking last year because Emily had asked her to, because smoking could kill you, they said at school. At the time, Emily did not want Mother to die, but now that did not seem like a bad thing. It was a fun thing, really. Regardless, Mother was smoking again. She smoked one cigarette after the other and when the phone rang, she sometimes cried out. She would answer it, but her voice was always very funny. Emily went to answer it once herself, but Mother stopped her just in time.

Still, there were fun games to play.

Mother told Emily that if someone came to the door, she was to go hide down in the cellar. Emily had never liked the cellar. Especially the old coal bin with its dirt floor and dank smell and stone walls threaded with spider webs. But the new Emily liked it just fine. She spent a lot of time in the coal bin. The door was big and heavy and it creaked when you opened it. Just like a crypt. Emily liked to play down there. She liked to pretend that it was her tomb. She would lay on the dirt floor and cross her arms over her chest just like dead people on TV. She dug herself a grave and sometimes she laid in it. She took her old dolls down there and buried them too.

It was great fun.

Those first few days people came and went. Emily's funeral had been ten days before, but still the people came. They still brought cards and casseroles, plates of ham and pies.

So much that Mother started throwing it away. She rarely ever ate and then only when her head was spinning and she couldn't stand up. She told Emily that she had no appetite.

So sometimes Emily would hide in her tomb in the cellar—a place Mother would not go, which was good because Emily had buried some parts of George down there which were getting green and delicious-smelling—or sometimes in the spare room upstairs when people came to visit. Then she would watch them leave through the parted curtains. Mother told her not to do that, but Emily liked to. One time, when Aunt Doris stopped by, Emily had been watching her leave through the curtains and Doris had looked up and saw her. At least, Emily thought so. Doris took one look and ran to her car and did not come back.

But Emily did not tell Mother about that.

And she didn't tell her about the kids in the neighborhood. She liked to watch them through the curtains, too. Mother would not let her go out and play with them. She said Emily was sick. Maybe another day. But Mother was lying and Emily knew it. So she just watched the kids. She knew all of them, used to play with them. Sometimes Missy Johnson from down the street, Emily's old best friend, would ride her bike past the house and look up at it. A couple times she stopped out front and just stared. Then she rode away fast. Emily knew Missy was crying. Missy was sad because Emily was dead. Emily thought that was funny.

But Emily was getting sick of staying in the house.

She wanted to go out. She wanted to see her friends and tell them all the secrets she knew. They would like that.

But Mother made her stay inside, so she played alone and listened to the people passing by on the walks. The mailman and the neighbors, her friends riding their bikes and rollerblading and skipping and singing songs. She wanted to skip and sing with them. Next door, she could hear a baby crying. It was Mrs. Lee's new baby that had been born just a couple weeks before Emily's funeral. Emily liked to listen to it cry. She had always liked babies. She still liked them...but for other reasons.

She wished she had a baby of her own.

A fat, squealing, pink little baby to play with.

Maybe one night, Emily would go over there and play with it.

*

Nearly two weeks after Emily had been out of her grave, the house was filled with flies. They were attracted by Emily's special smell and despite all the sponge baths and perfuming Mother did, that smell remained. Finally, when some of Emily's skin came off in the tub, Mother stopped doing that. She just got used to the flies. Emily didn't mind them. They liked to cover her like a blanket, always buzzing and nipping. Sometimes when she opened her mouth, flies flew out. There were things burrowing under Emily's skin, too. Some were in too deep for her to get at, but others were close to the skin and she could dig them out with her nails. There had been a big swollen spot at the side of Emily's neck and when she scratched it open, dozens of fat white worms came squirming out. Emily kept them in a jar, but they died.

Mother spent a lot of time out of the house.

Usually when she came back she was drunk. She was worried about George, she said, because people were starting to ask questions about him and there might be trouble if they didn't stop.

But Emily didn't care about that.

There wasn't much of George left now. Just some bones and scraps and Emily was getting hungry again.

When Mother was gone, sometimes Emily would put on dress-up clothes and look at herself in the mirror. Feather boas and tiaras, wedding gowns and long evening coats that did not fit very well. Emily was no longer just white, she was gray now. There were patches of furry stuff growing up her cheeks and around her neck. It itched something terrible. Sometimes when she combed her hair, locks of it would come out. There were lots of white squirmy things in her scalp.

One afternoon, while Emily was alone, there was a knock at the door.

She hid upstairs. Whoever it was just wouldn't go away. They finally opened the door and came in. It was Aunt Doris. "Liz? Liz, are you here?" she called out. She waited for an answer but didn't get one. But she didn't leave. She just walked around and Emily could hear her saying things about the smell in the house, the flies, and the mess.

Emily hid at the top of the stairs, watching her.

But Aunt Doris must have heard her, because she turned around and said, "Liz? Liz, is that you?" No answer again. Emily giggled, even though she did not mean to. Doris just stood there. "Is someone there? Who's up there?"

Emily ran off to hide.

Doris came up the steps and Emily could smell the fear on her. It was getting so that she liked that odor. It made her hungry. It was like good odors coming out of the kitchen when supper was cooking in the old days. Emily remembered that she had never really liked Aunt Doris. She was always pinching Emily's cheeks and kissing her and her breath always smelled like garlic and her perfume was just awful. It would linger in the house for hours. Mother sometimes called Aunt Doris a "no-good nosey Nelly." Emily had thought that was funny.

But now she understood.

Aunt Doris was being nosey. She had no business here, but she came anyway. So Emily waited in the hall closet for her. She tried not to giggle, but it was not easy. Aunt Doris was walking back and forth, looking in rooms. Emily could still smell the fear on her. It was a thick, sour yellow odor that Doris was not even aware of. She walked around, muttering things to herself. Emily hid in the darkness. It was like playing hide-and-seek. She wondered if Aunt Doris liked hide-and-seek. Smiling, Emily rattled her fingers on the inside of the closet door.

And that got Aunt Doris' attention.

She stood outside the door. "Is someone...is someone in there?"

Emily giggled.

Aunt Doris opened the door. She opened it very slowly, breathing very hard now, then threw it open all the way.

"You're *it*," Emily told her.

Aunt Doris screamed and fell down, clutching her chest and writhing on the floor. Emily could hear her heart struggling to find its beat, but it was skipping, speeding up and slowing down. And she kept screaming, of course.

So Emily jumped on top of her and banged her head on the floor until she stopped moving. Then she dragged her down to the cellar and buried her in the coal bin.

Mother would never know a thing.

The night after Emily knocked Aunt Doris unconscious, then tore out her throat in the cellar, Mother started acting very peculiar. More peculiar than normal, that was, because Mother was always very peculiar. Mother used to work very hard to keep the house clean. She'd scrub and wash and wax, make big dinners like roast beef and flank steak, but these days she never cooked or cleaned. She liked to drink whiskey, smoke cigarettes, and take pills. She was very thin and shaky, sometimes she cried and sometimes she held a pillow over her mouth and screamed into it.

But that night when she came home, she started asking questions about Aunt Doris.

"Emily...did she come over today?"

Emily just smiled. "She might have, but I hid just like you told me."

"You...you didn't hurt her?"

Emily shook her head. "I never hurt anyone. But sometimes I make them be quiet."

"Oh, Emily...did you?"

"Did I what, Mother?"

But Mother could not ask the question. She needed to drink and smoke and talk to herself for awhile. She liked to do that. Sometimes she would curl up on the floor for hours, mumbling and staring off into space. Those were the times that Emily went down into the cellar for a snack. She would disinter all her dolls and they would have a little tea party. Emily would pretend they were eating, too.

Emily waited until Mother passed out and then she went and sat in her room. She could hear the Lee's baby crying next door. It sure liked to cry a lot. When it was dark, Emily went out her window and over to the Lee's house. She saw Mr. and Mrs. Lee watching TV through the window. They were very nice people. The baby had the room in the back of the house. Emily stood outside its window. Everything was done in blue so she knew it was a boy.

"Hello, baby," she said through the window screen.

But the baby was sleeping and Emily knew that babies needed a lot of sleep. Carefully, she pulled the screen out of the window and went inside. She was very quiet. She did not want to disturb Mr. and Mrs. Lee. The baby was sleeping in a little blue onesie and diaper. He had a teddy bear in his crib and a Winnie the Poo mobile that spun round and round.

"Hello, baby," Emily said.

She picked him up and he began to squirm. She held baby close to her and he squirmed even more. Then he began to cry and cry. As much as Emily cooed to him and sang songs under breath, baby would not stop struggling and crying. That was not good. If Mr. and Mrs. Lee came, they would not let her play with baby. They would take him from her and she did not want that. Baby was so soft and warm and chubby. Emily wanted to kiss him and touch him and suck the breath from his little mouth.

"Stop, baby," Emily told him. "Stop making noise."

But baby wouldn't, so Emily made him be quiet. His little fat neck broke beneath the caress of her gray, flaking hands. Carrying baby by the feet, she slipped out the window. Long before Mr. and Mrs. Lee came into the nursery and the screaming and commotion began, Emily had baby down in the coal bin. She showed him to Aunt Doris.

And then she began to play with him.

*

Mother was gone the next morning and the phone kept ringing and ringing while Emily was playing dress-up. Mother did not want Emily answering the phone, but it kept ringing and ringing and Emily could not stand it anymore. Her hearing was very acute since she left the grave. She liked things to be quiet now. She liked things cold and damp and silent.

But the phone kept ringing.

Finally, she pulled it off its cradle.

A voice on the end said, "Liz? Liz? Liz, are you there?"

It was a voice that Emily had not heard in a long time. A very sweet, patient voice that belonged to Grandma Reese, Mother's mother. Emily had always liked grandma whenever she came to town which was only a few times a year. Usually at Christmas and sometimes in the summer. She would always bring Emily gifts.

Emily liked to hear her voice, yet that emptiness inside herself would not let her feel happy or sad, just coldly indifferent.

"Liz? Liz, are you there."

"Hello, Grandma," Emily said.

And on the other end there was a gasping and a great commotion as the phone was dropped and grandma began to wail in a high, unnerving voice.

Emily hung up.

She did not like those kind of sounds.

Afterwards, Emily went back to playing dress up. She put on a white sparkling lace gown that looked very much like her burial dress. She wore a floppy straw hat with a big flower on it like rich ladies sometimes did at Kentucky Derby. Pearls and bracelets and long white gloves. In the mirror, she thought she looked very nice even though she was all swollen-up and blackening, worms crawling under her skin and flies covering her face. Her left eye had fallen out of the socket the day before and she could not find it. A great flap of skin hung from cheek now and you could see the skull beneath. When she grinned, her smile was all yellow teeth and gray gums, her lips shriveled away.

It was Saturday and on Saturday afternoons, Emily and Missy Johnson used to go play in the vacant lot across the alley. There were stands of trees to every side and it was like their very own kingdom. They liked to play very dramatic games as all little girls did. Usually, they would pretend they were sisters and their parents had died in a plane crash and they were hiding from the bad people who wanted to kill them. Or they would pretend one of them was dying from an incurable disease and the other was a doctor or a nurse trying to save them. But in the end, the sick one always died. And that was funny, because now one of them had *really* died.

Out the window, Emily saw Missy riding her bike down the alley. She had her plastic Barbie case with her. You opened it up and it was a little salon with mirrors and a wardrobe, lots of little dresses and shoes. She was going over to the vacant lot.

Mother had warned Emily that she was never to leave the house, but since she was all dressed up, she decided it would be okay. She went out into the backyard and right away Mr. Miller's beagle down the alley began to howl. Emily walked over towards the vacant lot, her high heels clicking on the concrete. She saw Missy there. Missy had her back to her. She had her Barbie case open and was singing as she dressed Skipper and Stacey.

Emily came up behind her like she always had. "Boo," she said.

Missy turned and screamed like Emily had never heard her scream before. She scrawled away on all fours and ran, screaming the whole while. Emily called out to her, but she wouldn't stop.

Emily went back home.

On the way, Mr. Miller drove down the alley in his car and she waved to him. He just kept staring...staring so much, in fact, that he drove his car right through his own fence.

*

The neighborhood was busy after that.

Cars drove up and down the street and a lot of them were police cars. Lots of people gathered outside the house with Mr. Miller. Missy's mom and dad were there, too. By the time Mother came home, there were people everywhere and lots of policemen in uniforms. They tried to stop Mother, but she ran from them and came inside.

"What did you do?" she said to Emily. "What did you do?"

"I went outside," Emily said.

Mother locked the doors as fists pounded on them, wanting to be let in. There was a lot of shouting and yelling as night came.

"We have to get out of here," Mother said. "We have to go somewhere safe."

"The cemetery," Emily said.

"Yes, that's where we'll go."

But then there was more pounding at the door and finally something kept ramming it until it came off its hinges. Then the police came charging in and Mother ran right at them, screaming and fighting.

"Run, Emily!" she called out. *"Run!"*

So Emily did.

She ran out the back way and almost made it to the vacant lot when she heard the barking of big dogs. Men were running through the neighborhood with flashlights. Emily went into the vacant lot and hid in the grass. She dug up Mrs. Lee's baby where she had hidden it in the dirt under the big rock, brushed the crawly things off it. Then the men came and put flashlights on her, blinding her.

"Dear God in heaven," one of the policemen said.

Emily shook her headless baby at them and hissed, showing her long teeth.

The dogs that were with them were howling and baying and snapping at their handlers. The men let them go. The dogs came right at Emily, sinking their teeth into her, tearing open her dress-up clothes and biting free flaps of flesh and crunching bones. Lots of people cried out, but they didn't come any closer. The dogs chewed and rent and split Emily, yanking off her limbs which kicked and clawed in the grass, fingers looking for something to grab. The dogs did not stop. They were mad and frothing and snapping and biting.

Emily kept screaming until there was nothing left to scream *with*.

Then there was just silence and the growling of dogs and people whimpering.

So fifteen days after Emily came out of her grave, what was left of her was shoveled back in there again.

DIS-JOINTED

It was raining when they murdered Pauly Zaber.

And it was coming down in buckets and pails when they dragged his corpse from the trunk of Specks' Buick. Zaber had been a big man and he made a big corpse. Wrapped in sackcloth, a lot of it, he was roped up like a steer. Getting him in the trunk was tough business and getting him out was something else again.

"Just grab hold," Specks said. "He's dead for godsake, he won't bite you."

But maybe Weams and Lyon didn't quite believe that. Sure, they'd helped Specks murder Zaber and their hands were just as red as his, but now handling the body after it had been cooling an hour...there was just something obscene about that.

Lyon reached in there, taking hold of the ropes, started yanking along with Specks, drawing the dead man up. "I'm doing my bit," he said, raindrops beading on his face. "Tell Weams to do his."

Weams was going to tell him to go to hell, maybe tell both of them that, but instead he reached into the blackness of the trunk, started pulling, feeling that awful weight shifting under the tarp. He kept his lips pressed in a white line and he wasn't sure if that was because of what he might say or to keep himself from screaming.

Because that was a real possibility.

"On the count of three, girls," Specks said. "Up...and...out..."

It was nasty work.

The rain hammering down, the ground gone to sluicing gray mud. The trees rising up around them black and gnarled, ribboned with crawling shadows that were viscid and horribly alive.

Weams kept imagining that maybe Zaber was still alive, that three rounds from a 9mm hadn't been enough to put that pig down dead. That under the tarp, maybe he was awake. Maybe he was thinking things.

Zaber made a big corpse, all right. A huge, porcine man whose idea of eating light had been a porterhouse smothered in clam linguine. He tipped the scales at 400 pounds. A big, meaty fellow with eyes just as black as coal dust and a vicious temper. People said he once ate a guy that didn't pay up on a loan...but you couldn't believe everything you heard. There was only one thing for sure about Pauly Zaber: he was a loanshark and if you didn't make your payments, he would hurt you.

But now he was dead, cold, had eaten three slugs from a 9mm and that's all she wrote.

Specks, Weams, and Lyon were grunting and puffing, swearing and groaning, but finally they got their sackcloth package up onto the lip of the trunk, balanced precariously. And that's when one of Zaber's huge arms slipped out of the canvas, his hand landing on Lyon's own with a wet slapping sound.

Lyon screamed.

You could say it was shock or superstitious terror, but all that mattered was that Lyon screamed like a little girl with a high, shrill wailing sound. He let go of Zaber and the sudden weight of the corpse overwhelmed the other two and it fell to their feet, slopping in the mud...both arms out now.

"He touched me!" Lyon stammered, rubbing his hands on his wet pants. "Jesus, he touched me, he *touched* me!"

Specks took hold of him and shook him. "He's dead, you idiot, he can't hurt you now! He's no more dangerous than a side of beef."

"But cold...damn, he's so cold..."

Weams wasn't hearing any of it. He was just looking down at that lolling, grisly bundle, thinking how with those flabby white arms hanging out of the sackcloth Zaber looked like something being born, trying to pull itself free of a placenta.

"Lend a hand," Specks said.

They took hold of Zaber's legs under the canvas and dragged him through the muck down the trail. The undergrowth was wet and dripping, the trees tall and skeletal. The night was damp and cool and ominous. When they made the shack, Specks unlocked it and they dragged Zaber inside and deposited their burden on the plank flooring.

Specks found a lantern on a hook, lit it.

"Nobody uses this place," he told them, the shadows crawling over his face in the flickering yellow illumination. "It's perfect."

And maybe it was. Just a desolate tumbledown shack far from the city nestled in a desolate stand of woods like a pea in a poke. The sort of place that stood for fifty winters and might stand for fifty more, or just fall to jackstraw ruin next month.

Specks said, "I'll be back in a minute with the goodies. If he moves...just scream good and loud." He thought that was funny. "But not loud enough to wake the dead."

Then he went back to the Buick to get the tools, leaving Weams and Lyon alone with Big Pauly Zaber, the former syndicate shylock that had made all their lives hell. But he wasn't going to be doing much of anything now.

"I think," Lyon said, "I think we screwed up big here, I'm sure of it."

Weams chuckled low in his throat. "Do you really think so?"

"Fuck you."

Zaber's corpse shifted in the sackcloth, one hand sliding free, knuckles rapping on the floor.

Lyon sucked in a sharp breath and did not seem to be able to exhale. Weams just stood there, filled with a gaping terror that was oddly blank and dreamlike. He couldn't seem to get his mouth to close.

"Gravity," Lyon said, like maybe he was trying to convince himself.

The shack smelled of moistness and age, black earth and mildewed leaves. It was a heavy, vaporous odor that got thicker by the moment. Both men just looked at each other, then away, their faces gaunt and chiseled by stress, their eyes jutting from their skulls, glassy and unblinking.

Then Specks was back.

He handed out crowbars and hammers from his sack of tools, left the shovels leaning up in the corner. By the shifting lantern light, they yanked up the rotting planks one by one until the clotted black earth below was revealed and a fetid, loamy stink filled the shack.

"Okay, girls," Specks said, stripping down to his undershirt—a tank top, of course, to show off all his gleaming muscles—and grinning like a skull in a basket. "You know what happens now."

But Lyon shook his head. "I just don't know if I can."

"Oh, you will," Specks told him. "By God, you will. We're in this together and together we'll do what has to be done."

Specks told them to start digging while he unwrapped their package. He used a knife, cutting the ropes free from the sackcloth, exposing Pauly Zaber's huge, naked corpse like a grim surprise under a Christmas tree. Zaber had gone white as lace, distended and obese, a thickset rage of chins and pendulous tits, an immense belly like some fleshy beach ball inflated to the point of bursting. And everywhere, just bleached and rolling. The only color on him was the tattoo of an eagle on his chest...and that looked like something hit by a truck now, a mangled crow at best. The artwork had been shattered by blackened bullet holes, streaks of gore that oozed and dried.

He hadn't bled very much and Specks was quick to point out that was because one of the bullets had shattered his heart. When it stopped pumping, he said, Zaber stopped bleeding.

Weams said, "Look...look at his face..."

It was a white, greasy mass, thick-lipped, one eye open and staring, the other retreating into a pouch of fat. Maybe it was rigor mortis or something, but his mouth was drawn into a lurid, toothy grin. There was something vile and perverse about that.

Specks had a hacksaw out. "Who wants to go first?"

Lyon made a whimpering sound and almost lost his lunch when Specks laid the teeth of the saw against Zaber's pudgy gullet and began to draw it back and forth, back and forth. Weams had to take him outside. And when they were both there, the night closing in and the rain on their faces, they both got sick, the nausea boiling up and out of them in tangled, gagging tides. But it was more than just what Specks was doing in there, but the *sound* of it. That shearing, meaty sound like a crosscut saw ripping into a ball of suet. And when Specks struck bone...Jesus.

Weams and Lyon had a smoke out there, pulled from Specks' flask of whiskey, and wondered to high heaven how they would ever purge this night from their minds. When they went back in, Zaber's legs and head were missing. Specks had cut them off and bagged them in green Hefty garbage bags. There was blood soaking into the soil, blood smeared right up to Specks' elbows.

Weams looked down on that legless, headless torso and felt a clawing madness in the back of his skull. Zaber was now an immense, fish-white blobby thing with arms still in place, head sheared to a stump, legs gone where they entered the hip. He could see the grizzled meat in there, marbled and red like fresh beef, the sawed knobs of bone trailing streamers of white ligament.

It was too much, just too much.

"Lyon," Specks said, enjoying himself, "take off his arms. Me and Weams will go dump this trash in the river."

Lyon was shaking. "No, no, no...Jesus, you can't...you can't leave me alone with that thing..."

Specks started laughing. "All right, Weams you stay. You each do an arm. Start cutting in the armpit, it's soft there. I'll take this stuff down to the river, fill the bags with rocks and sink them. By the time the bags rot through, won't be enough left to float."

"C'mon, Specks," Weams said. "Let's just dump him in the hole as is."

"No. Arms are hooked to hands and hands to fingers. Fingers have fingerprints. If anybody finds the torso, I don't want them matching fingerprints to it. And Zaber has a record. He did time. So cut him up."

He told them to put the torso in the big hole they'd dug and to bag the arms, bury them off in the woods. Before he left, he said, "And don't let me down, boys."

He tossed Zaber's legs over his left shoulder and even bagged in that green plastic, they could see that the undersides of his knees were resting atop Specks' shoulders.

"Man," he said. "These legs gotta weight eighty a piece."

He picked up the bag with the head in it and off he went.

Which left Weams and Lyon alone with the torso, watching it, not wanting to look, but unable to stop. There was a grim magnetism to the thing. So they watched and waited—maybe for it to move.

"I don't like this," Lyon said. "I don't like any of it."

"It doesn't seem to bother Specks," Weams said.

"That's because he's a fucking animal." Lyon went to the door, peered out, then closed it again, making sure Specks wasn't out there eavesdropping. "I mean, c'mon, whose idea was it to kill fucking Pauly?"

"Specks'. But we went along with it."

"Sure we did. And whose idea was it to slice the body up? Specks'. He's too easy with all this, man. He's done this shit before."

Weams had been thinking that, too. Specks did the shooting. He'd known exactly how to bag up the remains and he seemed to know exactly how to cut them up. "Specks has been around. He's a bad boy. But he got us out of some ugly shit with Zaber. I mean, shit, I was into the guy for almost twenty G's."

Lyon sighed. "Me, too. But still...we should have thought about this. Killing a guy...Christ, that makes us no better than Specks. He's done time before, but we haven't. I don't think I could take it."

Weams didn't say so, but standing there with that massive legless, headless corpse spread at their feet, he was thinking that prison was the least of their worries.

"Okay, we're part of this now. No going back. But I'm not going any farther," Lyon announced. "I won't butcher a...a corpse."

"Me either," Weams sighed.

They pushed it into the hole with their boots and it landed with a flopping, rubbery sound that made them both gasp. Then they buried it, smoothed out the soil. They dug a dummy hole out in the woods, buried it back up. It would convince Specks...unless he wanted to paw around in there.

When he returned, they were fitting the floorboards back in place, nailing them tight.

"How was it, girls?" he asked, rain dripping from his hair. "Messy?"

"Let's not talk about it, okay?" Weams said.

"Sure, sure, whatever you say. The arms?"

"Out in the woods," Lyon said.

Specks seemed satisfied. "Well," he said, "I guess that's the last we'll see of Pauly Zaber."

But Weams had to wonder.

Later, the night thick as soup beyond the windows of the old house, Weams was watching Lila mix him a vodka martini. Just watching her, you knew she had been a bartender once. Too smooth, too easy with it.

Just like Specks with a dead body.

Lila was all dolled-up in a short skirt and sequined top, a gold chain teasing her ample cleavage. That was Lila: all dressed-up and nowhere to go. And she knew damn well why there was nowhere to go: no money, no nothing. Just that old creaking house and Weams, her husband.

Lila handed him his drink. "Let me guess," she said, her eyes frigid and brittle like black ice, "you were out with Lyon and Specks? Stop me here if I'm wrong. Out playing the ponies, working the slots, dropping a few hands of blackjack. Am I close on this?"

Weams sipped his drink, heard his wife, but only saw a blubbery white thing falling into a grave. "I guess. Maybe...what did you say?"

"How much this time?"

"How much what?"

"How much money did you drop?" she wanted to know, those eyes not black ice now, but something colder, maybe absolute zero where even oxygen freezes. "And, better yet, how much did you borrow from that loanshark, from—"

"Change the record," Weams snapped, sweat beading his brow.

"You have a problem," his wife said. "You're an addict. You need help."

"I'm fine."

"Are you? You know what I heard? Lyon's wife is leaving him and he's about to lose his house. Does that little bell ring familiar?"

Weams' hands were shaking and it took both of them to get his drink to his mouth. "Leave Lyon out of it."

"How about Specks...how is Specks doing?"

Weams slammed his drink down on the coffee table. "Why the hell are you always asking about Specks? Do you like the guy? You got something going on with him?"

"That'd be the day," she said. "He's a creep and we both know it. An ex-con. How can you associate with a guy like him?"

"He's okay."

And Weams almost started laughing. *Sure, he's okay. And Pauly Zaber? He was okay, too. Salt of the earth. Just normal, hard-working guys.*

Lila laughed. "Me and Specks. Don't be ridiculous."

But Weams didn't think he was being ridiculous. He just stared at his wife, his complexion pasty, his eyes red-rimmed and fixed. "Sometimes I wonder about the two of you."

"You don't look good," Lila said, crossing to the picture window and looking out across the darkened yard, the trees blowing in the wind, the gate creaking open and shut on the fence. "You look sick. Maybe you should tell me about it."

"About what?"

"About what happened tonight? Did you sign away the house? The car? Is it that fat loanshark? What's his name? Zab—"

"I'm fine, dammit!" Weams told her, brushing perspiration from his face. "I'm perfectly fine! Can't you see that? Can't you see how fine I am?"

*

When the phone rang just after midnight two days later, Weams came awake with a scream on his lips. He held it in check, shivering and sweating, trying hard not to remember what he'd been dreaming about. Lila was gone. Out God-knows-where with God-knows-who.

He stumbled over to the phone. "Yes? Hello?"

"Listen, Weams, you got to get over here." It was Lyon and he sounded funny. Drunk? Crazy? Maybe both. But there was something in his voice, a sharp-edged dread that was positively frightening in its urgency.

"C'mon, Lyon...do you know what time it is?"

But Lyon didn't seem to care. "You have to get over here. I mean it. Something's happening and, God, Weams, you gotta help me..."

"Calm down, will ya? Just take it easy. Tell me about it."

Weams could imagine him over there, clutching the phone in a sweaty hand, alone in that house now that his wife had left and just white with terror...but terror of *what?*

Lyon's voice went down to a whisper, a gritty rough sort of whisper like he was afraid somebody was listening. "It...it started about midnight, no eleven-thirty...I'm not sure, but that's when I first heard it."

"Heard what?"

"Something scratching at my door."

Weams' belly felt loose. "Scratching? Like what? A dog? A cat?"

"No, nothing like that...just a scratching like...like maybe nails being drawn over the outside of the door." He paused there, as if he was listening again. "It kept on and on and, God help me, I was scared for some reason...I didn't dare look out there..."

"But you did?"

Lyon swallowed. "Yes." Swallow. "Yes, I did. I...I crept up to the bathroom window and looked out on the porch—"

"And?"

All he could hear was Lyon breathing, licking his lips. "Out there...I wasn't sure...something fat and white like a body, Weams...something that didn't have a head and didn't have legs...it was scratching the door with its fingernails..."

Weams just stood there, sweat running down his spine. He wanted desperately to fall over like a post. He was dizzy and nauseous and his throat had constricted down to a pinhole. His breath came in short, wheezing gasps. "Lyon...you're losing it...do you know what you're saying to me?"

But then the phone was dropped and there were sounds over there. The sound of shattering glass. The sound of something thumping and crashing around, something wet and heavy.

And, of course, there was also the sound of Lyon screaming.

*

An hour later the police were all over Lyon's house, snapping pictures and taking measurements, asking questions and getting few answers. But mostly just pulling their peaked caps off and rubbing their eyes, trying to get the sight of what they'd seen out of their heads.

Specks pushed past the big cop at the door and Weams followed right behind him, right into the slaughterhouse. It was bad. It was more than bad. Besides the shattered glass on the floor and the ragged curtains billowing in, there was a lot of blood. Looked like someone had butchered a steer in there. But what both Specks and Weams saw was the form on the couch with the bloody sheet thrown over it. The sheet had slipped off Lyon's face and it was marble-white, eyes staring up at something nobody else could see.

The bad thing was the sheet ended right where Lyon's legs should have been.

"Where...where are they?" Specks said in an empty voice.

"Can't find 'em," one of the detectives admitted.

Specks looked around—through the debris and drying pools of blood, the clods of black earth on the floor—like maybe he might catch a glimpse of them. Shoved under the couch or tucked behind a chair.

The cops started hammering them with questions and Specks said he was just a friend, didn't know anything more about it. Weams told them about the phone call. About Lyon saying something was scratching outside the door. But that's all he said. He wasn't about to go farther. Not then. Not yet.

The cops seemed to believe them, but they studied the two men, gave them some funny looks. Maybe they saw how pale they were, how they shook, the way they fumbled their words and started at the slightest sound like they were expecting something. But Specks and Weams had just lost a friend and that's all it was, that's all it could be.

Outside, Weams had to fight not to get sick. That metallic, sour stench of blood was all over him, he couldn't seem to get it out of his head.

"You know, you know what this means—"

"Shut up," Specks warned him. "Just shut the hell up."

The coroner's people were examining the broken window in depth by flashlight. With forceps, they were pulling strands of something from the shards of glass still in the frame. Looked like strands of tissue.

An old lady was standing under a tree with a cop. She was a slight thing with a wrinkle for every year. Looked like a good wind would send her sailing over rooftops and trees like a sheet blown from a line.

"I saw something," she was saying. "I don't know how you'd exactly describe it."

"Do your best," the cop said.

"A big white monkey," she said.

The cop just looked at her. "Ma'am?"

"Yes, sir. That's what I thought. It was hopping down the walk like a monkey, like one of those apes in a circus, you see? Using its hands to push it along, swinging its body and slapping along with its hands...but it was white...funny..."

"How so?" the cop said and you could see he thought it was all a waste of time. Christ, pink elephants next.

She hugged herself against the night breeze. "Well, sir, it didn't seem to have a head nor legs, just those long arms and a big, fat body."

"Anything else?"

"Yes, I believe it had a tattoo on its chest."

*

On the way out to the shack in Specks' Buick, Weams spilled it, said those words, hated the taste of them on his tongue: "We didn't do it, Lyon and me. We didn't cut Zaber's arms off, we just threw him in the pit. That's what we did. That's exactly what we did."

"Should've known better than to trust you idiots."

"Yes," Weams agreed, "you should've."

"What the hell's that supposed to mean?"

Weams chose his words carefully...carefully as he could. "Me and Lyon were amateurs, Specks. You knew that. You damn well knew that. Not like you."

"Oh, you think I do that shit all the time?"

"No, but we saw you. You were experienced. You knew exactly what to do."

Specks sighed, lit a cigarette. "Maybe I did. Maybe I spent too much of my youth with the wrong people. What of it? I'm not a fucking psychopath. What I did, I did for us all. You boys agreed. You're as deep in this shit as I am, Weams. Don't you dare forget that."

Weams didn't think he ever would.

Specks pulled the Buick off the highway, onto a gravel road that turned into a rutted dirt track a few miles down the line. Weams didn't say a thing, he just remembered it all, watched the headlights limning those big twisted trees that hung out over the road. He didn't say a word, but he thought plenty.

"All right," Specks said when they reached the field. "This is it."

Weams stuck tight to him as they followed that meandering trail through the dark, brooding forest. There was terror in him, hot and white and knotted, but not for what they might find, but for what mind find *them*.

The shack was still there, still waiting.

Then the lantern was lit and Specks and he began yanking up the boards. They didn't bother being careful this time, they went at it all-out, splitting the boards and tossing them aside until there was a circular, rough-hewn hole through the plank floor. Weams held the lantern down there, his blood gone to a cool, gray sludge. The dirt of the grave was undisturbed. Or so it seemed.

"Keep that lantern steady," Specks said, taking a shovel and giving his 9mm to Weams.

He began pawing through that moist, rank soil, flinging shovelfuls aside wildly, not caring if he sank the blade into Zaber's corpse, not caring much about anything but proving to Weams how very wrong he was.

Four feet down there was nothing.

"We didn't go any deeper than that," Weams told him.

"You must have," Specks said, sweat streaking down his dirty face. Weams felt something happening, something that made him instinctively cringe away from that hole as if a snake was going to show itself or a tiger was going to come vaulting out with gnashing teeth. "Specks, dear Christ, get out of there, get—"

Too late.

Specks looked down into the pit where his feet were, saw they were slowly sinking into the bottom of the grave. He couldn't seem to work them loose. He let out a shriek, thrashing and fighting and finally falling over. And by then he had sunk to his knees in that rippling, bubbling soil. And he was still going down, like a man drawn into quicksand.

"Help me!" he cried. "Help me, Weams!"

Weams took hold of one of his hands, then let go.

"What're you doing, Weams?" Specks whined, tears running down his face, drool flying from his contorted mouth. "Help me, for godsake! Help me! Help me! Get me outta here! Something's got me, *something's pulling me down*—"

Weams' eyes were huge and wet. "Tell me, Specks. Tell me about you and Lila. Tell me about what you have with my wife."

But Specks was beyond simple conversation. He had sunk to the waist now, screaming and moaning and gibbering and all that did was sink him farther. Sink him until two bloated white arms rose from the muddy earth, pudgy fingers taking hold of him and dragging him down and down. But before his mouth was filled with soil, Weams heard what he said.

Heard it very well.

Zaber, he'd said. *It was Zaber, not me.*

*

Lila came slinking home an hour before dawn.

Sneaking, stealing lightly, her high-heels in hand, she slipped through the front door and Weams was waiting for her. He had Specks' 9mm and he pointed it straight at her.

"I've been waiting for you," he said.

She just stood there, looking a little worn around the edges from a rough night of play, a cat creeping home, its belly full and satisfied. She started to smile, saw the gun, thought better of it. Then she didn't do anything but watch Weams slam the door shut behind her. And Weams could hear the loom of her brain whirring and clicking, trying to spin believable webs of lies, but unable to find any fresh silk.

"How long," Weams put to her, "how long were you and Zaber sneaking around behind my back?"

"Zaber? I—"

"Don't lie to me."

Lila was figuring that probably wouldn't be a real good idea either. Because she was seeing Weams, her husband of six years, seeing that twitch in the corner of his mouth, that mottled face, those eyes like windows staring into a madhouse.

"Not long," she said, then started to cry.

And, hey, she was good. You had to give her that. Right to the last drop. Those tears looked real and they made something soften in Weams. But not for long. "You wanna tell me why?" he said to her.

Oh, she was whimpering and chewing her lip, making with those big brown doe eyes. The sweet, precocious little girl who had done something bad, but would never do it again.

Weams laughed. Maybe it wasn't a laugh exactly...too hollow, too sharp, too agonized. "No, let *me* tell you why. *Money.* Plain and simple. It's always that way with people like you, Lila. Cash means so much to you, you'd lay with a pig and...ha, ha...I guess you did at that."

"Please...please," she pouted.

"Get moving," Weams said.

He marched her right to the cellar door, the gun on her the whole while. "Open it," he said.

She did. Her hands were trembling. All you could see down there were the steps leading into a mouth of blackness. Like the depths of a cave, there could have been just about anything down there.

"Go ahead," he said, far too calmly.

"Oh please, baby, you don't—"

"Go down...or I'll fucking shoot you," Weams told her, drooling now, a funny sobbing sound coming up from his throat.

Weeping, Lila moved down two steps, then three. Stopped. She turned and looked back up at Weams like he might change his mind. And as she did so, there was a sound down there...a fleshy, heavy sound. Something moving, something big.

"Enjoy yourself," Weams said, slamming the door shut behind her, locking it carefully.

He heard her scream.

Heard the sound of motion, somebody scrambling up the stairs. Lila's voice crying out, begging hysterically for help. A thrashing, a slapping of flesh, a rending. A manic scream dampened by something wet and slobbering and attentive.

Then, his mind just gone, Weams put the gun in his mouth and pulled the trigger.

It was easier that way.

*

A week later, the police busted into the house.

They were led by two detectives named Green and Dickson, both big brutes with topcoats and thick necks, identical oily gray eyes. When Zaber went missing and they found out that he was hooked up with Specks, it wasn't too hard to put it all together. They found Weams' corpse and Lila's down in the basement. It was a real ugly scene, but they were used to ugly scenes. They couldn't figure out who chopped off Lyon's legs or the whereabouts of Specks, but they had an angle on Zaber...or part of him.

"They finish the post on the woman?" Green asked a few days after the coroner's people bagged the bodies and took them away to the morgue where things were more intimate.

Dickson nodded. "They did. Doc says she was ruptured pretty bad, raped repeatedly by the looks of it. Vaginally, anally. Probably went on for days."

"Jesus. Bled to death?"

"No, not exactly," Dickson said. "There was a foreign object wedged down in her throat. She choked on it, asphyxiated."

"What was it?"

Dickson told him. "Doc said it looked like she bit it off and tried to swallow it. She must have been some kind of freak, because it was putrefied. Whoever it came from was dead for days before she put it in her mouth."

PIRAYA

As they pushed deeper into the Amazon Basin, following a winding series of tributaries, their guide told them one randy tale after another of what he called the *piraya*. He was a kind old Yagua Indian from the Javary named Rico Uara Valqui and had come highly recommended. He told them wild stories about the old Conquistadors who'd made the unpleasant mistake of wearing blood-red trousers in piranha-infested waters. About swimmers getting their nipples bitten off and skinny-dippers who'd gotten *more* than their nipples bitten off.

At that last one Jack chuckled, wiped sweat from his face, and gave Elise a jab with his elbow so she'd see it was a joke too. But Elise did not think it was funny. The others in the low-bottomed boat—Cutler and Basille—just smiled thinly.

"And all true, I swear," Rico said, crossing himself after telling a particularly lurid tale of a madman named Crazy Lupo who'd caught his limit of piranha by using his murdered wife's corpse as bait. Rico grinned, ran fingers through his stubbly white hair. "But it not all bad, eh? You wait, we catch our limit, conk-conk-conk, we knock the fight out them sumbitch *pirayas*, then we clean 'em out, slit-slit-slit, some the garlic, the salt, the spice root, then cook 'em up over the fire. Taste real good. You see, eh?"

"That's what I'm looking forward to," Jack said. "I heard they taste like catfish."

"Sure, like you say." Rico looked at him and grinned. "Hey, maybe Rico show you how to make *piraya*-head soup, eh? It make a man more a man. You eat the soup, Jack, your wife she not enough for you! You need ten wives!"

Elise sighed, waving flies away from her face. She hated fish in general. It was Jack's idea that she come. He told her that she'd never know Peru, the *real* Peru by hanging around the hotel in Pucallpa. And her answer to that was she did not want to know the real Peru. Pucallpa was bad enough with the bugs and the stench coming in from the docks, she didn't need to get devoured by man-eating fish to boot. But Jack had explained that there was nothing to fear. There were twenty-five species of piranha in the Amazon and most fed on other fish, on insects, on fruit that had fallen into the water. Only six species were true flesh-eaters and of those six, only the Red-Bellied Piranha and the larger Black Piranha were dangerous to man.

So here she was, deep in the backwaters of the Amazon with a guide who kept telling one raunchy tale after another, showing off the stump of the finger he'd lost taking a hook from a piranha's mouth. There was absolutely no breeze. The air was damp, the river stank like something dead. They had rubbed Vick's Vapo-Rub over their faces and arms so the clouds of mosquitoes wouldn't drain them dry. As it was, she was drenched with sweat, her eyes were burning, and Cutler kept staring at her.

From the moment they stepped into the boat—a flat-bottomed motorized skiff—Elise was aware of his eyes on her. His gaze was perverse. Something about it made her stomach roll. Not that she hadn't dealt with men like him before, but the way he looked at her, sizing her up like a tasty slab of beef, was just too much.

"Why don't you take a picture, it'll last longer," she told him.

Cutler grinned. His teeth were yellow, tobacco-stained, there was a sheen of sweat on his face. "Was I staring?"

"Yes, you goddamn well know you were."

Cutler shrugged, licked his lips, and stared out over the shimmering expanse of the upper Amazon. What he saw was pale green flora growing in and out of the dirty brown water, clouds of gnats rising and falling, broken stumps and dead trees rising up like monuments. A steam condensed above the water, rolling over its surface like a sluggish fog. Tanagers and barbets cried out in the treetops, insects buzzed and flies nipped. None of which was as remotely interesting to him as Elise and her fine cleavage which made him feel weak in the pit of his belly.

"Simmer down," Jack said under his breath and not for the first time.

Elise scowled at him. "If he keeps staring at me, he's going overboard."

"Quit staring at her, Cutler," Jack said, smiling. "I won't have it."

Cutler was one of his drinking buddies from Pucallpa. He was a small, wiry man with the eyes of a rodent. He made Elise's flesh crawl. Basille, the other occupant of the boat, was a round, portly businessman from Lima. The only thing that excited him was money.

Elise tried to ignore the both of them.

They were on the Ucayali River in central Peru, the main headstream of the Amazon formed by the junction of the Apurímac and Urubamba. A wild green world like something out of the Mesozoic: hot and steaming, clotted with palms and creepers and hanging vines, the jungles haunted by jaguars and poisonous snakes, black caimans and anacondas waiting in the stagnant river bottoms and flooded undergrowth.

They had come because Jack wanted to go piranha fishing.

And that was so like Jack, Elise thought. If he couldn't catch it with a hook or shoot it with a gun, he had no interest in it.

The jungle seemed endless as it pressed in from all sides. Rank, uniform, monotonous, licked by the foul-smelling serpentine river. Now and again they came upon clusters of palm huts belonging to families of Yorba Indians. But that was it. Rico moved the boat along, still telling stories, still making the men laugh. Elise sighed. He was exactly the kind of man Jack always seemed to find.

There was a sudden gagging stink of fleshy decomposition that put Elise's belly in her throat. She smelled it right through the Vapo-Rub and the pungent brown river. And from the looks on the faces of the others, they smelled it, too. Rico steered them around a few stumps, navigated a turn in the river and there—in the center of a wide channel—was the bow of a large boat rising from the murk. A wood stork sunned itself atop it. All around the bow were hundreds of dead fish floating, belly-up. There were flies all over them.

"What the hell is that about?" Jack asked.

Rico shrugged. "Some kind research boat...she sink. Hit something and sink. They suppose to come, tow her away. Ah, but the state...ha! Probably be year before they do!"

"What killed the fish?" Cutler wanted to know.

Rico shrugged again. "Chemical or something. It were a biotech boat out research things. Everyone get off okay. So no worry...except for them sonofabitch fishies, eh?"

Elise was holding her nose. The stink of those rotting fish was hot, nauseating. It crawled up her nose and down her throat, tried to drag her stomach back up with it. She noticed that there was a funny purple sheen to the water around the sunken ship. Something about that she did not like at all.

But no one else seemed bothered.

Rico steered them away from the main channel and into the *igapo*, or flooded forest. The meltwaters of the Andes overflowed the rivers between January and June, creating a weird world of flooded jungle. He steered them around huge vine-covered trees and clotted stands of foliage, finding the channel where he knew the fishing would be good.

"Yes," he said, "this will do. Them sonofabitch *pirayas* travel in schools, hundreds of them, eh? They come to the *igapo* because they know game in the water and the eating she is good."

Jack was excited. "All right, let's do some fishing."

*

As they made ready with the long bamboo poles, Rico told them that during flood season the *pirayas* were not truly dangerous. Their hunting range was expanded into the jungle and there was plenty to eat. They were only really a threat when there was no food. In fact, he said, during this time of year men wade into the river and spearfish, women wash clothes, and children swim in piranha waters without any harm.

Elise figured he was saying that for her benefit.

The jungle was primeval, silent, unbearably eerie. The channel they were in was maybe forty feet across, a stew of brown steaming water. Leaves and sticks floated on its surface. Trees grew from the water in tangled, knotted masses to either side, rising up on snaking roots and filling out, growing thickly until their twisted limbs joined together overhead like woven canestraw. The result was like being in a tunnel...a hot, smelling, claustrophobic tunnel of stagnant water and warm decay.

Rico tried to give Elise a pole, but she refused. The bamboo poles were about four feet long, set with six-pound nylon lines and triple-barbed hooks that were baited with chunks of raw beef and chicken liver. To attract the piranhas, Rico tossed some bloody chum into the water.

"They smell this for miles," he said.

The men tossed their lines into the water.

Rico rolled a cigarette, told a story about Isobel, his first wife, who was so crazy she'd once chased him down the muddy, winding streets of Cerro de Pasco with a baseball bat. She had been naked at the time. "And that, my friends, is no thing to be looking on first thing in morning." He shivered. "*Yah!*"

Then the waiting began. Elise sat there, beads of sweat rolling down her face. Swarms of gnats and mosquitoes hovered over the water. Dragonflies buzzed about. Howler monkeys wailed in the treetops. Elise listened to the blue macaws screech and watched palm vipers thread through the spoking branches.

Basille suddenly stiffened, his bovine face beaded with perspiration. "I...ah...I think I have a nibble," he said.

"Easy," Rico told him. "The *piraya* is sneaky little devil. Don't scare him off. Let him take good bite first...then he yours."

Basille waited, looking very nervous. Suddenly his rod jerked, then bowed as something below tugged at the line. He pulled up his bamboo pole and there was an oval-shaped fish on the hook. It was silvery, its belly a dull orange. Jack and Cutler cheered. Elise was the only one that saw something was terribly wrong with the fish. But as Basille swung it on board they all saw it. On one side the fish looked like any other Red-Bellied Piranha, though maybe faded in color, but on the other: just bones. The head was intact, but it was just bones straight down to the tail.

"You hooked a dead one," Cutler said.

Jack laughed.

"It wasn't dead," Basille said. "You saw how it attacked my bait."

Rico swallowed. "Yes...but they are the cannibals, them *piraya*. They attack one another. You hook a live one, but its fellows...*ha!* ...they strip it before you pull him in."

And that seemed a perfectly logical explanation...but then the fish *moved*. Stripped to bone on one side or not, it began to flap its tail and writhe on the line, its hooked jaws snapping.

"That's not possible," Jack said.

Elise was getting a real bad feeling now. She didn't believe for a moment that other piranhas had cannibalized this one, at least not recently. Because the fish stank...it was putrescent.

Basille, a look of horror on his face, just stared at the fish dangling over his lap. Then a slender green worm slid out of its side and dropped into his crotch. He tossed the pole, shrieking, brushing the corpse worm off him and smashing it beneath his shoe.

Cutler jumped away from the dropped pole and what flopped on the end.

Rico, looking dead serious now, grabbed it and threw the line overboard. He slashed out with his knife and cut the piranha free. The fish hit the water and swam away like it was perfectly healthy. Nobody said anything for a time. They listened to the jungle. The silence was deadly, ominous.

Then Jack's line was hit. Cutler's, too. Both men looked at each other, for the first time in their lives almost afraid to see what was on the end of their hooks.

"This not right," Rico said.

And then, from below, something hit the boat. In fact, several things hit the bottom of the boat in rapid succession. One after the other, like hammers. Then it stopped. Everyone just sat there, wide-eyed, the boat moving in a slow counterclockwise rotation from the impact. Then it started again and this time there was no stopping it. From below it was hit again and again and again, maybe hundreds of times. The boat shook. It canted this way and that. Bamboo poles were yanked from hands and dragged beneath the surface.

"This is crazy!" Basille cried out. "We're being attacked!"

Jack held Elise to him, either for her protection or his own. He looked frantically at Rico. "Croc? Is that what it is? A croc? A big fucking croc?"

The boat was hit so hard from beneath that it jumped an inch out of the channel and came back down with a cascading splash of murky brown water. Basille lost his nerve. He screamed, elbowed Cutler out of his way in a frenzied attempt to get out of the bow. Cutler took hold of him. They wrestled, they swore. Rico shouted for them to *stop it, stop it, stop it*—

But it was too late.

Tangled together, they fell over against the lip of the boat and it flipped up out of the water from the sudden shift in weight. For one frightening second it hung there, its side parallel to the river, while everyone tried to hang onto the seats for dear life.

Then it flipped right over and all five of them went into the drink.

*

Elise surfaced, her legs bicycling and arms thrashing. She spat out a mouthful of water that was brown, slimy, and warm like some primordial ooze. Rico was only maybe five feet away, pulling himself up onto the overturned boat. Crying out, she swam towards it as it drifted away from her. She could see several fish attached to Rico's legs as he dragged himself out of the river. They had bitten right through his pants and blood was blossoming from the wounds.

Somebody shoved her forward and she was never sure if it was Cutler or Basille. She heard Jack shouting out in a high, almost girlish voice: "Swim! Elise, swim for the boat! Swim! Swim! *Swim!*" His voice broke into a note of absolute terror.

Elise pounded through the water to the boat. She felt something bite into her knee. Her ankle. Her hip. Then she was at the boat and Rico hauled her aboard by grabbing her hair and yanking her up out of the water with considerable strength. She flopped onto the bottom of the overturned boat, glad to feel the hot sun upon her. She spit out more water, coughing and gagging. Cutler pulled himself aboard and so did Basille, both men tearing biting fish off their legs. Rico grabbed the one chewing on her knee. It was bloated green, eyeless, its triangular teeth red with her blood. It was so rotten it went to a soft, oozing pulp in his fingers. He tossed it away.

"Jack!" Cutler cried. *"Jack!"*

Elise, shocked and trembling, looked for him. In her panic she had forgotten about everything but survival, everything but getting out of the water and getting away from those flesh-shearing jaws.

Jack was still in the water.

For whatever reason, he had been thrown out farther from the others. The drift of the overturned boat had put him even farther away. He was closer to the trees so he swam for them. They saw him grip the solid spiraling anchor roots rising from the water. He got his hand on one and pulled himself to it, then up out of the water and it seemed like he was going to make it, he was really going to make it—

And then, as he pulled his upper body out of the slop, the water around him began boiling like a pot, seething in a great fountain of thrashing silver bodies. Jack screamed. Screamed with a wild, almost animal sound of agony and horror that echoed off into the jungle and sent a flock of birds winging into the sky. *"Help me! Help me! Somebody fucking help me—"*

His cry turned into a moist gurgling sound as he swallowed water, fighting to pull himself away from all those razored, chomping jaws. But the limbs of the trees were damp, green with fungus and he couldn't quite get a grip. He'd pull himself up an inch or two, then slide back down. His body was shuddering as he was hit by hundreds of piranhas and the thrashing water around him gushed a brilliant red.

The agony.

Oh Jesus, the agony. When they first started hitting him, Jack felt the impacts, boom-boom-boom, and the nipping pinpricks of their teeth. And within seconds, not a nipping, but a biting, a ripping, a feeding frenzy. It felt like a thousand razors were slicing into him, carving him, slitting him open. The water was churning with red bubbles, foaming with blood and tissue and thousands of fish, gutting him to the marrow—

Elise was screaming.

Jack was making a gobbling, clotted sound in his throat as his own blood filled his mouth. The fish kept hitting him and with one last valiant effort he pulled himself up out of the water. Beneath the hips, he was nothing but bleeding red muscle, yellow ligament, and knobs of white bone. There were hundreds of fish hanging from him, biting and tearing. They were bloated green, looping with worms, many nothing but fleshy skeletons. They could not possibly be alive, yet the inborn instinct to feed was driving them on. Blood burst from Jack's mouth in a red mist, his eyes bulging, his face twisted in a silent scream.

Elise was hysterical.

Rico tried to hold onto her but she was hot and greasy in his hands, squirming wildly.

Jack was pulled down into the water, still trying to yank himself up, but the fight was gone and he slid into the boiling mass, his body thrown from side to side, jerking and jumping like some grisly marionette. He broke out of the water, a bleeding husk that had been shredded down to basal anatomy. A fleshless hand groped over the surface. He let out one last cry and everyone saw that the left side of his neck and face were eaten right down to muscle-covered bone. He looked like a living, bleeding shank of raw beef.

He went under.

Then he surfaced once again, more skeleton than flesh, fish clinging to him by their jaws. His skull was trembling as if there was still life in it, one single eyeball staring from its hollow of bone with a deranged look of absolute shock.

Then he sank from view leaving only a slick of blood and tissue.

*

Elise was hysterical and it was Cutler who slid over towards her and slapped her across the face. And he didn't just slap her once, but four times. Maybe he would have kept at it but Rico stopped him, shoved him away and almost into the drink.

"That enough, you crazy *punheteiro.*"

Cutler didn't like being handled like that, but he took it and kept his distance because, white-haired or not, he had no doubt that the old man would have given him the beating of his life with those rough, callused hands. They looked like they could split kindling.

Next to Cutler, Basille moaned.

"Easy now, lady," Rico said, pulling Elise to him. "There, my lady, easy now."

She was limp, face wet with tears, blood running from her mouth. Her shorts were stained red, her legs open in several places from the bites of the piranhas. He comforted her the best he could even though he himself was leagues beyond comfort.

She kept shuddering, shaking her head from side to side. All she could see was Jack, Jack, Jack—

The school of living dead piranha hitting him again and again, chewing and tearing, engulfing him in a primal bloodlust of cutting teeth, and that look in his eyes, that terrified, agonized, insane look in his eyes as they reduced him to a bleeding pulp.

She sat straight up and screamed.

Rico held her tighter. "Easy, you got to be easy now."

"You better shut her the fuck up," Cutler said. "We got enough problems here."

Rico gave him a look that burned right through him. It was easy to read. It said: *Just you and me alone, sonofabitch. That's all I ask. You and me alone and, God above, how you gonna hurt when I put my hands on you.*

He looked away. "I fish these waters sixty year," he told them in a wounded voice. "Never...never I see a *merda* like this."

Cutler offered him a sarcastic grin. "Zombie piranhas." He shook his head. "That boat...that research ship. They must've spilled something in the water, set some bug loose, a virus or something..."

Rico shrugged. "I not know. And what does these things matter, eh? God help us."

Basille had been badly ravaged and he kept moaning and groaning. He had lost consciousness now and was probably in shock. His white pants and shirt had nearly been ripped away. What remained were bloody rags. He was laid open in a dozen locations with deep, cutting wounds. Blood ran from him, pooled under him, and trickled down the boat into the water where it floated like a slick of grease.

Cutler stared at it, his face sunburned, blue-eyed, and stark with fear.

"We gonna get out of this," Rico said. "We gonna use shoes as paddles and get us to the riverbank. You see if we don't."

Cutler laughed with a dead, hopeless sound. "We ain't fucking going nowhere and you know it."

"You shut that mouth, *punheteiro.*"

Cutler turned away, staring at the blood seeping from Basille into the water. He started to make the connection. "His blood," he said. "It's in the water." He looked over at Rico, his eyes wide and glassy like he was out of his mind. "You hear me, you goddamn idiot? His blood...*it's in the fucking water...his blood is in the fucking water...*"

Rico got it, all right.

Blood in the water. Those devil-fish. And them floating on the overturned skiff, its flat bottom a scarce four inches above the river.

Elise snapped out of her fugue. "Listen," she said. "*Listen...*"

Yes, they heard it, too. Beneath, in the water, the piranhas were hitting the boat again, one after the other. The sound of their gnawing teeth on the wood was almost like a muted sawing. They were trying to chew their way through it. It was insane but that's what they were doing, driven by some malefic force to eat and kill. The water was filled with their darting bodies, slivery, scaly, discolored and putrefied...but alive, somehow alive.

"We have to get out of here!" Cutler cried out, beside himself with fear.

More fish now.

The water began to roil. The piranha were swarming like locusts, pouring themselves at the boat in a steady stream of teeth. They chewed from below, from the sides, so many pressing in that hundreds were pushed flopping up out of the water and hundreds more were pulverized by the greedy appetites of the expanding shoal. And they were not just centered around the boat, it seemed, but the *entire* channel as if there was not a school of hundreds, but perhaps a school of thousands or *hundreds* of thousands. The frothing of the water made the boat roll in the water like it was caught in a good swell.

The carrion fish were whipped into a wild eating frenzy, driven mad by the taste of blood dripping into the water. Sawdust was floating to the surface as they chewed at the skiff. The flat hull Rico and the others sat on was greasy with water and blood. They gripped each other so they'd didn't slide off.

All except Basille.

His unconscious form was sliding nearer and nearer the edge.

Nobody made to grab him for there just wasn't time. The boat was rocking under the onslaught of the fish, the water a churning maelstrom of snapping jaws and bones, piranhas and parts of them. And maybe the motion of the boat would have carried them to the treeline, but something happened first: the fish started leaping on board. Driven by a relentless hunger, they leaped out of the water and started landing among the survivors, grotesquely bloated and decayed, some little better than living skeletons held together by leathery sinew and ligament.

But dead or *undead*, they were united in a single purpose.

Rico shouted as he ducked away from two or three that sailed at him, swatted two more out of the air, and was hit by three more that fastened their sawtoothed teeth right into his flesh. He yanked them free, tearing out flaps of skin as he did so.

They landed on the hull, flopping and chomping their jaws.

Cutler kicked them back in, slapped at them, smashed a dozen to a foul putrid paste with his fists. But for every one he destroyed, there were ten more vaulting at him. They bit into his arms, his shoulders, his hands, dozens affixed to his boots, their teeth sunk into the leather. One caught him by the chin, biting deep.

The air was filled with fish, a steaming brew of blood and corpse gas.

They hit Elise, too. They fastened on her legs, her arms, one sank its triangular teeth right into her breast. She pulled them off, screaming, hitting and crushing them under her fists. She was completely out of her mind, ripping them free, kicking and slapping. She smashed them in her hands into a black gushing slime of drainage and tiny bones. She tore one off her left arm and the whole body came away in a pulping flap, but the small chambered skull remained, those serrated jaws holding tight, teeth punctured deep. She beat at it until it shattered to fragments.

And when one clamped its interlocking jaws on the knuckle of her pinkie, she attacked it without thinking: clamping its foul, festering body in her own jaws and biting down until it exploded in a gushing spray of putrescence in her mouth. More hit her, but she craned her head and vomited putrid flesh, scales, and tiny bones along with a few squirming, severed worms.

More and more were coming out of the water and there was simply no defense.

Cutler fought through the rain of fish, shouting, *"It's him they want...don't you see?"* He ripped piranhas free, tearing one from the end of his nose and leaving several teeth sunk into the cartilage. "THEY WANT HIM! THEY WANT BASILLE! NOT US! THEY DON'T WANT US—"

And with a sideward kick, he knocked Basille's body into the foaming water.

It was the sort of deranged diversion only a psychotic mind could come up with, but there is no sanity in survival. The water instantly went red in a swirling eruption. It frothed and boiled like a cauldron. Basille's body was covered in a living, biting tarp of the monsters...and somewhere during the process, he came awake, thrashing and screaming, gulping in water, his own blood, and piranhas. His body rolled over and over in the churning wake, voracious jaws shredding him as the others watched. He was like a shank of bloody meat tossed into a shark tank.

But it worked.

The diversion worked.

The school enveloped him and no more fish dove at the skiff. In fact, the very act of the piranhas abandoning the boat left the water roiling and this pushed it out of harm's way, precious feet from the devouring shoal.

Out there, you could not even see Basille any longer. He was buried in thousands of fish, their teeth in constant industrious motion in that simmering sea of blood. And when they finally fell away, glutted, there was nothing but a freshly-picked skeleton that bobbed to the surface for a moment or two, then sank from view.

*

Maybe Cutler expected some gratitude. Maybe in his crowded, twisted little mind what he had done to Basille was seen as an act of selfless heroism. But once the remainders of the biting fish were disposed of, gratitude is not what he got from Rico and Elise.

Bitten, ravaged, bleeding, they came at him with hooked fingers and eyes glazed with madness. To them, sacrificing one of their own to those hideous little monsters had never been an option. So they came at him with murder in their eyes.

"Wait a minute!" he told them. "I saved us! Not just myself, but all of us!"

Elise just glared at him. "You sick bastard! It was murder! Murder! You fucking murdered that poor man!"

Cutler's face was bitten, scratched, stained with blood. But now all the color ran from it because he knew, he *knew*, that they were no longer in their right minds. They were going to throw *him* overboard.

"Don't even try it," he warned them.

"Killer!" Rico said, "Dirty stinking killer!"

Cutler was right on one thing: they *weren't* in their right minds. Had they been, they would never have considered throwing him to the fish. But they had been through too much, suffered through unimaginable horrors, been strained to the limit, and now they were thinking survival and nothing more.

Cutler edged as far as he could away from them on the flat hull, sliding his ass through the blood and water. "I swear to God! You try it! Either of you try it and I'll flip us all in! *I goddamn well fucking mean it!*"

But they didn't seem to believe it. They kept inching forward. In their minds, they already had Cutler pegged for the selfish, narcissistic piece of shit he was. He wouldn't sacrifice what he loved best even to thwart his enemies. They knew it. And, sadly, he knew it.

Elise honestly didn't want to hurt him. Maybe Rico did, but she was really just taking out her frustrations by putting a scare into him. And maybe that might have worked...had the situation not been so damned desperate. When she got within a foot of him, Cutler looked out at the slopping brown water, the dry islands rising up in the channel—maybe wondering if he could reach them in time—then turned back quick. And before Elise could react or even think of it, he hit her in the face with everything he had. Her head snapped back and she would have went right into the drink had Rico not grabbed her.

That was it for Rico.

He was Yagua Indian and where he came from, you did not hit women. But the men who struck them? Oh yes, you beat them silly. He came right at Cutler and Cutler threw a few sloppy jabs at him that seemed to bounce right off that old, seamed brown face.

And then Rico had him.

He bounced Cutler's head off the hull two or three times, then hit him barefisted again and again. Cutler's face was a mess now but still he fought. He shook and raged, trying to hit the old man, trying to deflect those huge callused hands. They grappled. The boat rocked uneasily. Grinning with pure wicked delight, Rico hit him again.

But he didn't see Cutler fish the lockblade knife from his pocket, snap it open.

Elise did. She shouted: "Rico! Look out! He's got a—"

Too late, Cutler brought the blade up and sank an easy three inches of it right into the side of Rico's neck, severing the carotid artery. Rico, looking stunned and shocked, fell away grasping a hand to the wound. The artery was laid wide open, blood squirting between his fingers. He fell onto the hull face-first making a moaning, gurgling sound in his throat. His blood was everywhere, pools and rivers of it flooding their banks, vivid red and shining.

Elise launched herself at Cutler and he slashed her across the arm. "Next time it's your throat," he promised her.

Rico tried to pull himself to his knees and slid on the greasy spill of his own blood. He tried again and Cutler lashed out with his foot, caught the old man in the ass and propelled him forward.

Blood bubbling from his wound, Rico tried to stop himself and was only partially successful. His hands found purchase so he didn't go all the way in, but his head and upper shoulders went under and the rest of him followed right to the waist. The piranha hit him like bullets. Their teeth punched right into him as he tried to pull himself up. But his blood in the water drove them to new heights of mania. His head was still underwater in the churning mass of feeding piranha, hands hooked into claws, splashing and flaying madly. Each time an arm came out of the thrashing water, there were more decaying piranhas on it. And each time there was less flesh.

Screaming, Elise took hold of one of his ankles, trying to pull him back on board. But he was a big man, under attack, and fighting with everything he had. Cutler would not help. He stayed as far away as he could. The more Elise pulled, the more Rico seemed to slide deeper into the seething pool of teeth. Blood and water splashed against her as the jaws of the living dead fish cut into him like buzzsaws, pulverizing his flesh, puncturing him.

And it was bad for her...but those scarce seconds underwater were an absolute horror for Rico.

From the moment his face and upper body submerged, they were at him. Their slimy, putrefying bodies, teeth slicing into him like knives. They hit his face, his arms, his shoulders, but especially his throat. Dozens of them fighting their way in, chewing and sucking at the hot flow of blood, drilling into him, gnawing through muscle and tissue. But what was worse, was that as he fought, his mouth open screaming and gargling in the water, they swam right in. Right into his mouth, chewing his tongue away and biting their way into his throat, deeper, deeper, filling him, making him gag—

Rico came out of the water with a fierce backward lunge, knocking Elise aside. He came out fountaining water and blood. From the waist on up, he was bitten, mangled, simply laid raw. There were dozens and dozens of piranha in every state of decomposition hanging off him, jaws shearing, tails flapping. His face looked like the surface of the moon, cratered down to shining white bone from hundreds of bites. His eyes were gone, his nose chewed down to a hollow, his lips gnawed down to the bleeding gums.

He thrashed about like some obscene zombie, spraying blood and drainage and fish in every direction, a horrible gagging sound coming from his pitted throat. And then his abdomen, so bitten and torn, seemed to dissolve before Elise's eyes. It exploded outward as the fish that tunneled down his throat ate their way back out, macerating organ and muscle and membrane, scissoring jaws rupturing through like drill bits. A slopping, slimy tide of blood and carrion fish and half-eaten tissue came flooding out and he flipped back into the water where the real devouring began.

Elise reached out, managed to grab a hand as he was caught in the surging maelstrom. He nearly dragged her in, but she pulled back with everything she had left and, to her surprise—and horror—he came up. Or his hand did. It was clutched in her own, the wrist gnawed to a bloody stump.

She screamed and threw it, hysterical and shaking.

The rest of Rico sank away in the foaming scarlet water.

*

On her hands and knees on the blood-covered hull, Elise called out his name again and again and again.

But he was gone.

She was alone with Cutler and even being eaten by the living dead fish seemed preferable to that. When she turned back, Cutler had the knife in his hand and he was making his way toward her. "Now it's your turn," he said. His face was an absolute atrocity: a gouged and chewed waxen mask, streaked red and lit by two blazing hungry eyes and a grinning mouth of pink-stained teeth.

Elise could see it in on him.

There was no mistaking it.

He had been watching her ever since they got on the boat like a child molester watches a schoolyard. He knew what he wanted and even the misery they'd all been through had not vanquished the flame of lust burning in him, it had not dulled the perverse edge to his soul. He had a knife. They were alone. There were no witnesses. She had a choice: she could either give him what he wanted or he'd take it.

But he'd have it. There was no doubt of that.

She sneered at him. "YOU FUCKING ASSHOLE! YOU FUCKING SLIMY DISGUSTING PIECE OF SHIT!"

The words meant nothing to him.

As he came forward, the knife edge catching the sun, his eyes were wild, filled with a shocking animal delight.

"You can either enjoy it, Elise, or I can make it worse than anything you can imagine," he told her.

"Get away from me!"

He laughed. "You know better."

He reached out to touch her and she slapped his hand away. He sliced at her with the knife, again and again, pushing her closer to the edge and the waiting jaws. She had no choice now. There was nothing left but to allow it...as vile and repellent as that would be.

She shoved him away.

"ALL RIGHT! ALL RIGHT!" she said, tearing her blouse open, exposing the cones of her breasts. "IS THIS WHAT YOU WANT? IS THIS WHAT YOU FUCKING WANT?"

It was. It was obvious that he had been thinking of nothing else. With Jack alive or Rico he would never have dared to do what he was now going to do. But now all bets were off. He was practically drooling. He unzipped his pants and he was already hard. Not letting go of the knife, he squirmed his way out of them until they were down past his knees.

And Elise, her belly flooded with a warm rush of nausea, stripped the rest of the way and stood up so he could get a good look at her. Although bitten and bloodied, it was easy to see that the only place she wasn't tanned was where her bikini had been.

"Get over here," Cutler said.

She went back down on her knees, knowing that what she must now do was the only way. She sucked down everything inside herself, forgot about such trifling things as self-respect, dignity, and honor. She replaced it all with something that was dark and grim. Maybe Cutler saw it in her eyes for just a second, for he cringed.

"Now," he said.

"On your back," she told him. "You want this, we do it my way."

He was so excited he didn't question it. Not for a moment. Elise went right over to him and felt his grubby, scaly hands roughly fondle everything she had. Then with a crooked, salacious grin she took him by the shoulders and forced him down on the hull. She squatted over him, gripping his hard little penis and then forcing herself down upon it. She gasped. He trembled. He had forgotten his knife now. Forgotten everything but what he was getting which was all he'd ever dreamed about. Elise rode him until he came, making a good show of it, the whole time thrusting down hard on him and sliding his body across the greasy hull ever closer to the water.

"Oh God," he said. "Oh God that was good..."

"I'm glad you enjoyed it," Elise said and then sprang on him, shoving him with her weight and every ounce of muscle she had. Her strength was irresistible and especially to a man who was as spent as Cutler.

She forced him over the edge of the hull and he immediately started shouting, swinging, trying to throw her off. But she pinned him down with her legs and, grasping his throat, forced his head into the water...then beneath it.

The piranhas struck right away in wave after wave of shearing jaws.

Cutler thrashed, gyrated, but Elise clung to him, straddling him and locking him into place. She barely felt his fists as they bounced off her head or his nails that laid her face open.

She was only aware of the churning water and the swarming fish, how Cutler jerked with each attack.

Even submerged she could hear them feeding: the tearing of flesh and soft tissues, the chomping of muscle and connective tissue, the dull crunching of bone that sounded oddly like someone chewing on ice cubes. They bit at her fingers, too, which were just under the surface, but their main interest was the head.

Cutler died horribly.

It did not even occur to him that the cunning bitch had led him into a carefully baited trap until she shoved his head underwater, into that murky brown water, and the searing, unbelievable agony began. He could not see them, just a darkening mass of seething bodies that covered his face and head as the water boiled red. Their jaws snapped, tore, cut, ripped, and ultimately rendered him to bone. But he fought, oh how he fought, striking at the evil bitch and tearing at the biting fish that went to corpse jelly under his fingers. But it was futile, of course. A school of living piranha can deliver 1200 bites in less than a minute and who could say about these monsters? Their jaws punctured his face, sawed and bit and stabbed. His eyes went fast as did his tongue and lips. *His nose and ears took a little longer. All in all, his head was devoured to a ball of fleshy mucilage in thirty seconds.*

After maybe fifteen seconds, Elise fell away, gasping, sobbing, studying the ruin of her once long attractive fingers. Just bloody stumps now, worried right to the bone.

Cutler's head finally came up out of the water and it was really little more than an eyeless, earless, scalpless skull covered in pink, rutted, well-gnawed tissue. He rose for a second, his head bobbing like some gruesome Halloween prop and then he fell backwards and splashed into the drink. The school finished the job they had started.

Elise watched until there was nothing but a bubbling scum of blood and fragments on the surface. Then lying down on the hull, she closed her eyes.

*

The moon came up over the Amazon River basin.

Elise woke, raw and hurting, aware of nothing but the agony that pulsed through her body in punishing waves. Botflies had laid their eggs in her wounds. Clouds of mosquitoes had drank their fill. Gnats and chiggers had feasted on her throat.

Out in the rainforest, night birds cried out and snakes slid through the wet leafy loam. Spiders spun webs larger than men in the branches and huge Amazonian leeches clung to the thick cable roots just under the water. Moths fluttered over the clotted surface of the channel and crab-eating raccoons chattered in the jungle.

All was well in the hot, misty night world.

Elise went to the edge of the hull and peered into the water. What the moonlight showed her should have been shocking, but she was well beyond things like shock or fear. She was bruised, bitten, slit, peppered with dozens upon dozens of swelling insect bites. Botfly larva were already wiggling in her wounds. She knew only agony and misery and there was no light at the end of the tunnel. Only nature at its fiercest and a channel filled with unnatural things. This is what the moonlight showed her in the water: the piranhas.

Hundreds and hundreds of them surrounding the overturned skiff. Just waiting. Row upon row of them breaking the surface, their jutting jaws wide open. Greening things, bloated things, wormy things, glaring evil skulls. They were not alive and had not been in some time so they did not need to swim

to force oxygenated water through their gills.   The leaking
chemicals from the biotech ship that poisoned the school also
resurrected them.   Once they had been alive, filled with a
rapacious vitality.   Social creatures that lived to defend the
school. Not truly dangerous to man except in the dry season
when food was scarce. But now they no longer mated and swam
for the glory of the school.   Now all they had left was an
insatiable appetite.

And this is what they offered Elise: their appetite.
Serrated rows of triangular teeth activated by powerful jaws.
The sort of jaws that could bite through fishing nets and steel
hooks. It was all they had and they offered it to her now.

Elise looked down at them surrounding her little island.
Like loyal subjects surrounding their queen.   And they were
loyal. She did not doubt this.

They waited.

They knew she would come to them.

Finally, staring out across those yawning, tooth-studded
jaws gleaming in the moonlight, all open in her honor, she said,
"Please, I hurt so bad, so terribly bad...let it be fast."

Somehow, she knew they would make it so.

She thought then of Peruvian cattle herders. Jack had told
her how they would sacrifice a cow downstream in the dry
season to the hungry piranhas so that the rest of the herd could
cross safely upstream. Elise knew then that she would be such a
sacrifice.

Sucking in a breath, she slid into the water and submerged
amongst them and they accepted her. And true to their promise,
as the water gushed red with her blood, it was mercifully quick.

The skiff drifted on upstream.

A giant otter splashed in the distance.

And in the treetops, a pygmy owl screeched.

THEY WALK BY NIGHT

When the phone rang I was sleeping like a body in a freezer, cool, dead, and easy. When it finally jarred me awake, I bolted upright, my heart pounding, my head full of spun cobwebs. How long it had been ringing I didn't know. I seemed to remember dreaming about phones. Maybe for hours.

My hand fumbled it off its cradle. "Steel here," I said into the receiver, my voice full of sand. "Make it good."

"Vince? Where the hell you been? I been calling you all goddamn day."

I knew the voice. Knew it well. It was everyone's favorite homicide detective, Tommy Albert. Tommy and me went way back. Years ago, before I picked up my private cop's license, I'd been on the force with him. He didn't call me unless it was important.

"I've been sleeping, I guess. I like to do that sometimes."

I looked at the clock. Christ. I'd been out for almost fourteen hours straight. Not surprising, really, when you took into account that for the past three weeks I'd been chasing an errant husband and his twenty-year old mistress throughout the tri-state area. And for those three weeks I bet I hadn't slept more than three or fours hours a night. The entire case was a comedy of errors, a comedy with me as the lead clown. Not exactly duck soup but I'd brought the duo in and it had paid off in heavy green. Good or bad, it was how guys like me made our meat.

I cleared my throat. "What the hell's so important? You know I gotta get all the beauty rest I can."

"And then some," he said. "I was about to send a couple uniforms over there, have them kick in the door and drag you over here."

"I don't think I'd like that."

Tommy went on to tell me he'd been calling me just about every half-hour all day long. "It happened this morning," he went on. "Our boy...surely you remember the one that decided his wrists would look better laid open with a razor? Yeah, well, guess what? Guess what happened this morning?"

"You remembered you were engaged to him?"

"Ha. No, and let's keep that between us, shall we? No, I'm afraid our boy disappeared from the morgue."

I was awake now. "What do you mean *disappeared?*"

"Just what I said."

It hit me hard. Like a hammer to the skull. "You telling me those county ghouls lost him?"

"Yup. Either misplaced him or someone took him. Unless you think he might've wandered off on his own," Tommy said. "But you gotta remember how sweet he was on you, Vince. Probably out dragging his dead ass to a florist, buying something special for you."

The man we were talking about was named Quigg. And he was sweet on me like I was sweet on razor blades in my shorts. He hated me and I hated him and wasn't the world a beautiful place to live?

But let me tell you about this guy.

It was a homicide case. Strictly something for the precinct boys, definitely not the province of a private dick like me. I got pulled into it when the sister of one of the victims hired me to do what the police weren't doing: tracking down the killer. And, somehow, *killer,* doesn't seem to really cut it here. Maybe a better word would be *maniac.* Our boy here, you see, was a cannibal. Yeah, he was killing 'em with a knife—post mortem knife it turned out—just as sharp as you please, slitting open their throats like the bellies of hogs and having himself a spot of cold lunch when they were down and out. I saw a few of the bodies. Tommy Albert showed me the crime scene photos of the others. It was enough to put you off red meat for life. The bodies were all the same—young women, throats slit, meat from their bellies and thighs cut free with a knife, throats and faces and wrists chewed-up. The bodies were generally drained of blood. Thing that we never did understand is why he cut the hearts out. No other organs, just the hearts. Maybe he was eating them. That was the general presumption. But even then, I didn't believe it.

I'd been on the case a month when the eighth and final body in as many weeks turned up. I had narrowed down my cast of revelers to three men by then—one was a former mental patient, another just a big mean bastard with a history of sadism, and the third, a mild mannered guy who just happened to be a professor of anthropology of all things. It turned out that our boy was Quigg, the professor. I caught him in the act. I got there too late to save the girl's life, but at least I stopped him from carving her up like the Christmas ham at grandma's house.

I'll be the first to admit that I worked him over pretty good before I called in Tommy and his boys. When the black and whites finally rolled in, Quigg was in need of some prolonged dental care. But the fact that this twisted, sick piece of shit was even breathing when the bulls slapped the bracelets on him was testament to my self-restraint. Given what he'd done, I should've made him the suck the end of my .45 like a 10 cent lollypop before I urged his brains out the back of his skull.

Anyway, Tommy's boys took him away. His lawyer—some hot shot greaseball garbage-eater with all the morals of a child molester—tried the insanity plea, but Quigg was convicted and sent upstate. His first night there, he opened his wrists and the angels sighed.

And that's all she wrote.

Or was it?

"Who the hell would spring a stiff?" I said.

Tommy said, "Who knows? But I'm just bringing you up to speed here. All that happened twelve hours ago, chum. It's what's happened since that's yanking my chain."

He dropped the bait and I bit.

And it was worse than I thought.

2

An hour later, after a hot cup of Joe and a hotter shower, I pulled on my rags and went uptown to the townhouse residence of the district attorney, Bobby Tanner. He was a good egg for a prosecutor. He'd hired me numerous times to do background checks on cases he was working on. We were tight. Bobby's family had money like geese have feathers: he could've stuffed mattresses with it. Bobby had attended some ivy league college, but had decided to go into public service much to the chagrin of his people who wanted him to join some upscale whiteshoe firm on Fifth.

But that was the kind of boy Bobby was: honest, decent, principles so high you would've needed a ladder to climb over them. Problem was, Bobby didn't have anything anymore.

Bobby was dead.

His living room was crawling with cops and coroner's people. They were thick as eels swimming upstream. Tommy and I were standing over in the corner next to a bookshelf, smoking, not saying a hell of a lot. Bobby wasn't just another stiff, he was our friend.

The condition of the body was eating at us...much the way someone else had been eating at Bobby. He'd been partially devoured, you see. Most of the flesh had been stripped from his face and throat. His belly had been ripped apart. His head had been opened like a can of soup and sucked clean. His left arm was missing beneath the elbow. This time, the killer hadn't used any tools, the coroner informed us, he'd used teeth and nails.

"I know what you're gonna say," Tommy said to me, "but there can't possibly be a connection between Quigg and this."

"And why not?"

"Because he's dead."

"He's also missing," I pointed out.

"That don't buy beans," Tommy said.

And maybe it didn't. I started thinking about Quigg. It was something I dearly wanted to put out of my head forever. But now it all came back like a bad rash. The same old questions that I never could answer, but ones that I knew were important. Somehow. "I'm still wondering about Quigg," I said. "What did we really know about him?"

Tommy just stared at me. His was a big fellow, went an easy three-hundred plus, was built like something that could've pulled a beer wagon for a living. He wasn't pretty. He was balding, his face a roadmap of Death Valley, a cigar butt shoved in the corner of his mouth. Maybe not campaign poster material, but effective as hell. Only reason he hadn't brought in Quigg himself was that Quigg, though under suspicion, was connected like the water works.

"He was a sick sonofabitch," Tommy said. "He ate goddamn people and now he's dead. And don't start with any of that 'cult' bullshit with me again. I'm not in the mood."

It had been my pet theory.   You see, Quigg, although technically employed by City College as a professor of anthropology and folklore, had been on the last leg of a five-year leave of absence at the time of his arrest.   According to the college, he had been gathering information for some paper he was writing.   He spent two years in Haiti, another in Ecuador, and two more hopping around Asia and the Middle East.   I'd never been able to connect up any of that unless he had learned how to be a cannibal from some jungle tribe.   But I knew there was a connection.   I could feel it like a fat man can feel cool air blowing up through a hole in the seat of his pants.

But the cult angle?

One of the few witnesses to the murders claimed he saw not just a lone man leaving the crime scene, but a group of people.   And when I was following Quigg around he was always in the company of three or four others.   And that night I found him doing his thing...well, I could've sworn I heard footsteps running off as I approached.   Many of them.   I hadn't bothered following because I'd thought I had my man.

But were there others?

Was Quigg operating alone?

Somehow, I started to see a connection here.   Whatever Quigg was part of, maybe it was still in operation.   But why Bobby? Why a high-profile victim like the district attorney? It made no real sense...or maybe it made all the sense in the world.

"I'll be in touch," I told Tommy, heading towards the door.

"Where the hell you going?"

"Following a hunch," I said.

Tommy looked at me. "I don't give a rat's hairy ass how you spend your free time, Vince, but don't get yourself in trouble.   You know how you are.   When you get going, things happen."

"Things?"

"You know what I mean.   Try and keep the body count low, will ya?"

But I was already out the door.

3

It was midnight and rain was pissing down from a slate sky and I had spent the past three hours parked in the darkness.   I was watching the house of Marianne Portis.   Why? Because she was really all I had. Marianne was a slight, pale woman who looked like central casting's idea of a librarian. She didn't look to me as the sort that could hurt a fly...but you never knew. She showed up every day at Quigg's trial and, more than once, I saw the two of them pass secretive looks. So I'd had her checked out. When Bobby bought it, I thought of her right away.

But nothing was happening. I didn't know what I was expecting or hoping for, only that when it happened I'd know it. It was getting on one in the morning and I was starting to nod off when a black sedan rolled up. Marianne came out and hopped in. They drove off and I followed them all the way over to the East Side where they pulled into a small parking lot behind a funeral home. That definitely raised my curiosity a notch. Traffic was light so I didn't hang around. I drove up to the next block and parked my heap across from some second-rate clip joint and struck out on foot.

The funeral home was stuck in between a boarded-up factory and a row of old houses. It was a two-story brick job with withered ivy climbing all over it like hair on a monkey's back. There was a gray and weathered sign out front which proudly proclaimed it was the Douglas-Barre Funeral Home and had been since 1907...in case I was counting.

I strolled casually past the front and then circled around back. I came through the alley, a chill wind blasting rain into my face. My overcoat flapped around me like a flag on a high pole and rain ran off the brim of my fedora in tiny rivers. It was so wet even the rats were staying home. I positioned myself beneath the overhang of a warehouse loading dock, hiding in a pocket of shadow like a spider in a crevice.

I waited over an hour before something happened, cigarette butts gathering at my feet. The delivery/receiving doors at the back of the funeral home were opened and secured. There were two cars parked back there and neither of them were hearses. Just that sedan and a wood-paneled delivery wagon.

Cigarette dangling from my lower lip like a steaming icicle, I watched. Two men carried out a body—and I could see by the way they carried it that it was just as dead as my mother's virtue—and unceremoniously dumped it into the back of the wagon. Then the doors were closed and the wagon drove off, followed by the sedan and Marianne. I could've made a mad dash for my heap, but I decided I wanted to look around first.

I was curious.

I wanted very much to know where they were taking the stiff, but there was no real chance of catching up with them at night. Not in this city. Not without breaking a few traffic laws and having coppers crawling up my backside like mites. And I didn't want to spend the night in the jug.

Those delivery doors were locked, but the lock wasn't much. I took out my little case of picks and went through it in about a minute. Inside, the place was lousy with shadows. All the darkness in the world was gathered here. It stunk of sweet flowers and age. I made my way through winding corridors and past darkened viewing rooms. All I could hear was the rain on the windows and the beat of my own heart. Don't get me wrong, I'm not afraid of dead people. Death and me go way back. I've sent plenty of business His way. But places like this always remind me of my mother buying it when I was eight...or of Helen. Helen was my wife. Three months after we were married we were still nuts about each other and then she got sick. Two months later, we planted her. The cancer. Got into her blood. She was two weeks shy of her twenty-fifth birthday. But that's the way it works sometimes. Guys like me aren't designed to be happy in life, we're designed to stumble drunkenly from one scene to the next like a two-bit actor without the benefit of a script.

I looked around and didn't see a thing worth noting. Then I went upstairs, found the offices, some storage rooms. In one of the offices, one that had been recently occupied judging by the clouds of cigarette smoke hanging in the air, I found an address book in the top drawer...after I jimmied it open, of course. There were notations and phone numbers scribbled down. Names of florists, mortuaries, a few business cards clipped to the back cover.

What intrigued me I found in the back.

It read:

H. HILL 2:00 A.M.

H. Hill?

I jotted that down in my little notebook. It must've been a meeting with someone, somewhere. It was a vague clue, but something told me there was relevance simply because funeral directors, to my knowledge, didn't conduct their business at that hour of the morning—

"What the hell you think you're doing?"

I looked up and there was some guy standing in the doorway leaning on a broom. His mouth was hanging open wider than a hooker's at a convention. He was as ugly as a platter of fried dogshit. Looked like someone had heated up his face and pressed it into a Mr. Ugly mold. Thing was, it cooled all wrong. Another thing was, I knew him.

"*You,*" he said when he saw my mug. "Steel. What the hell are you doing here? I better call the cops in."

"Slow down, Junior," I told him.

His name was Junior Styles and he was a wrong number from the soles of his flat feet to the top of his pointy head. He'd had a pretty good racket going at one time. He had a couple girls working for him, young stuff mostly he'd bullied into it. They'd pick up johns at bars and bus stops, you name it, and bring 'em back for a quick roll. Thing was, Junior'd be waiting there with a rod and he'd rob 'em blind. Threaten to tell their wives or families if they squealed to the cops. I hadn't seen him in about five years; he'd been upstate doing a nickel. I knew. I helped to put him there. And I could see he remembered it, too.

He screwed up his mug and said, "I've been thinking about you a long time, Steel, you dirty sonofabitch. Breaking and entering. Ha! I like that."

"Zip it, pimp," I told him. "If anyone's gonna call the bulls in it'll be me."

He paled some at that. He knew I'd been a cop and he knew a lot of my friends were cops. And he was a petty criminal and an ex-con. We both knew who they'd believe.

"Never figured you for a broom jockey, Junior. Good to see you found your place in society."

"Fuck you, Steel. This is just something I'm doing for awhile."

"Yeah? What's your grift? How'd you get tangled up in this mess?" I said.

"What mess?"

I shook my head like I knew what I was talking about. "They'll put you away for keeps this time."

But like a skinflint, he wasn't buying it. He swung the broom handle at me and it whistled past my cheek. I stepped in hammered him two quick shots to the chops. He took 'em, spit blood, and cracked me in the ear with the broom handle. I saw stars and clipped him under the jaw. Before he could answer that one, I took hold of his shirt and sank my knee into his stomach. I repeated that maybe three times until he was curled up harmless as a kitten in a box.

He gagged and spat and called my mother a few unsavory names. But all that got him was a couple more kisses from my left.

"Dirty...sonofabitch," he growled.

"I'll do the talking, Junior. I'll ask the questions and you'll do the answering. Savvy?"

He glared at me with eyes like runny egg yolks. "Go...screw...yourself."

I laughed and pulled a switch out of my inner coat pocket. It was a special pocket I'd had sewn in the back, at the bottom, right where the seam was. Even if somebody took my gun, I was still armed. I thumbed the button and six inches of double-edge Sheffield steel was at my disposal. I took my pal by the shirt and hoisted his dead weight up. I slammed him up against the desk and pressed the blade against his crotch.

His eyes were wide, his face trembling. "What the hell you doing? Jesus, Steel."

"What am I doing? I'm about to slice off Uncle Johnson and the twins unless you start singing a tune I wanna hear."

"For chrissake! What do you wanna know?"

I sketched it in for him, real slow and simple-like. Didn't want to tax that dishrag he called a brain.

Junior nodded, started humming a few bars. "All I know is that I was told those people would be coming for a body...that they knew what they were doing and I was to stay out of their way. That's what the man said."

"And who's the man?"

"The man? Barre...Franklin Barre. He owns the place. Christ, you gotta believe me."

And I did. I let him go and he slid to the floor like lard down a hot pan. He just sat there, covering his friends with his big mitts, and hating, just hating me.

"We'll finish this talk another time," I promised him.

I picked up my lid off the floor, brushed off the brim and put it on my skull. Then I got the hell out of there.

4

Next morning I was sitting in my office pouring hot tar down my throat when the blower rang. I'd been sitting there thinking about H. Hill and what it might mean as I answered it.

"Yeah?" I said, setting my coffee down.

"Vince?" Tommy Albert said and I could hear it in his voice again, that sense of disgust like he'd just found out his mother had the clap. "Well. My friend, this ain't getting any better. In fact, it's getting a hell of a lot worse."

"Lay it on me."

I could hear him striking a match and I could almost smell that turd he was smoking. "You recall a guy named Buscotti? Tony Buscotti?"

I did. Tony "The Iceman" Buscotti, a.k.a. "Frankenstein", a.k.a "The Headhunter". Big Tony, as he was also known, was an enforcer and a torpedo for the Italians. He was one of the main cogs in their protection rackets. He was the guy who collected late payments from bookies, loanshark customers, and a variety of other businesses the wops decided needed "protecting". He was also the guy the mob gave contracts to. A stone killer, Buscotti very often used a knife on his victims. His specialty was a few slugs in the knees to cripple his prey and then some fancy knifework to finish the job. He was a big fierce man, part human and part grizzly bear. Rumor had it he ate raw meat. And when you were nearly seven feet tall and weighed around four hundred pounds, you could do any goddamn thing you wanted to. He made the toughest cops on the force want to wring out their shorts.

Or had, that was.

A year ago he'd been convicted of some seven homicides and sent to the big house for the hot squat. Two weeks ago, he sat down in that chair and put the funny hat on and they fed him the juice. Worm meat now, but the memory persisted like a bean fart in a closet.

"He's dead," I said. "Nobody showed at the funeral. Hard to understand, he was such a sweet kid...when he wasn't using a baseball bat on someone's jewels."

But Tommy wasn't in the mood for that. "His body's missing."

I almost spilled coffee all over my lap. "Missing?"

"Yeah," Tommy said. "I'm out here at the cemetery. You better get out here. I think we're developing a pattern."

I was already pulling my coat on. "Which boneyard are you at?"

And then he said it and I knew: "Harvest Hill," he said.

5

By the time I got there they were pretty much finished with the grave.

They had opened it and found Buscotti's casket empty as my wallet and now everyone was standing around looking grim as graverobbers. The day was the color of dirty laundry: dingy and gray. Last night's rain had turned the boneyard into a mud sea. It was everywhere, clotted on the bull's shoes like they'd just tiptoed through Mother O'Leary's cow pasture.

Tommy Albert said, "They had this special coffin made for this ape." He flicked his cigar butt down into the black, yawning grave. "Had to be twice as wide as usual and longer than your standard box. Like the service and the plot, it was paid for anonymously. You know what I'm saying, Vince?"

I did.

It was all paid for by the Outfit. They couldn't come right out and put their names to it because that wasn't how they did things, but everyone knew who sprang for it all the same.

Tommy and I turned away and walked through the sloppy earth, weaving our way amongst headstones, stands of leafless trees, cracked slabs. In the bleak shadow of an ornate burial vault we found more diggers at work. We got there just as they struck wood.

Tommy looked at me. "Eddie Wisk," he said. "Numbers runner. He was gunned down three weeks ago."

The workers brushed dirt from the lid of the casket and opened it. They didn't have to bust open the catches because somebody beat them to it. Wisk was gone, too. You could see the grayed impression on the silken pillow where his head had been. A beetle ran across it. But that was all.

Tommy's boys jumped down there and started dusting for prints.

"Gone," Tommy said. He shook his head. "This is connected, ain't it, Vince?"

"Has to be."

"Still clinging to the 'cult' theory?"

I sighed, slapped a nail in my kisser and gave it some heat. "I'm not sure of anything just yet." Quickly, I filled him in on

115

my visit to the funeral home. "I'm thinking whoever wrote that is the one that was here last night."

"And you think it's this Franklin Barre character?"

I blew out smoke. "Just a guess. It was his office I was in."

"I'll have him brought in. See what we can sweat out of him," Tommy said. "What about this Marianne Portis broad?"

"I think you should hold off on her for now. Give me a day or two."

Tommy looked at me. "You know what kind of shit I could get into if I did that?" He shook his head. "Two days. That's it. This stinks, Vince. Stinks bad. I got pressure on me now like you wouldn't believe. I got uniforms out looking for Stokes too."

Stokes was the night watchman at Harvest Hill. Nobody seemed to know where he was and maybe he wasn't tied up in this, but neither Tommy or I believed that for a minute.

Conspiracy? You're damned right. One that involved killing prosecutors and robbing graves and making off with dead bodies in the still of the night. But what was the thread? There was something, but I just couldn't make the connection.

"See ya, Tommy," I said walking off.

"Where you going?"

"I gotta see a guy about a grave."

6

Thirty minutes later I was in Little Italy. Parked just up the street from a warehouse called Frenzetti & Sons. For all intents and purposes, it looked like a warehouse and was: inventory in the form of furniture came in and went out. But if you happened to know the right people, you could get invited down below into the basement where the Italians operated an illegal casino. Blackjack, roulette, craps, slot machines, high and low stakes card games—you name it. The mob ran it and took a lucrative cut of everything that went down. The mob, in this case, being Slick Jimmy Conterro. A guy I grew up with and who happened to be an underworld soldier. I never held that against him and he never held being a cop against me.

I knew that right now, Bernie Stokes, night watchman of Harvest Hill boneyard was down in the casino. And would be for fifteen or twenty minutes more.

I knew I could go down there and get him anytime, but I didn't. I've gambled at Jimmy's place plenty. Lots of cops do. He gives good odds. Better than you'll get in Vegas. He runs clean games. But I also knew Jimmy wouldn't like me barging down there and manhandling a customer. You didn't make waves in this neighborhood; even the cops were on the payroll here.

So I sat there in the heap chewing a salami on Jewish rye and dipping my bill in a quart of beer. The minutes ticked by. I finished the sandwich, the beer, was halfway through my second butt when Stokes came out.

You should've seen him.

Looking over his shoulder, keeping his head low trying to blend into the crowd. But he blended in like a nun in full habit at a stroke parlor. Maybe it was how he acted—so jittery and afraid—but the guy was marked. You could see that.

I called him over and he almost left his skin lying on the walk.

"Jesus, Bernie," I said. "What gives? You don't look so good."

"Don't feel so good," he said, sliding through the passenger side door.

He was a tight little guy with a beak on him like a doorstop. Good guy as far as that went, but you could trust him like you could trust a rattlesnake in your shorts. He stank of hair oil and cheap rum. His eyes were red as the setting sun and his face hadn't seen a razor in a week or more.

"I got my problems, Vince. You know? I got my problems." He kept his eye on the rearview. In fact, he kept an eye out everywhere. "You can't be too careful these days."

"Give you a ride somewhere?"

"Sure. Uptown. You know the place."

I did. Bernie had a place over an Irish saloon. "Somebody after you, Bernie?"

He was trying desperately to light a cigarette, but his fingers were trembling too much. I lit it for him. His face was pale as a whitewashed fence. "Yeah, somebody's following me. I know it."

I wasn't sure what that was about. Jimmy's goons weren't known for their subtlety; they wanted you, they kicked right through the front door like the First Marine Division hitting a beach. "Probably cops, Bernie."

"You think so?" He was even paler now.

"I know it." I explained to him how I was unofficially working with the precinct. "It's this bit about Tanner. The papers didn't have the particulars, Bernie, but he was partially eaten. Chewed up like a drumstick."

"Jesus."

He looked like he was going to be sick, so I turned the screw a bit.

"They want to talk to you about what happened out at Harvest Hill. Some ghouls hit it last night, snatched a couple stiffs. Caretaker found the graves all messed-up this morning."

Bernie stared off into space. "You think they'd put the graves back in order when they were done."

Some cabbie laid on his horn and I gave him the finger. "Who are *they*, Bernie? Listen, you might as well be square with me on this bit. Better me than the bulls, you understand? They put the pinch on you, you'll be wearing a state suit."

"I don't know nothing about nothing," he said.

But he knew. He knew, all right. "You know a cop name of Albert?" I asked him. "Big ugly flatfoot? Know the guy?"

"Never heard of him."

I smiled...then frowned, shook my head before he saw me. "Well, this Albert, this big ugly shit-eating ape, he's really something. He's handling all this. You sure you never heard of him? No? Damn, guy gives me the creeps. They should've thrown him off the force years ago. Things he does to guys...*boy*. Anyway, he's in charge. He'll be coming to see you real soon. You can count on it."

Bernie looked at me. "What...what kind of things this Albert-guy do? I mean, what? Knocks guys around? Rubber hose or what?"

I laughed and shook my head. "Only if they're lucky. See this Albert...boy, he's something. Some kind of pervert, I guess. Likes to get a guy alone. Strip search him and stuff. But that's just the beginning with this freak...man, makes me sick, Bernie. I just hate the idea of him pawing you up and all. Forcing himself on you—"

"*Christ!*" Bernie said, desperate now. "I'll just talk to you, okay, Vince? You can keep him off me, right?" He dragged off his cigarette and he could barely hold it still. "All I know is these people come to me. They say they'll pay me a hundred just to look the other way. But when I found out what they want...I'm, no sir, no goddamn way..."

"Not unless they up the sugar?"

He shrugged. "Well, you know how things are these days. So five-hundred they give me. I tell 'em, okay, just put everything back the way you found it. First couple times they did too."

I swallowed. "How many times this happen?"

"Three, four times. I don't know what their thing is. Don't wanna know. Last night, though, Vince, that was my night off. They must've just come in and did what they wanted."

"Who watches it when you're off?"

"No one. They were all by their lonesome last night."

"Who are they, Bernie?"

He shook his head. "I don't know. Didn't get no names and didn't give 'em mine. There's two of 'em—a man and a woman. Creepy, I tell you. Both of 'em. But they just handle the business end. This truck pulls up and men get out, do the digging. It's dark, I never see what they look like."

"Why these hoods, Bernie? Why are they after these dead criminals?"

He just shook his head. "They know who they want and where to find 'em. I didn't have nothing to do with that."

He told me a few more things, but nothing of any value. I brought him back to his place even though I knew the cops would be waiting for him. But it had to be done. They had to put Bernie in custody...if somebody really was following him, he might not be around in a day or two.

Two uniforms jumped out from behind a parked car and put the elbow on him. He was like jelly in their hands, trembling, shaking, loose as a bag of poured rubber. Completely boneless. Tommy came walking up and nodded to me, then he turned to Bernie.

"You Bernie Stokes?" he said, flashing his tin. "Yeah? Well, I'm Detective-Inspector Albert. I need to have a word with you. Alone."

You should've seen Bernie then. Christ, he came alive like a sack of cobras, twisting and writhing and fighting. The uniforms could barely hold him. Me? I had all I could do to keep a straight face.

"Put him in the car," Tommy said. Then he turned to me. "What the hell's wrong with that sonofabitch?"

"Search me." I quickly filled him in on everything I'd gotten out of Bernie. "You better put him under protective custody, just in case."

Tommy nodded. "He'll be safe."

"He's not a bad guy, Tommy. Just a little sleazy is all. He'd make a good little rat. Let him skate on this and he'll be more than happy to finger these people for you if we can bring 'em in."

"Yeah, okay. Sure was acting funny...not a hophead, is he? No?" A look passed over Tommy's face. Then: "You didn't happen to tell him I was some kind of pervert, did you?"

"Me?"

"You bastard. You goddamn bastard, Steel." But he thought it was funny as always. "Listen. Do the names Yablonski and Sumner mean anything to you?"

They did, but I couldn't place them

"They were two of the jurors that put Quigg away," he said. "They found their bodies this morning. Same as Bobby Tanner."

I just stood there, the color running out of my face slow and steady. "It's connected to him. It all is. But how?"

"That's what we're gonna find out tonight, sunshine." Tommy put an arm around me and grinned at me salaciously with a face uglier than a boar's backside. "You think I'm a pervert? Good. Because me and you got a date."

"What should I wear?"

"Come as you are. We're pulling the night shift out at Harvest Hill."

7

Truth was, we weren't alone.

Tommy and me were staked-out in a stand of dark bushes that bordered a family plot of leaning marble headstones. Roughly dead center of the graveyard. Two uniforms were hiding out by the north wall and two more near the gates. Tommy's instructions were simple: nobody moved until the ghouls were in place and digging. It was a clear, cloudless night. Cool and breezy, but with a big old moon riding high in the sky and painting down the cemetery in a white, even glow. It was a good night to do what we were doing.

I lit a cigarette, cupping it in my hands to cut the light same way I was taught in the Navy. "This is a hell of a date,

Tommy," I whispered to him. "No wine. No steak. No music. Not even a goddamn movie. You think you're getting into my pants, guess again."

"Shut your yap, Steel," he said.

I had an ugly feeling I wouldn't be seeing my bed this night. I wasn't sure if this was going to work or not. I just kept watching the headstones dotting the hills, jutting from the dark earth like teeth, angled and white. A sudden gust of wind blew leaves in our faces.

And then we heard gunfire.

Someone shouting.

A police whistle.

Screaming.

It was coming from the north end. Tommy and I were already running, ducking through the marble forest of tombstones. I leaped over slabs and leapfrogged markers. Guns were still shooting and men were still shouting. We came around a stand of gnarled elms and saw shapes in the darkness.

I pulled my .45 out of the speed rig under my left arm and almost started pumping metal into a pair of stone death angels flanking some rich guy's grave. And then suddenly there was a third angel, only it was no angel. The guy advanced on me with an upraised shovel. I yelled at him to drop it, but he waded right in. I put three slugs in him and it dropped, but he didn't. I tried a fourth and fifth but I might as well have been plugging a bag of wet cement for all the affect it had. Suddenly he was on me and I was bathed in a putrid stink like a morgue drawer full of spoiled beef. He took hold of my arm and nearly broke it he was so goddamned, unnaturally strong. He tossed me around like a scarecrow stuffed with straw. And at 6'3 and over 200 pounds, I'm no lightweight. I punched him and he didn't even notice so I went for his eyes, clawing at his face...and it came apart under my fingers like dry, rotting plaster. My nails scraped the skull beneath and then he tossed me through the air and my head struck a stone and Goodnight, Irene.

A few minutes later, Tommy was pouring a flask of whiskey into my mouth. I came awake coughing and gagging and swinging, completely disoriented. I felt like I was sewn up in a bag of black velvet. The mists parted and Tommy helped me up.

"They got away," he said in a hopeless voice. "Never seen nothing like it. I gave one of them four rounds, point-blank, and that meateater went through me like nobody's business."

He brought me on a quick tour of the carnage. One cop was dead. His head was nearly twisted from his shoulders. He was laying on his back, a broken arm tucked under him. But to see his face, you had to flip him over. Two other cops were beaten and busted-up.

Tommy scanned the area with a flashlight. In the distance I could hear sirens. We came up to a body sprawled in the grass, arms outstretched to either side. There were so many bullet holes in it you could have used it as a watering can. Tommy put the light on the face. It was decayed, gray, and flaking, eaten away in places as if by insects. There were tiny worm holes in the nose. One glazed eye stared up at us.

Tommy looked at me. "You know this guy?"

I nodded dumbly. "Yeah...I think...I think it's Johnny Luna."

"Yeah, it's him, all right," Tommy said in a dry voice. "And Johnny Luna died six months ago."

8

The next night, I stuck to Marianne Portis like a birthmark.

I sat there in the darkness, my brain spinning like a top in an oil drum. This was all connected to Quigg somehow. The D.A. who'd convicted him was dead. Now two of the jurors. Tommy had placed cops at the houses of the others. But there were other people involved in putting that headcase away—the judge, Tommy, me, plenty of others. And how did all that tie in with glomming corpses and, worse yet, with walking dead men? Two days ago, you asked me if I believed the dead could walk I'd have laughed in your face. Now I wasn't so sure. I didn't know what to think.

But I did know a few things.

One of which was that Franklin Barre was missing, presumed dead by Tommy and his people. The links to this business were being cut like apron strings and I had a feeling it wouldn't be long before I got snipped. And Marianne Portis? We now knew she was a colleague of Quigg's. At one time she had been chairwoman of the City Folklore Society. We also knew she was somewhat respected in the field, publishing assorted papers on folklore and the occult in various trade magazines.

But what did it all add up to? Anyone's guess. That's what.

Just before midnight the black sedan rolled up again. Marianne came out and got in it. I followed at a discreet distance. They drove slowly through the city traffic, but like a hooker paid by the hour, they were in no hurry. I followed them down the main stem over the bridge and right out of town. They hit the highway and then cut down a few deserted country lanes. My lights off, I followed at a safe distance.

I started to get that feeling in my gut. The one that tells me I'm onto something, that things are about to become...*relevant*. Either that or the salami roll I had for supper was starting its march to the sea.

Out in the middle of nowhere, the sedan whipped through a set of black iron gates and into yet another cemetery. I waited a few minutes before following. Just another boneyard—lots of monuments and scraggly trees. I piloted my heap down the lonesome dirt drive, shadows reaching out and clawing over the ruts. Above there was no moon, just gray clouds and skeletal boughs scratching against them. I got lost. I'll admit that. I'll also admit I was starting to get the creeps just driving around and around, maybe half wondering if I'd ever find my way out. Wouldn't that be a goddamn set-up? Stuck in some spookworld where I drove endlessly through a cemetery?

But, eventually, I found the sedan.

It was way out back. There was a big mausoleum crowning a barren hill. Two stories of rectangular gray stone set with huge black windows. A real inviting place...if you were a corpse. I killed the engine on the heap and coasted into a stand of trees, just off the drive. The sedan was parked up there pretty as you please. There was a delivery wagon and a truck up there, too. I sat there, smoking in the dark, wishing I had Tommy and his boys backing me up. But I was alone, so I did the first fool thing that popped into my head: I walked on up there.

The front door was a massive affair you could've driven a tank through. I went around back and cased the joint. I could see lights in a few windows, but there were drapes covering them so I couldn't see what my pals were doing. I started checking doors and windows, but they were all locked. Then I found a cellar window that tilted up. I slid through like a greased eel and landed in the darkness. I sat there waiting for a reception committee, but none came.

So far, so good.

It took my eyes awhile to adjust to the darkness. I had a flashlight with me, but I didn't dare use it. I could see that I was in a storage room of sorts—crates and boxes stacked up, a few metal barrels against the wall. It was all pretty pedestrian, except for that funny smell which I knew was formaldehyde. There were other odors, too. A sweet, sickly stink of decay and death hung in the air. And something like a spice cupboard that had been shut up for too long.

I kept moving around down there, feeling up the walls like a teenager under Mary Jane's sweater until I found my way into a cement block corridor studded with doors. Way it was stinking down there, I just didn't feel really curious about what was behind those doors. Finally, I found a set of steps and went up. I was in a marble hall, the walls of which were studded with brass nameplates bearing the tags of the deceased. It was cold in there. I kept going, wandering down more and more corridors until I saw lights and heard voices.

I cracked open a heavy oak door just a bit and the gang was all there.

I could see Marianne and another thin, cadaverous-looking guy with a face only Frankenstein could love. Next to them were three or four other people, their backs to me. I couldn't hear what they were saying, but I sure as hell could see what they were doing. The room was set up like an embalming chamber...or so I thought at first. It was dimly lit, but there was no mistaking the metal drums of chemicals or the hoses and suction devices, floor pumps, trays of instruments. Just as there was no mistaking the stiff spread out on a metal table like Sunday's wash. He was rancid. About as fresh as a wormy hamburger on a hard roll.

Marianne and the others all had aprons on and little surgical masks. I was ready to ask if I could borrow one before I heaved up my dinner. To this day, I still can't be sure what it was they were doing exactly. I saw them douse the body with chemicals. I saw Marianne take a syringe and shoot something in the cadaver's neck. I saw another sprinkle powders and rub the graying flesh down like a Christmas goose. And then I saw them dump what looked like bloody meat the entire length of the body. The stink of whatever they were using overpowered the death smell. Reminded me of biology class in high school.

Maybe I can't really be sure about any of what they did. My heart was hammering like Gene Krupa and my belly was full of jumping frogs.

So, I can't be sure.

But I am sure of what happened next...the body, that goddamn stiff they'd dragged out of some moldering grave, *it began to move.* It began to shudder and writhe like there was a high voltage cable shoved up its ass. About the time it sat up and let out a mournful, agonized shriek, I was on my way out. Back down the stairs I went, drenched now in cold sweat, scared like a kiddie at a monster show. At the bottom of the steps I walked right into something (I don't know what) and it tipped over and shattered. Glass sprayed everywhere. I froze up like a Roman statue, just my heart thumping away.

But everything was still quiet.

I tried to negotiate my way in the darkness. It was no easy trick. Maybe if I'd had half a brain I would've broke out the flashlight. But I didn't. Not yet. I found a door and I was sure it was the one. I slipped into the mulling darkness and the room was colder than a meat locker. That awful stink of putrescence and formaldehyde was stronger. In fact, it was gagging. It was like being trapped in a body bag. I bumped into something again, but nothing fell. And, dammit, I'd had quite enough. I pulled the flashlight out of the pocket of my overcoat and clicked it on.

And then instantly wished I hadn't.

I was in another cellar room, but not the one I'd landed in earlier. No, this one had tables arranged in rows from end to end with little walkways in-between. They were like mortician's slabs, each draped in a white sheet. And there was no doubt what was under those sheets: I could see the forms easily enough. Now and again, a hand had slipped from beneath its covering, dead fingers dangling in midair. I could see the toes of some of the taller ones. Quickly, I went from slab to slab, looking down on those ruined faces. I recognized quite a few.

It was about that time, my skin all clammy and my fingers stiff as pencils from the cold, that I first sensed it. I don't know how to adequately describe it. It was like the air around me had changed, was charged with something. I could feel the hairs along the back of my neck stand up. Gooseflesh spread down my spine like ripples in a pond. The air was suddenly full of static electricity, thrumming with it, some noxious stored potential was beginning to vent itself. I caught a sharp aroma of ozone like lightening was about to strike.

And then it did.

My head reeling with that savage smell, that dark and rising sweetness, the bodies on the slabs all began to sit up. I saw sheets shudder and slide from sunless, graveyard faces. A lot of them were little more than skulls knitted with tight dry flesh like tanned leather.

I didn't wait to see what came next.

There was a window on the other side and I went for it, smashing through it with my flashlight and diving into the cool grass. And then I was running and stumbling and sliding down the hill on my ass. I could see my heap waiting for me and then I saw the two heavies next to it.

Unarmed, smelling like a litter pile in a death camp, they came at me. My .45 slid out from the speed rig and I started drilling those bastards, knowing that you can't kill something already dead, but sometimes you can sure give 'em a bad day.

I emptied the clip and drove them back and then I was in the heap. I had barely started rolling when she was hit hard. I thought a truck had rammed into us. I was practically knocked against the passenger side door. Another thud and that old Chrysler went up in the air a few feet, balancing on two tires and then hammering back down, the shocks squeaking like honeymooner's bedsprings.

Then I saw.

It was no truck that hit me. It was worse.

Out of my window I saw *him* standing there, his huge and moonish face grinning like a skull in the desert: Tony "The Iceman" Buscotti. Remember him? He was the human ogre and former syndicate hitman that was supposed to be feeding the worms out at Harvest Hill in that grave big enough to drop a Steinway into. Yes, sir, old "Frankenstein" himself. Big Tony could have given Karloff the cold sweats.

His hand smashed through my window and I covered my face against the implosion of glass shards. His hand—big enough to palm a football—came snaking in, fingers clawing for purchase. And those fingers...I could see the bones popping through the knuckles, the skin hanging in ropy loops. I slammed down on the accelerator and almost went right into a tree. I threw her in reverse and mowed down the other two goons that

I'd given the gift of my bullets to. I rolled right over one of them. Then Big Tony was there again, the yellow of his skull showing through the holes in his face which looked like a wormy shroud hanging from a clothesline. Those gargantuan hands took hold of the door and at the exact second I gave the old heap the gas, there was a sudden lurching and screeching metallic groan as Big Tony ripped the door clean off the driver's side.

Then I was peeling away in a spray of dirt and that big, dead hulk was standing there with the door in his paws like a cue card. I don't remember very much of my escape. Only that I sideswiped tombstones and bushes as I thundered down that winding maze of dirt road. Drenched with fear-sweat, I exited those black gates like a train rocketing from a midnight tunnel. Then the road. The highway. The city lights.

And me, shivering like a sick kitty in a high wind.

9

Ninety minutes later, after half a pint of rye, I was back out there.

This time Tommy Albert was with me. Him and about twenty cops, local johns—sheriff's deputies—and assorted whitecoats from the coroner's office. The place was wriggling with badges. You know what we found? Squat. Yes, that's right. The bodies were gone. As were Marianne and the ghoul glee club. But they hadn't completely sanitized the place. There just wasn't time.

Downstairs we found the slabs. We also found the room where they did their thing with the stiffs. All the equipment was pretty much in place. We found blood everywhere. Sticky fluids. Scraps of raw animal meat. A linen bag of human bones so fresh they still had red-brown stains on them. But that was pretty much it.

"It happened," I was telling Tommy. "Don't look at me like some kind of freak. I saw it."

He stopped looking at me. "I believe you. Maybe I shouldn't, but I do."

I dragged off my cigarette. "These guys never will."

"They don't have to, Vince. What we got out here is more than enough justification for me to call in all these boys." He stuffed a cigar in his mouth. "I gotta pick up that Portis broad. You know that. She's behind all this and only she can fill in all the holes."

Holes? Sure, we could've dropped most of the Midwest through the holes there were in this one. Graverobbing. Cannibalism. Murder. Walking dead hoods. Any minute now, I expected Chaney and Lugosi to be brought in for routine questioning. That's how bad this mess was. It stunk worse than a trucker's underwear.

A uniform came running in from the outside. "Inspector, we gotta a dead cop," he said to Tommy. "In the city."

Then we were back in Tommy's Ford sedan screaming towards the concrete jungle, lights blaring and siren shrilling. There was no more to do out at the mausoleum. Those already there could handle it. Once we had the streets beneath us and the concrete and brick wrapping us up like mama's arms, I started to feel better. On the West Side, down near the docks, was where the cop was. He was sprawled in a pool of his own blood.

There was a sheet over his body, reporters barely held at bay by a defensive perimeter of uniforms. Another detective—a thin, asthmatic guy named Skipp—was breathing through a handkerchief. You could smell the wharfs, the docks. That stagnant fishy smell of the bay blowing in with fingers of mist.

Skipp pulled the sheet back. "This your boy?" he said.

Tommy nodded. "That's Mikey Ryan. He worked vice."

I knew Ryan. We'd gone to the academy together. We'd pounded a beat together, drank out of the same bottle, raised hell. I was at his wedding. Now he was dead. Another good cop gone in a city that can't afford to lose too many.

He hadn't been mutilated. He'd been stabbed, though. Skipp said he'd been stuck at least fifteen or twenty times. "Took the last jab right in the pump," he told us. "Then as an afterthought, his killer did this."

Ryan's neck had been snapped. The side of his throat bulging with a shank of protruding bone. "Wasn't an easy way to go," Skipp said and resumed breathing through his hanky. It sounded like there was a whistle lodged in his throat every time he sucked in a breath. "Goddamn night air...it's not good for me."

"It's even worse for him," I said.

"He didn't die right away, though," Skipp said.

He held up Ryan's hand, it was wet with blood. That didn't mean a lot until you saw what was scratched in blood a few inches away:

"He lived long enough to leave us a message."

Tommy just kept staring at it, shaking his head. "L-U-N...what in Christ you suppose that means? Could be a plate number...could be just about any goddamn thing."

But I knew. There was no doubt in my mind. "He was telling us who did this to him," I pointed out. "LUNA. As in Johnny Luna."

Tommy looked at me. "He's in the morgue."

But I just stared at him, boring holes in his face.

10

It didn't take too many phone calls to find out Luna was missing from the deep freeze. The attendant on duty covered his ass by saying maybe he was picked up by a private mortuary. And it sounded good. But Tommy and I knew different: Johnny Luna had walked out of there. Only good thing was nobody saw him do it.

11

The next day, after a sleepless night in which gaunt shadows reached out for me in the darkness, I did some checking. I went about it real casually. I had a photograph of Marianne Portis and I started showing it around very selectively.

About three, four hours later I struck gold.

I struck it with Louie Penachek, a degenerate gambler who was always into the loansharks for three or four figures. There wasn't much he wouldn't do for a buck. He was obsessed with the ponies. Sports betting. Card games. Any possible way he could wager on the outcome of something, he was into.

Barely five feet, slick as an oiled weasel, I found him out at the track, betting on the Danes. He was jumping up and down and screaming at the top of his lungs. By the time I'd reached him, he was leaning up against the railing, defeated.

He saw me, said by way of greeting, "Sonofabitch should've been a winner, Vince. It had all the markings. I had an inside tip on this one. Damn! Twenty clams down the old pisser."

I flashed the cabbage at him: a couple fifties. "I need some info," I told him. "You tell me what I want to hear, you got em."

He licked his lips, looked like a sailor finally coming into port, catching his first glimpse of a cathouse. "Sure, sure, sure, Vince," he said. "Ain't much I don't know about."

I showed him the picture of Marianne.

His face dropped like mercury on a cold day. "No, no, no." He held his hands up. "I can't get involved in that. How would it look?" Then he looked at the bills again. "That's some rich gravy." He licked his lips again. "All right, goddammit, you bastard, Vince, you asked for it."

And he told me.

12

What I had to do had to be done at night.

So I waited.

And waited.

When the sun was down an hour, two, I was still waiting. Still thinking. I'd talked to Tommy, but I hadn't told him what Louie told me. I was saving that until I was sure. I had to be sure this time. Tommy told me that Mikey Ryan had been undercover, following around bagmen who ran money for the Italians. The money was from gambling, prostitution, extortion. He was mapping out their haunts, their routes, how often they came and went. All in advance of a big raid by vice.

But now he was dead.

How did that factor in? I wasn't sure just yet. I laid there in my rack, listening to the clock tick, traffic on the street below. I smoked and watched the neon from the bar downstairs light up my room, latticing me with sharp shadows.

That's when I heard my door open.

Feet went pounding away. Very casually, I went for my .45 on the nightstand. I didn't know what to expect. The lights were off. Carefully, I turned the gooseneck lamp on the stand so when I clicked it on it would illuminate the intruder, temporarily blinding him. It would give me the edge.

Breath locked up tight in my lungs, I waited. A trickle of sweat ran down one temple like ants to a picnic. My finger was hot and damp against the trigger of my Browning. I caught a whiff of something sharp and pungent like spices, like age. I could hear the intruder moving through my living room, approaching my bedroom door.

The door swung in.

I saw a shadow...filmy, almost transparent.

I clicked on the light. And it could've been a lot of people standing there, arms outstretched. I could've given you a grocery list of sorry bastards who wanted me dead. But I never would have guessed this.

Helen was standing there.

Dead these two years, but shuffling forward all the same. She was a mummy. Nothing more. I still recognized the diamond choker around her withered throat. She was naked and her flesh was papery, shriveled, it clung to the skeleton beneath like wet decoupage. Except it wasn't wet, but dry and rubbed with spices to keep it from crumbling away entirely. As she drifted towards me, stick arms extended and twig fingers clutching, she seemed to be disintegrating, flaking away. Motes of her danced in the shaft of light from the lamp.

Her skull-face attempted a grin but it was the grin of mortuaries and death houses, the grin of something long-buried beneath shifting Egyptian sands. Eyeless, her fine nose collapsed into the nasal channel of her skull, her teeth gone black, she attempted speech...but her vocal cords had long ago succumbed to worm and dust. What came out was a dry and hideous croaking.

My insides gone to sauce, funeral bells gonging in the drum of my skull, I sat forward and, letting out a piercing shriek, I put two slugs in her head. She folded up like a house of cards, shattering into dust and pitted bone and rags as she struck the floor.

My brain full of her stink, my mind full of an insane screeching, I fell next to her, sobbing.

This was their latest game.

But it hadn't scared me off; it only made things personal.

13

It was a huge and rambling Tudor a mile outside the city lights. In a neighborhood where the yards sprawled half a city block and the driveways were circular and flanked by weeping willows. This is where I came. This is where it would end. The place was surrounded by a low stone wall.

I slid over it and dropped into the grass.

I waited for dogs, for guards, for worse things. But nothing or no one came. Surprised? I wasn't. The egos of the people behind this ghastly little game couldn't or wouldn't accept defiance of any sort. The drive was choked with Rolls-Royces and Mercedes...but there were a few low-class sedans and wagons. I saw the car that had spirited away Marianne Portis and smiled. I also saw a delivery truck. I knew without a doubt that the dead ones arrived in that like troops.

I was glad she was there.

I wanted her to be part of this.

As I was casing the joint, some guy—an Outfit soldier— stumbled through the hedges probably in search of a place to relieve himself. He saw me and went for his gun, but never made it. I popped him three, four times in the face, dropping him. Then I punted him in the head and turned his lights out. I gagged him with his own hanky and tied him up in the hedges with his own belt.

I wasn't careful going through that cellar window.

I kicked it in and dropped through with my bag of goodies. Using my flashlight, I made a quick inspection of the place. Kept looking and looking until I found the furnace room, taking special interest in the fuel oil tank against one wall. It held over 200 gallons and it was nearly full. And then I knew how it would end for them. Not with a whimper, but like the Fourth of July finale. I'd found what I was looking for.

I opened my bag and got to work.

During the war, I served in the Navy. In the UDT to be specific. Underwater Demolition Teams. You probably read about us, they called us frogmen. We swam around and planted bombs on boats, docks, beachheads. Sometimes we came out of the water for quick commando raids. Like any good UDT man, I knew explosives better than I knew my own mug. I taped together ten sticks of TNT with electrical tape and attached a blasting cap to it. Then I ran a positive and negative wire from a battery-operated alarm clock to the blasting cap. Then I set the timer. I gave it ninety minutes. I was in no hurry and according to Louie Penachek, these little gatherings went on all night.

When I had attached my bomb to the fuel tank, I went right up the stairs.

It was a big house by any stretch of the imagination. But it only took me a few minutes to locate the people. There were a couple hatchetmen outside the door and I shot both of them down and kicked my way through the double oak doors and there they all were. Marianne and her crew. An assortment of high-ranking hoods from the Italian mob. Because you see, that was my plan: I wanted them all in the same place.

A couple tough guys went for their rods and I killed them where they stood. Then I aimed at the leader of the rat pack: Carmine Varga, the boss of the syndicates. He was an obese, swarthy guy with a face like congealed grease. He seemed to glisten with oil and evil. He was so fat they should've hung an orange triangle on his ass. I had seen pictures of him in the daily rags, but none of those did this guy justice. All my life I'd wondered when I'd meet the guy with the patent on ugly and here he was. I kept my rod on him while his hoods bristled like the pigs they were. They all wanted to make a try for me, but he stopped them with a slight shake of his head.

"Vince Steel," he said like we were old pals. "I wondered when you'd show."

I glommed a nail and burned the end, blew out a cloud of smoke. "Where are they?" I said to him, looking around, taking it all in—the long tables of culinary delights, the imported champagne, the works of art that hung on the wall. All things stolen or bought with blood money. "Where are the dead guys, fatso?"

He sneered at me, quickly gathered himself. "Dead guys?" He laughed. "Whatever are you talking about?"

I looked at him flat and mean and hungry, the way a rattlesnake might look at you right before it sunk its teeth into your throat. "You know what I'm talking about, you fat piece of shit. Are they here? Are they downstairs? Upstairs? Answer me and don't even think of lying, because if you do I spray that morgue photo you call a face all over the fucking room."

Marianne Portis stepped forward, her eyes were iron balls—cold and rusty. "Mr. Steel, you have no idea what you're involved in here...put that gun away while you still can."

I smiled at her. She had a cute way about her...like a hungry leopard coming at you in the dark jungle. "Shut that pisshole you call a mouth, sweetheart, and tell me where that festering collection of roadkill is. You know the ones I mean, I think."

The gaunt man with her took a step forward in some vain attempt to protect his lady love. Maybe. I had to admit that Marianne—with her hair down, dark and lustrous, some make-up on, and a tight-fitting evening gown that left little to the imagination—was a pretty swell dish. I bet she'd been in more beds than a hot water bottle.

"Easy, Dracula," I told him. "I don't think it'll take a wooden stake in your heart to put you down."

"Drop that gun, Mr. Steel," Marianne said.

I stared at her. "That was a nice trick you had, sending my dead wife over. Sickest piece of work I've ever seen."

She smiled like a cat disemboweling a mouse. "My gift to you."

"That's sweet. And here's one for you," I said and put a slug in that fine expanse of belly.

She made a gagging, coughing sound and dropped to the floor, a blossom of blood spreading over her dress like a red flower. She glared at me through the pain, blood running from her lips. The gaunt man came at me and I gave him a pill in the face, point blank, spraying the others with the contents of his skull. I was throwing lead like a maiden aunt tossing rice at a wedding, but I didn't care.

"It's a hell of a way to die, sweetheart," I told Marianne. "Gutshot. Could take hours and hours before you cash in."

I sensed motion at my back and the welcome wagon rolled in with a maggoty stench. Johnny Luna. Tony the Iceman. I emptied my heater into them and Tony, his face hanging like confetti, gave me a shove and I went to the ground. And then, of course, they were all over me.

First things first. Varga's hoods gave me a good beating, made me spit some blood and make obscene comments about their mothers. But then they had me subdued, tied to a chair. But despite all they did to me, I kept smiling.

"You won't be smiling long, you sonofabitch," Varga told me. Guy smelled like fish oil and grease. "Not when we're through with you. But let me explain."

I spat some blood. "No point. I already know what your mother does for a living."

That got me a couple more knocks. When the fog parted, I was still smiling. How much longer before the place went up? An hour? Maybe a little less? Hee, hee, hee. Boy, were they in for a surprise.

Varga swept his hand around the room indicating the living ones. "I won't bother with introductions. These are my people." Then he looked at Marianne on the floor, bleeding like a slit pig. Her friend with that hole in his face. A few others including some broad who looked like Peter Lorre in drag. "These people here. They're the ones that put this little thing together. You might remember a guy named Quigg. You do? Of course, you do. See, our good Mr. Quigg, he spent years bopping around to all them weird places putting together all this..."

He gave me the rumble and I listened.

Quigg had lived amongst sorcerors, witch doctors, shaman, you name it, all around the world, studying and learning. What he was interested in was nothing less than resurrection. After devoting most of his life to it, he succeeded. Or almost had. I kind of messed that up when I tracked him down and helped put him away. But Marianne, apt pupil that she was, carried on and put on the finishing touches. But she needed money. That's where Varga came in. He bankrolled it all and was pleased with the results. See, through Quigg's neo-science, he had an army of dead hoods at his disposal—killers, bagmen, enforcers, thieves, racketeers. Guys who could pull jobs and never be prosecuted because they were already dead. Even if they left fingerprints, what possible difference did it make? Eye witnesses? Who'd believe 'em?

It was perfect.

"...and it was out of respect to our Mr. Quigg that I had some of my boys take out the D.A., a couple of the jurors. That cannibalism bit was just a cosmetic touch. Yeah, but those three are only the beginning. Before we're done, they'll all be doing the deep six: the judge, your friend Tommy Albert, even yourself. We do that out of respect for the man that made this all possible."

The walking dead goons parted and I almost shit a pearl.

Old Quigg came shambling forward, a bag of graying bones. His eyes were like yellow moons setting in that shrunken face. "Yes. Mr. Steel," he managed, his voice dry as sandstorms. "And soon you'll be joining us. First you'll need to die, then we'll need your heart—"

"Kiss my ass," I said and then something hit me and I fell into darkness.

14

Thud.
Thud.
Thud.

That's what I woke to. My head was throbbing, but I came awake sharp and ready. I came awake in panic. In the darkness. In a box. It wasn't a fancy casket they were burying

135

me alive in, just a plain wooden packing crate. I tried to move, to thrash, to fight, but it was no good. This was Quigg's revenge— let me die like this and bring me back like one of them. Trying to think, I pushed up at the lid with everything I had. It moved up two, three inches, but that was all.

The dirt kept raining down.

The sound of it was muffled and I knew my coffin was covered now. If I was going to do anything, I'd have to do it before too much dirt piled up on top. I flicked my lighter and saw that the lid was roped shut. At least it wasn't chained or nailed. After some squirming and banging my knees and head, I got my switch out and began sawing through the ropes. It took less than a minute, but a minute was a lot when you were running out of air.

When the ropes were free, I began putting everything I had into getting that lid up. The dirt was still loose above, but it was still heavy as all hell. I got it up enough to start forcing myself through and then I was free, trapped in that cocoon of shifting black earth. I was able to draw air from pockets. I began clawing my way up real slowly, making progress, but not wanting to come bursting out of there before the gravediggers were done. But soon enough, the air was getting harder to breathe and I had to strain it through my teeth, drawing in ranks clods of dirt. That soil was rich and black and wormy. With everything I had, I clawed my way up. About the time black dots were dancing before my eyes, my fingers broke free. Then my head and shoulders.

The gravediggers were gone.

My throat and chest aching, I gulped in lungfuls of fresh air. When I could think again, I looked around. I was in a stand of trees out back of Varga's Tudor. In the distance I saw retreating shadows and figured they were my gravediggers. From the way they walked I could see that they were zombies.

Pulling myself to my feet, I checked my watch.

Less than fifteen minutes until showtime.

15

When I'd brushed myself free of dirt, I made my way around front.

Varga was just climbing into his Mercedes and the others were getting into their respective vehicles. I dashed from shadow to shadow and came right up to Varga's door. Before his driver even knew that the shit had hit or what it smelled like, I had his boss's door open and I dragged that fat gob out onto the grass. A couple kicks to the ribs and the fight drained out of him like piss through a leaky drainpipe.

I threw him up against the car just as the troops moved in.

But I already had my knife against his soft, white throat. "Tell them to fade or I'll slit your throat," I ordered him.

He made a few pathetic wheezing sounds. I pressed the knife home until a trickle of blood ran over my fingers. "Do it," I said. "Tell 'em all to get back in the house. The dead ones, too. Everyone."

"You stupid—"

I kneed him in the kidneys and he yelped. "INTO THE FUCKING HOUSE!" he cried out. "ALL OF YOU!"

I watched them file in. Marianne's little club...what was left of it. Then all of Varga's hoods, at least twenty of them. Finally Quigg and the zombies carrying the bodies of Marianne and her boyfriend. In they went. The door closed.

"Any of 'em come out of there," I hissed, "and you die, understand?"

He shook his head carefully. "They won't. Not until I come for 'em."

"You sure?" I said, pushing that cutter against his pipes.

"Yeah, I'm sure, tough guy."

I dragged him up the drive and over to the wall.

Maybe my timing was a little off, because we'd barely made the wall when the fireworks began. There was a huge, rending explosion that pitched us to the grass. And the Tudor came apart like a house built of Popsicle sticks. Great sections of it vaporized as gouts of fire and rolling clouds of flame blasted through the windows and engulfed the roof. The air was raining charred wood and missiles of glass and burning fragments. They showered down all around us.

Varga sat up and just stared at his house, slowly shaking his head. "You sonofabitch," he said, sounding like he needed to cry. "You dirty sonofabitch."

I started laughing and couldn't stop. "It's all over, asshole. All of it."

But then I wasn't so sure. A huge figure stumbled out of the burning wreckage, lit up like Roman candle. He made it a few feet and fell into a blazing heap. You could've roasted wieners off him.

I figured it was Big Tony.

A few minutes later the fire department arrived along with dozens of nosy neighbors. There wasn't much to do but watch it burn to ashes. They asked me and Varga questions, but we had no answers.

Finally, Tommy arrived. "Jesus H. Christ, Vince," he said. "What in hell's name did you do this time?"

He dragged me away to his car after warning the mob boss not to move. He gave me a belt of bourbon from his pocket flask, stuck a cigarette in my mouth, and waited. Just waited. It was going to be good and he knew it.

"Well?" he said. "You wanna tell me about it?"

"Depends," I said, blowing smoke.

"On what?"

"On whether you like horror stories or not." I took another drag. "Because if you do, Tommy, boy, have I got a beaut for you."

MORTUARY

Weston said his people were ready to kick ass and take names and Silva knew the moment had come. A lot was riding on what he did in the new few minutes. The decisions he made now—or didn't make—could haunt him for years.

"We're going to do this right, understand?" he said to Weston. "This operation is not going to become another Waco or Ruby Ridge. I'm not about to become the subject of a Senate investigation."

And now that it was time to break the standoff between the FBI and the religious crazies down in the compound, Silva was wondering for the first time in his career if he was the right man for the job.

Using a nightscope, he was looking across that open stretch of field, thinking the complex looked like something from an old prison movie. A sprawling, flat-roofed collection of rectangular buildings quarried from a dirty gray stone. The windows were tall and narrow, set with iron bars. The grounds were barren, the perimeter wrapped up in a high chain-link fence topped with coiled barbwire. A very utilitarian sort of place. About as cozy as a Victorian madhouse.

A helicopter buzzed overhead, a mounted searchlight scanning over the darkened, interconnected buildings.

Silva didn't like it. Didn't like the feeling twisting in his belly.

And he liked even less what was going to happen within the next ten minutes or so.

Things went well and nobody got hurt...well, careers were going to be made here tonight. But, if on the other hand, the whole thing went south...somebody's ass was going to get hung out to dry. And Silva pretty much figured whose ass it would be.

Silva was an FBI Assistant Director for the Critical Incident Response Team, the CIRT. He was in direct charge of the Bureau's elite Hostage Rescue Team. The HRT was a Tactical Support Branch of the CIRT, a highly-trained paramilitary force used in every delicate situation from hostage rescue and high-risk arrests to mobile assaults and the search for WMDs.

One of their specialties were raids against barricaded subjects.

Something they were going to be practicing real soon now.

Down in the compound were members of the Divine Church of the Resurrection, a shadowy cult led by a psychotic messiah name of Paul Henry Dade. Dade's specialty was kidnapping new recruits, brainwashing them and putting them to work in his domestic terror network which he funded with everything from narcotics trafficking to the sale of illegal arms.

This guy was so fucked-up, Charles Manson had openly called him a *fanatic* in a taped interview two months before.

And for once, old Charlie was right.

Night had fallen now and the immediate area around the police blockade was a hive of bustling activity. Hostage negotiators on loudspeakers were trying to get Dade's people to give themselves up. Floodlights were sweeping the compound. Armored trucks and support units were pulled up at the ready, ambulances and fire engines behind them. And to the immediate rear, the county sheriff and his people keeping the press and the curious at bay.

Jesus, it was like a circus, Silva thought.

He got on his walkie-talkie: "All right, Weston," he said, his voice oddly shrill, "tell your teams to prepare to stage."

A balding agent named Runyon came running up, leaping from the back of a tactical support van. He wore a midnight blue windbreaker like Silva with the letters FBI stenciled on the back in day-glo yellow.

"Sir," he said, "thermal imaging still isn't picking up a goddamn thing down there."

"Dammit," Silva said. "I knew we should have kicked the door in two days ago."

But it wasn't his decision. The timing of the raid was his, but the actual decision came down from the Attorney General. The standoff had been going on for nearly a week now and the administration was in no hurry to get anymore bureaucratic egg on their faces. So they'd held back. Until tonight. And that was just plain bullshit because thermal imaging had told them the worst possible thing since early that morning: no infrared signatures.

Meaning, if there was anything alive in the complex, it must have been hiding pretty damn deep.

Silva thumbed his walkie-talkie. "Weston. Deploy your teams. Repeat: It's a go. Take it down..."

*

There were three HRT tactical teams: Red Team, Blue Team, and Green Team. Each had four operatives. Blue Team came in from the rear, cutting its way through the chain link fence and blowing the backdoor with a shaped charge of C-4. Green Team was helicopered to the roof, put on standby. Red Team blew their way through the front entrance.

And waltzed right into the mouth of hell itself.

*

TAC unit Red Team was led by Weston himself, an ex-Delta Force commando. When the door was blown in, he charged through, LeClere, Becker, and Hookley right behind him. All the HRT TAC teams were dressed in black coveralls and Kevlar vests. They wore ballistic helmets with headsets and NV goggles, carried Colt M4 tactical carbines, assault shotguns, and H & K MP5 machine pistols.

They were loaded for bear.

The compound was blacker than the inside of a body bag, a labyrinth of corridors and rooms and staircases leading up and down. Dead-ends and cul-de-sacs and storage closets. The place had originally been a U.S. Army military complex in World Wars I and II, then a government warehouse, and now?

Now it was a trap waiting to be sprung.

No electricity, no water. No nothing. Just the unknown waiting in the damp darkness.

"Keep your eyes open," Weston told them over his headset, studying the corridor ahead through the green field of his NV goggles. "Not seeing any movement...not a damn thing..."

Becker said, "Not picking up shit on infrared."

They probed farther, weapons held out at the ready. The corridor angled off to the left and Weston came around the corner fast, ducking down low in a firing stance. Immediately he scanned for unfriendlies. Found absolutely nothing.

"Clear," he said.

The others came around the corner.

There were four doorways ahead, every one of them closed. The TAC unit took them down one by one. They were all vacant, nothing inside but some old packing crates, a few empty twenty-five gallon drums. Red Team moved to the end of the corridor. There was a heavy iron door blocking their progress and it was locked.

Becker slapped a charge on it, set it, and the TAC unit stepped back.

The charge went with a peal of thunder, nearly stripping the door from its hinges. Red Team moved in, taking up firing positions. It was a big room, dank and chill, about forty-feet in length, thirty in width. The air was rancid with a pall of moist bacterial decay.

And there was a very good reason for that.

Infrared told them there was nothing alive inside and, God, how true that was. The place was like a slaughterhouse. But instead of carcasses of beef, human bodies were hung from meat hooks chained to the ceiling, dozens and dozens of them. Naked and stark, they'd been skinned, disemboweled, carved and plucked. Men, women, children. Some had no limbs, others were lacking heads. They twisted in the air with a slow, dreadful motion, a dance macabre.

Their body cavities had been quite neatly hollowed out.

The TAC unit just stood there, the stink of death rubbed in their faces. All those sightless, staring eyes and empty sockets glaring down at them with an almost primal hunger.

"Jesus Christ," LeClere finally said. "It's like a morgue in here."

"All right," Weston managed. "It's bad...but we've got work to do here."

Red Team slid their NV goggles back up onto their helmets, slipped protective goggles over their eyes and clicked on the tactical flashlights bracketed to their weapons. They played the lights around, gigantic shadows jumping over the walls.

Weston reported what they found to AD Silva as the TAC unit moved through the carnage, their faces pale and corded. The bodies were hung in neat rows, the sweeping beams of the flashlights making them seem to move and creep, duck away and dart forward. Shadows crawled over those bloodless death masks, making them grin and leer with a macabre life.

Together, the troopers moved down the rows of bodies and saw there were not just bodies, but arms hanging from those chains as well. Hooks inserted at the meat of their elbows, they were colorless things spattered with dark spirals of old blood.

Nobody was saying anything now.

Only hard-edged discipline, unit integrity, and months of tough training kept the men from bolting out of there. Weston would not have blamed them if they had. Not really. Because he was examining the bodies much closer than they were and he knew what those gashed punctures he was seeing were.

Teeth marks.

These bodies had been gnawed on. Faces and wrists, legs and necks. Something had been at them. And from the arrangement of the bites, Weston had a pretty good idea it hadn't been animals.

As they moved down the rows, Becker bumped into the corpse of a woman and she bumped into another who bumped into yet another, until that entire row was swinging and twisting and gyrating. It was a horrible thing to see. The shadows pooling and jumping, those bodies filled with a hideous animation, looking as if they were trying to pull themselves free.

The men could barely take it.

Weston had not expected anything like this. He could feel the horror and revulsion coming off his men in raw, sickening waves.

There was another door beyond the dancing cadavers which led into another room much like the first. Instead of a meat locker, this one looked more like a warehouse. Deep shelves ran from floor to ceiling on either wall. But the shelves were heaped with things.

And Weston wanted to know what, despite himself. He just had to know. And not out of morbid curiosity, but because it was his job.

The shelves were stacked with bodies. Dozens and dozens of corpses wrapped in plastic sheeting or stained shrouds. Men, women, children. Cultists and kidnapped victims. Some newly dead and others severely decomposed...maybe dead for weeks, if not months, faces boiled right down to muscle and ligament and knobs of bone. Some were zipped in bags and others...what there were of them...secreted in buckets.

As they went about their grim business, pawing through the remains, making one grisly discovery after another, the TAC unit found worse things. Not just cadavers, but parts of them...hands and heads and torsos.

This place, the entire place, not just a mortuary, but something worse. A dissection room. An anatomical theater...only Weston knew it was far worse than that. For there was a rhyme and reason to this carnage, a secret truth that he feared was so awful it would lick his sanity straight into the void if he had to look it in the face.

And he was not a man who frightened easily.

But something was happening here and it was leagues beyond dead cultists. For he could feel it building in the air around him like a scream, a heavy and electric sense of...*activity*. The air had gone thin as ether and the shadows were slithering around them like fat-bodied vipers coming out of a snake pit.

Gripping his weapon tightly, he said, "Stand ready..."

*

About the time Red Team announced they had found bodies, AD Silva was on the radio with Blue Team who'd come in the back way. Clark was in command of Blue.

"We got something here," he was saying over his headset.

"What?" Silva wanted to know. "What're you seeing in there?"

Clark was slow to respond.

Silva could hear him chatting with Platz, Tuchman, and Seaver. Their voices had an unpleasant, almost frantic edge to them.

"What the hell's going on in there, mister?" Silva demanded.

Clark said, "We...we're in a large room here, sir, looks...yeah, looks like some kind of old hospital ward or something...I'm not sure. Beds are lined up against either wall, bodies on most of 'em, covered in sheets."

Standing there in the command van, Silva felt his throat constrict tight like a snake. "Bodies?"

"Yeah," Clark said, his voice oddly thick. "Yeah...gotta be thirty beds here...most of 'em have bodies on 'em. Men and women...some kids, too."

"Dead?"

"Yeah...yes sir, AD, all dead." He paused. "I got...shit...I'm seeing bullet wounds, entry wounds to the chest, the vitals. All their throats, they've been slit ear to ear. Mother of Christ. Some of them, they've been dead for weeks, maybe months I'm thinking. Damn, that stink..."

"Any sign of Dade?"

A long drawn-out silence. "Yeah, he's here with the rest—"

*

And he was.

Clark was looking on that face that he'd poured over for hours and hours in photographs. It was pallid as flour, the eyes wide and staring, the mouth hooked in a contorted gruesome smile. Like maybe Dade knew the punch line to a real funny joke, but he wasn't ready to share it, not just yet.

"We got a live one over here," Platz announced, pulling off his helmet and going to a woman who was sitting up.

Clark saw her face in his flashlight beam, in the beams of the others...but she couldn't be sitting up. Her throat was slit ear to ear. And maybe Platz didn't seem to realize that or maybe he was realizing it now because she made a hissing sound and took hold of his arm in one gray claw, drawing him closer before he could do much more than scream. Before the others could stop her, she produced a jagged shard of glass and slid it into the side of Platz's throat.

And then the shit truly hit the fan.

Platz was on the floor, making a bubbling sound as blood washed down his throat and he vomited red to the floor, slipping and sliding in it.

Tuchman opened up on the woman with his MP5, gave her two three-round bursts to the chest. The rounds ripped holes through her, spattered the walls with her meat, but she kept coming, a toothy, demented grin on her face. The TAC unit watched in abject, stunned horror as she fell on Platz. As she pressed her fissured mouth against his own and came away, chewing on a bloody strand of tissue that had once been his lips.

Platz never screamed; he was way beyond that.

And then flashlight beams were flickering and bobbing, men were shouting and swearing, weapons discharging.

Because they were all waking up.

Sheets were sliding from ravaged faces and licking black tongues. Bloated hands reached out, teeth gnashed together.

The TAC unit was shooting and screaming for back-up, but it was simply too late.

A door slammed open on the far side of the room.

Shapes, forms, figures...they came hobbling through the doorway with a putrescent grave stench. The strangers were rotting and crumbling, sporting beards of mold and cobwebbed faces. Some lacked limbs and others lacked faces, but they were united for a single purpose and as Clark and the others watched, it all became horribly clear what that was.

His people started screaming and shrieking, drawing guns and trying to run, shooting and shooting, and on came their killers. He saw Tuchman smash the butt of his machine pistol into one decayed face and put two rounds into another. But like swatted mosquitoes, the dead were instantly replaced by others. Tuchman fought and kept fighting until a fleshless face darted in and tore out the soft meat of his throat. And then they had him and he disappeared in a noisome sea of fungus-covered bone and chattering, ripping teeth.

Clark could hear Silva shouting, demanding to know what was happening.

But there was no time to tell him.

Clark emptied his Colt carbine into a wall of deadwood faces, then fished a 9mm Steyr auto from his vest and fired on a gray and withered stickwoman who literally disintegrated as if she were made of dehydrated clay. And then skeletal fingers were on him and he was thrown to the ground. He saw Seaver— his face a drooling, demented mask—start spraying down anything that moved with his submachine gun.

And on it went, bullets ripping through the air and mouths screaming and everywhere the stink of cordite and violated tombs. It became a nightmare shadow-show of darting figures and slashing teeth, muzzle flashes and clutching fungous fingers, atrocities captured in the strobing flashlights. Yellow-eyed faces with flesh hanging in loops and mouths vomiting froths of black putrescent slime.

Clark fought bravely through that barrage of gnarled hands and chomping teeth, saw his men go down in bloody seas, saw them unzipped and eviscerated and divided by thrashing fingers and tearing red mouths. The dead yanked out ribbons of greasy entrails and fought like starving dogs over them, biting and chewing and sucking and slurping.

And then something looped around Clark's throat and snapped tight like a garrote, collapsing his windpipe as lewd mouths bit into his legs and crotch and belly. But all he was really aware of was his mind falling into a coveting blackness as that cord strangled him.

Finally, ultimately, he went down.

Not knowing that a woman dead some three weeks had strangled him with a loop of her own viscera.

*

As the zombie woman woke up and stabbed a shard of glass into Platz's soft white throat, Green Team, waiting up on the roof, got the word. They crashed through the skylights, rappelling down on ropes into that claustrophobic blackness. They climbed out of their harnesses and regrouped, prepared to deploy.

Oliverez was in charge. He said, "All right, don't bother with the NV goggles. We need all the lights we can get. Red Team and Blue Team have made contact with unfriendlies, but they're not armed."

"At least not yet," Rice said.

Johnson and Turner slid tactical goggles over their eyes, checked their weapons quickly, flexed their hands in fingerless gloves. Oliverez was going on about what Silva had said, the chatter from Red and Blue that he'd monitored.

"I don't know what kind of clusterfuck this is, but be ready."

They moved out, Rice taking point, his big Remington 12-gauge police shotgun held out before him. The flashlight attached to the barrel cut through that roiling tenebrous darkness, showing everyone an empty corridor.

They slipped single-file down a set of iron steps and came

into another corridor which split off ahead to the right and left. They could hear the other TAC units crying out, opening up with their weapons, calling out for back-up...but Green Team did not rush to their aid. They had orders to proceed with extreme caution and they followed them.

They came to the T in the corridor and Rice spotted a form shambling in their direction. At first he thought the guy was drunk, but as he closed in, Rice saw he was dead. His face had been blasted down to meat and bone like it had been used for target practice and he was carrying what looked to be coils of linked sausages.

"His fucking intestines," Johnson said.

The man kept coming despite being told to get on the floor and Oliverez said, almost too calmly, "Rice? Put that peckerwood down."

Rice closed the gap between them, got a real good look at the man's face...what there was of it. He had no eyes, no nose to speak of, his face hanging from the bone beneath in bloody tethers.

"*Hey*," the mutilated man said in congested voice like his throat was full of wet leaves. "*My sister's going to love your ass...you see if she don't...*"

Rice said, "Sonofabitch," and gave him a load of buckshot at point blank range.

The impact knocked the zombie over, nearly split him in half. But instead of lying down and waiting for a box and grave, he sat back up. His ragged shirt was smoking from contact burns, flames climbing up his collar. His guts were gone now, as was one of his hands. There was a gaping black hole in his abdomen and you could see right through it. Plumes of smoke were wafting from it.

The air was redolent with a stink of incinerated meat.

Rice made a funny, strangled sound and blew the dead man's head to shards of bone that tinkled down the hallway like broken crockery. He fell over, his face missing from the nasal cavity on up. His jaws were still there, though, and they were snapping open and shut in rapid succession like a set of wind-up chattery teeth.

"Move out," Oliverez said, not wanting the men to pause long enough to let any of this insanity sink in. Because if it did, they were done.

He led on to the left—the gunshots echoing louder from

that direction—and the others fell in behind him. They came to an open door and saw candlelight flickering in there, throwing weird hopping shadows and bathing everything in a dirty orange light.

He came low through the doorway and saw a woman sitting cross-legged on a bed in there, the candle next to her on a little nightstand. She was humming. Utterly naked, she rocked back and forth, back and forth.

"Lady..." Oliverez managed.

She looked up at him, fixing him with a malignant leer...with her right eye, that was, because the left was just a blackened socket from which fed a moist pelt of yellow-green fungus that covered the left side of her face like a caul. She kept humming and rocking, flaking lips pulling back from narrow discolored teeth.

And it was bad, certainly.

But it wasn't what made Oliverez's stomach clamp tight like a vise.

What did that was what the woman was *holding*...an infant. It was gray and bloated and putrefied, like something pulled from a lake. It was sucking on her left breast with a sloshing, repulsive sound. The woman's other breast was also moving, but that was because of the pockets of larva feasting within.

Then the infant pulled away from that gray nipple, looked over at the TAC unit and made a gurgling sound. Maggots were wriggling free of the woman's tit and this is what the baby had been feeding on. Its face was distorted...bulging and sunken and eyeless, great holes torn in it and through them you could see the worms boiling within.

Oliverez never gave the order.

But everyone opened up.

Submachine guns and carbines and Rice's assault shotgun were pumping lead in a lethal volley. They kept shooting until they'd emptied their magazines and the obscenity on the bed...and its offspring...were reduced to clots of glistening flesh. Bits of the dead woman and her child were plastered against the wall, dripping from the headboard, pooling in the sheets and the stink was revolting.

Oliverez ordered his men out of there.

"What...what...*what in the fuck is this?*" Johnson demanded.

"We ain't here to figure that out," Oliverez snapped at him. "Now lock and load, we're moving out."

They all had questions, yes, but they did not ask them. Maybe they didn't dare to. Ten minutes into the compound and they'd already seen enough to give them cold sweats and nightmares for a lifetime.

And it didn't get any better.

Two more zombies came out of a room to meet them. They were both large men with black boots and camouflage pants on. Shirtless, their bodies were of an almost phosphorescent whiteness and neither of them had a head, just frayed stumps. The one on the left was carrying the head of a woman by the hair. A living head. Her face was fissured and livid with purple blotches.

"*There,*" she said with a grating, airless squeak of a voice. "*These are the ones, right ahead now...that's it, straight on...bring me to them, bring me to them...yesssss...*"

The TAC unit started shooting again, getting a little smarter this time around. They took the two men down at the knees, blowing their kneecaps to fragments. The woman's head was dropped, rolling across the floor, hair whipping and voice grunting.

The headless men began crawling forward, dragging their shredded legs like bleeding confetti, but on they came. The TAC unit opened up with everything they had as the woman's head shrieked and cackled and snapped its teeth.

Rice stuck the barrel of his shotgun in her mouth and she clamped down on it, biting and biting, trying to sink her teeth through the metal. He pulled the trigger and blew that hideous thing to slush. But still they could hear her voice...maybe in front of them or behind or maybe just echoing through the drums of their skulls...taunting them and telling them how they were going to die.

But there was no time to consider the madness of that or the two men who had been blasted to creeping slats of bone and tissue, for another zombie came down the corridor at them. It was a boy carrying a shoulder sack. He was giggling, digging into that sack and throwing things before him, like a girl tossing flower petals at a wedding. The TAC unit first thought they were spiders he was throwing...crawling albino spiders.

But then they saw they were *human hands.*

Living human hands severed at the wrists.

By the time they put the boy down, there were dozens of hands hopping and skittering and jumping. And pretty soon they were on the TAC unit and men were screaming, trying to pull iron fingers from their legs and ankles.

Johnson lost his mind as one of them ran up the leg of his coveralls. Followed by third and fourth and a fifth that found his crotch and gripped it with a crushing strength. Another got up his pant leg and others under his Kevlar vest. He jumped up and down, spun around in circles, slammed himself into walls like a man covered in nipping ants, anything to pull those grasping hands off him.

The TAC unit was shooting as they backed away, just white with a rolling terror now.

And though they beat off the zombies, the hands were something else entirely.

Johnson choked to death on one as it got in his screaming mouth and lodged itself in his throat, curling up there in a fleshy ball.

And the other TAC unit troopers let him die as the hands came on and flashlight beams cast dizzying flashes and weapons were discharged. And through it all, Oliverez forgot about the crawling heaps of bones. Until he fell down and they swarmed over him, that was.

*

Hell in a handbasket.

AD Silva had heard the expression, but until that fateful night at the compound he had no idea of the reality of it. His TAC units had been deployed and what he was hearing over the radio just could not be.

The living dead?

Zombies for the life of Christ?

It couldn't be, it just couldn't be. He could not accept the idea that his men were being attacked by hordes of the walking dead. Every cheap, low-budget horror film he'd ever seen as a kid was coming back to him now, coming back to roost and his flesh was crawling and a buzzing whiteness was droning in his head.

The agents piled into the back of the comm van were all watching him now, their faces drained of color, their mouths hanging slack. Silva could not look at them. He clutched his headset in shaking hands and licked his lips and watched the monitors and wished to dear God he wasn't in charge.

"Okay," he said, "okay. Let's get some back-up in there."

Men started to scramble out of the back of the van, glad to

be doing anything other than sitting there and imagining what must be going on in that lightless mortuary.

And that was when Silva started laughing.

You see, he'd finally gotten the joke. Finally gotten Paul Henry Dade's little joke and it was a doozy, yes sir. The Divine Church of the Resurrection. *Resurrection.* Ha, ha, ha. Yeah, it was a good one, all right.

And Silva just could not stop laughing.

Even when they finally took him away, he was still laughing his ass off.

*

What happened to Red Team was this:

Moments after Weston began to feel something building in the air around him, the dead began to wake up. In the panning lights of his TAC unit, the dead were coming to life...or some blasphemous semblance of it engineered by Paul Henry Dade and his crazy cult. It started with the crinkling of plastic and the squeaking of vinyl as the dead on the shelves began to make themselves known.

Corpses zipped in body bags sat up.

Corpses wrapped in plastic began to claw their way free...sheets were sloughed like snakeskins...long-armed shapes rose up...heads snapped their teeth and hands in buckets began to scratch and whisper and spill to the floor.

Chains began to clink and creak as the bodies on the meat hooks in the other room began to stir and fight, thrashing and writhing and trying to wrestle themselves free.

LeClere screamed.

Screamed and ran as the dead stepped off the shelves. He made it into the other room, running straight into that swinging menagerie of hanging cadavers. Bodies bumped into him, arms swatted at him, faces nipped and spit and licked at him. His light was bobbing and flashing, cold hands caressing him and finally he was locked in a tangle of clutching hands. All those arms hanging from the hooks had him, crushing him in an embrace of cold white flesh and putrescence.

The rest of Red Team had no time to help him.

They had their own problems.

It was pandemonium.

Becker fought his way from the clutching hands of two skull-faced assassins—their fingers coming away with him—and brought out a massive .44 magnum. Another cadaver shambled in his direction, hands held out like bailing hooks and Becker began jerking the trigger frantically. The slugs ate huge and gaping holes in the cadaver, making a sound like a hammer into dry kindling as they blew their way through. Even though much of the cadaver's wasted anatomy was blown across the shelves, it crept forward. Becker stared into ruined eye sockets, saw black beetles congregating in that skull and then hands like raw, cold liver caressed him and began pulling him apart like a screaming gingerbread man.

Hookley kicked his way free of several corpse assassins and saw the bloody ball of a snapping head roll across his boots. Then he was up and wanting to run, but there were simply too many. A dark and hulking form of a large corpse with an insect-ravaged face tossed others aside to get at him. Hookley emptied his carbine into the monstrosity, then hammered the death'shead with the butt...the flesh falling away like sheets of balsa wood. It looked like termites had been at this one. His seamed face split in a sardonic grin, hating, hating. One eye was but a blackened, festering socket and the other housed a milky opal that glistened and cried tears of worms. Skinless fingers reached out for Hookley and that face of furry gray-green mold swam in for a kiss.

Hookley screeched and brought the stock of the carbine down in a powerful arc. It struck that bobbing skull with the sound of damp, rotting wood splitting. The puckered forehead shattered, the cranium collapsed and within was a nest of feeding maggots.

Hookley, cackling insanely now, brought the stock down again and again. And that graveyard face came apart like a moldy house of cards and the body stumbled blindly past him and fell forward stiffly.

Hookley fought through two or three others, could hear someone making a deranged, wet shrieking sound, but he never guessed it was himself. He fell to his knees, drooling and pissing himself, and then he saw his executioner.

A woman—or something that had once been one—slithered forward with a slime trail of moist soil. She had no legs, no nothing beneath the waist, just a few moth-eaten rags that might have been flesh and ligament once. She propelled herself like a slug, grinning with a moldering flap of face. The empty holes of her eyes found Hookley and the gray mouth smiled, the pitted stumps of teeth gnashed and chomped.

But Hookley was beyond it.

He held himself, rocking, discordant laughter belching from his throat as the woman swam in, that worm-holed face oozing slime and falling into itself like a rotting Jack-o'-Lantern.

And then he was wrapped in a blanket of putrefaction, those jagged teeth opening his belly and biting down on what they found there.

Weston was squeezed into a corner just beyond the shelves.

The room was on fire now. Maybe from stray rounds or a tossed incendiary grenade. It didn't matter. Flames were licking up the shelving, throwing a wavering, surreal illumination.

It was light to die by.

A ring of zombies was pressing in closer, their threadbare hides punched with smoking bullet holes. Ravenous and ruined, they marched forward with skeletal fingers outstretched. Weston watched them come and wished he'd saved one round to use on himself.

The cadaverous sea parted and Paul Henry Dade stepped forward, his face hanging in fluttering tatters, gouts of black blood drooling from his lips in streamers.

Weston let that atrocity get in close, then he pulled his knife and sank it into Dade's belly, slitting him to the throat. A tide of viscous ichor drained from the wound like puss from a festering boil. It splashed over Weston and he saw it swam with worms.

Then Dade's cold hands were on his shoulders, tightening with a grave rictus. Weston cried out as he felt his bones snap, as his mind released itself in a whimpering tirade.

Dade was trying to tell him something, but all that came out was a bubbling, slopping sound, his crypt-breath sour and sweet and sickening.

Dade split Weston lengthwise like a sausage and fed on the hot, salty bounty within. He chewed and tore and ripped and sucked. And much later, painted red with blood, stepped away and held Weston's bloody head high. The agent's viscera decorated the shelves like Christmas garland. He was divided and scattered and mutilated, his bones broken open and leeched of marrow and stacked in a tidy heap on the floor.

And all was silent then, save for the crackling of the fire and the sound of bones being gnawed and bowels being nibbled. The floor was a bloody, stinking stew of flesh and meat. Some of it was still, but much of it moved and pulsed and hungered, unable to die as such.

*

Rice of Green Team was not dead.

Hell, no.

He was bitten and clawed, bruised and bleeding, but surely not dead. Problem was, he was mostly fucked and knew it. His helmet was gone, his assault shotgun history now. He'd used every last round putting down the mutiny of the dead hands, tossing the Remington when the hands were replaced by zombies that flooded down the corridor.

He'd been hiding ever since.

He did not know if anybody else was alive.

Right then, he didn't really care. All he cared about was a quick way out. He was hiding in a closet with a Colt 9mm handgun clenched tight in his fists, trying to remember the TAC leader, Weston, going over the map of the compound that was tacked to the wall. Problem was, the map was World War II vintage and there had been a lot of remodeling since. Stairways were gone. Hallways sealed up. Walls knocked down. So, yeah, Rice was trying to think his way out, but it didn't look good.

He hadn't heard any gunfire for awhile now, maybe ten or fifteen minutes. He could smell the death in the compound...like pressing your face into roadkill, filling your nostrils with that rank green smell and swallowing it down in reeking rivers. He could also smell the cordite and something like wood smoke, which told him the complex was burning.

But who lit it up?

The zombies? The FBI? Helicopters buzzed the roof from time to time and loudspeakers were broadcasting muffled appeals for Dade's people to surrender.

And that was pretty funny when you thought about it.

Rice thought: *They ain't gonna surrender unless you bring a hearse.*

He sat stiffly in the darkness. He had a small tactical flashlight and his Colt nine, that was about it. But maybe he could just wait this out, maybe—

Footsteps.

Something like them.

A lumbering, heavy sound. Like a bull was coming down the hallway, smashing into the walls, grunting and puffing. It passed by the door, then paused and Rice was certain it was sniffing, making a wet snorting sound.

The doorknob jiggled.

Jiggled again.

Whatever was out there stank like an open grave and it was strong, God, very strong, because it was yanking on the door now, rattling it on its frame. There was a groaning, crashing sound and the door was ripped from its hinges in a rain of wood splinters.

Rice made a choking sound in his throat and put the flashlight beam on it. But what was he seeing? A man...or something like one, immense and distended...white and black, swollen and mildewed and rancid. It was grotesquely bloated with gases, its eye sockets fluid with maggots and yellow bile.

Rice emptied the Colt into it and it took hold of him, dragged him down the hallway.

It opened an iron door and tossed him through, slamming it shut behind him.

Rice had the flashlight, but he didn't dare turn it on.

Because he wasn't alone in there. He could smell the others, hear them chewing and sucking and licking. Something damp brushed his arm, something like a tongue licked the back of his neck.

He turned on the light.

Yes, they were all around him, the zombies. Disfigured, grotesque, rotted to mush. Some were missing limbs and others looked like they'd been burned. One of them had a meat cleaver instead of a hand and another—a woman—was pregnant, or had been at the hour of her death. Her blue-black belly was voluminous and heaving, split wide open. There was something like a wormy fetus coming out, pulling itself out in a wash of noisome jelly, a crawling gray carrion.

It splashed to the floor, inching itself forward like a leech, leaving a trail of slime in its wake. The others dropped the limbs they'd been chewing on and watched what was about to happen. Grinned with disfigured faces like raw beef.

Long before that undulating, boneless thing touched him, Rice had gone raving mad.

*

Turner was the last TAC member alive.

He crawled through a slick of blood, his eyes wide and staring, his jaws clamped tight. He still had his Colt tactical carbine, but he was down to his last magazine. On hands and knees, he peered through a doorway, crab-crawled over there, breathing hard, his face beaded with sweat.

He was doing everything he could not to panic, but it was no easy bit.

With what he'd seen, experienced, even all that rigorous training wasn't enough to keep his mind from melting into slush.

But he would stay alive. Somehow, some way.

Dear Christ, he would not be like *them*.

He would not allow himself to become something that fed on corpses and human flesh, something that should have been zipped in a bag or slid shut in a drawer. No, dammit, he would kill himself first.

He'd been pretty much on the dodge since Green Team was attacked by those hands. He saw it now in his brain, like some nightmare one-reel cartoon that played over and over until it all became almost laughable.

But it was not funny.

Johnson had gone down under those hands and Oliverez had been inundated by the crawling remains of the headless men. But you could give that old, leather-faced bastard credit, for even knitted with a blanket of surging carrion that tried to engulf him like a pustulant jellyfish, he fought on. As Rice and Turner evaded their asses out of there, Oliverez stumbled along, fighting the abominations which covered his head and upper body.

Somehow, he'd gotten loose, tossed his attackers.

Screaming and covered in an ooze of corruption, he ran right past Rice and Turner, vaulted through a doorway and disappeared before they could catch him.

They found him, though.

He'd gone through a doorway, trying to make his way down a flight of emergency steps...and that's as far as he made it. Something captured him there. Something that sent Rice running and burned a scar across Turner's mind.

Even now, stroking his carbine and remembering, Turner could not believe it, could not stomach that poison memory.

At first, they'd thought Oliverez had stumbled into a spider's web.

The sort of thing some gigantic arachnid mutation might have spun in a cheap 1950's B-movie. But it was no spider. What Rice and he saw was an intricate network of knotted bowels, strung together in an oily web at the bottom of the steps.

Oliverez had wandered right into it, got tangled up in those rubbery strands. Might have fought his way free, if something like a skinless girl hadn't come racing down that network and chewed his face from the skull beneath.

Because that's what was happening when Rice and Turner showed.

That skinless girl...maybe twelve or thirteen...was eating Oliverez. His face was gone and her own was buried in the cavity of his belly, pulling out coils of viscera and chewing globs of yellow fat with teeth that were not teeth, but shards of glass hammered into her jaws.

Turner stared at her in the beam of his light. She had eyes, but they were dangling out of her sockets by bleeding optic nerves. Yet, they moved and saw. She looked upon him with such a ravening lunacy, it made his guts slink in cold waves.

Rice ran off.

Turner gave her a few rounds, had been hiding ever since.

And the fact that he wasn't laughing at it just yet told him he was not crazy. Maybe tomorrow or next week, but not now. Horror and revulsion and hot-blooded anger that God would allow a travesty like this...these things kept him hanging on, kept his edge polished and sharp.

He could hear sounds coming down the corridor, echoes of voices, dragging sounds, scraping sounds. But in that maze of corridors, it could have been around the next bend or upstairs.

Thing was, Turner was lost.

Even when he came to a room with a window, it did him no good: they were all barred like prison cells. But he could see that everyone was still out there beyond the blockade—cops and medics, journalists and the curious kept at bay behind them.

Wishing he still had his headset, Turner kicked open a door and plunged in there, flashing his light around with the sweeping motion of the Colt's barrel. Nothing, nothing, nothing. He was in a little apartment with a bathroom off to the side.

He came around through the archway, saw a toilet that was filthy and stained brown with ancient rust stains. The sink. A mirror with jagged cracks in it. And—

Someone was in the tub.

At first he couldn't tell if it was a man or a woman, only that they were entirely red from head to foot, red and glistening, like a stick man (or woman) dipped in blood and bowels and decomposition, splashed down with a bucket of waste from a slaughterhouse. The tub was filled with human meat, the zombie chewing on a corkscrew of intestines, totally unconcerned that Turner was standing there.

He gave him—or her or *it*—two three-round bursts that splashed its anatomy off the bone beneath. Slowly, like a ship going down in a sea of blood, the zombie sank beneath the stinking, quivering sea of remains.

Turner got out of there.

He moved down the corridor, came to a room with a zombie splattered in the center of the concrete block floor. *Splattered.* Looked like he or she had been dropped from some great height, though the ceiling was only eight feet up. The body lay there, a gored plexus of meat webbing out in all directions, strands and streamers of it snaking about. And drowning in that still-pulsating ocean of pulp and tissue was a bleeding skeleton that trembled, seemed to be trying to breath.

It was too much.

Turner ran out of there, paused before another doorway, wondered if he'd ever find sanctuary in this morgue.

Then two slender hands reached out and yanked him into the room, threw him headlong to the floor. The door was slammed shut, a lock was turned. He brought up his carbine, training the light on his attacker.

A woman.

She was naked.

Tall and willowy, her hips nicely rounded and her breasts firm and jutting, she had a sweep of red hair falling down one shoulder. Her lips were moving as if she were trying to find words.

Turner eased his finger off the trigger.

"Please," she said. "I...I was kidnapped...please don't kill me..."

She fell to her knees, sobbing and shaking. Turner studied her closely. She was very pale, but not rotted or discolored. A scent of withered roses came off her in a sweet breath.

Turner lowered his weapon.

Jesus, she looked so much like Dierdre.

Too much like Dierdre.

He knew it was not because Dierdre had been dead seven years now. Leukemia. Turner had been with her through it all. Saw his love, his only true reason for getting up every day, slowly eaten away by the disease. And then she was gone and he turned his mind hard, tried out for the HRT so he could spread some of his pain around, give it back to bad guys and terrorists.

Turner felt cold and hot and confused, didn't know what to say or even how to speak. It took time to fill his lungs with air, to wrap his mouth around some words that would make sense.

He licked his lips, said, "They...they'll be storming this place, maybe they already are. I'll protect you..."

Turner saw a candle on the table and lit it, loving the light and warmth it threw. He went to the woman.

She was still shaking and whimpering, all that lustrous red hair in her face. Turner set his weapon down, went to her. Was surprised...or maybe not at all...when she threw her arms around him, put her lips against his.

He felt her in his arms then, pressed up against him and she wasn't dead and how could this possible be? She was cold and shivering under his hands and he felt his penis unfurl in his pants. Jesus, now and of all places. But the woman seemed to want it, too, for she was kissing him harder, pushing her tongue into his mouth.

Turned pulled away, said, "Not here, we can't—"

"Please," she said, kissing his face, his throat. "Oh please." And then her tongue was at his ear and she was saying things and unzipping his Kevlar vest. Turner was helping her, pulling his coveralls off and growing dizzy then as she began to stroke his cock.

He took one nipple in his mouth, licking and tasting it and feeling a strange sort of warmth spreading beneath the skin. And it was exciting and liberating and, dear God, she had been right. In a situation like this, what better thing could a man and woman do for one another?

Turner pushed her onto her back and spread her legs. She hooked her ankles behind his back and guided him in, positioned him properly. But she wouldn't let him enter her. She gripped the globes of his ass, teased his cock with her moist sex and then, staring into his eyes with a voracious appetite, she thrust him into her with a delicious force and—

And Turner screamed.

Screamed as his penis was impaled on something in there, ripped and gouged and slit. He tried to pull out, to push off her, but her legs were wrapped around him and she clung to him tenaciously. He saw the blossom of blood at their hips, saw that raging demented hunger in her eyes.

Like the others, just like the others.

Thrashing together, trying to fight and only succeeding in wounding himself further, Turner ignored the white-hot blades of pain and felt his fingers brush the stock of his Colt carbine.

She saw him bring up the weapon and fixed him with a raw, unflinching hatred. Her eyes oozed filth like infected sores. Turner brought the stock down on her face again and again and again until it split open like a knife-cut, until the skull beneath cracked open and what was inside, was exposed. Worms. Knotted, squirming lengths of blood-red worms moving in and out of her brain, slipping now from her eye sockets.

Turner fell off her, his penis hanging in shreds now, blood running down his legs and pooling at his hips. Shards of razors were still embedded in it. The woman had stuffed herself with them. Turner crashed to the floor and closed his eyes against the agony, the defilement.

He did not open them again.

*

Now that Silva was taken away in an ambulance, heavily-medicated because it was the only way to get him to stop laughing at the wonderful joke he kept trying to share with the others, Runyon was in charge.

He did not want to be in charge.

He had been in the comm van when the truth was told first by Red and Blue Teams, then by Green.

Runyon did not want to believe it, felt himself slowly going mad, but given the fact that the TAC units had not been heard from in nearly thirty minutes now, he had no choice.

Something had happened in the compound.

Whatever it had been, it was bad enough to take down twelve highly-trained, highly-motivated men. Take them down and silence them. And Runyon had a feeling, it was far worse than mere cultists.

So Runyon rallied his troops—two back-up TAC units, some thirty sheriff's deputies and state troopers, and an infantry platoon from a local National Guard base. Armed, pissed-off, and scared, they moved in formation at the compound. Armored vehicles knocked the barbwire fences down and Runyon's army followed in their wake.

The siege was about to begin.

And it was about that time, that the zombies started

coming out of the compound. Zombies led by members of TAC units Red, Green, and Blue that still had their limbs. The living dead poured from the diseased carcass of the compound like worms out of pork.

And the real battle began.

EULOGY OF THE STRAW-WITCH

It was in Boone County, Nebraska, that Strand first heard tell of Missy Crow, the old straw-witch what could call the dead up out of their graves. And if it hadn't been for the fact that Mama Lucille had passed of the consumption not two days before, Strand probably wouldn't have paid such a tale any mind.

He never had before.

Boone County was hot as hell's own skillet in the summer and cold, white, and bitter from December to first thaw. And maybe those extremes did something to people there. Boiled their brains to mash and made 'em start thinking funny things. Things they might be ashamed of by day.

But at night it was different.

The wind would come moaning across the plains without much more than a few silos or a cottonwood thicket to stop it. The corn would rustle with the sound of hollow breathing and the shadows would creep and whisper. And if you listened to the wind speak, you might hear scraping voices telling you things you did not want to know or hear a low malevolent howling from the dry ravine. These things worked a dark alchemy on the soul and, soon enough, gathered in bunkhouses and at firesides, tales were told of things that lived that should have been buried and things that walked that should have crept. Yarns would be swapped of deserted farmhouses and the pale loathsome things that crawled in their dank cellars or stared out from the rotting hay of crumbling barns with peeled, yellow eyes.

And sometimes, you just might hear about Missy Crow, the straw-witch, and the things she could do and those she would never attempt, which were few. Such stories might get you to thinking impure thoughts and particularly if you'd just buried your mother two days before.

*

That's how it was with Strand.

At the Broken Arrow Saloon, well into his cups, grief punching a hole in his belly like an awl, he listened to a skinner name of Lester Koats and heard all he needed about the old straw-witch and her wicked ways.

"Missy Crow were born of straw-devil and witch-wife," Lester said, his boozy breath hot and sour. "She can call the dead up out of their graves with a song and whistle demons to her hearthside like a hound brought to heel. She talks with ghosts and commands vile spirits and has herself rode through the holes between the stars themselves with evil shadows that feed on men's souls."

Lester kept on with the tale-spinning until Sheriff Bolan came over and broke the whole thing up, letting Lester see the hard gleam in his eye and the nickel-plated Army .44's that rode his hips. Lester took the hint and disappeared out the batwings like a bad stink.

Bolan put one callused, thick-fingered hand on Strand's arm, said, "You don't want to be listening to that fool nonsense, son. Stump-water hag like Missy Crow can only bring you six inches closer to hell. So do yourself a favor, just go on home and mourn your mama proper."

Strand told Bolan that he would do just that, yes sir, straight away.

But he had no intention. Grief can be an immense and stark machine. And once caught in the terrible grinding of its gears, your sense of perspective can be worn smooth as those teeth bite into you and empty you.

When he got home, he told Eileen his intentions.

"But that's...that's blasphemy, Luke," she said. "It's unholy, it's witchcraft! You can't be a party to that! The dead have to stay dead...it's not natural to bring them back."

But Strand did not listen. He could not explain what fever burned in his brain or how since his mother's death there was no shine left in his soul, only a terrible dark graininess.

So he went up to the Oak Grove Burial Ground with a shovel and exhumed Mama Lucille with that big old harvest moon grinning high above like something hungry.

And maybe that was an omen.

*

It took three days of hard riding to find the straw-witch.

Three days in which a hot wind of crematoriums blew across those range grasses and buzzards circled in a sky the color of dead bone. Scarecrows creaked in rustling corn patches, smiling and pointing the way, always pointing the way. Strand rode alone through that lonesome far country, swatting at flies and mopping sweat from his sunburned brow. He searched every dusty corner of Boone County. And in the wagon, Mama Lucille was still stitched in her linen shroud, resting silently in the crate which had brought her grandfather clock some years before, packed in dry ice so she would not turn.

"Don't you be worrying none, Mama," Strand would tell that soundless box at the evening's fire as the wind walked and talked. "I'll get you fixed up proper, see if I don't. We gonna find that straw-witch. Maybe tomorrow."

But it was a long pull and a lonely one, just Strand and Mama Lucille's crate, and those gloss-black geldings that were none too happy about what they were carrying in the wagon.

Along the way, Strand asked farmers and range hands about Missy Crow and he heard high tales of the sick being cured and storms being raised and fevers being conjured. But when he inquired of the dead being raised up, he was met with a stony silence as if he were mad. And maybe he was. He did not linger any one place long, for once he started asking questions, folks seemed to be sizing up his neck for a swing from the sour apple tree.

Three days into it with a little advice bought with trade whiskey, he found the straw-witch's cabin on a distant fork of the Loup River, just sitting there all by its lonesome in a wild hayfield like a headstone in the heather. There was no road going in and none coming out, just a bumpy ride across the hay meadow that smelled hot and yellow and crisping. And maybe another smell, too, one that made the geldings whinny and splutter, but Strand was gladly ignorant of.

The witch's cabin was a simple affair with log walls and a sod roof, plank shutters banging in the wind, the whole thing congested in chokecherry and bracken, knapweed and wild sumac so that it looked not like something built, but something *grown*. It was shaded by a single spidery and dead scarlet oak whose branches were strung with what seemed hundreds of bones and bottles. When the wind kicked up, the bones rattled and the bottles moaned.

That's a witch-tree, Strand told himself when he saw it, something inside him running hot and acidic. *That's a conjure-oak.*

And maybe it was at that.

For as that warm-dry Nebraska wind exhaled across those empty miles, those bones rattled like they wished to walk again and the breeze blew across the mouths of those bottles in a lonely, hollow dirge.

As Strand dismounted before a low, sloping porch, he noticed that there were a half dozen scarecrows woven from cane straw nailed to uprights twisting from side to side in the breeze. Lots of other things dangled from the porch overhang, like sculptures of twine, straw, and sticks. An old woman sat beneath them in a wicker chair, rocking back and forth. She wore a patchwork calico dress and a denim scarf at her head, a clay pipe locked tight in her seamed lips.

"Well, well, well," she said, exhaling a cloud of smoke that stank like burning pine, "so ye've come, have ye, Luke Strand? Just as I knewed ye would."

Strand stood there in his rumpled suit and dusty bowler, his throat dry as fireplace soot. "You heard? You heard I was coming?"

The old lady spat off the porch. "I did not and I did not need to, son. I know things as I've always knowed things. I knewed you was coming just as I knewed what you would bring in that wagon. How? Mayhap I divined it in the bowels of hog or from the bones of a stillborn child or sprinkled moondust in an open grave...and does it matter?"

Missy Crow had a face fissured and flaking-brown like that of an Egyptian mummy. When she grinned with that awful rictus, it seemed that face would split open like dry brushwood. There was a jagged pink scar running across her throat and disappearing behind her ears and it looked like a crooked mouth that wanted to open up and spit at you.

"Yes, Luke Strand, that there scar is from the noose," she said in that voice of deserts and dry washes. "Tyler County, West Virginny, it was. The good and god-fearing folk there strung me up for witching and the practice of necromancy, which be the conjuring of spirits. They left me to swing near on three days from a black elder with birds pecking at me and flies nipping, until some good Christian gent cut me down and planted me proper. Three days later, aye, I kicked my way out of the grave and visited them what had done me harm. But ye haven't come to hear my yarning, have ye?"

Strand swallowed. "I heard you can do things. Things like in the Bible."

The straw-witch pulled at her pipe. "Did ye now? Do ye hear that I call up plagues and storms of locusts? Boils and frogs, blisters and blights? That I can cure yer firstborn and curse yer adultering wife? Is that what ye heard, Luke Strand?"

Strand shook his head, not liking those eyes of Missy Crow's upon him. They were just as dark and oily as coffin varnish. They seemed to look inside you and know all the things you had done and you would yet do. "I heard...I heard you can raise up the dead."

Those eyes were on him hard then, looking into him and maybe right through. Eyes that were mystical and cabalistic, peering out from shadow-riven glens, sacred groves, and misty mountaintops where the witch-clans gathered and sang their songs, flew through the air on hackberry rods and hickory shafts, casting the runes and harnessing malignant spirits and malevolent elementals.

"And ye wish that I raise up yer dead mama, eh? Call her from the damps of the grave and from beyond the pale?" Missy Crow spat again. "Do yerself a favor, Luke Strand. Forget such vile doings. Take her home and bury her proper, say a prayer to Jesus and the saints."

"But I brought money," he said. "Everything I could get."

"Did ye now?" She put those eyes on him that were open sores and secret cancers. "Then say the words, Luke Strand, say them words that will damn yer immortal soul straight to hell. Say unto me what ye would have done."

"I want you to raise my mama...from the dead," he managed, his breath catching in his throat.

"Ye wish a resurrection?"

"I do."

With no help from Missy Crow, Strand brought the shrouded body of Mama Lucille into that dank-smelling cabin. Through the warped plank door knotted in a tangled profusion of woodbine and trumpet creeper. A place of shadows and sheeted forms; tables crowded with alembics and retorts and dried animal scraps; corpse-fat candles guttering on shelves amongst bones and jars of fetal things floating in brine. It smelled of spices in there, of ashes and tanned hides, wormseed and devilpitch, rotting coffin linings and graveyard soil.

"Now, Luke Strand, ye kindly step outside while I cut and sew and snip, whilst I remove things and say words and sprinkle essential salts and warm this barren clay."

It took about two hours.

Then the still sleeping form of Mama Lucille was placed back in her box, smelling of dampness and carbolic, preservatives and cold rain.

Missy Crow the straw-witch took the money, and whispered something into the shroud. Then to, Strand himself: "Take yer mama home and bury her, son. Two days of seasoning in the ground, she'll ripen like slaw and then just maybe...just maybe...but if she moves, if she walks above again, no salt and no meat. Remember that, Luke Strand, and I bid you good-bye. And may the Lord have mercy upon yer heathen soul for the things ye have done and those ye will yet do."

*

Two days later.

The cemetery.

What Strand did he did in silence, he did alone, he did with a madness tickling at the base of his brain and a spade in his hands. And in that sullen graveyard, there was the rustling of unknown shadows, somber light winking off leaning tombstones, spiders tickling the dark with silken threads. High above, that ancient moon slid through the sky like whispering casket silk as something far below ripened and readied itself.

It was a night of resurrection beneath that same glowering, bloated moon. A night of digging and clawing, of the moist skin of the earth cut by the surgical blade of a shovel as a hideous gestation reached its peak. As the swollen belly of the graveyard delivered a grim parody of life from the moldering oblong box of its womb and cold meat was given breath and colder clay given sterile animation.

Strand worked that shovel, tossing out clods of black earth and squaring off the grave meticulously as was his way. He could feel it below him, waiting in the thick and swelling blackness of his mother's coffin: a dire breathing in those damp confines of decay, a life, a death, the undead and poisoned milk of the charnel yard filling that box and needing to spill out in noxious tangles.

When he struck wood, found that fine gumwood coffin with the iron bands, he brushed dirt from it, whispering something under his breath just as he was certain something inside was whispering to him.

Was that...was that the sound of ragged fingers scraping from within? A thudding and a shifting like a child announcing itself from its mother's belly? No, not yet, not yet.

As Strand reached for the catches on the coffin lid, his hands pulled back and some dread voice in his mind demanded to know what he thought he was doing, in this place, down in this claustrophobic darkness.

And that stayed him for a moment or two, long enough for him to hear the chortle of frogs from the ravine and the sing-song shrilling of whippoorwills and the droning of night things. But then his fingers were at those catches, undoing them, curling along the seam of that lid as an earthworm coiled fatly beneath his hand.

It's time, mama, he thought with a buzzing sibilance in his head. *It's time to wake and rise up and—*

Then the lid was swung open and there was a rush of moist putrescence and fetid gas that made Strand gag. Mama Lucille was laying there in her silk burial gown, gray hands folded neatly at her bosom. Her face was pallid and drawn, the skin there thin and tight as if the skull beneath was trying to push its way through. Blackened lips pulled back from narrow teeth in a livid corpse-grin.

She was dead, she was not alive...yet, there was almost a repellent and lewd vitality to her that did not belong. There was a sentience, an awareness that was practically obscene. Like seeing a wooden window dummy smile and wink at you. Life did not belong in those remains, yet it was there.

This was when Strand truly realized he had made an awful mistake.

Then Mama Lucille's eyes flickered open, luminous yellow sacrificial moons.

She grinned and those withered fingers reached up, skeletal twigs scratching at an October window.

Strand started screaming.

It was a week later when he stumbled into town, gibbering and mad, his eyes wide and reflective like wax pennies. He made it to Sheriff Bolan's office and collapsed into a chair, his face grimy, leaves and sticks braided into his hair. When he tried to speak, all that would come out was a dry gibbering. And when he tried to make Bolan understand with just his hands, those fingers shook with violent quakes.

No, Bolan did not know what had happened to him, not then, but he knew it was bad. Luke Strand was thin and wasted, drooling and delusional. Whatever had taken hold of him it had done so with claws and teeth and appetite. Chewing up the man and shitting what was left out the other side. You could smell the fear and the insanity running from him in a sharp juice. He was like some demented ghost haunting the bones of his life.

"Okay, Luke," Bolan finally said. "We'll do it my way then."

Bolan was a big man, hard and wiry with sure hands and a cool head. And if there was one thing he believed in, it was whiskey. It was the only medicine he used and the greatest curative in God's creation. No greasy, slick-talking Yankee snakeoil salesman could touch good Kentucky whiskey and that was the plain truth. So he got out his bottle and he started pouring it into Luke Strand along with hot black coffee that was so strong it could've made a blind man see or a seeing man blind.

After a time, incrementally, Strand relaxed. All those compressed springs and taut wires loosened slowly, slowly, and he began to speak. He was still out of his head. So far out that try as he might, he could not find the way back in again. But he was lucid. And that was something.

"Eileen's dead," was the first thing he said. "She was murdered."

Bolan sat down, nodded, rolled himself a cigarette and gave it some fire. "Did you do the killing, son?"

But Strand shook his head so violently it looked like it might fall right off. "No, sir! It weren't me...it was, it was...*my mama.*"

Bolan pulled off his cigarette, his eyes narrowed to razor cuts. He knew that Strand was not pulling his leg; he could see the sincerity in his eyes and it didn't sit well with him. There were certain things that could be and others that could not. "Your mama's dead, Luke. I saw her put in the ground."

Strand's eyes were glassy and staring like those of a stuffed elk. "She was in the ground, sheriff, then I dug her back up and I took her...took her to Missy Crow..."

Bolan grimaced and a slight tremor passed through his hand. An understanding passed through his eyes, a recognition as if he knew this dark path all too well and where it led. He sat there silently, smoking, looking as if what he had chewed for lunch was chewing on him now. "I told you to leave that goddamned hag out of this."

But, as Strand explained, he could not.

He told Bolan what it was like with Mama Lucille being gone, how it had all pulled out his guts, emptied him, the grief stuffing something else back in there that was poisoned and foul. He told Bolan how he had gone to the straw-witch and paid her and all the rest.

"Then I dug her up and she was dead...but she was alive," Strand said.

But not really alive, he admitted. She was animate, but not human anymore. After she had woken up down in that grave, he climbed out of there, his mind just gone to sauce. He ran home and hid in the farmhouse and Mama Lucille followed him.

Strand was running his hands through his hair roughly like he wanted to yank it out by the roots. "She...she wasn't mama, she was something else. Like a living scarecrow, something that should not walk but did. Not human, not like me and you. Not warm and feeling, just a cold shell...*walking, breathing meat.*"

She would not speak, Strand said.

She made funny hissing sounds and grunting noises like a hog rooting in soil, but that was about it. She did not sleep. She walked around the house, flies nesting in her hair and mouth and she did not seem to care. She would stand in the hallway for hours staring into space or in the corner just looking at the wall. At night, she would pace back and forth, that black flyblown stink hanging on her. Once, she got outside and laid down in the turnip patch. By the time Strand found her, there were beetles and ants tunneling in her.

"I...I tried to pretend she were really mama, sheriff, I know it's blasphemy and I'm going to rot in the bowels of hell, but I just weren't thinking right," he said in a squeaking, childish voice. "I *wanted* her to be mama, I *needed* her to be mama. I tried to get her to eat. I gave her soup and bread and taters with no salt just like Missy Crow said, but mama wouldn't touch it. Then...then two days ago, I dug a grave out in the field and I made her lay in it. I buried her down near five feet. She was dead, she was walking carrion, stinking and rotting and always chattering her teeth like she were hungry. But she was dead so I buried her.

"I thought that would be the end of things. That she was dead and she would stay dead. Eileen had left me, she never saw none of it. When I went to dig up mama she just left, went back to her people, I reckon. I was thinking that the madness had passed and things could be sane again. But that night...that night I was lying in my bed and I heard Rafe Short's old hound begin to howl down the road a piece and I knew what was going to happen, I just knew it. Then I heard the creaking of those loose boards out on the porch and the door opening. Then those slow, heavy footsteps coming up the stairs. I think...I think I screamed when the door opened. Mama stood there in the moonlight coming in through the window and I smelled her long before that and heard all them flies buzzing on her. She stood there, just dirty and moldering and wormy, clods of earth falling off of her. She was holding out her hands to me like she wanted something, chattering her teeth, just chattering and chattering those teeth...but I knew what she wanted, God help me, but I knew what she wanted."

Bolan looked a little sick himself by that point. He crushed out his cigarette under his boot. "And what was that? Tell me, boy."

Strand licked his lips. "Meat. She wanted meat. She wanted salt. Missy said not to give her none, but I did. I had a joint of beef, raw and bloody, and I gave it to her. I dumped salt all over it. She chewed it right down to the bone...just gnawing and chomping on it, then licking it. When I tried to take it away from her, she snarled at me, she hissed and there was something in her eyes, something evil, Sheriff. It hadn't been there before. Something black and godless and...and *hungry*."

Strand said she went down in the root cellar with her bone and he could hear her down there nibbling on it. He ran out of the house and did not come back until the next night, which was last night. Eileen must have come home and found Mama Lucille...and Mama Lucille found Eileen.

"Oh dear God, Sheriff," Strand said, barely able to catch his breath. "I came home and right away I could smell it...that bloody, raw smell like you get around butchering time. I found mama with Eileen. She had bitten most of the meat off her face and eaten her fingers. She was chewing on her leg when I got there."

"What did you do?"

"I hid in the corn patch all night," Strand said. "I thought she would come after me, too. Then I got on my horse and I rode off. I was heading out of Boone County and never coming back. Then a couple hours ago, I thought I better come and see you."

Bolan thought it over for a long time. Then he stood up and strapped on his Army .44s. "All right, we better go take care of this, son. Ain't no one but us that can."

*

Missy Crow was sitting on her porch when they rode up. "I warned ye, Luke Strand. Did I not warn ye, boy, what ye were bringing onto yerself by calling up the dead? Oh, I knowed, God, how I knowed! I knewed ye wouldn't listen! I knewed ye'd feed her the salt and the meat!"

Bolan dismounted his dappled mare, tying her off at the hitch post. "Then you know, don't you, you old hag? You know what you've brought to being here? What terrible things you've set into motion?"

The straw-witch pulled off her ash pipe, grinning like a stuffed ape. "It's not what I set into motion, Sheriff. It was that fool there! He's the one! His mind and his hands and his heart! I was not the fire that burned down his house and damned his soul!"

"But you struck the match, you old witch," Bolan told her, trying desperately to keep his hands from his guns.

Strand was beyond fear now, beyond retribution. He was just pale and small and lifeless. "She were not human, Missy Crow. She killed my wife...she et her..."

The straw-witch laughed with a booming, unpleasant sound like thudding from inside a buried box. "Ye gave her the salt? Ye gave her the meat? I cain't help ye now, boy, ye brought this on yerself! She were a dead, mindless thing before, but now she's something else! There's things out there, boy, hungry and evil things that were never meant to be born...but now ye have birthed one and it's in yer mama, hear? A scratching, hungry pestilence! Ye have to bury her deep in a chained box! Let her go back to death, let her feed on herself, starve until there's nothing left but bones!"

Bolan had pulled one of his .44s now. "I should put you down right now, you goddamn hag."

"Yes, maybe ye should, Sheriff. But ye won't. No sir, ye won't. It's not in ye to kill an old woman even if she be the devil's own." Missy Crow leaned forward in her rocker, her eyes blazing and sulfurous. "Hear me well, Sheriff Bolan. Ye might be thinking of mayhap riding up here with a posse tonight or tomorrow to burn me out. But ye better think on that careful. I know yer wife is with child. Didn't know that, eh? Well, she is, boy, she certainly is. I knowed what's growing in her now and I also knowed what *could* be growing in her if I make it so! Something with teeth that would bite her from inside. Now ye don't want that, do ye?"

Bolan was taken aback, but not for long. "Listen to me, you hag. You've existed in this county because I'm a tolerant man. Now I give you fair warning: get out. Get out of my county before that posse does come, you hear me?"

Missy Crow just nodded. "I hear, Sheriff. I hear just fine."

*

It was sundown by the time they reached the Strand farm.

And just riding up there, Bolan could feel something like fingers unfurling in his belly, white and cold and clutching. If there had been doubts seeded in his brain, looking for soil to spread their roots, they were gone now. There was something spiritually defiled about the farmhouse, a palpable sense of rottenness that was not sensed with only the nose. It crawled and coiled like it was looking for a throat to wrap itself around.

The wind rustled the corn and the branches of a dead cottonwood tree scraped together overhead like knifeblades.

Lighting a coal-oil lamp, Strand said, "She's in there, Sheriff."

"Maybe you better wait out here."

But Strand shook his head. "Missy Crow's right: I am to blame. I have to see this through."

He was so completely calm about it all it was disturbing. Bolan wondered if there was a limit to what the human mind could suffer before the cogs of horror were worn smooth and there was only acceptance...indifferent, long-suffering acceptance.

Stepping up onto the porch and pushing the door open with the barrel of one of his .44s, he could smell that tomblike, violated atmosphere just fine. It was not just a stink of decay and organic corruption, it was something far worse. It was the odor of black earth and mildew, of bone piles and spoiled meat and creeping vermin, but something else too. Just a fathomless black stench of darkness beyond mere darkness, the smell of buried graves and crumbling pine boxes, the oily blood of deep rank earth dripping and running and settling into the mold of ages.

Bolan sucked in a breath, that smell repulsive to not only his belly but his brain. He wanted to vomit, then scream. Maybe both at the same time. The shadows were thick and oddly bunched, slithering and heavy and aware. The air was grainy, it seemed, hard to breathe and Bolan knew it was the air of crypts sealed for decades and centuries. The air the dead breathed, suffocating and damp.

There was blood in the hallway.

Oh, just buckets of it sprayed and smeared and splashed around like a pig had been gutted and drained in there. Bits of meat and tissue and hair were stuck in it. It had dried now to a sticky film like a membrane of cooling molasses, but the stink of it was all-too recent: raw and savage and coppery.

Strand was breathing very hard and it took everything he had to continue on.

The trail of gore led to the cellar door.

It was standing open, bloody handprints all over its panels like some kid had gotten into the red paint. The steps leading down into that hot, seething charnel darkness were stained with more blood and scraps of flesh. A few white, gleaming bones that might have been from fingers. In the orange, flickering glow of the lamp, Bolan saw a single, fine hand laying on the fifth step down. The light gleamed off of Eileen Strand's wedding band.

"Listen," Bolan said.

Yes, he was hearing something now. A wet, tearing sound and maybe it was just in his head, but he did not think so. It was the sound of a bear gnawing on a meaty bone in the darkness of a cave. A nibbling and sucking sound.

When they got to the bottom of the steps, they saw the wreckage of Strand's wife. The scattered bones carefully suctioned of meat. The husk of her trunk emptied of its dripping goodies. Her head smashed open, brains licked out, eyes plucked free like candied cherries. Her bowels were looped around the uprights of the stair handrail, chewed and slit and then carefully, expertly woven through those posts like Christmas garland.

"Show yourself," Bolan said.

And then she did.

Or something did.

Mama Lucille was a wraith. A wraith that had bathed in blood, swam in rivers of it. She was filthy and ragged and rotting, her burial dress and her gray flesh hanging in tatters and strips so it was hard to say where one began and the other ended. As she lumbered forward, you could see the rungs of her ribs jutting forth. Her face was gray and puckered and infested with worms—they boiled in her left eye socket and squirmed from the innumerable holes in her face and fell from her mouth. Flies buzzed in her hair and from deep inside her belly. Her teeth chattered and her stick-like fingers sought meat to pull from bones, that one good eye gleaming a wet, translucent yellow.

Strand screamed...screamed and lost his mind.

He dropped the lamp and went right to her.

Bolan said something he wasn't even aware of and grabbed up the lamp, just in time to see Strand get taken into his mother's arms. Those worm-eaten cerements engulfed him, those fleshless fingers pulled flaps of skin from his shoulders, and that black yawning mouth went to his throat, blood spraying out over her ruined face. She was a sea of carrion that flooded over him and pulled him down, drowning him in a dark sepulchral sweetness.

Bolan did not hesitate.

He shot right through Strand to get at her. Strand went down right away and then Mama Lucille, bleeding graveworms and soil and diseased bile from her wounds, turned on him. Those split, discolored lips pulled back from blackened and narrow teeth that snapped and chattered, ropes of tissue and gore hanging from them. She exhaled a cloud of fat meatflies. That eye found him and held him, yellow and reptilian, a dead-end noxious universe of ravening, insane appetite. And Bolan knew she would gut him like a salmon and bathe in his blood, tear his viscera out in hot, bleeding handfuls and suck the salty marrow from his bones...if he let her.

"Lay down, Lucille," he told her. "Just lay down."

But she came on, noisome and malign, a carcass peppered with insects and riven with maggots.

Bolan sighted in on that eyeball and pulled the trigger twice. The punch of a .44 at close-range is devastating. The first round blew that eye and the skull that housed it to fragments and the second round split her face right down the middle. She hissed and screeched and fell straight over like a plank.

And then lay still after a few shudders swept through her.

Laying there in a contorted, shattered heap, it did not seem possible that she had walked. She was just putrescent and blackened, a dirty and fleshy heap of bones and rags boiling with worms. A cloud of blowflies lifted off her like a vapor of swamp gas and that was it.

Bolan made it upstairs and then tossed the coal-oil lamp against the wall and let that mausoleum burn. He sat on his horse and watched the flames consume that ramshackle old farmhouse, knowing there was purity in fire.

As he rode off, he knew there would be another burning that night and he wondered how quickly straw would catch.

MONKEY HOUSE

In late March the army swept through the city putting the living dead back in their graves for a final time. They came with heavy machine guns and .50 caliber sniper rifles, flamethrowers and 7.62mm miniguns mounted on armored personnel carriers which cut the dead down in waves. Mop-up units followed, eliminating the stragglers, and searching house to house for those infected by the Necros-3 virus. The infected were put down; the uninfected were given injections of the experimental antiviral Tetrolysine-B, which inhibited the replication of the virus within the host body.

Necros-3 had put two-thirds of the world's population into the graveyard within seven weeks and nearly all of the dead had returned searching for flesh to eat.

Tetrolysine-B, which had been developed for use against HIV, proved to be the magic bullet. The pestilence was stopped dead in its tracks, but by that time the cities of men were cemeteries.

*

Emma Gillis was ready to leave.

She'd watched her neighbors sicken, die, then return to feed. No one would ever know how many people they slaughtered and Emma tried not to think about it. Gus had fortified their house, turned it into a bunker with gunports, a generator, and a razorwire perimeter that was carefully mined.

The dead had never breached it.

But now the war was over and Emma had had her fill. For the past three months she'd been stuck inside their trim crackerbox house cum-bunker and she was ready to leave.

"It's just time, Gus," she told her husband who watched the streets through one of the gunports, hungry for enemy activity. "Time to move on."

"I'm not leaving," he said.

Good God. He was still in the Marines. He was living some prepubescent G.I. Joe fantasy. The zombies had been vanquished. There was no reason to hole up like this any longer.

When the Army came—and Gus, of course, had warned them off until they trained antitank guns on the house—they said that out at Fort Kendrix there were hundreds of people—men, women, children, all rebuilding their lives. They had fresh meat, fresh fruit and vegetables. Water that didn't taste like metal. And medical care. Real medical care. And the guy in charge, Captain McFree—handsome, dashing really, with his black commando beret and pencil-thin Errol Flynn mustache—said they had electricity and a DVD library.

"Gus, be realistic. It's time to go."

He looked around, pale and paunchy and unshaven, camouflage pants worn and dingy. "I'm not leaving all this. I'm not leaving my home."

Emma sighed. "Home? This isn't a home, Gus, it's a barracks."

There were cases of MREs fighting for space amongst iron crates of ammo and jugs of purified water, the guns and first aid supplies. A survivalist's wet dream, but hardly a home. The walls were tacked with maps, the windows boarded over and criss-crossed by duct tape so they would not shatter. The brass coat tree by the front door was hanging with gas masks and waterproof ponchos and web belts.

Home?

Sure, *Good Housekeeping* as seen by *Soldier of Fortune*.

Emma didn't bother arguing. She packed up what she could in a suitcase and a nylon duffel and dumped them before the front door. "I'm going now, Gus. The war is over. Time to put away our guns and pick up shovels and saws and rebuild."

"Fuck that," he said.

Emma felt sad. She had watched a good man degenerate into this paranoid wreck. And as he degenerated, so had her love and respect for him.

She threw the bolts on the door and stepped out onto the porch. Gus slammed it immediately behind her, fumbling locks into place.

"You'll come back," he said.

No, I won't.

"You're making a big mistake, Emma," he told her through the mail slot, using that calm and authoritative voice of his that had been so effective in the past for everything from getting money to getting into her pants. "You won't make it out there. You'll be dead before you reach the Army base. You're not a survivor type and you know it."

She didn't argue with that. "The survivalist thing is you, Gus, it's not me."

"You just don't have what it takes, Emma."

"You're right," she said, leaving the bunker.

If surviving means becoming a rat afraid to leave its den, then I'll be a victim, Gus, and be happier for it.

It was wonderful to be outside again.

The clean-up crews had hauled away the bodies and remains and for the first time in weeks and months the breeze did not smell like it had been blown from a morgue drawer. It was coming from the south and she could smell sweet odors of spring growth, lilacs and honeysuckle. The sun on her pale face was warm, inviting.

She moved down the walk and stopped beneath one of the big oaks out there.

Thank God, thank God, thank G—

The wind shifted direction and soured right away, bringing with it a vile odor of bacterial decay and corpse gas. It was not old, but recent, very moist and organic like rotten meat shoved in her face.

Emma froze up.

She dropped first one bag, then another.

The sun was behind her.

Her shadow was cast over the walk as was that of the oak. She could see its twisting limbs and threading branches...and in them, hunched-over shadows like gargoyles.

Something hit her in the back of the head.

She heard a high chittering sound.

She turned and something hit her in the face.

Something wet and crawling and stinking.

She clawed it away with her fingers...bloody meat that crawled with bloated white grave maggots. Gagging, she tossed it away, the stink of putrescence putting her down to her knees.

With a gore-streaked face she stared up into the tree.

She saw a grinning, demonic visage staring down at her. It snapped its teeth at her.

Emma screamed.

*

Through the gunport slit in the living room wall, Gus watched his wife walk away. She was making a big mistake and he was angry that she did not know it. Angry that a bright woman like that did not realize the fix they were in.

And after all he had done for her.

Betrayal.

He didn't need the Army.

He didn't need Fort Kendrix.

Everything he needed was here in the shelter where he was master and commander.

He lit a cigarette. It was stale but he didn't even notice anymore. He blew smoke out through his nose and scratched at the stubble on his chin. Automatically, obsessively, his hands roamed his body making a quick inventory: .45 Smith in the holster—check; K-Bar fighting knife in its sheath—check; extra magazine for the—

What the hell is she doing?

Emma had stopped on the walk. She had dropped her bags. She made a gagging sound, digging something from the back of her head that was tangled in her hair.

Gus grabbed his M-14 sniper rifle and ran to the door.

He threw the bolts and was outside in seconds.

Emma was sitting there on her ass as something dropped out of the tree not five feet from her.

The thing saw him, hissed, and charged in his direction.

Gus just stood there, shocked at what he was seeing.

A baboon.

A *baboon* of all crazy fucked-up things: thick-bodied, compact, covered in a down of shaggy brown fur. Its eyes were shining a tarnished silver like dirty nickels, huge jaws wide open, fangs bared. It left a trail of slime in its wake.

There were huge ulcers eaten through its skin.

You could see its bones.

Zombie.

When it was ten feet away, Gus automatically shouldered the M-14 and fired just as he'd been taught at Parris Island so many years before. He popped the ape in the left eye socket with a .308 round that blew its skull apart in a spray of gray-pink mucilage and sent its corpse tumbling through the grass. A jelly of worms bubbled from its ruined head.

"EMMA!" he called out. "EMMA! RUN!"

Two more baboons dropped from the trees, then a third and a fourth. There had to be a dozen more up in the branches. They were shrieking and growling, absolutely enraged.

Gus heard a scratching, scrambling sound and turned. Two more were up on the roof. They were leaping from the trees onto the top of the house.

He dropped one that was five feet from him, pivoted, and knocked another off the roof that had only one arm.

He could hear Emma screaming.

The baboons were coming at him from every direction.

They looked like the remains of test animals that had been slit and bisected, poked and peeled and drained: grave-waste. He saw one lacking legs that swung its torso forward with its arms and others that seemed to be missing sections of flesh as if they'd been biopsied.

They all had huge holes eaten through them, bones jutting from their maggoty hides, meatflies rising from them in clouds. Baboon faces were skinned to pink meat or gray muscle, some were chewed to the bone by carrion beetles.

He dropped two more and then there was no room to shoot as they nipped at him, raking his legs with sharp skeletal fingers. He used his rifle like a club, swinging it, bashing in heads and smashing snarling faces to pulp until he was sprayed with rancid gouts of brown and red fluids.

The baboons circled him, gnashing their teeth.

He waited, the M-14 encrusted with gore and dripping a foul corpse slime.

He knew Emma was out there, but he didn't dare look for her. He couldn't even hear her now over the wailing and yipping sounds of the baboons.

Claws laid his knees open as he smashed the butt of the gun into a baboon face that was threaded with a filigree of mildew.

Then one of them bit into his ankle.

Another vaulted forward and bit into his left hand.

Crying out, he dropped the rifle, pulling the Smith .45 with his good hand.

A big baboon with a reddish-brown pelt and a pronounced white mane charged in at him, scattering the others. It had no eyes. The flesh was eaten away from its face revealing a cadaverous simian skull, jaws yawned wide to expose gleaming yellow upper and lower canines, each long and sharp enough to lay an artery open.

But what Gus noticed mostly was that its belly and chest had been completely shaven, a Y-shaped incision running from crotch to shoulders.

Autopsied. This thing had been autopsied.

Bleeding and hurting, Gus faced off with it while the others formed a tight and cohesive circle around them.

"EMMA!" he shouted. "GODDAMMIT, EMMA!"

The beast kept snapping its teeth at him, making a shrill staccato whooping noise.

Gus put three bullets into it and all that did was piss it off.

It charged and so did the others. The baboons hit him from every side and he felt himself go down under a sea of maggoty hides.

*

Emma, of course, saw Gus charge out of the house with his rifle, heard him call to her, but she was otherwise occupied.

The baboon in the tree above her was amused.

It was making that weird chittering sound that was chitinous and strident.

Staring up at it, Emma knew instinctively it was a female as were the others in the higher branches. She knew this just as she knew the males had gone after Gus.

Wiping slop from her face, she did not dare move.

The baboon stared at her with glassy, fixed eyes, grinning that toothy clownlike grin that made it look very much like some deranged pygmy looking for meat to skewer. There was some morbid growth like a grave fungus that consumed most of the left quadrant of if its face and was creeping in on the right. It seemed to be moving.

Emma heard Gus cry out.

She felt his voice slide through her heart like a needle.

He was shooting.

The baboon in the tree showed its teeth, letting out a piercing reverberating cry that was chilling and deranged and sounded very much like wild hysterical laughter.

It threw something at her that splatted on the walk. Meat. Greening meat threaded with corpse worms. It made that laughing sound again when it saw or *sensed* the revulsion coming from her. Then it slid its black leathery fingers into a gaping bloodless wound at its belly and pulled out more rotten tissue and threw it at her.

Emma ducked away.

The baboon laughed.

Her heart thumping in her chest, she stared at the horror with its greasy, nappy fur and yellow fangs and carrion eyes. Her terror pleased it, made it grin with an idiotic bestial splendor. And this more than anything not only disgusted her, it offended her.

It pissed her off.

It made Emma get to her feet, the ancestral apex predator within rising for battle.

The baboon in the tree stopped cackling now, it made a threatening almost territorial barking that got all the other females worked up. They all started screeching and baring their fangs, beating and scratching at themselves, pulling out clods of fur and necrotic tissue, throwing it like monkeys throwing shit.

Emma was pelted with the stuff.

She heard shooting, fighting, the constant screeching of the baboons.

"GUS!"

She backed away from the tree, made to turn and go to Gus and a baboon leaped through the air and tackled her, knocking her into the grass where she rolled to a stop, coming up not ten feet from the razorwire enclosure and its perimeter mines.

The baboon that attacked her came forward on all fours.

Its face was a mass of scar tissue and suturing that was bursting open from internal pressure, oyster-gray pus and pink jelly pushing its way through. The skin around its mouth had been surgically incised in an oval patch, leaving its speckled gums and fearsome teeth on display.

Emma knew she was no match physically for the beast, living or undead.

There was only one thing she could do.

As the beast roared and leaped on her, she waited it for it. And when it landed, planning on sinking its fangs in her throat, she kicked out and caught it in the chest, flipping it end over end through the air. It hit the ground on its rump, bounced, and came down inches from the razorwire.

There was a resounding explosion as it triggered a mine.

The creature was vaporized into a rain of blood and meat.

Clots of it fell over Emma and she madly pawed it free, stringy pink meat caught in her hair.

She started to scream.

*

When the baboons hit him from all sides, Gus lost his .45.

He hit the ground and they converged on him.

He never even had time to pull his knife before dozens of sets of teeth bit into him, tearing out chunks of meat and severing arteries and splintering bone.

He screamed.

He thrashed.

But it was no good.

There were too many ravenous baboons seizing him by then and he was laid open in too many places.

A large male went right for his soft white throat and found it, seizing it and tearing it open. Gus's scream became a moist gagging sound as those teeth sank into his neck, sank in deep.

The baboon shook him by the throat like a terrier with a rat, blood spraying in every direction, its muzzle stained red right up to the eyes.

The sound of Gus's vertebrae snapping was loud as a pistol shot and still the beast kept at it, driven mad by the blood and the taste of meat and maybe something more.

When it finally dropped him, Gus's throat was torn out, nothing but a ragged bloody mass of sheared muscle and ligament in its place, a few fingers of shattered white vertebrae showing through.

The others kept biting into him.

Chewing on him.

Pulling strips of skin free, tearing out quilts of muscle and sinewy tendon. A set of teeth pulped his genitals, two sets of blood-dripping jaws yanked out his bowels and pulled them in opposite directions, fighting and snapping over them as others ripped out organs in meaty masses and hopped off with their prizes.

As Gus lost consciousness, he could feel them pulling him apart and gnawing on his internals.

The male that had torn out his throat, sank its long ensanguined fangs into his skull, piercing it, impaling his brain.

It kept at it, applying pressure, until his skull was crushed and its mouth was filled with gushing blood and tissue.

*

Still pawing rancid bits of baboon from her, Emma crawled off.

She got to her feet, stumbling.

As she got clear of the tree, a male baboon came loping in her direction on all fours. It had a silver-gray mane and trailing beard that was fouled with dried blood and curdled marrow.

The females screeched with excitement.

Emma stared at the dead thing coming at her.

The fur and flesh at its back had been peeled to pink muscle, as had the flesh of its face. Jutting from the surrounding orbits, its eyes were like eggs translucent with fresh blood.

It snarled at her.

Emma tensed.

It attacked.

She aimed kicks at it, trying to keep it off her so she could at least make the door. Her defense worked at first—her boots struck it in the mouth, alongside the head, driving it back. The baboon was enraged, spinning in circles, growling and barking while froths of pink saliva rained from its mouth like vomit.

Emma knew how powerful the creature must be, resurrected or not. If it got hold of her, she'd never escape its iron embrace or those gleaming fangs.

She had to keep it off her as she backed towards Gus and the door.

Several females had dropped from the trees and were yipping with delight. They went down on their bellies and offered their hairless, callused, maggot-infested asses to the male.

Emma kept kicking at the baboon.

But it began to second-guess her, began to anticipate her moves. It ducked away from a flurry of kicks and came right in, seizing her right calf in its bloody jaws and putting her down.

Emma was screaming and fighting, kicking out with her left leg while pain threaded through her right in white-hot waves. The baboon wasn't just biting her...it was *chewing*, tearing, rending. Her pantleg was shredded, her calf muscle punctured...as those teeth came down again and again and again.

Screaming, crying, Emma engaged in one last act of defiance.

Instead of trying to kick out, she brought her leg closer to her body, dragging the baboon in with it by its teeth. And by that point it had worked a great flap of meat from her calf and it dangled from the baboon's jaws like a bloody cutlet.

Her mind erupting with blades of white-hot pain, Emma took hold of the animal by the ears and yanked down with everything she had, snapping its head sideways. The agony of its teeth being ripped so crudely from her leg was enough to make black dots parade before her eyes, but something in her—some primal, instinctive barbarism—fought on.

Acting instinctively, she jammed her thumb into its eye.

She buried it right to the second knuckle and the eye went to a soft mush like a rotten grape.

The baboon went wild.

It whimpered and howled, contorting and thrashing, tossing her onto her back and then jumping up on top of her, growling and snapping its jaws.

An inky fluid dripped from the ruined eye and the stench was like rotting fish.

It held her down and she could feel its blunt, stubby penis pressing against her thigh.

On the ground as she was with the beast hovering above her, she could see beneath its shaggy beard. There was a perfectly symmetrical bald patch circling its throat. She could see the gray flesh beneath and it had been sutured...as if the creature's head had been removed, then sewn back on.

With a scream she grabbed hold of its shaggy head mainly to keep those teeth from her. The baboon was extremely powerful, but she held on. Beneath the dirty fur, the flesh of its skull was spongy and soft. Emma dug her fingers in and they slid through meat and tissue soft with putrid decay.

The baboon cried out.

It trembled spasmodically.

She dug her fingers in deeper, a black sap running down her arms. Her fingertips scraped along the inside of its skull and she squeezed gray matter to mush in her fists, yanking out clods of brain that spurted between her fingers like oatmeal. Gouts of black blood fell into her face.

The baboon dropped away, whining and hissing, the top of its cranium crushed to a globby slush. It crawled in gyrating circles on the ground, leaving a slime trail of mucus behind it, its entire body contorting madly as if every neuron was misfiring.

Emma pulled herself away, wet and stinking.

The females hopped and shrieked and beat the ground with their skeletal fists. One of them had no eyes. In fact, the sockets had been stitched closed.

What the hell is this about?

Bloody, agonized, bile spewing from her mouth, Emma dragged herself towards the doorway. Blood, oh so much blood everywhere. In the grass. On the concrete. Sprayed in loops up the siding.

She looked for Gus.

But he was gone.

Piecemeal, he had been dragged off.

*

Emma crab-crawled up the steps onto the porch, trying to work the doorknob with blood-greased fingers.

The Primate Research Center, that's what this was about.

It stood just outside the city. Animal rights activists were always protesting there. In the chaos of Necros-3, it had been forgotten. But the virus must have jumped species and reanimated these...*things.*

She could hear the yelping and barking of the baboons.

They were coming for her.

Her fingers kept slipping on the knob. She pulled herself to her knees, her damaged calf sending fingers of agony right up into her chest.

She got the door open.

She pushed herself through, leaving a trail of blood behind her that marked her progress from the yard to the porch.

The baboons yammered hungrily behind her.

A gun. There were many and she had to get one.

She slammed the door shut behind her, throwing her weight against it and the baboons hit it from the other side, one after the other. She jerked with each impact, her back against the door, trying to keep it closed with all her strength as her fingers reached shaking for the lock.

The door burst in and she went down.

She scrambled across the floor, nearly blacking out from the pain. She could smell the hot green wave of putrefaction the zombie baboons pushed before them. It was moist and heady and repulsive.

Gnarled fingers scraped against her ankle.

The sound of them squealing and piping was cacophonous echoing through the house.

One of them grabbed her ankle and she kicked back, freeing herself.

More fingers raked her leg.

She grabbed wildly at the rifles in the case and they fell over like dominoes from her searching fingers, a .12 gauge pump coming free, bouncing off her head, and then she had it just as the baboons seized her and began to drag her back to their voracious waiting mouths.

She swung around, the shotgun in her hands.

There were three baboons gripping her legs.

One of them was missing the top of its head, just a gleaming dome of exposed skull that was punctured with holes as if from primitive trepanning. Another's face was pitted from probes and cutting.

They opened their mouths, howling, diving in for the attack and Emma fired, pumped, and fired again.

The faces of two of the baboons splashed off the skulls beneath, the third riddled with blazing holes that lit its fur on fire. It hobbled away, smoldering.

Emma cut another in half and blew the head off yet another.

The one that was cut in half did not die.

It pulled itself forward, its legs and lower torso forgotten, dragging ribbons of flesh behind it. It made a sharp hissing sound in its throat, its eyes lit with a crimson blaze, mouth open and ready to bite.

"C'mon," Emma panted, tears running down her face. "COME AND GET IT! C'MON, YOU MOTHERFUCKER! LET ME SEE WHAT YOU'RE MADE OF!"

The baboon, of course, needed no prompting.

It slithered forward and Emma blew its head to confetti. That stopped the others. With all that meat sprayed around, they lost interest in her. They began to feed on the remains of the others, slurping up blood and nibbling on brains and gnawing on bloody bones.

They were occupied.

Now was the time.

She looked down at her torn calf, the blood pooling around her leg. God, she needed to do something with it before she got woozy from the loss of blood.

The baboons were ignoring her.

Very slowly, she moved towards the first aid kit near the gun rack. Calmly, she took hold of the plastic box, opened it. With shaking fingers she wrapped her calf and then taped it up.

Now and again, a baboon would look up at her with a blood-stained muzzle and snarl, but that was about it.

Next, she had to get out of there.

But Gus, oh Jesus, what about Gus?

No time for that. She shut her mind down. Went cold. Emotionless. This was survival now, it was war to the teeth. The easiest way out would be through the dining room and into the kitchen. If she could make that, then she could slip out the back door and hobble to the garage. The keys to it and the Jeep inside were in her pocket. Then a quick spin out to Fort Kendrix.

Swallowing, she began to move towards the archway that led into the dining room.

She scooted herself along on her ass.

The baboons still ignored her.

She got to the archway, took one long last look at them to satisfy herself that they had no interest in her. They didn't. There was plenty to eat and that seemed to be the primary motivating force: hunger.

The shortwave radio was in the dining room.

But she didn't dare send a message.

That would mean speaking at full volume.

She pushed herself into the kitchen. Almost there, by God, almost there.

Into the kitchen.

More of a warehouse now with stacked crates of MREs and purified water and flares and radio parts and—

Emma heard a scuttling noise.

A ragged breathing.

She swung around on her ass and an especially large ape was waiting there, puffing out its chest.

A Mandrill.

It was a large shaggy baboon-like beast with an olive pelt, its nose a brilliant bright red, vivid blue spokes fanning out over the cheeks. Emma found herself staring into its eyes. They were a cool, watery scarlet. The top of its head had been cut away, its brain exposed.

She did not want to think about what they had been doing to this animal just like she did not want to think about what it could do to her.

It stepped forward on all fours with an almost swaggering, arrogant stride.

It bared its teeth, yawned its mouth wide and let loose with a high-pitched scream that was instantly answered by a dozen other screeching voices.

Emma licked her lips.

There was a gaping hole in the beast's midsection and she could see right through it, nothing but bones in there. It couldn't possibly be moving, but it was.

She brought up the shotgun.

The Mandrill charged.

She pulled the trigger.

Nothing.

She worked the pump, pulled the trigger again, and in the back of her mind a small voice counted off the five rounds she had already fired.

Five.

Here's what you need to remember about the Mossberg 500, she could hear Gus saying to her. *It has a five-round magazine so if you're going to use it, carry a back-up. It's a devastating weapon, Emma, but not if you run out of shells.*

Shit.

Hopelessly, Emma tried firing it again.

Then the Mandrill was on her.

It took hold of her with great strength, pushing her down and bouncing her head off the floor to take the fight out of her. Then it grabbed her by the hair and swung her like a Barbie doll, smashing her into cupboards, the kitchen table, a green metal cartridge box.

By then she was barely conscious.

The Mandrill seemed pleased.

For alive or dead, it liked its females submissive.

Emma looked up with bleary eyes.

She saw the Mandrill's bright red penis squirt cold urine into her face, marking her. It gushed over her cheeks, burning her eyes, bringing an acidic, nauseating taste to her lips.

The stench more than anything made her pass out.

The Mandrill, grunting happily, dragged her from the room.

*

When Emma came to she was in the cellar.

She was sore, threaded with pain, but the worst part—

What the hell?

She was face-down and something was humping her from behind. Her first instinct was to fight, to scramble free. But she was still dressed so it wasn't like she was being penetrated.

Wait.

There were several baboons gathered around, but keeping a respectful distance and that was because the Mandrill had her. Mandrills were not baboons, she knew, just close relatives, the largest species of monkey in the world and this one was the alpha male of a pack of baboons.

It was humping her to show its dominance.

It screeched.

The baboons yelped and barked.

The females were busy picking maggots from each other's hides and eating them.

Emma knew she could not panic.

A lot depended on what she did now.

She cast an eye around. There was the woodstove, the carefully stacked kindling. The axe. Double-bladed, kept very sharp by Gus. You could slit paper with it.

The Mandrill leaped off her.

The baboons growled at him and he snarled and shrieked, driving them off and up the stairs. He sat back on his haunches. There were insects crawling in his fur. He studied the females.

His harem.

And Emma was now one of them.

She gathered her strength. It was now or never. She had to reach that axe and if she couldn't, that would be it.

The Mandrill was turned away from her.

Now!

Emma dove to her knees, ignoring the pain it brought. She scrambled over to the woodpile. The females made baying sounds. The Mandrill roared and came after her.

Emma grabbed the axe in both hands and swung it with everything she had.

The Mandrill came at her with jaws wide.

The axe came down.

It cleaved the beast's exposed brain, slicing deep into the cerebral fissure separating the right and left hemispheres. The Mandrill hopped this way and that, clutching at the axe buried in its head. It shook. It convulsed. It vomited out a bubbling black jelly and then it pitched forward, dead once again.

Two of the females ran.

A third turned to fight.

It dove at Emma.

She never had time to get the axe free from the Mandrill. The female knocked her down and then they were fighting and scratching. The female was powerful, but Emma fought with a manic frenzy. She clambered onto the female's back and did the only thing she could do to win.

She bit into its throat.

Bit deep until blood that was black and tarry filled her mouth.

The female squealed and shook, but finally went down under Emma's weight.

Covered in baboon blood and drainage, she pulled the axe free and chopped off the female's head.

Then she sank to her knees and vomited.

*

When she came upstairs, she braced for battle.

Her shirt and pants were blackened with baboon discharges, blood encrusted over her face and neck. Tissue caught in her nails.

The other baboons did not attack.

They kept well away from her.

They grunted and yelped and whined when she passed them.

Emma stank of decay and corpse slime and baboon piss. Maybe they smelled the Mandrill on her and the blood of their own kind.

Outside, there was a rumbling.

Gunfire.

The Army had returned.

Thank God.

Emma moved past the cowering zombie baboons and to the door, still clutching the gore-streaked axe in one hand. She was limping, beaten, scratched, bitten and bruised, but still standing.

You're not a survivor type and you know it.

You just don't have what it takes, Emma.

The hell I don't, she thought as she stepped out onto the porch and saw the dead baboons laying everywhere, several dangling from tree limbs.

She waved the axe to the soldiers in the APC.

One of them put the minigun on her.

"Wait..." Emma started to say.

The minigun could lay down something like six thousand rounds per minute and in the scant few seconds between when Emma was first hit to when she pitched over dead, some two hundreds chewed through her, pulverizing her.

What hit the ground were fragments.

Emma was gone.

"Never seen a zombie with an axe before," the soldier on the minigun said.

Captain McFree laughed. "You see it all in this business, son."

The APC rolled up the streets as the mop-up continued.

THE MATTAWAN MEAT WAGON

The kid's name was Blaine. He had heart, but his head was no good. Naïve as all hell and Cabot took every opportunity he could find to remind him about that. About how things worked and his place in the larger scheme of things and how he better not fuck up because too much was riding on it.

"I don't get it, though," the kid said. "Why me? Why do I pull something like this? Did I piss somebody off? I mean, shit."

Leaning up outside the warehouse door while the meat was loaded in the back of the truck, Cabot lit a cigarette and sighed. "Everybody gets a shot, kid. It's nothing personal. But in Hullville we all pull our share. You, me, everyone. I make this trip once a month."

"Yeah, but in the back of the truck—"

"You don't worry about what's in the back of the truck."

Cabot knew the kid wasn't liking it, knew he thought maybe it was a little barbaric and maybe more than a little uncivilized. But those words had lost their meaning here in the brave new world. Ever since Biocom started sweeping people into the grave and waking 'em back up again, things had changed.

Morality, ethics, humanity...abstract concepts. The country was a cemetery now.

No, he wasn't going to beat that drum.

The kid wasn't real bright, but he wasn't that stupid. Cabot wasn't going to remind him what his life had been like before a patrol found him out there in the Deadlands and brought his sorry ass into Hullville. How the town had patched him, smoothed out his rough edges, put food in his belly, a pillow under his head and a roof over him. They did it because they needed him and he needed them and he seemed like an all right kid.

The Council did right by him.

And now, favor for favor, it was time to earn his keep.

Chum came out of the warehouse, his overalls grimy, his eyes looking like open wounds that wanted to bleed. "Okay, Cab. You're loaded. Take it easy."

"That's my way," Cabot sad, grinding out his cigarette and watching the fog coming in off the lake.

Chum hooked his elbow, said, "I mean it, Cab. Watch the kid. Watch him."

"Sure."

Then Chum was gone and Cabot was standing there feeling a little weak in the knee. He cleared his throat of fuzz. "Okay, kid. Let's get this show on the road."

Blaine kept trying to swallow but it just wasn't happening. He froze up and Cabot took him by the arm and led him over to the steel-reinforced cab of the big Freightliner.

"Relax, kid," he said. "Just pretend you're delivering beef to the butcher's. Because that's exactly what you're doing."

*

It was funny, Cabot got to thinking as he drove. Just five years ago the world was full of cities with people in them and now there were just a lot of graveyards and ghost towns out there swarming with the walking dead. A few far-flung burgs like Hullville and Moxton, walled-up medieval towns protecting themselves against a coming siege. Once humanity ruled the Earth, now they hid in ratholes and crossed their fingers, made offerings to the Wormboys to keep them happy.

After the gates were closed behind them, Hullville faded into the fog and there was desolation. Ruined little towns and collapsing farmhouses, overgrown fields and wrecked cars, overturned trucks. Day-glo skull-and-crossbone signs set out, warning the unwary away from the Deadlands. Not much else. Just the fog and the night and whatever waited in it.

"How far?" Blaine wanted to know.

"To the drop-off?" Cabot shrugged. "Twenty miles. We gotta go slow in this soup. Be a real pisser if we crashed into an old wreck and had to hoof it. That would be a real hoot."

"It got a name? This place?"

"Not anymore. Just a ghost town now."

Cabot drove on, feeling the Freightliner purring beneath him. She was solid and steady with a 220 Cummins under her hood. Medium-duty, she was small compared to some of the rigs he'd handled, but she'd do in a pinch. The cab had been reinforced with riveted steel plating and the side windows weren't much more than gunport slits now, the windshield only slightly larger, all of it shatter-resistant and impact-resistant plexiglass. The cab was armored like a tank and with where they were going that was a good thing.

The fog grew thicker, tangling and twisting, flying past them in fuming pockets and sheets. Got so they couldn't see much out there in the headlights but the jagged contours of gnarled black trees, a few rusting cars on the side of the road. Nothing else but that mist, enclosing and enveloping, blowing out at them like steam from a pot. Now and again, Cabot spied shapes and shadows moving through it but he didn't dare mention it. Kid was getting nervous. Starting to shift a lot in his seat, looked like he was about to have a litter of puppies.

"Why do you do it, though?" Blaine asked him.

"This? Because I was a truck driver before and that's what I'm good at. You need a load run through hard country, I'm the guy for the job. I ain't worth a shit at anything else." Cabot told him how it was in the old days, running freezer trucks of Texas beef up from Kansas City, flatbeds of harvesters into Boise, tankers of hi-test down to Little Rock. "Been everywhere and hauled everything, kid. This ain't so different. Not really."

Blaine studied the rack of pump shotguns. "Oh, it's different, I think."

Cabot shrugged. Maybe the kid wasn't so dumb after all.

He drove on, cutting through the fog, keeping the truck in creeper gear all the way. Just too damn much wreckage and debris on the roads. They'd used a big loader a few years back to sweep all the wrecks into the ditch or onto the shoulder, but now and again some fool tried to cross the Deadlands or skirt them and he plowed his pick-up into a rotting hulk and created yet another driving hazard.

Blaine sat up straight, looked out his window port, tried to catch something in his rearview. He stared at Cabot. "You see that?"

"What?"

Kid swallowed. "I don't know...I thought I saw some woman standing there by that wrecked van. Looked like she was holding a kid."

"Out here?" Cabot stepped on the accelerator, got them moving a bit quicker. "Ain't no women or kids out here."

"But I thought—"

"Maybe you saw something, but it sure as hell wasn't a woman and what she was holding was no kid. You know better than that."

"But she didn't look...*bad.*"

"Some of 'em don't, not until you get up close and see their eyes, smell the stink coming off 'em."

There he went being fucking naïve again. Jesus. Kid knew the score, all right. He'd gotten his ass into a bind out in the Deadlands when he and some other survivors tried to slip through in a van. They'd blown a tire outside Carp River of all places. That town was just as infested with Wormboys as a dead dog was with maggots. And, yeah, the comparison *was* appropriate. The kid got away, but the others were butchered out there. He hid out by night, ran by day for over a week. That's when a patrol from Hullville out mopping-up stragglers came across him and brought him back—

Cabot jerked the wheel to the right to avoid a smashed minivan and nearly put them right into an overturned Greyhound bus rising from the ditch like a missile from a silo. He jockeyed the truck a bit, jerked the wheel this way and that, got her under control. Just as he did, a blurred form appeared out of the fog. They both saw it for maybe a split second before it thudded off the Freightliner's grill and was gone.

"Christ!" Blaine said. "You're gonna kill us!"

Cabot laughed. "Don't worry kid. I could thread a fucking needle with this baby. Relax."

But the kid was past relaxing and Cabot saw it.

He couldn't seem to sit still like his shorts were full of ants. He was tapping his fingers rapidly on his knees, shifting around, peering out the port of his window. Cabot could hear him breathing real fast like he was ready to hyperventilate. There was a sheen of sweat on his face.

The radio crackled and the kid jumped.

There was static, then: "Seven? You alive out there? Talk to me."

Cabot grabbed the mic. "Hey, Chum. We're about ten minutes out."

"How's that fog?"

"Like soup."

"Anything to report?"

Cabot peered out into the soup. "Not much. We got a wrecked bus that's a hazard. Seen a couple stragglers, no numbers, though. Sweet and clean."

There was silence for a moment. "How's your guest doing? How's Blaine?"

Blaine sighed and shook his head.

"He's not liking it much, Chum," Cabot said, winking at the kid in the dim cab. "Sitting over there with a sour look on his puss like he's got about seven inches of cruel loving up his ass and he can't shake it loose."

Chum giggled over that. "Okay, don't be a stranger, Cab. Out."

"Why'd you have to say that?" Blaine asked Cabot. "It sounds gay."

But Cabot never answered him because in the back of the truck there was a sudden thudding sound, a thumping. Then something which might have been a hand slapping against the rear door, a low moaning like someone was in pain.

Blaine had balled his hands into fists now. He was shaking.

"Just our cargo, kid," Cabot told him, grinning. "They must be waking up back there. Dope must've worn off. It does that. We better push it, get our piggies to market."

*

It began with a microbe in Clovis, New Mexico.

A robotic satellite called BIOCOM-13 was sampling the upper atmosphere for microorganisms of possible extraterrestrial origin. Somewhere during the process, it found the microbe, analyzed it, sealed it in a vacuum jar, then proceeded to get cored by a rogue meteorite. Long before a maintenance crew could get up there, BIOCOM-13 fell into a rapidly decaying orbit and plunged to Earth.

It crashed outside Clovis, its sample jars bursting upon impact. Several were bacterium of terrestrial origin, a few exotic mold spores, and a virus. The virus would come to be known as *Biocom* after the satellite. The virus, it was later learned, was not from Earth. It had drifted here, scientists theorized, perhaps stuck to a rock or a speck of cosmic dust, on a trip through deepest space that might have lasted ten-thousand years or ten million.

It probably would never have made it down if the satellite hadn't grabbed it.

NASA exobiologists had long said that the possibility of pathogenesis resulting from contact with an alien microbe was minimal. That extraterrestrial agents such as bacteria, fungi, protozoa, and multicellular parasites evolved differently and would share no common biochemical or cellular traits with terrestrial types. Ergo, it was more conceivable for a human being to get infected with Dutch Elm Disease or wheat rust than an alien microbial agent. But Biocom was a virus. And NASA had left viral agents out of the loop. Viruses have no cellular machinery of their own; they convert that of the host organism to reproduce themselves. So a virus is a virus is a virus, regardless of where it comes from. It adapts to any chemistry.

And nobody knew where Biocom came from.

First contact was in Clovis and from there it spread in every conceivable direction, mimicking pneumonic plague and putting two thirds of the world's population into the grave within six months. But they didn't stay there.

They started rising.

They got out of their graves, feeding on the dead and the living and spreading the virus like the common cold. If you got bit, you died. And if you died, you came back with a whole fresh slate of culinary impulses.

Of course, nobody believed it at first.

Zombies? The dead rising? Utter bullshit. File it away with those aliens on ice at Roswell and Bigfoot shitting in the Oregon woods. But the stories did not go away: they proliferated. From Florida to Maine, Michigan to Texas, the dead *were* rising. And it wasn't long before videos of the same showed up all over the internet. One in particular was posted to YouTube. It got so many hits it crashed the server.

What it showed was Clovis, New Mexico.

At first glance, the grainy video taken with a night-vision device looked almost comical, like something from a Gary Larson cartoon about the living dead: men in bathrobes and fuzzy slippers, women in fluffy nightgowns with curlers in their hair, all wandering the streets in the dead of night. Then some daylight footage was added and things got spooky. Men, women, children. Some stark naked and some dressed in burial clothes, pallid, decaying, infested with vermin. They were rising from cemeteries and crawling free of mortuary slabs and morgue drawers. Their faces were gray and seamed, their eyes flat dead white or lit a lurid red and filled with a cunning, evil intelligence, narrow teeth jutting from shriveled black gums, chattering and gnashing, looking for something to bite.

This is when people started to worry.

And when they saw the video of the naked little boy with the glaring black autopsy stitching running from throat to crotch feeding on the dead cat or the bloated woman breastfeeding her swollen, blackened infant while grave maggots wriggled in her dirt-clogged hair...well, panic ensued. The authorities denied it all, but still the stories spread and nobody believed what they were told because by then, they had all seen the walking dead. Biocom overflowed the graveyards and deceased loved ones came washing out, knocking at doors and windows in the dead of night with grim appetites.

Six months later...the world was gone.

Biocom was the great eraser that washed the blackboard clean. A world that had been a struggling, unruly child lost its innocence almost over night and became a deranged adult that shit and pissed itself hourly, its mind lost in a sucking black whirlpool vortex of dementia, madness, and resurrection.

The plague filled the cemeteries and emptied them again and that's the way it was. Many contracted the plague, but survived it. But even survival left a little parting gift: sterility. No man or woman over the age of thirty came away able to reproduce. The young and virile became something to protect and covet. Without them, there was no children and with no children, no future.

And that had been five years ago. Five long, hard, cruel years.

This was the reality that Cabot and the others in Hullville lived with day in and day out. It was a bitter pill to swallow.

Some people just couldn't keep it down. They lost their minds, they raged, they pulled into themselves, they became sightless breathing shells. And more than a few slit their wrists or ate the gun.

But for all those, many more did not roll up like frightened pillbugs. They survived. They accepted. They adapted and overcame. Not just in Hullville, but in towns like Moxton and Pick's Valley, Slow Creek and Nipiwana Falls. They accepted the reality that the new world was not the world they or their parents had known. The new world offered the survivors nothing; everything from food to shelter to a bucket to piss in had to be fought for, had to be wrenched free from the hard earth or taken from those that held it.

Survival.

A simple concept and one the human race was very adept at.

Graveyards and ghost towns.

A few struggling pockets of humanity trapped in-between. In Hullville, things were run by the Council. They made all the decisions. Guys like Cabot didn't like the idea of driving the sick, the weak, the old and diseased out to the Deadlands and ghost towns, but there was no other choice. If the Wormboys weren't given meat, they'd come for it.

So Cabot, like so many others, did what he was told.

For in the end, it was always better to be in the front of the truck than in the back.

*

The ghost town came up out of the fog like a clustering of tombs blown with fingers of white vapor. The headlights speared through the mist, but neither man looked too closely at what they might reveal in the deserted lots and leaf-blown streets. A pall of age and shivering malevolence hung over the town, just as thick and palpable as the fog itself.

"This is it, kid," Cabot said, his voice dry and rasping. "This is where we dump our load."

Blaine said nothing.

He hadn't said a word in some time now. He was just as still and silent as the mist-shrouded streets spreading out around them. Cabot had been keeping an eye on him and, mile by mile, he had gotten more tense, every muscle drawn taut, his jaws clamped tight, sweat beading his face.

Cabot pushed the truck further into the ghost town.

Out of the corner of his eye he caught shapes pulling back into the fog, thought he saw eyes once that reflected red in the headlights. He'd done this so many times but it never got any easier. He fumbled another cigarette into his mouth with a shaking hand, his fingers trembling so badly he could barely fire it.

The Freightliner's lights revealed the town inch by diseased inch: the dusty windows of empty shops, the spiderwebbed windshields of abandoned cars rusting at curbs, rotting houses leaning precariously on lawns gone wild with weeds. Everywhere, desertion and desolation, the American dream gone to rot and ruin.

In the back of the truck, the cargo was thumping and bumping around in the darkness, trying to shake off a drugged stupor.

Cabot pulled off his cigarette, pretending he could not hear them back there. Pretending he could not feel the flat, evil atmosphere of the town invading him and turning him cold and white inside.

"Another block," he said. "We'll be in the village center. That's where we'll get rid of our load."

Blaine muttered something under his breath.

"What's that, kid?"

He swallowed, then sighed. "I said it hasn't changed much. Just older. Decaying."

Cabot looked over at him. "You been *here* before?"

Blaine nodded. "This is Mattawan. This is where I came from. This is where we were running from that night our van puked out."

"Why didn't you ever say so?"

"Nobody ever asked me." He shook his head. "Whenever I started talking about it, people shut me up. In Hullville, they all shut me up. You're here now, they'd say. Where you came from don't matter. We all came from somewhere."

Cabot didn't like this. He was getting a real bad feeling stirring in his guts.

"We hid out in a basement for three years," Blaine said. "We foraged by day. The dead were in the streets then, too, but not as bad as at night. Ever notice how they're so sluggish and stupid during the day? But then at night—"

"Kid, you should've told someone."

"Nobody'd listen. Now I'm back. I'm home."

Cabot was wiping sweat from his own face now. "Sure, kid. But this ain't home. Not anymore. It's a graveyard."

And then Blaine reached over and quickly popped the lock on his door, threw it open and leaped out. Cabot cried out, caught the kid's elbow, but he pulled free and was gone.

"Shit!"

Cabot hit the brakes and brought the truck to a stop. It rocked back and forth on its leaf springs. He shut the kid's door, smelling the vile and polluted stink of the mist out there.

Then he jumped out himself, looking around in every direction.

"KID!" he called out. "GET THE HELL BACK HERE! DO YOU HEAR ME? GET THE HELL BACK HERE!"

His voice echoed off into the misty darkness, but there was no reply. Fog filled the headlight beams and brakelights, swirling and steaming. Shadows clustered in warped doorways, the air damp, heavy, and moldering.

Cabot wiped a dew of sweat from his face, his breath coming fast.

Maybe Blaine was naïve and just plain stupid, but *he* was not. He knew this was not just some empty dead town. *They* were out there and they were out there in numbers. Even now he could feel their malefic eyes crawling over him, sizing him up.

They wanted what was in the back of the truck.

But they would take whatever meat they could get.

Cabot started first this way, then that, stopping each time, daring to go further. There was a park across the way. He could make out the shapes of slides, swingsets, an upended teeter-totter rising up in the fog like a derrick. This more than anything said all that needed saying about the wasteland the town now was, the extinction of the people who'd once lived there.

A little house bordered the park and Cabot wondered if maybe the kid had gone in there, wondered if it could be that simple.

He stepped over the curb into the long yellow grass that climbed up above his calves. His breath would barely come. He could hear the truck idling, a stray breeze in the trees overhead. Shadows were crawling everywhere and death waited in each one. The house was sagging, weathered and gray. A lone monolith wreathed in darkness.

He moved further into the yard, the crackling of dry leaves under his step making something pull up tight inside him. He saw a birdbath in the yard. It was sprouting withered creepers. The front door of the house was hanging from its hinges, the darkness beyond sinister and pooling.

That's when Cabot saw he was not alone.

From one dusty window above, a white face was staring down at him. Its eyes were black and glistening. He almost fell over backing away. The figure up there began slapping its hands against the window violently.

"Shit," Cabot said and ran back to the truck.

He got inside and threw the locks, started breathing again.

He was shaking worse than the kid himself now, everything inside him gone loose and watery. He knew how things worked. He knew exactly how they worked. The kid was valuable to Hullville. They needed the young and the strong because they could still bring babies into the world and Hullville needed babies. They needed a next generation or they were done. He would be sixty himself come next birthday and his procreating days were long over. He was just as sterile as the rest. Not as valuable as the kid. He wasn't old, but it was coming and when you no longer had a use in Hullville you went in the back of the truck.

That's why the patrols went out.

They needed bodies. They found anyone they could and brought them in. Then the Council decided whether they were useful or not. Lots of them were. People with trades, doctors, carpenters, bricklayers, engineers. But others...alcoholics, drug users, the old, the lazy, criminals, the sick...they were culled off, went into the back of the truck for the trip to the ghost town. That kept the Wormboys happy.

And now Cabot had fucked up.

He had lost the kid.

The Council wouldn't like that. He thought about calling it in, but he was afraid to. He could hear Chum now: *You lost the kid? Well, that's a real pisser, Cab. He was set to marry up with Leslie Rule next month. They'd a had some beautiful babies, I'll bet. Oh well. Shit happens. Dump your load and head in. Council will want to talk to you.*

Shit.

Council will want to talk to you.

"Like hell," Cabot said under his breath.

He pulled a pump shotgun from the rack and filled his pockets with extra shells.

He was going out there.

Out into the graveyard of Mattawan.

He was going to find the kid.

*

Night and fog.

Cabot moved through the mist, having no idea where he was going. It was a fool's errand and he knew it, but to go back empty-handed...well, that just wouldn't do. He eased by picket fences spotted with black mold, crossed overgrown yards where children's plastic toys bleached colorless by the grim roll of years were tangled in weeds. He slipped by rows of rotting houses with broken windows and rooflines fringed with mold.

So far, so good.

He scanned the darkness with a flashlight, the beam reflecting back off the rolling fog. Sometimes he saw shapes out there. Sometimes they were just trees or bushes and sometimes they were something else. He used the flashlight sparingly, turning it on and then clicking it off just as quick. The Wormboys were out there. Mattawan was dark, lit only by the mist and the pale moonlight filtering through it. Light of any sort would draw them right away like moths to a streetlamp. They didn't like light much, but they knew it meant prey when they saw it.

Cabot tried to focus his mind, tried to come up with some sort of plan.

Where would the kid have gone? He had lived somewhere in this gutter, only he was never particular as to where that had been. And what had happened in the truck? Had he been planning this all along or had the sight of the place just unhinged him?

He couldn't have known we were going to Mattawan. Nobody calls it that anymore. Ever since it died it's just been the ghost town.

But there was no time for that.

Cabot decided right then and there that all he could do was sweep around the general area, be quiet about it, then make for the truck before he became lunch. If he couldn't find the kid—and he was starting to feel pretty sure he wouldn't—then he'd make up some story, anything to throw him in a good light and shade the kid in a bad one.

Sound thinking.

Cabot moved down a street that was crowded with rusting cars and trucks. Some were smashed up against trees, others had popped the curb and died on lawns. Many had bird-picked skeletons behind the wheels. The town was wild, hedges and bushes consuming lots, ivies engulfing garages, yards lost beneath uprisings of weeds and straw-yellow devil grass. Tree limbs had fallen everywhere.

He kept moving, keeping a wary eye out for anything alive...at least, anything *moving*. The mist distorted everything. Turned trees into stalking figures, shaped fire hydrants into crouching forms.

He stopped.

Behind him there were footsteps...slow, measured.

He whirled around, tucking the flashlight into his pocket, both hands on the shotgun now. He waited behind a hedgerow, ready, ready. A warm stench like spoiled pork wafted through the air and sweat ran down his face. He caught a momentary glimpse of a hobbling stick-like shadow melting into the fog.

The footsteps faded into the distance.

Cabot waited another few minutes, then he was moving again. Stealthy, alert, his muscles drawn taut like piano wires, his blood pulsing hot in his veins. He moved over grassy lawns, frost-heaved sidewalks yellow with rain-plastered leaves. The mist was damp and chill about him, moving, swirling, encompassing. His heart was pounding in his throat, his temples.

Off to the left, a branch snapped.

He froze, unsure whether to go forward or go back.

There was a scraping sound now...like something sharp dragged over the hood of a car.

He smelled a sweet and high odor like rotting hay. It grew stronger by the moment. He brushed sweat from his face, licked his paper-dry lips. The world around him was painted gray by the mist. Tree limbs creaked together in the breeze. He looked around, peering through blankets of fog, terrified at what he might see coming at him.

The stink was overpowering now.

He turned, ready to run, ready to give up his position by making a mad dash for the truck and then—

Someone was standing not ten feet away.

At first, Cabot was not even sure that he was looking at a man. Dressed in a black coat that was feathered with moss, his back twisted and body contorted, he looked like a dead, gnarled tree growing up from the weedy soil, his skeletal hands reaching twigs, his face corded like pine bark. "Please, friend," he said in a rasping tone. "I am so hungry, so very hungry..."

Wormboy.

Cabot just waited there, the shotgun in his fists. "Get the fuck away from me," he said.

The Wormboy dragged himself forward, grinning happily. His face split open with it, tissues tearing and tendons popping like dry roots. His eyes were blank and white, rimmed with red, his mouth hanging open to reveal pitted gums and black teeth. A dark slime oozed from his lips like running sap.

Cabot shot him.

He caught him in the belly and nearly tore him in half. But what was left, like stringy pink and gray meat, kept crawling in his direction.

Cabot ran.

Off into the shadows, trying to find that little park but what he found were shapes, long-armed shapes, dozens of them moving at him out of the mist. They were coming from every direction. He was in a nest of them. Grinning faces bloated with putrescence swam out of the fog. Spidery fingers clawed out for him. Gurgling voices called out. They were ringing him in, gliding forward like swarming insects.

Cabot turned and fired, ran to the left, fired, to the right and fired again. Fingers tore at his jacket and he swung the shotgun like a club, felt it smash into something soft and pulpy. More were coming and he needed to reload, but there just wasn't time.

He dove through a knot of Wormboys, hammered his way clear. He leaped over a hedge, crawled on his hands and knees through the grass. On his feet again, across a yard, around a house, down an alley. Behind him, they were coming, screaming and squealing, the stench of their numbers gaseous and revolting.

He cut through another yard, paused and fumbled shells into the shotgun.

And then a voice said: "Hey, mister! Over here!"

Cabot felt his heart gallop to a stop, lurch painfully, then start beating again. He turned and there was a little girl standing there in what looked like a white dress that had gone dark with filth. It hung in rags. Her face was as pale as the mist, her eyes huge and black and glistening with wetness. She held a finger like a skeleton key to her lips, said, "Sshhh!"

She began backing away between two ruined houses, arching a finger at him to follow. His breath lancing his throat, Cabot listened to the Wormboys gathering out there, sniffing out his trail. The girl could have been one of them and then, maybe not.

"Hurry! Or they'll get you!" she said.

He followed her, some electric instinct telling him to run, that this was a trap, a trap, but he was too scared to listen.

He followed.

The girl kept backing away, through the grass, around bushes and trees. Without even turning, she vaulted a heap of dead leaves. Cabot went after her, praying under his breath. He stumbled through the leaf pile and there was a sudden, unbelievable explosion of white agony in his ankle.

He went down, screaming, fighting, the shotgun going one way and he going the other.

The girl turned away, made a high whistling sound like a wind blown through catacombs. And as she did so, Cabot saw in his pain that the back of her head was mostly gone. Strands of dirty hair fell over a gaping, rotten chasm that boiled with meat flies.

She whistled again.

Dear God, she's signaling the others, calling out to them...

Cabot thrashed, trying to break free.

The pain tossed his mind into darkness and then yanked it back out again. His eyes irised open, blinking away tears, and he saw the girl. Just standing there, giggling softly, looking very pleased. Her eyes were larger than ever, oily and moist, filled with a raw-toothed hunger. A fly ran over her threadbare lips and she caught it with a gray tongue, sucked it into her mouth. Then she ate it, gums shriveled away from teeth that were black and overlapping, filed sharp.

As her insane laughter echoed into the night, Cabot reached down to his ankle to see what held it. The pain made white specks flash before his eyes.

A trap, oh yes, a trap.

A bear trap. The spikes were buried in his ankle, buried deep like the jaws of a tiger. He tried to force them apart and he nearly went out cold from the pain. His hands came away dark and dripping.

Two more figures came out of the darkness.

They stank like tombs.

Cabot screamed, but a pulpy, moist hand squeezed his mouth shut. Somewhere during the process, he fainted.

*

He woke later to the sound of humming.

Humming.

A woman's voice, but cracked and dry-sounding like her throat was packed with dirt and dead leaves. His eyes opened, shut, opened again. He was in a room that stank of old blood and rancid meat, a shocking rank odor. Candles were flickering on a mantle throwing greasy, wavering shadows in every direction.

The humming went on and on.

Beneath it was the near steady drone of flies.

Something crawled over his face but he dared not move.

He tried to remember, to make sense of it. There were only fleeting, maroon-tinged images of the fog, the things hunting in it. Then that evil little girl. The bear trap. Then...Jesus, just some distorted nightmare of him being dragged through the mist, dragged by the trap that snared his ankle, the agony throwing him into darkness.

You're in their lair, he thought then. *They've got you good.*

His leg was numb from the knee down and he didn't know if that was a good thing or not. But he knew the trap was gone. Without moving, without daring to give indication that he was even alive, he peered around. It looked like he was in a living room...or what had once been a living room. Stainless steel traps hung from chains on the walls. Old blood was spattered everywhere in loops and whorls. It looked black in the dirty light.

What the hell is this?

But by degrees, he began to understand.

He was dumped on the floor, resting in a pool of blood gone sticky and cold. All around him were hunched shapes, silent, stinking, netted with flies. Gutted torsos, gnawed limbs, sightless faces peeled to the bone. He was in a litter pile of human remains. He felt something inside him run wet and warm as he realized it. Not just the mantraps on the walls, but tables gleaming with cutlery, saws and axes. Candlelight was reflected off puddles of dried blood clotted with tissue and hair.

Flies filled the air in clouds, rising and descending to feed. They investigated his lips, his nostrils, dozens of them crawling over his wounded ankle. A maggoty head was at his left elbow, a cleaver sank in its skull.

A slaughterhouse.

He would have screamed, but what was the point? He had never been alone in his life as he was now. That humming. He craned his head precious inches. He saw a woman in the guttering light. Her hair was long and colorless, matted with tallow and dried blood. Her face was an obscenity. There was a skullish hollow where her nose had been, some cancerous ulceration chewing it away and spreading, leaving a gaping fleshless pit in the center of her face. A black chasm in which carrion beetles spawned. Her eyes were dark and glossy, her teeth jutting from a lipless maw.

She was humming.

Working on something.

Cabot craned his head a bit more and saw. She was kneeling before a cadaver, working it with a knife like a woman preparing a chicken for Sunday dinner. Sawing, cutting. She yanked out moist loops of bowel and glistening lumps of organ, separating them, threw a snakelike ribbon of entrails over her shoulder. Flies covered her, covered what she was working on. She hummed happily. Now she was reaching into cloth bags, sprinkling things into the hollowed belly. Seasoning it. Now stitching the gut closed with needle and thread.

Dear God.

Cabot was trembling. He couldn't help it. Then through the door came a man in the same shapeless, shroud-like rags the woman wore. His face was white and pulpy, threaded with segmented green worms. They didn't seem to bother him. He looped a rope around the cadaver's ankles, threw the other end over a roughhewn beam overhead. Together, they pulled and pulled until the body was dangling in the air, fingertips just brushing the floor.

They tied the rope off.

And that's when Cabot saw its face: Blaine.

It was the kid. Stupid, dumbass fucking kid. This is how it ended for him in this cannibal's lair, as meat. The knowledge of this made things unwind in Cabot until he felt hopeless, calm, senseless. The kid was just livestock to be slaughtered, dressed out and seasoned, aged for the dinner table.

Cabot knew he would be next.

The girl that had trapped him came hopping through the door on all fours. She went right over to him, pressing her vile flyblown face into his own. She licked his cheek with a scabrous tongue. Nibbled at his throat, his exposed belly, then downwards towards his ankle.

Oh not that, don't wake that ankle up.

The woman turned, putting red gleaming eyes on the girl. "Nah! Nah!" she cried out in a rasping voice that was full of grave dirt. "Not et one! The finding of the meat! The getting of the meat! Must be aged, must be soft!" She threw something towards the far wall. It might have been a heart. The girl scampered after it, began chewing and sucking on it.

So this is what it had come to? This was the malignant, loathsome sort of evolution that had been going on in graveyard towns like Mattawan. The dead were not just shambling in the streets and hiding in the shadows or hunting in packs...they had formed familial bonds of a sort, basal tribe-like hunting units. This is what had been going on in the shadows, the mortuaries, cellars and ruined houses. Breeding and evolving like crawly, slimy things beneath rotten logs.

Evolving.

Cabot did not move. He had not moved when the girl tasted him and he would not move now. They thought he was dead, so he would be dead. They were letting him cool before they dressed him out.

The man stumbled away and the woman followed him, muttering about the finding of meat, the stocking of meat, and the tasting and filling of meat. The girl tagged behind, crawling on all fours like an animal. Cabot heard stairs creaking as they went up to the second floor.

He waited.

Flies covered him, biting him, laying their eggs. Beetles crawled over his face.

He did not move.

*

Later, when Cabot opened his eyes, there was only silence.

The zombie family was gone.

He listened for a long time and only heard the flies, the rats that came out to feed upon the dead. He sat up, a brilliant thunderclap of pain in his leg. He dragged himself away from the corpses, through sticky pools of blood. Using a table, he pulled himself up. He could not put weight on his leg. He found a shovel in the corner.

A shovel? *Yes, of course a shovel. They've probably opened every grave in the county. When the truck comes from Hullville they probably get their share and bury it until it's soft and wormy the way they like it.*

He knew it couldn't be this easy.

He couldn't simply walk out of there without them knowing. But he did. He hobbled out of the room and through a door that was hanging from its hinges. The night air was damp and sour-smelling, but fresh compared to the house. His breath did not want to come, his ankle was throbbing, his body knotted with aches and pains, but he kept going. Even with the shovel as a crutch, he was every quiet. Through yards, across streets, down alleys. Moving by instinctive sense alone, he found the park.

The dead were not there.

He looked for them, but the mist was empty. Just decaying houses, collapsing fences, leaning and splintered telephone poles whose lines hung limp as spaghetti. The truck would not be far. He would find it, get in it, get away. Yes. He would pull the lever that opened the doors to release his cargo. The Wormboys would take care of the rest. Then he would go back, make up a story. Maybe crash the truck and call for a pick-up on the radio, say the dead had attacked, he'd released the cargo to draw them away.

Yes, yes.

Through the mist, the latticing of shadows.

The truck would be just ahead.

He stopped, suddenly roped tight with fear. He could hear...yes, grunting sounds, sucking sounds, chewing sounds. The stink of blood in the air was violent and overwhelming. He crept through the fog, knowing he had to see and then, hidden behind a bush, he did.

The doors were torn off the truck.

Jesus...look at that.

The rear door was open, lift gate down. The Wormboys were everywhere. They had released the cargo and fell on them in a starving mass. It was a sea of blood and bodies and entrails out there now, the dead squirming in the waste like worms, feeding and fighting, blood-slicked faces snapping up meat. A feeding frenzy. They bit the bodies in the streets, one another, even themselves.

Now was the time to get out.

Cabot hobbled away into the mist until he found the sign marking the perimeter of the town. Only then did he dare rest. But not for long. He moved down the road, weaving through the auto graveyard out there. And then...lights.

Headlights.

They were coming for him.

Thank God.

He stepped out, waving his arms. A truck. It slowed. Cabot fell over, just worn out and used up. He lay there, half-conscious, just breathing, just alive. Not much more.

"Help me with him," a voice said.

"Where...where you from?" he heard his voice ask.

"Moxton," the man said. "Moxton."

Hands on him. He was lifted gently into the truck. It was warm in there. He drifted off, feeling safe at last. It was good.

*

Later, Cabot opened his eyes.

There was darkness all around him. He heard people mumbling and sobbing, pushing against him, crawling over him. He tried to get up and he was knocked flat. He tried to talk to the people with him but he was not heard. With a slowly dawning horror, Cabot understood. Understood how that truck was from Moxton and not Hullville and in Moxton they did what they had to survive.

A great clicking. A groaning.

Moonlight pushing in as the rear doors of the truck opened.

People screaming.

Mist flooding into the bay like toxic steam. And in that mist, hulking shapes and morgue shadows with reaching arms and graying fingers. Graveyard faces specked with flies, faces gone to wormy white pulp, all grinning with long gnarled teeth and leering with glossy red eyes.

Cabot closed his eyes.

And waited his turn.

MORBID ANATOMY

"Who shall conceive the horrors of my secret toil,
as I dabbled among the unhallowed damps of the
grave, or tortured the living animal to animate
the lifeless clay?"

—Frankenstein, 1817

I

An Introduction and a Horror

Of my experiences in the Great War with Dr. Herbert West, I
speak of only with the greatest hesitation, loathing, and horror. For it
was to the flooded, corpse-filled trenches that we came in 1915.
Perhaps I held some naïve patriotic and nationalistic motives of
serving mankind and saving the lives of the war wounded—a state of
mind induplicable once the truth of war is known—but with Herbert
West it was never the case. Openly he disparaged the Hun, but secretly
our commission in the 1st Canadian Light Infantry was merely a means
to an end. You see, my colleague's motives were hardly altruistic.
Though a surgeon of exceptional, almost supernatural skill, a biomedical
savant and scientific wunderkind, West's lifelong obsession was not
with the living but the dead: the reanimation of lifeless tissue and
particularly the revivication of human remains. And in the war itself
and the horrid by-products it produced like some great fuming factory of
death, he saw the perfect environment for his arcane research...not to
mention unlimited access to plentiful raw materials.
I came to the war as West's colleague, yes, but I felt deep inside
that I was answering the subtle call of a higher power, that I—and my

surgical skill—were the instruments of good in a theater of evil. I arrived with high ideals and within a year, I departed Flanders, hollow-eyed, broken, my faith in mankind hanging by a tenuous thread. For many months, the memories struggled within me, stillborn shadows of pestilence—living, crawling, and filling my throat until, at times, I could not swallow nor draw a solitary gasping breath.

If that seems a trifle melodramatic, then let the uninitiated consider this:

Flanders, 1915.

A cramped, claustrophobic maze of waterlogged trenches cutting into the blasted earth like deep-hewn surgical scars. Throughout the long misty days and into the dark dead of night, machine-guns clattering and high-velocity shells bursting, the thumping of trench mortars and the choking cries of gassed soldiers tangled in the barbwire ramparts. The stink of burned powder, moist decomposition, and excrement. Rotting corpses sinking into seas of slopping brown mud. Rats swarming atop the sandbags. Flares going up and shells coming down. And death. Dear God, Death running wild, sowing and reaping, gathering His grim harvest in abundance as the bodies piled up and the rain fell.

It was just the sort of place where a man of Herbert West's peculiar talents would thrive.

Unlike I who held faith in the existence of the human soul and its ascension, upon death, unto the throne of God, West held no such misconceptions (as he put it). He was a scientific materialist, a confirmed Darwinist, and to him the soul was a religious fantasy and the Church existed only as a political entity to oppress and control the masses for its own remunerative ends. Life was mechanistic by nature, he claimed, organic machinery that could be manipulated at will. And if I had doubted such a thing, he proved it repeatedly with a reagent he had developed that galvanized life into the dead...often with the most unspeakable results.

Even now, these many years later, I can see West—thin, pale, his blue eyes burning with a supernal intensity behind his spectacles—as he sorted through the piles of corpses, whispering off-color remarks to me and giggling with his low cold laughter as he scavenged about like a butcher selecting only the finest cuts...a clot of gut, a stray undamaged organ, a particularly well-proportioned limb or the rare intact cadaver. I can see corpses floating in flooded bomb craters and the black clouds of seeking corpseflies. And I can see the terrified eyes of young men about to go over the top in search of their graves.

I can see Flanders.

I can see West's workshop—a converted barn—part surgical theater and part laboratory of diabolical creation. I can see things in jars and vessels of bubbling serum...remains that should have been dead but were horribly animate with a semblance of ghoulish life. I can see the headless body of Major Sir Eric Moreland Clapham-Lee that West had reanimated. And I can hear the Major's head crying out from its vat of steaming reptile tissue right before German shell-fire brought the structure down in a blazing heap.

But worse, far worse, are the dreams that come for me in the blackest marches of night. For I see Michele. Articulated, wraithlike...she comes to me like a jilted lover in the night. She wears a white bridal gown like a flowing shroud. It is spattered with mud and gory drainage, threaded with mold and infested with insects. I can clearly hear them buzzing and clicking. I can smell her odor which is flyblown and fusty, equal parts mildew and filth and grave earth. She comes to me with outstretched arms and I seek her as fast. Her bridal train is discolored, ragged, worried by plump graveyard rats whose stink is the stench of the darkest, moldering trenches of Flanders. When her arms embrace me I shiver for I can feel the grave-cold of her flesh, the coffin-worms writhing in her shroud. I gag on her stink.

She does not kiss me.

For she has no head.

2

The Walking Dead

Creel had been in Flanders for four months, embedded with the 12th Middlesex, when he got invited on a little raiding party that was being thrown together. No volunteers were asked for. The sergeants went down the forward trench, picking men at random like apples from a barrel and none of them were too happy with the idea.

Somehow, he had thought there would be a little more military precision involved in such a thing, but it was no different than anything else in that war. *Eenie, meanie, miney, mo.* Looking at the dour faces of the selected, Creel asked Sergeant Burke what would happen if one refused to go.

Burke got that pained expression on his face that Creel so often seemed to inspire. He was Creel's aid. His job was to stay by Creel's side, keep him in one piece if possible and keep him out of trouble...if such a thing were feasible.

"Well, they'd replace him, wouldn't they?" Burke said. "Then they'd march him out and shoot him."

Creel wrote that down, amused by his own question.

Being a journalist, he was there out of the mutual suffering of the general staff and the line officers. The Brits already had their own carefully-controlled correspondents, they didn't need some Yank from the Kansas City *Star* coming in and mucking things up with his glib tongue and saucy manner, but President Roosevelt had pushed the British on the matter. Saying that if American correspondents were not embedded with British and Canadian units, it would harm the war effort...in other words, if the proper spin wasn't presented to the American public *by* Americans, he'd never be able to get the public to swallow the idea of committing troops and dollars.

So the British Expeditionary Force submitted and the BEF did not like submitting to anything.

There were four men in the raiding party: Sergeant Kirk, Corporal Smallhouse, Privates Jacobs and Cupperly. In addition to his Enfield rifle and fixed bayonet, Jacobs carried fifty rounds of ammunition. Kirk was the grenade man. He carried a haversack filled with Mills bombs. Smallhouse was a grenade thrower, too. Last in line was Cupperly, another rifleman with fifty rounds in his bandolier.

Two other raiding parties led by two other sergeants would be going out as well.

"We're going to go out and play naughty schoolboy," Kirk said, grinning. "Our job is to annoy, disrupt, and cause trouble. A burr in the Hun's behind, that's us. A merry lark it shall be."

Creel found it interesting how Kirk, who was a pretty decent guy by all accounts, really enjoyed these raids. There was a mischievous gleam in his eye and a crooked smile to his face like the appointed task was a bit of boyhood deviltry like tipping over privies or putting wormy apples on the teacher's desk.

With Burke and Creel tagging behind, they went over the top at nightfall and into the muddy, corpse-strewn waste of No-Man's Land. Faces blackened, moving like shadows, they crept at a low crouch or crawled through the mud, legions of corpse-eating rats moving in dark rivers around them. On his belly, Kirk cut them a hole through the wire and within minutes they spotted two German forward sentries. Jacobs and Cupperly took them out silently, rising like shades behind them and clubbing them over the heads with the butts of their rifles, then bayoneting them in the throats. It took very little time and the only noise was the impact of rifle butts against helmets and the sound of blood bubbling from gored throats.

Silently then, the raiders dropped into the first line of trenches which were well ahead of the main German trench system. They crept their way through, moving from bay to bay, tossing grenades when they heard movement. They killed half a dozen Hun this way. It was quite efficient, Creel thought, and the element of surprise was a big part of it. There had been an artillery barrage less than an hour before which drove the Germans from their trenches and into their sandbagged dugouts on higher ground. The only men left behind were sentries and they paid with their lives as all three raiding parties moved fast, clearing trenches and stealing equipment, destroying anything they couldn't take with them.

Burke told Creel later that it was a near-perfect raid, for usually the Germans heard them cutting through the wire and opened up with machine-gun fire.

The three parties combined cleared over four-hundred feet of trench before they heard a German reaction force mounting a counterattack.

The raiders slipped out of the trenches with three prisoners, running and stumbling back to their own lines. All in all, it was a crazy, heart-pounding sort of way to spend a few hours.

One of the captured Germans was an old white-haired sergeant with only two teeth left in his mouth. He had surrendered instantly, throwing up his arms and shouting, "Kamerad!"

"Lot of them give up easy like that," Burke said. "Just glad to be out of this bloody war."

The prisoners were taken into one of the British dugouts where they could be interrogated by the intelligence officer. Creel and Burke and a few others waited there with them. Creel gave the old sergeant a cigarette and he grinned with those near-empty gums. He smoked the cigarette, muttering, "Kamerad," under his breath again and again as if to reinforce the point. But after a time, he began to look very grim, jabbering on incessantly and pointing in the direction of No-Man's Land. "Die toten...die toten!" he began to cry out, his eyes as dark as burnt cinders. "Die toten...die toten dieser spaziergang! Das tote wandern! Die toten dieser spaziergang!"

"Quit yer yabbering," Burke told him.

But if it was yabbering, then it was some of the most unusual yabbering that Creel had heard in that war. Maybe his German wasn't the best, but what the sergeant was saying was all too clear and the fear behind it unmistakable.

The dead, he was saying. *The dead that walk.*

That's when Creel began to get a few ideas and getting them, smelled blood in the water.

3

Memento Mori

The Germans mounted a small, inconsequential, half-hearted offensive that left their corpses scattered about the perimeter like rice after a wedding. The rain fell, bloating the corpses, puffing them up into particularly unpleasant white mounds of decomposition that flowered weird growths of fungi. Though the stink of them was no worse than the usual smell of Flanders, they did season things up to the point where the officers were complaining and that got action. A small group was sent out to bury them in a mass grave.

Creel went with, taking his little box-shaped Brownie camera with him and getting some nice shots of the cadavers. He had quite a collection by that point: corpses blown up into trees, tangled in the wire, sinking in the mud, nested by rats, and—his favorite—a Hun officer who'd been machine-gunned but was held upright in a casual sort of stance by a sharp oak branch that had speared him through the back. When Creel had snapped that one, many months after the First Battle of Ypres, the officer had been nearly picked down to bones by the local ravens and buzzards—sparrows nesting in his ribcage and skull—and he looked very much like a skeleton on a jaunty afternoon stroll, steel helmet tipped at a rakish angle.

It became an obsession for Creel in that war to collect photographs of the dead as it had in other wars he had covered. The Tommies either politely ignored him or were openly offended by what he was doing.

"Why?" Burke asked him one day. "Why do you want pictures of that? Your paper won't print such things."

Creel had laughed as he always laughed at the question: a cool, bitter sort of laugh. "I do it because I don't understand death. I don't understand the process of life becoming death."

"Nothing to understand, mate. You get it or you don't get it, saavy? Me mum would say it's God's province."

"Yes, God's province, but man's suffrage."

The day after the Hun were shoveled into a mass grave, the BEF put together their own little counterattack and with similar results. The trenchlines were stagnant and had been for months, the only thing that ever changed was the amount of corpses left to boil in the sun and melt into the mud of Flanders like wax effigies.

Afterwards, Creel watched the walking wounded coming in—grimy, mud-caked, fatigued, bloody—with their slings and bandages, none of them speaking as if the war had erased their voices and turned them into mutes. They shuffled along, limping and hobbling on swollen feet, a procession of the maimed and he got the feeling that when they signed on beneath the grim shadows of Kitchener posters (WE WANT YOU!), they hadn't expected it to be like this. All of them had the same dead tombstone eyes gray as puddles of rain. The only difference between them and the dead spread across No-Man's Land is that they were walking.

Die toten dieser spaziergang?

Without a doubt.

The stretcher bearers brought the real bad ones over to the ambulances for a trip to Battalion Aid or the Casualty Clearing Station and most of them would die before they got there. Creel liked to hang around and catch whatever after-action gossip he could. He listened to three men, blinded by gas, eyes patched with gauze, discuss what they had seen out there and it was more of the same. The gas came down on them in a mushrooming, rolling green cloud, they said, that appeared a luminous yellow by the time it reached them, blown by eastern winds. Then the Hun let loose with a massive barrage of shell-fire and smudge canisters that enveloped the battlefield in a pungent white smoke thick as London fog. Men got lost. They charged in the wrong direction. They fell into flooded shell holes and drowned. Some sank without a trace in the yellow-brown mud. The combined gas and smoke smelled like sulfur, one man insisted. No, more like ether, yes definitely ether, said another. But the third claimed it was the odor of rosin. They could not agree on that but they did agree that hundreds died, both Hun and BEF hard-chargers, suffocating on the fumes, choking, gagging, lungs dissolved to yellow froth that spilled from shrieking mouths.

Creel walked amongst the wounded and discovered that some of them had been out there for days following the last offensive, lying in craters in the falling rain, no food, no water, fighting off the rats who were attracted by the raw, meaty smell of their injuries. Many of them were stark mad and many others in good spirits despite the fact that their wounds were crawling with maggots.

Long after the stretcher bearers and ambulances had moved on, Creel was still standing there in the gray afternoon drizzle listening to the distant thump of artillery pieces and the much closer flapping of sheets that covered the dead at his feet. He took snapshots of them and particularly those where his own dark shadow had fallen over them like Death coming to collect His due.

Smoking a cigarette and muttering things under his breath that even he was not aware of, he stood amongst them, breathing in the cool coppery odor of shattered anatomy and the hot smell of infection, filthy dressings, and corpse gas.

He did not feel as if he were alone.

An asphyxiating, cold-crawling fear took hold of him and he could not put a name to it. Only that it was all around him, a pall of rising black death, an unearthly possessed malignant intelligence that seemed to be standing just behind him and breathing cold catacomb breath down the back of his neck. He felt like he was bathing in it. When it passed, he was on his knees, panting, shaking, ignoring a wild, insane urge to lay down with the dead and close his eyes so he might know what they knew.

And in his head, over and over and over again, that German voice: *Die toten dieser spaziergang.*

4

Corpse Rats

At night, the rats would come out.

Like some black pipe had ruptured, they'd flood out in numbers from hidey-holes and warrens, filthy nests out in the barbwire and crawlspaces beneath the sandbagged ramparts. Some of the Tommies said they lived inside corpses out in No-Man's Land, chewing a hollow in the belly where they could bring their young to term in putrescent darkness.

Regardless, they'd come surging out, swarming, infesting, feeding off the dead, biting the living, scavenging for food scraps, crawling through refuse heaps, and even eating leather boots and belts...quite often while some poor bastard was wearing them. Numbering in the millions, they knew no fear. They ran through the trenches in numbers, crawling over men whether asleep or awake. They were huge, gray things, fattened on carrion, rabid eyes beady, pelts greasy with slime and drainage, teeth forever gnawing and chewing and nipping.

They were a constant of war. When there was a lull in the action and the Tommies got bored scraping their tunics free of nits, they'd shoot rats off the sandbags or bait them with bacon on the muzzles of their rifles. When a nest was found, they'd kick the rats to death with their heavy boots and stomp the young...not that it thinned their numbers any. Sometimes enterprising young officers, new to the trenches and horrified by the idea of sharing them with mulling rodents, would rat-proof the dugouts with wire netting, spending hours and hours at it only to discover four or five rats crowding under their dinner table looking for scraps.

War produced refuse and human wreckage and that brought the rats. It was a vicious cycle and there was only one cure for it: peace.

5

Casualties

The Germans broke up a fierce dawn raid by the 12th with a chemical attack, a combination of mustard gas and chlorine. Quite a few men had gotten enveloped in yellow clouds of death before they got their masks on. Creel volunteered to go out that night beneath the light of the moon with a burial party. The Germans would be doing the same and it would be something of an unofficial ceasefire while what could be collected was collected.

"Bloody hell," Sergeant Burke said when he got wind of things. "What the hell'd you get us into this time? A pissing burial detail?"

"Come on, Burke," Creel said. "Just a little walk out into No-Man's Land."

"I've been out there more times than I'd like to recollect."

"This time no one will shoot at you."

Burke grunted. "So says you."

That afternoon, they took a ride on an ambulance with the last of the gas survivors to Number Four Rest Camp. There were wounded aplenty amongst the neat rows of peaked hospital tents, but most of the men seemed quite fit, Creel thought. Groups of Tommies were in the fields digging graves, sweating rivers, while a sergeant-major stomped about swearing at them and snapping a riding crop against his leg.

"What gives here?" Creel said.

Burke laughed. "Oi, don't be so bleeding silly, mate. What you think is going on here? These boys is got the jack, near everyone of them."

"The jack?"

"Aye, the clap, the crawlies in the ballies, the old Syph. The pox."

Creel got it then: syphilis. As they toured the camp they learned in bits and pieces that there was something of a pandemic of venereal disease laying unit after unit low. The War Office was losing its patience with the situation and there was a posting on the notice board from Lord Kitchener himself saying something to the effect that in the future, any man rendered unfit for active duty because of VD would suffer an appalling fate: his wife, parents, or relatives would be informed in writing of his condition and *how* he had contracted it.

Those with the pox were in camp to go through a new German treatment called 606 which involved mercury injections.

Creel scribbled it all down in his notebook.

"You don't think they'll let you print that, now do you?" Burke said and Creel told him that one day the war would be over and he would be back in the states and when that happened he was going to write a book about it, tell it the way it was not the watered-down, censored claptrap the press corps allowed.

The problem with VD, Creel was told by the Medical Officer, was that many French women were in a desperate state. Their men were off fighting the Hun. Even old men were being conscripted, anyone that could hold a rifle. So these women had no way to buy food or feed their children, so they turned to the oldest trick in the book.

A cheeky private from the Royal Artillery told Creel exactly how it worked: "You get these old haybags what will put anything inside 'em, see? You give 'em a five-franc note and they takes you into this dirty old room with a dirty old bed in the corner. Then, quick as you please, sir, she undoes your fly and has herself a feel and a squeeze to see if you've got the pus or any such foulness. Then off come her knickers and such a sight that is. If it don't cool yer business, then in you go. And when yer done sweatin' and puffin', she has herself a boiling kettle and gives you a cuppa with herbs and brews and what not for disease's sake."

Creel wrote it all down already figuring on a chapter reserved to prostitution and vice in his book. It was going to be a good one and when he told Burke about it he couldn't stop laughing.

"Your brain is not strictly right, Mr. Creel," he said.

Creel took a few shots of the men burying the dead because he could not help himself. He was drawn to it. Burke got him out of there as some of the diggers looked ready to add another corpse to their collection.

On the way back to the front, he tried to get Burke to speak of his experiences with the London Rifles. He'd won the Victoria Cross at the Battle of Aisne for single-handedly capturing a German machine-gun and dispatching the crew that manned it, then turning it on the Germans themselves and mowing them down in ranks. But Burke didn't want to talk about that.

Instead:

"A lot of the boys had dysentery so bad they slit open the arses of their trousers so they could shit while they were fighting," he said without a trace of humor. "Nothing can take away a man's dignity like fouling himself every five bloody minutes. You're sent here to fight in the trenches with rats and lice, corpses rotting at your feet, and you get trench fever and dysentery. What kind of fucking war is that, I ask you?"

He went on to tell a tale of the men of the London Rifles fighting with their trousers at their ankles, so riddled with dysentery—or "the screaming squats" as he called it—were they. A sergeant named Holmes that they'd all cherished for his wit and common sense and fatherly, fair treatment of the boys in his platoon had gotten dysentery so bad that he could no longer walk. He crawled about, white and trembling, his pants down, his backside and shirt fouled brown with his own shit. They kept watch on him but he'd crawled off to the latrine trench at some point and been so weak with it, that he'd fallen into the slime and hadn't the strength to climb free. He'd drowned in a vile, fly-specked pool of excrement.

6

Burial Detail

By six that night, Creel and Burke were back at the trenches and then it was off with the burial detail which Burke was still grumbling about. Sergeant Haines formed up his burial party and they went over the top into No-Man's Land. They carried gas masks because gas was still clinging to hollows and low spots. German burial parties came within a few yards of them but were ignored as they ignored the Tommies.

The mud was thick and slopping when they stepped off the duckboards, sinkholes sucking men right up to their waists at times and it was a real struggle pulling them back out. The corpses were everywhere, some jutting from the mud and some floating atop it, all of them yellow with gas, blistered, limbs contorted, death-white fingers clutching at their throats, bubbling tangles of yellow vomit hanging from their mouths along with regurgitated chunks of their lungs.

It was ghastly work.

Since sniper fire was not a worry, the men carried shaded lanterns with them and more than once they stopped as scurrying trains of rats came up from flooded burrows and bomb craters, immense things that paid them no mind, squeaking and chewing on the dead, dipping their snouts into freshly gored throats and tunneling into the bellies of corpses.

Twice the burial party paused when the wan circle of light revealed hundreds of leering red eyes watching them.

If I only had my damn camera and some light to shoot with, Creel thought.

The rain fell in a clammy mist and pockets of groundfog twisted around their legs as they pulled their boots out of the muck and carefully took yet another step, the noxious stench of the unburied dead fuming about them. They saw lots of bodies or fragments of the same that had been there a long time, most of them nothing but well-gnawed skeletons. They found the skull of a German in the barbwire, its helmet still in place...someone had put a cigar butt in its teeth. Battle-ravaged cadavers rose from the sucking yellow mud like leaning white tombstones, rats moving in black verminous armies around them. One of the

226

Tommies stepped into a pool of mud and sank into the soft white mush of a dozen bloated Hun corpses. He nearly went out of his mind before they yanked him free.

The night was tenebrous, the air dank and cloying. Now and again, they could hear the Germans cry out as they made some grisly discovery.

"Bloody hell," Burke muttered when he stepped on a body and three or four oily rats escaped the abdomen with meat in their jaws.

Creel found a corpse that was moving and Haines, using his bayonet, discovered why soon enough: there was a rat nest inside it. Worked into a mad frenzy, he slashed the adults into ribbons and stomped the blind squirming pups to paste.

Haines told them to don their gas masks when they started to see dozens and dozens of rats creeping about on their bellies like great fleshy slugs. They'd all been poisoned by the gas and were dying in numbers. A couple of the Tommies started kicking them like footballs, giggling as they went sailing away into the brown slop.

About thirty minutes into it, they found three corpses tangled together at the edge of a run of duckboard. They were men from the 12th and Haines and the others recognized them, despite the fact that they were covered in yellow slime.

"Look here," Haines said. "Rats again."

The bellies of all three had been hollowed out quite thoroughly, even the flesh of their throats were missing. Haines and the others stood around in their bug-eyed masks, swearing and kicking at anything handy while Burke had a closer look. He waved away clouds of flies that were thick as a blanket.

"See?" he said to Creel, out of earshot of the others, pointing to great gashes and punctures in the bones of exposed ribs by lantern light. "Ain't no rat ever born had teeth like that. Too big."

"Dogs?"

But Burke just shook his head and would not say.

"Footprints over here...small ones," one of the Tommies said.

They went over to the duckboard and there was a crowding of muddy footprints on it which was not so surprising except for two things: they were the prints of bare feet and very, very small.

"Children," Burke said. "Children's prints."

"Out here?" Haines said, stripping off his mask and mopping his sweaty, mottled face. There was something quite akin to stark horror in his eyes. "No kids...not out here..."

But the evidence was unmistakable: children had been out in No-Man's Land stalking about barefoot. It seemed inconceivable, but to each man standing there, there was no denying what they were seeing. Sometimes mud could expand in size with the dampness, make prints larger than they were but certainly not smaller.

Nobody said anything for some time and Creel thought that moment would be burned into his brain forever: the Tommies standing around, ankle-deep in the Flanders mud, rain running down those grim gas masks, mist coiling about them, corpses rotting in the muck.

And as he framed that moment in his mind with something quite near to hysteria, a voice in the back of his head said: *The prints of children. Children are out scavenging No-Man's Land by night. Barefoot children. And these bodies have been eaten by something that is not rats or a wild dog, Burke says. You don't dare make the connection because it would be insane to do so....yet, yet you know something is terribly, dreadfully wrong with this scenario. You can feel it in your guts, in your bones, in the shadowy recesses of your soul.*

"Heard a story once about—" one of the Tommies started to say and Haines jumped on him, took hold of him and shook him wildly. *"You'll shut up with that talk! Do you hear me? You'll shut up with it!"*

After that, solemn as only undertakers can be, they finished up their work quickly, each man suddenly very aware of the long shadows stretching around them and what might be hiding in them. They wasted no time in getting back to the trenches.

For there was something damnably unnatural haunting No-Man's Land and they all knew it.

7

Tall Tales

The Tommies, when they gathered in the dugouts to warm their fingers about the glowing little coal brazier at night, their bellies warmed from the daily rum ration, would start telling crazy tales by the light of the moon. And maybe sometimes that was because they had a story to tell and sometimes because they just needed to hear their own voices.

Creel understood that part of it just fine.

After a particularly violent barrage in the Le Touquet sector by German 18-pounders, whizz-bangs, which blew sandbags into fragments, a young private from the 2nd Lancashire Fusiliers with eyes like smoked glass kept touching his arms and legs and chest in the observation trench.

Standing there, knee-deep in the frozen mud, Creel said, "It's okay, son. You're still intact."

"Oi, it's not that, sir," said the private, touching his grime-streaked face. "It's not that at all, you see. It's just...well, I'm making sure I'm *solid* and what, not a ghost. One minute you're solid as brick, the next naught but a ghost drifting about."

In the trenches where death came so swiftly there was a real need to prove to yourself that you were truly alive, a thing of flesh and blood. When you spent week after miserable week living in what amounted to sandbagged ditches with freezing drizzle raining down on you, ears ringing from machine-gun fire, the pitted landscape a cratered run of barbwire and unburied corpses lit at night by flickering green flares...it all became very surreal. And the need to prove to yourself that you were not in some desolate hell or purgatory whiling away eternity became very strong.

Creel had felt it himself more than once.

Scribbling down the vagaries of life in the trenches, the madness was always there and he was mute witness to it. Very often, it vented itself in the form of stories. Particularly after a fierce action or raid, like bad blood that had to be lanced.

He'd heard about monstrous packs of rats that took down living men. About visions of Christ and the Virgin Mother in the trenches. The phantoms of dead men patrolling the perimeters. And from one particularly terrified sergeant of the King's Royal Rifle Corps, he'd heard about a creature half-bird and half-woman, a hag that fed on corpses (later he learned that was an old one, so old it had hair growing on it, a twice-told battlefield tale that predated the days of Cromwell).

But he was a realist.

Seventeen years as a combat correspondent will do that. It will leech the poetry from your soul and sometimes that's not a bad thing. War, any war, is bad enough without a fertile imagination complicating things.

But after the burial party...and what that German sergeant had said...he began thinking differently.

It was the state of those corpses and the footprints that haunted him for days afterwards. Maybe it meant nothing at all...yet, his mind would not let go of it. Over and over again, it went through what he'd seen out there and he began to get that feeling in his gut he hadn't had in years...the sense that he was onto something. And when that feeling grew strong, when he smelled the blood in the water, he knew he'd have to track it to its source, one way or another.

But he went slow.

He went easy.

When you were in his position, there by the good graces of the BEF—even if their reasons weren't exactly altruistic—you could not make waves. He wasn't like some of the British newsies, guys like John Buchan or Valentine Williams, Henry Nevinson or Hamilton Fife, established accredited war correspondents. They had been selected by the Brits to shovel out the propaganda and were doing a bang-up job at it, steering the British public away from the godawful truth of the war and finely tuning their misguided perception of a valiant struggle against the bloodthirsty savage Hun (with only light, acceptable losses, of course). If they knew the truth of what was being done with their sons and husbands, brothers and fathers in the meatgrinders of the trenches, there would be rioting in the streets.

Creel was offended by censored news.

Maybe his own stories were watered down, but he did manage to keep a somewhat despairing undercurrent to them. He would not be a tool of corrupt politicians regardless of what side of the Atlantic they spawned on.

But he knew he had to be careful.

He had to step light.

So he didn't make much noise at first, he just listened.

And he kept hearing the same thing again and again: there was something out there. Something that wasn't a man. Something that fed on the wounded and dying. He jotted it all down in his notebook, thinking it was the sort of thing that might spice up yet another dreary account of war.

Then three men of the 12th disappeared from a listening post a stone's throw from the German forward trenches. And this after not one but two wire-cutting parties failed to return.

"It's nothing but the Jerries," Sergeant Haines said. "They snuck up on 'em, took 'em prisoner. Them Jerries is quite good at things like that."

It was always possible. But Sergeant Stone, who'd led the three, was extremely capable.

"So when are you going out?" Creel asked him.

"Tomorrow," Haines said. "We'll have a bit of a look. Be a morning mist coming in."

"I want to go with."

"You?"

"Yes."

The sergeant sighed. "All right. But you carry rifle and kit like the rest. If you lag, you're left behind."

8

No-Man's Land

Haines was right about the mist: it came with the dawn, white and fuming, a perfect enveloping wall that obscured everything, turned all the wreckage out in No-Man's Land to gray indistinct shapes. As the sun rose higher and higher, it did not dissipate. It seemed to be steaming from the broken, mud-slicked ground itself. It fell over the trenches like a shroud and visibility was down to ten or twelve feet. Creel could hear the men and the clank of their equipment but not see them.

There was no time to admire the fog as the officers and sergeants called for the men to "stand to" and up on the fire step they went, bayonets fixed to guard against a dawn raid. It was the same every day. Afterwards came what the Tommies called the "morning hate" in which both sides exchanged machine-gun fire and some light shelling just to relieve the tension of waiting. It didn't last long. The soldiers stood down, cleaned rifles and equipment, were inspected by the officers.

"Hear you're coming for a walk with us," Corporal Kelly said to Creel as they breakfasted on hard bread, bacon, and biscuits.

"Thought I might," Creel told him.

"Won't be good out there, sir," Kelly said, shielding his rations from a light falling rain. "If I was you, I'd change me mind. You don't have to go but we do."

There was no getting past the dread underlying his words, but was that the understandable fear of the enemy or was it something else? Creel didn't ask. No sense getting any of the boys worked up and nervous like he was.

"The bloody situations you get me in," Burke said to him as he had a cigarette. "Think I'd be safer in combat."

"Something's going on out there," Creel told him, "and I have to find out what."

"Still on that, mate?" Burke said.

"Yes, and I'm going to be on it until I figure it out. You can't tell me you don't sense it like I sense it. It's there. Something incredible. Something unreal."

That made Burke laugh. "You believing them stories? Old Creel? The kingpin of cynical bastards everywhere? Cor, I didn't know you had it in you."

"You saw those prints. You felt something out there."

But Burke wouldn't have it. "Not me, not me. Didn't feel a thing. And I didn't on account I like to sleep at night."

The mist still held thick after breakfast and Haines gathered them together—Creel, Burke, Kelly, and a Private known as Scratch because of his lice infestations—and they climbed up on the fire step. Captain Croton scanned the perimeter with his trench periscope. "Right," he said. "Good time as any."

As they went over the sandbags, Creel understood the fear that ate at every man on the line. As foul and disgusting as the trenches were, there was safety in them and out beyond was death waiting, hiding in every draw and pocket. They crawled over the muddy ground, slipping through breaks in the barbwire ramparts that were tangled with bird-picked skeletons, and soon enough they were out in No-Man's Land.

Though the fog was still heavy, Creel could see the shattered landscape of shell-holes, oozing pink clay and pooling brown mud, heaps of pulverized brick. There had been a forest or wood here at one time and now it was just a wasteland of stumps and limbless trees rising up like telegraph poles amongst sucking black mud holes crisscrossed by duckboard.

"All of you stay behind me," Haines said. "Stay on the duckboard and be quiet."

"Do what the bloody git says," Burke said under his breath.

"What was that?"

"Nothing, Sergeant," said Burke, grinning.

Gripping his Enfield, sixty pounds of fighting kit on his back, Creel did as he was told as they moved single file down the duckboard which seemed to sink into the mud as their weight pressed down upon it. Dirty water sloshed over their ankles and the stink of putrescence rose from pools of muck that were inundated with assemblages of corpses, maggoty and green, white bone shining through graying hides. Corpse-flies filled the air with a steady low buzzing. Out in the mist, he could hear the splashing and squeaking of rats.

How Haines navigated, he did not know. No sun, no stars, nothing but the repetitious expanse of stumps and sinkholes, the rain coming down in sheets, bomb craters bubbling with brown water, a muddy slime sluicing over the duckboard itself. But Haines was an old hand. He'd been in the trenches since the beginning, fighting amongst the slapheaps and pitheads of the Mons coalfields and leading suicidal charges against German Jager Battalions at the Battle of Marne. Maybe he had the intelligence and personality of a toad, but he knew his business.

The duckboard sank away just ahead but they stayed on it, feeling it beneath them as they waded through thigh-deep water that was cold and heavy, floating with branches and abandoned ration tins and empty rusting cordite cans, all matter of refuse. Rats swam from one heap to the next, huge things, bloated and greasy. The duckboard carried them up out of the swamp and soon enough there was no more duckboard—just the remains of the forest ahead, the shafts of blackened trees like graveyard monuments, crowded, leaning, strung with rusting barbwire, mist like white lace drifting about their trunks.

Haines led on and the muck was up to their knees but thankfully got no deeper. The sergeant let them rest a moment while he took a bearing with his compass. There were rags and bones, boots and helmets everywhere as if the moist, steaming earth had regurgitated a meal of men. Scratch and Kelly sorted around a bit, finding shell casings and old Lewis gun drums, scaring carrion crows from the remains of Hun soldiers.

"Look at this," Scratch said, holding up a German helmet with a bullet hole channeled neatly through it. "He took it in the head, poor bastard."

"Aye, but it was quick, weren't it?" Kelly said, gnawing on some canned Bully Beef.

"You eating again?" Burke said.

"I'm hungry."

"Swear you got the worms or something."

"Pipe down," Haines told them, reading his compass.

Creel sat there smoking, clicking off a few shots of the wreckage around him with his Brownie. He did not need to be there at all and he knew it. He could have had a soft, cushy job back home in Kansas City. He rated an editor's job, but here he was in this misting netherworld of rats and crows, carrion and mud. He didn't belong here...then again, he hadn't belonged in the Balkan Wars or the Mexican Revolution, the Second Boer War or the Boxer Rebellion, but he'd been there and now he was here.

War and the litter it produced, always drew him.

Sighing, he watched Kelly and Scratch.

Just kids. That's all they were. Maybe the atrocities of the trenches had bleached the innocence from their eyes and replaced it with a perfect hollow glaze of indifference, but they were still kids. He watched them scavenging, playing in the mud while Burke just shook his head. They found the fully articulated skeleton of a Hun officer gripping a tree trunk for dear life. They could not pry him loose...he had grown into the tree with ropy tendrils of decay like the fibers of woodrot threading through a deserted house.

Haines gave the word and they moved on, splashing through the muck, rain running from the brims of their steel helmets. It grew very quiet. Nothing moved. Nothing scurried. Water dripped from the trees, but little else. The mist blew around them in churning clouds. Creel wiped a mixture of cold sweat and colder rain from his face, very much aware of the beat of his heart. His greatcoat and mud-slicked boots seemed like concrete. He thought if he stopped completely he would simply sink away. He was seeing things moving around them, but he knew it was imagination...ghosting, long-armed forms at the periphery of his vision.

"Down," Burke suddenly said.

They crouched in the mud, not seeing anything or hearing anything...then three ghostly forms emerged from the fog: a German reconnaissance patrol, faces blackened, bayonets fixed. They moved with an eerie silence over the boggy ground, not muttering a word. They faded into the mist and Creel could not be certain that they hadn't actually *been* ghosts.

Ten minutes later, fighting through mud pools and crawling over the exposed roots systems of blasted trees, they sighted the trench system and ruined dugout Sergeant Stone and his men had been using. Creel could see a nearly-obliterated sandbag rampart enclosing a series of trenches flooded with a slimy yellow muck which bobbed with rat corpses. There was a crumbling brick wall that looked like the remains of a house or hut that had taken direct hits from heavy artillery. A single dead tree rose up above it, hooded crows gathered on its remaining branches.

They moved closer, spread out now so that a single volley of machine-gun fire could not cut them all down in a single sweep.

A crow squawked.

Rain fell.

And for each man, dread moved in their bellies.

Creel put a cigarette in his mouth and it was sodden with the rain almost immediately.

"Go easy here, gov," Burke told him, a guiding hand on his shoulder. "My back's up. We're being watched. Sure we are."

Creel looked around but could see nothing. Yet, he could almost feel eyes, watching eyes, staring out at them from the gathering fog.

Rats scratched over the sandbags, dozens of them sitting atop the broken wall as if waiting for something. Creel nearly stepped on a bloated white corpse and then jumped back when he saw not two but three rats come out of the torso in a steady march. They hissed at him and went on their way.

"Kelly, I want you off to the left flank," Haines said. "Scratch...the right. Secure the area. Creel, with me."

Burke went along. Haines did not include him by name because he did not like him. Burke had the VC and Haines was livid with jealousy.

Creeping over the sandbags, they moved up on the dugout.

A hot stench of decay wafted out at them. Inside, it was shadowy and dim, black swarms of flies rising in clusters, crawling over their faces and hands. There was three feet of water inside, rubble and refuse, and Sergeant Stone. He was leaning up against the wall like he was about to catch a smoke...only he was slit open from belly to throat and perfectly hollow within. Not a scrap of viscera or meat could be seen.

"Rats?" Creel said, amazed by that point that anything could sicken him.

But Haines shook his head, breathing hard. "He wasn't bitten open, you fool...*he was slit*. He was opened by a trench knife, maybe, then gutted, cleaned out like a bloody fish."

Again, Burke examined the body and flashed Creel a look. "Like the others," he said.

"What the hell is that supposed to mean?" Haines demanded.

"It means, you great bloody gob, that Stone was chewed on by something that wasn't a rat nor a dog," he said, glaring into the man's eyes. "These teeth marks...they're from something else. Something, I'm thinking, that walks about on two feet like we do."

"Idiot," Haines said, crawling up and out of the dugout.

"Scared stiff, ain't he?" Burke said, pointing a thumb at the sergeant's hasty retreat. "Don't blame him, I don't. Not at all."

Creel found himself staring at Stone's face which was a grinning grave rictus, lips pulled back from discolored teeth. There were maggots in his eye sockets. In the tomblike silence of the dugout you could actually hear the industrious suckering sounds of them feeding.

"Enough," Burke said.

They moved back over the crumbling wall, the bricks tumbling away beneath them. Scratch was waiting there with his rifle, surveying the flooded trenches and the swimming rats crossing them. There was a Hun corpse at his feet.

"Look at this," he said. He pressed his foot down on the corpse's chest and the blackened tongue slid out from between the lips. He lifted his boot and the tongue retreated. He kept doing it, giggling, human remains having lost all shock value for him.

And the war will end, Creel thought, taking a snapshot of the body, *and he'll have to go back home, his mind a black sore of corruption.*

"Kelly!" Haines called out, just above a whisper but firm. "Kelly!"

They looked around and he was nowhere to be seen. They moved off to his last position but there was nothing.

Swearing under his breath, Haines led them off, circling around the post in an ever-widening search pattern.

Kelly was gone.

"We better be off," Burke said. "Whatever got him is still out there. I can...I can *smell* it."

And the absolutely crazy thing was so could Creel. What was that odor? Sharp, pungent, like a stench beyond death.

"Oh, Christ," Scratch said. "He was there...I saw him..."

Creel studied Haines. This was a judgment call now and he could almost hear the gears whirring in his head. Did they retreat back to the trenches and leave Kelly or did they stay and risk their own lives in what might be a vain search? Maybe the reconnaissance patrol took him out quietly. Maybe he sank in the mud. Maybe he wandered off. The grim possibilities were endless.

Scratch's face was white as cream, flecked by specks of mud. His squinting eyes like knife scars, his mouth trembling. Haines peered about like a hunting hawk. Burke was listening. The rain came down in gray sheets, chill and clammy.

"Quiet now," Haines said, picking up on something.

Creel felt it and feeling it could not be sure of what it was...just a vague unformed terror that seemed to be swelling inside him, filling him up and making him go bad to the roots. He studied the devastation, the falling rain, the plumes of mist creeping over the ground.

"It's coming," Burke whispered.

Creel was hearing it, too...something out there in the fog, something moving in their direction. Slowly. At first it was just a muffled sound and then it became clearer: footsteps in the mud. Squishing sounds of feet—many feet. Stealthy, relentless. Then something else that sounded just beneath the falling rain like a hissing but soon revealed itself to be whispering, voices whispering.

Creel felt an irrational terror move inside him. His mouth was so dry he could not swallow. Those footsteps were coming from just ahead, to the left, to the right, as was the whispering. It was growing in volume but it was completely unintelligible. Like pressing your ear to a bedroom wall trying to make out voices in the next room that were purposely hushed.

"Ain't the Hun," Scratch said, his voice squeaky like a rusty hinge.

The whispering was practically on top of them.

Soon, any second now, what was out there would step out of the mist and Creel did not know what that could be. He could not wrap his rational brain around it, could not make himself believe it was men...for in his mind he saw specters and flesh-eaters, things with eyes like seeping red wine.

"Withdraw," Haines said under his breath. "Pull back...pull back for the life of Christ..."

And they did just as forms emerged from the fog. Neither Haines nor Scratch saw them and Burke had turned away, but Creel did. Just for a second before the fog enveloped them again. What he saw were...small, elfish, wraith-like things that looked very much like children.

He clearly saw a boy and his face was that of a stripped skull.

9
Dr. Herbert West

I had assumed, and maybe even hoped, that following the destruction of West's laboratory in the barn that his research would also come to an end. That it was obscene and blasphemous, I did not doubt. That by taking part in it I had damned my eternal soul, I firmly believed. After the barn crashed down and burned into a smoldering heap of timbers, I implored West to stop. As fascinated as I was by his compulsions, his obsessions, his almost preternatural scientific acumen, I fully believed that it needed to come to an end. That the shelling of the barn was akin to the finger of God. An omen. A portent. Call it what you will.

When I broached these thoughts to West two days after the shelling as he amputated the leg of a man with considerable dexterity, he laughed at me. "Stop now? Now when I stand upon the threshold of ultimate creation? I think not. Now is the time for more intensive study than I have yet undertaken," he told me, that cruel gleam in his eye. "Now, if you would kindly step down from your moral high ground and abandon your lofty ethics, Lieutenant, there are wounded men here that require attention."

Typical West to a fault—arrogant, egotistical, superior. As if I was the one who was derelict in his duty. No matter. On the orders of Colonel Brunner, the A.D.M. S. of our sector, I was sent down to the battalion aide post as Medical Officer and I was glad to be away from West and whatever might be going on behind those glacial eyes of his. My duties at the front were fairly routine. I started my day with the morning sick parade where those thought to be too ill for duty were examined. There was the usual amount of malingerers, but many serious cases as well. The soldiers seemed to feel better with an M.O. at hand though in many situations, there was very little I could do.

The trenches were generally broken up into three sets—the forward fire trench, the rear trench, and the extension trench. The forward, I discovered, was nearly always about waist-deep in water while the rear had about two feet in it and the extension was flooded to nearly five feet in depth. As M.O. I had to slog through like the rest, barely keeping my footing on the slimy mud beneath.

The German trenches occupied higher ground so the rain washed downhill into our own as well as the drainage from their lines. The sanitary conditions of the trenches were abysmal. The Tommies fought, ate, slept, and relieved themselves in these flooded, narrow cuts of foul water. Empty ration cans were used when possible for feces and urine and tossed from the trench, but it all drained back down in copious amounts. Wounds exposed to that filth became infected and often necrotic in a very short time. The officers had the men dig drainage ditches, but it did little good.

There were decomposing bodies everywhere that drew millions of flies and thousands of scavenging rats which the Tommies called "corpse-rats". I do not exaggerate when I say they were the size of tomcats. They were fat from feeding off the dead, spreading typhus, ratbite fever, and lice infestations and it was this louse whose feces caused numerous cases of trench fever. This, I must add, in addition to the suffering already caused by hunger, fatigue, shell shock, and raging cases of enteric fever. Prolonged submergence in the vile water caused feet to blister and swell with trench foot, often to two and three times their size if not treated immediately with dry socks and dry boots which were a rarity at the front. Sometimes boots had to be cut off infected feet very carefully as the skin was white, puckered, and suppurating, and often peeled free in great morbid sheets of tissue. The Tommies told me you could drive a bayonet through your foot when it was well-advanced and not feel a thing. Trench foot gangrene was common and resulted in amputation.

So the problems were numerous and the treatments few.

We had a terrible gas attack my first week and many men did not get their masks on in time. Dozens of them were brought into the aide post by the ambulance bearers. There was little that could be done. Those with some scant hope of recovery were sent rear to the Casualty Clearing Station. The others...dear God...they were burnt and blistered, covered with ulcerated lesions, blinded, eyelids stuck together.

They vomited out great chunks of lung tissue, gasping for breath as they slowly suffocated.

The shelling went on nearly daily and I removed shrapnel and amputated limbs, gave morphia and treated wounds with antiseptics. But it was often of little use. Abdominal injuries were nearly always fatal. Many of the men were so disfigured they prayed for death.

After three weeks I returned to the rear, feeling defeated and worn and without hope.

West was far too devoted to his research to back away on any "superstitious whim" of mine as he called it. He relocated his chamber of horrors to a deserted farmhouse about a half a mile from the Casualty Clearing Station near the shelled ruin of the monastery at Abbincour. Apparently, unknown to me, he had been involved in this move for some time. Even before the destruction of the barnlike edifice by shellfire. Apparently, there had been certain inquiries into his activities.

At first, West would not allow me join him and I was not disappointed over this.

"You've become far too squeamish of late. Your archaic medical ethics are standing in the way of scientific progress," he told me when I asked of his new laboratory.

"Herbert," I said, "how long do you think you can keep this up? Sooner or later word will get out. What if somebody stumbles in there?"

He smiled at me. "Then they'll be in for a bit of a surprise, won't they?"

Despite myself, I was drawn to the man. His intellect was almost godlike. His surgical skill often quite literally took my breath away. I witnessed him saving life and limb that no other medico could even hope to attempt. I learned more in one afternoon with West than I could in any five years of medical school or surgical practice. He was uncanny. He fascinated me. He frightened me. He made me feel like some Medieval sawbones with a jar of leeches.

As horribly, insufferably dismal as the war was, there was one bright spot for me which was my guiding light and my strength and my hope: Michele LeCroix. She was the daughter of the mayor of Abbincour. Dark of hair and eye, an exotic beauty that made my knees week simply to gaze upon her. That I was in love there could be no doubt. West, of course, did not approve. "You have a good brain," he told me, "but you're wasting it on simple animal need."

But he did not understand nor could he ever understand.

I decided to ask her for her hand in marriage. When I told West of it he laughed at the idea. "A marriage? In this godforsaken hellhole? It's absurd. It's high comedy." Then he must have seen the look on my face and sighed. "But...never let it be said that I stood in the way of romance. Of course, I'll stand with you."

Some days I had hope for the man, but very rarely.

As I said, I had little contact with him, then he again sought me out, dragging me away in the night to view his new workshop. In the past two months, I discovered, he had been very, very busy indeed. How shall I tell of what I saw there? The bones scattered over the floor...the buckets of seething anatomical waste...the spreading foul-smelling stains...the still sheeted forms atop slabs...the articulated skeletons hanging from wires...the dissected monstrosities...the revolting stench of the charnel. The walls were covered in anatomy prints, shelves crowded with skulls and books and arcane tubular glassware, bottles and jars of unknown chemicals and powders, grim preserved things in casks and tanks of oily fluid.

Amongst profuse biochemical apparatus which seemed a combination of modern scientific equipment and the wares of Medieval alchemy, I saw that his research was following perverse lines that were nearly unspeakable. What I viewed was a warehouse of the dead: large glass vessels filled with body parts—heads, arms, legs, hands, various organs...and dare I say that none of them in their baths of preservative and vital solutions were as dead as they should have been? That I saw a perverse and diabolical movement amongst that collection of morbid anatomy?

West was convinced that there was an ethereal, intangible connection amongst various parts of a body, that even severed from nervous tissue the attendant parts of a dissected form would answer the call of its brain. I knew it was true. For I had seen such evidence in the barn with the headless trunk of Major Sir Eric Moreland Clapham-Lee, who had been decapitated in an aeroplane crash then successively reanimated by West...head and body.

So, yes, I saw the most unspeakable and hideous things in the farmhouse. Whilst his research into the vagaries of perfect reanimation continued, he had involved himself in certain side projects, the nature of which turned my blood to ice. There, atop at table, in a metal wire cage surrounded by beakers and flasks, a maze of glass tubing and what appeared to be archaic alembics and retorts and spirit chambers, I saw a grotesque fleshy thing that was not one rat, but six or seven that had been shaved of fur then expertly sutured together into a common whole—a flaccid, pulsating mass of tissue with various clawed appendages scratching for escape and several heads with yawning jaws, bleary red eyes staring out at me with a voracious hunger.

"It's horrible," I said. "Why, Herbert? Why in God's name would you do that?"

He laughed as he sank several eyeballs in a jar of brine. "Why? Because I can, old boy, because...I...can."

We moved amongst tables set out with dissection instruments, surgical knives, exotic curcubits and glass pelicans, beakers and flasks and distillation units. Nearby was the head of a monkey resting in a jar of serum. Pale and hairless and shriveled, it floated in bubbling pale green plasma. Merely a specimen, I thought...and then out of some ghoulish curiosity I touched the jar and it was hot against my fingertips. A few oblong bubbles emerged from the puckered lips of the ape...and it opened its eyes. One eye, yes, for the other was stitched closed. But that eye, rheumy and pink and filled with a malevolent vitality, looked upon me and the lips parted, revealing yellow teeth that began to grind against one another.

"Toothsome little thing, isn't it?" West said.

There is madness in war, but the story West told me was beyond that. There was an officer, a Captain Davies, with the West Surrey Regiment, who routinely tiptoed over the top of the sandbagged parapet, whistling "Tipperary" with his pet monkey tucked safely under his arm. No one doubted that he was a lunatic for he often charged into battle stark naked. One evening, a German shell exploded as he walked the parapet, the shrapnel neatly decapitated his monkey and reducing him into an unrecognizable mess of red meat. Somehow, of course, West had gotten his hands on the monkey's head.

And what he did with it you can well imagine.

I would be remiss at this point if I did not write of the massive bubbling vat that was secreted in the very center of the workshop. I likened it to some massive aluminum womb that was connected via an intricate spider-webbing of glass tubing and rubber hoses to various immense glass tanks and vessels that hung from the ceiling in swaying harnesses, all filled or half-filled with red and green and yellow solutions that bubbled almost continuously. Other snaking tubes led to upended vacuum jugs and what I was certain were athenors, sublimation vessels, and decomposition chambers straight out of the Middle Ages, all connected together and feeding into the vat with an intricate system of glass piping like organs connected by artery and vein. I saw what I thought was a primitive digester furnace alongside vacuum pumps and gas combinators.

A womb. No more, no less.

The centerpiece of that congested laboratory.

West had yet again cultivated a seething mass of reptilian embryonic tissue. It was steaming and fluid and pulsing. A terrible hissing came from it as it "cooked" in its own vile secretions. There was a steel lid keeping it in absolute darkness. West kept it at 100% humidity and at a stifling temperature of 102°. Mimicking some offensive tropical spawning ground, the vat was but a revolting noxious womb of wriggling fetal life. As I stood there, trembling, he dropped the corpses of six rats in there, a jar of carrion and something else he would not let me see.

"Soon enough," he said, ducking under the tubing and piping and ductwork. "Soon enough."

I did not inquire further though my scientific curiosity was nearly insuppressible with a desire to know. West showed me something that snarled in the corner, a thrashing nearly impossible thing that bayed like a hound in its reinforced cage. I dare not describe that fanged doglike horror, its jaws dripping foul-smelling saliva.

I was glad when we stepped away around tanks and heaped stacks of books.

What West wanted me to see was lying on a slab in the center of the room. He pulled the sheet back and I saw the body of youngish woman. She was pale, certainly, but in no way decomposed. She had the "freshness" that West always sought in his subjects and which we both knew from our experiments was the key to successful reanimation.

I found her disturbing.

Just another corpse one might say and I should have been quite used to such things by that point...but the sight of her unnerved me. She was like Death personified: emaciated to a frightening degree, her ribs protruding and her pelvic wings seeming to nearly thrust from the flesh, legs and arms like broomsticks. Her grinning skull was horribly pronounced, lips shriveled back from dirty teeth and discolored gums. She was a skeleton stretched with tight yellow-white flesh that was shiny and ill-fitting. I was reminded, and unpleasantly so, of the female from Grunewald's The Dead Lovers.

"A prostitute," West said, holding up one sutured wrist. "The poor thing tired of life. But, you and I, we'll give her the chance that her maker never would."

The idea that this wraith could stand and walk was unthinkable. The very notion made cold chills run up my spine like spiders, a feverish sweat break out on my face.

As I lifted her head up, West made a tiny incision at the base of her skull with a scalpel, then taking up his hypodermic of reagent, carefully slid the needle into the medulla oblongata at the sight of the inferior peduncle which was just below the cerebellum. There was no guesswork with West; when you had dissected as many bodies as he had and put them back together again, there was no such thing as chance. Once the needle was seated properly, he injected 8 cc's into the selected site.

Then I lowered the woman back to the slab and the waiting began. Perspiring, trying to ignore certain nameless oddities squealing and slithering in that anatomical sideshow, I timed it with my stopwatch. West claimed that this latest reagent—which now contained a certain abominable glandular secretion from the reptilian tissue that hissed in the vat—would give us, he believed, a near-perfect reanimation. I was skeptical, of course, remembering quite well the absolute horrors we had resurrected in the past. The very idea of them made something inside me clench tight.

There was nothing to do but wait. Sometimes reanimation was achieved within minutes, sometimes not for hours.

I wrote my observations in West's voluminous leather-bound notebook while he examined the body: "10:27 PM," he said. "Six minutes, twenty-three seconds since injection. No discernable reaction as yet. No evidence of rigor. Limbs are supple, flexible. Pallor mortis unchanged. Algor mortis has flatlined...temperature rising steadily now." He checked the stopwatch. "At seven minutes, forty seconds, body temperature shows a noticeable spike. Sixty-one degrees...now sixty-two."

West continued his examination while I wrote feverishly by lamplight, the shadows sliding around me. Above the infernal noise of the creatures in that room, I could hear the wind whipping outside, hear the creaking of a tree, the scrape of branches at the roof.

"Temperature up two degrees," West said.

It was happening and I could feel it as I had so many other times. How to explain it? It was as if something in the atmosphere of the room had subtly shifted, as if the very ether around us was being charged with some unseen malefic energy. I swear to you that I could feel it crawling over my arms and up the back of my neck like a rising static charge. The shadows thrown by the lamps seemed thicker...oily, serpentine shapes that cavorted about us. Those abominations in their cages seemed to sense it and they began what can only be deemed a whining/shrilling/baying/screeching chorus of bestial wrath and fury that was part fear and part near-human hysteria. The profane head of that primeval-looking ape began to move in its jar of serum, suckering flabby lips to the glass like a snail. And in those bubbling vessels of vital fluid, the various limbs began a mad, hellish dance, thumping and bumping, hands wiggling their fingers and swimming around like waterlogged spiders. And in that vat of pestilential tissue, that seething firmament of fungous, godless creation, there was movement and hissing, weird slopping sounds. The metal lid began to rattle as if what was inside desperately needed to get out.

And then—

Through that bacchanalian cacophony of fleshy monstrosities, I heard a tapping. A single finger on the woman's left hand trembled. It was tapping against the slab as if impatient. Then her body jerked stiffly, her back arching, bones straining beneath that thin veneer of skin, and a low mournful moaning came from deep in her throat. "Aaaaaaa," she said. "Gaaaaahhhh." It was a dry and scratching sound like claws on concrete, like the rustling of ancient wrappings in a violated tomb.

"Nine minutes, thirty-two seconds," West said above the din. "Reanimation achieved..."

I was terrified to come into contact with her, for my fingers to brush against that shining, near-phosphorescently pallid flesh. And I say to you now, she sensed my unease, filled herself with my anxiety and tremor. For the eyes peeled open in that skullish face and they were glossy pink orbs, translucent like egg yolks, set with tiny pinprick pupils. She looked right at me, titling her head slightly and offering me a charnel grin of yellow, narrow teeth and blackened gums. It was a mirthless, sardonic grin of sheer malevolence that made me take a step back.

"You must not get up," West told her as if she were any patient that had just undergone a difficult procedure.

Licking my lips, fear-sweat running down my spine, I said, "Tell us...where have you been?"

She began to shudder, limbs contorting, fingers gripping the edge of the slab out of sheer unbridled terror. Her mouth opened into a wide oval and she screamed, screamed with a tortured voice that echoed up from the bleak cellars of hell: "YAAAAAAAAAAHHHHHH!" It rose the hackles on both West and I. She looked around frantically like a caged animal. "I saw it...I...saw...IT..." she finally managed.

"What?" I said, my heart pumping in my throat. "What did you see..."

"....IT...IIIIIIIT!" she cried out. "IT! IT! IT! The jagged face...it was coming for me, it filled time...it filled space...EYAAAAAAAAAAAHHHHH!"

I had no idea what she was speaking of, but my mind cavorted with the most dreadful imagery. She had seen something. Something that terrified her and no doubt had shattered her mind. I could not know what. We all wonder what lies beyond the grim edges of death. We all hope it to be our savior, our deceased loved ones, the ultimate good...but what if it is something else? Some forbidding evil anti-human essence of malign corruption?

A mad terror took hold of me as she climbed from the slab, hugging herself with those stick-thin arms. I trembled so badly I thought I might swoon. And it was because she said my name. Looking at me with those eyes like suppurating pink ova, she said my name clearly, but with the mocking flat tone of a parrot. Her grinning mouth like that of a hooked fish...dead, blank.

Stumbling along with a pronounced stiff-legged gait, a foamy red-tinged saliva running down her chin, she descended on West who suddenly looked frightened. As she moved, snaking ribbons of saliva swung back and forth at her chin, her face a distorted, seamed fright mask made of white gossamer flesh like spider's silk. Her eyes were sunken, pustular pits of wrath. She reached out to him with white-skinned, blue-veined hands that were like reaching, gnarled twigs.

Though an icy fear gripped me, squeezing my heart with cold fingers, I knew I must do something as she moved at my friend with her jerking, mechanical walk. I came up behind her and took her by the bare, bony shoulders and her flesh felt like thawing meat beneath my fingers.

A black slime running from her mouth, she turned and fixed with me with those eyes that had seen Death. I trembled in the cold lamplight of her gaze.

I used the only weapon I had: "Where have you been?" I asked her.

She backed away, clutching hands to the side of her head, greasy strands of hair hanging over her face which was frozen in a silent, wasting scream. "IT," she said with that grinding, subhuman tone. "IT...IT...COMES..."

With that, she whirled away from me, running from the room, knocking a table of glassware to the floor, her entire body jumping with wild spasms and contractions as if every neuron in her brain were misfiring. We heard the door open above the shrieking animals and heard the night, heard the woman crying out as she found the darkness of oblivion and it found her.

And it was at that moment, as she fled, that we both felt something in that room, a presence, a force, a darkness beyond death, moving around us with the whisper of casket satin, the flutter of shrouds. I think it was IT: the Angel of Death. It was there, so palpable that it flooded the room with an unspeakable despair and darkness...then it was gone as if it never were.

West, the master of understatement as always, said simply, "Why, I think she was out of her mind."

And yes, she truly had been out of her mind until we called her back. Out of her mind in some unknown place, but with WHAT?

I came as close that night as I have ever been to full blown lunacy. And it was only West's quick thinking and his good whiskey that saved me before it was too late. But even now I can feel that place, those things clawing in their cages, smell the chemicals and putrefaction, that steaming miasma in the vat, and, above all, I can hear that doglike thing in the corner.

Why wouldn't it be quiet?

Why did it have to keep screaming?

10

The Graveyard

The moon that rose over the battlefields of Flanders was a luminous, disapproving eye and the darkness was a cracked egg breaking over the land, spilling a creeping black yolk of shadows that filled trenches and shell-holes, rain-dripping dugouts and the cemetery of No-Man's Land. Like the ever-present rain of Flanders, it flooded the countryside and sank it in a perfect stygian blackness disrupted only by the frosted moonlight gleaming on spent shells and polished white bone.

Creel watched the moon come up and the darkness settle in, thinking, remembering, and shivering white inside as he tried to make sense of what he'd seen out at the devastated listening post.

You can't be sure what you saw, he told himself. You saw something...something that looked like a boy...a boy who'd laid in a grave moldering for a week, rats chewing the good red meat and pink skin from his face. But, surely, it was a trick of the light, the refraction of the same through the mist. But not...not what you thought.

You're too damn old to believe in ghosts, aren't you?

But he didn't know, he just didn't know.

Not after the burial party...those tracks, those damn footprints.

Die toten...die toten dieser spaziergang.

Yes, it haunted his every waking moment and turned his nightmares into ugly, black affairs.

His cynicism, his pragmatism...even they could not save him this time. He had been skeptical, of course, because he was skeptical about everything. One war zone after another, year after godawful year of poking his nose into the grim machinery of death, it had turned something inside of him, chased away light and filled those hollows with darkness.

All those fine young men.

Battlefield after battlefield, the politics might change, but the faces were always the same: boys of eighteen and nineteen living with fear and horror day by day until it scrubbed the color from their faces, trading young flesh for old, lips gone rigid and bloodless, eyes leeched of youth and replaced with a wizened desperation. All of them aged, worn, shattered, old before their time, used up before they saw twenty. Creel had seen them again and again, war after war, the survivors returning from the latest action, ears still ringing with shellfire and the screams of the wounded, limping along, shoulders slouched, backs bent...like old men, old broken men.

That was war.

Some months back, following the Battle of Neuve Chapelle, after a particularly fierce bombardment by German heavy guns, Creel had watched as burial parties came in carting the dead in stretchers, laying them out on the cracked pink clay of the ground...a dozen, then two dozen, then three times that many. The bearers looked at him with a boiling hate in their eyes only it wasn't for him, but for the war and the wreckage it produced. He stood there for a long time, unable to turn away, unable to pull his gaze from those tormented, gored faces. Their eyes were open, staring right at him, and he'd felt a cutting guilt open inside him.

During the battle, the trenches had been packed with Tommies, four-deep, firing rifles and machine-guns and trench mortars, trying to repel the German assault. The Hun poured in, wave after wave, and the guns roared and the shells erupted, and the bodies piled up, hundreds caught in the barbwire entanglements or sinking in the mud as high velocity rounds sought them out. The Germans had gotten so close that you could hear their individual screams of agony, see the fright and torment etched into their young faces...and afterwards, dear God, the bodies. They lay there for days, nesting with flies and maggots, worried by rats, a white and red patchwork of corpses that seemed fused into a greater whole of festering carrion gone green and gray and black. During the night you could hear the buttons popping off their tunics as they swelled with gas. The stink was unimaginable and it was more than the stench of death but the sharp, sour smell of an entire generation exterminated for no good reason.

There had been a fast, fleet-footed runner named Collins. Nice kid, naïve as hell, always giggling and sure of himself, untouchable as all the young Tommies thought they were untouchable, completely possessed by the idea of playing soldier, content with his speed which was impressive. After the battle he returned from the rear in time to see the killing fields. Ten minutes of it and his young skin was mottled, his eyes nearly rolled up white, the entire left side of his face hitched up like he'd just suffered a stroke. He started screaming and nobody could get him to stop.

Later, they got the kid calmed down and Creel looked in on him. His eyes were black starshot. "Ghosts," he said, "oh dear Christ, all them...ghosts...out there..."

Yes, ghosts. And the older Creel got and the more of it he saw, the more certain he was that they were there, sliding around him, shadowing him...pitying him, hating him, jealous of the life he had that he wasted in the graveyards of combat.

Sometimes he wondered if that's why he kept taking pictures of the dead—some fanatic, vague hope that he'd catch one of *them* on film. Some hollow-eyed ghost slipping away from the corpse that had housed it.

And why not? he thought as he waited in the stinking mud of the forward trench. *Why the hell not? Who has a better right to see ghosts? Who has spent more time with them than me?*

In the pale moonlight, he could see out beyond No-Man's Land, into a stripped forest that lay far beyond. The same one they'd passed through on their way to the listening post. Not dozens of trees, but maybe hundreds or even thousands, all of them de-limbed, de-barked, and soot-blackened from shellfire. They stood up straight or leaned over or collapsed into one another in great pillar-like deadfalls. Creel had been through them, had stood amongst them one bright day when the Germans had been pushed back and there had not been a single green shoot or leaf or so much as a solitary songbird. A dead place. The trees were like a thousand-thousand battle-worn skeletons climbing up out of that blasted inky-black soil that was rank and burnt smelling, so thick in your nose and throat it was like breathing ash. Ten minutes into it he'd began to suffocate, the good air sucked away and replaced with that gritty, powdery crematory ash that blew and blew and filled his lungs with sand.

Yes, death everywhere and would it be that insane to believe that here in the netherworld of the battlefield where life was extinguished so casually and ghosts roamed so freely that maybe death had turned back upon itself? That the dead were eating spilled life, filling themselves with it, so they might walk again?

Dead children that walk and feed on corpses? Are you willing to accept that?

The rain started coming down again, pooling, sluicing, filling the trenches with yellow-gray slime as the sky above scudded with black clouds that split open. In the dying moonlight, the rain was like falling crystals, billions of falling crystals: shiny, reflective. It drenched him, ran down his face and lips, dripping off his steel helmet. But it did not smell fresh, it only stirred up the rot and muck and filthy drainage bringing a rotten wet-dog smell to Flanders that sickened him to his core.

The rain subsided and there was silence for a time.

Listen.

Listen.

He was hearing it now, hearing it perfectly well: gnawing sounds. The sounds of teeth sinking into meat and scraping over bone. Too loud to be rats. He did not believe it was dogs. Things out there feeding, filling themselves, glutting obscene appetites.

"Just cover your ears," Burke whispered to him. "Maybe it'll go away."

The rain returned, coming down in sheets and Creel stared through it, certain for not the first time that just beyond the sandbags there were things moving out there, small twisted elfin forms taking advantage of the rain to feed on the dead.

II

Tomb Orchids

The dead waited.

In mud holes and bomb craters and shell pits, in skeleton forests and decimated villages and ruined cellars and filth-bubbling trenches, they waited. Moist with decomposition and sprouting tangles of green moss and rungs of polished white bone, they waited. In flooded ditches and muddy trench walls, in cheap plank coffins and beneath mildew-specked tarps, they waited and would wait. Steaming with rank corpse gas, netted in morbid sheaths of fungi, and exhaling the vile stench of the charnel and tombyard, they were patient.

The rain fell and the mud pooled and the slime oozed beneath a misting gray sky the color of gelatin. The swarming graveyard rats worried at the dead, fed on them, brought their degenerate pink-skinned brood to term in their bellies. The flies covered them in buzzing black shrouds two inches thick and the maggots erupted from mouths and eye sockets, orifices and the lips of green-furred wounds in boiling, squirming masses, ever-fattening themselves on carrion and decay until they burst with wing.

For the dead of Flanders there was silence and the death-watch ticking of eternity...but then something began to happen. Maybe it was in the black soil, the yellow-brown sluicing muck, the water, or the falling rain...maybe it was set loose when a certain barnlike edifice occupied by Dr. Herbert West and his grave-wares was shelled by German artillery. But it was there. It was active. It had potential. It was the catalyst that canceled out death and filled rotting husks with a grisly semblance of animation, a gruesome half-life. Day by day as it grew more concentrated, a toxic effluvium of resurrection, eyes winked open like marbles in tombstone gray faces and mouths yawned wide like clamshells and essential salts, so long dormant, were revitalized into motion. From the muddy, flowing, bubbling bog of No-Man's Land, faces like rotting weed and cemetery pulp peered into the night, ice-white fingers clawed in the slime as a great furnace of creation began to boil in the primordial ooze and warm amniotic mud of Flanders which was not so different from the primeval seas of earth where life first began.

By night, there was the sound of things pushing up from the swampy landscape, fingers breaking through the crust of graveyard mold, and ruined faces sliding from the mud. Each night, more and more. And beneath the wan, sickly moon of Flanders, in the gray rain and yellow fog and rustling shadow, there was a sound of feeding, gnawing and tearing, the noise of teeth on bone and lips sucking juice.

Each night it grew louder.

And louder.

The commanders of the London Irish Rifles had no true idea of how many men they lost in the abortive raid on the German lines at Lens that September day. The Battle of Loos raged for three days and early estimations were that some 20,000 members of the BEF had died and another 50,000 were wounded. That information was to be kept from the troops, but of course it reached them as everything did.

In charge after charge, the LIR had captured German trench systems only to be pushed back by heavy shelling and intensive machine-gun fire that raked the barren hills of Cite St. Auguste.

Creel and Burke were there, having taken their leave of the 12th Middlesex for a time. Each morning was the same: the men were fed an extra large ration of rum and then it was up onto the firestep with rifles and fighting kit, the sergeants crying out, *"FIX BAYONETS, BOYS!"* and then over the top, fighting a costly battle through No-Man's Land, stumbling over the bodies of the fallen, over twisted-up unburied corpses, leapfrogging bomb craters, slopping through the mud, hiding in shell holes, rising up to charge yet again across open fields and fighting through massive barbwire entanglements as they were raked by German sniper fire, volleys of shells and deadly accurate machine-gun strafing.

The BEF, lacking shells for true artillery support, used chlorine gas for the first time and the masked Tommies found themselves fighting through a rugged, scarred land that was obscured by rolling pockets of gas. One of the sergeants kicked a football ahead of him so his boys would charge in the right direction.

When it was finally over with and the smoke cleared, the offensive had been a disaster. For days, stretcher bearers and Field Ambulance companies moved the wounded rear to the battalion aid post and Ambulance HQ, the worst being shunted off to the Casualty Clearing Station. Both Creel and Burke worked hour after sleepless hour moving the wounded.

In the aftermath, Creel witnessed something he would never forget.

When the officers were in the dugouts, the men had a symbolic funeral for their fallen comrades: they arranged some thirty skulls in formation on the open ground beyond the support trench and paid homage to them. Who the skulls belonged to he did not dare ask, but such things were easy to come by in that war. The wind was blowing and little dust-devils were swirling about, coating those skulls with a fresh coat of age.

The soldiers, all with the same blank eyes, walked past, saluting. One guy they called Slivers—because he'd been a carpenter in Knightsbridge—openly broke down, went to his knees, and began to sob.

No one went to him.

The Tommies stood around in their mud-caked boots and filthy greatcoats, Enfield rifles slung at their shoulders. They were dirty, desperate, their eyes huge and hollow, faces like living skulls. They had lost the ability for pity.

Burke finally went over to Slivers and helped him to his feet and Slivers clung to him like he was something he had lost long ago and found again. "Got Dick, didn't they? He was my mate. He was right in front of me and the pissing Hun got him. Right in the fucking head, they did." He showed Burke a series of dirty smears on his uniform blouse. "That's Dick's brains. They sprayed on me. They was in me eyes and all over me face. This is what Dick thunk with. Poor old Dick. He was such a good mate. What am I supposed to do now, eh? What am I supposed to do without me mate?"

But nobody really knew. They were all shattered, fatigued, worn thin as wires and they didn't have the strength to do much but stumble back into the trenches and consort with their private hell.

"It was a mess," one of the sergeants told Creel later. "See, what kind of action is it when you've got no bloody artillery what to support you with? No bleeding shells for them bleeding guns?"

"Not good," Creel said.

"No, sir, not good." The sergeant looked up and down the trenches, that long stare in his eyes like he was looking for something he could never hope to find. "It was a real mess out there. Shells coming down and men dying, fighting for every inch of ground. Patrols bumping into patrols, companies getting tangled up with other companies and that gas coming down and which way was which and who was who...saw our own boys get gassed by our own shells. *Plunk, plunk, plunk,* they went and no warning. Our artillery, what there was of it, didn't cut through the Hun barbwire like it was supposed to and I was watching men, mates of mine, getting their boots tangled in it while the Hun cut them down. Ain't that the life?"

Creel gave him a cigarette, an American one, and he liked that. Started laughing at how American tobacco could make it to the front but no Americans.

"Country's divided," Creel told him. "Some want to fight, some don't. Lots of Americans joining the Canadians to get a taste."

"Nothing against your countrymen, mate. If I was them, I'd stay home. Enjoy life, ain't nothing but death here. We ain't winning and neither is the Hun."

As night drew on, Creel was in the dugout with a group of enlisted men and the stories started circulating as he knew they would and he knew he was going to hear things that he wanted...and dreaded...to hear. Lot of it, of course, was scattered recollections about the raids on German lines, just bits and pieces that shook themselves loose from the men's minds as they sat and contemplated. As Creel listened, he watched men stripping their shirts off, their backs scratched raw and red from flea and lice infestations. Some of them stripped naked and ran the flame of a candle along the seams of their underclothes and you could plainly hear the lice eggs crackling. It was the only sure way to get rid of them or keep them at bay.

"Funny bit, it was," a corporal was saying. "One night, the mist hanging heavy, we lost C Company's machine gunner and his two mates, see? We go up to the fortification, the gun pit, there's the Lewis gun, all the ammo boxes pretty as you please...but no men. All five of 'em are gone. How do you figure that? German sappers took 'em, they wouldn't leave the gun and ammunition, would they?"

"No bodies?" Creel said.

"Nothing, mate. Must've carted off the bodies even though it makes no bloody sense to take corpses and not weapons, now do it?" He shook his head. "Nothing there except them funny prints in the ground."

Creel felt something cold take hold of him. "Funny?"

"Sure. Bare prints, they was. You know, like somebody were walking about without boots on."

This would have been the point, Creel knew, that if the corporal's story was just a lark the men would have begun ridiculing it. But they didn't. They just sat about in the semi-darkness, smoking silently, their eyes shining in the murk.

"Were they...small prints?"

The corporal shook his head. "The prints of men not children. And the funny thing is they was full of worms, squirming worms."

Creel swallowed. "Worms, you say?"

"Sure. Maggots. Lots of maggots."

Creel did not interrupt as the stories made their rounds and each one—from maggoty footprints to skulking things like children that scavenged the dead to Hun that took .303 caliber sniper rounds and kept walking—only confirmed what he feared; that something absolutely incredible and horrifying was happening out there.

Later, he went out into the trenches and it was a quiet night save for the falling rain that went on for several hours before drying up. What it left in its wake was a sickening odor that was beyond dirt and mud, blood and filth and dank uniforms...it was the vile stench of rot, of tanned hides and dark sewers, sumps and mass graves and backed-up cisterns. He had all he could do not to vomit and was that because of the stink of war or was it because inside his own head he was smelling something infinitely worse, infinitely more pestilent, and infinitely more dangerous to his sanity?

He got away from the Tommies, leaning against the trench wall, mud up to his knees, smoking cigarette after cigarette, listening to the rats crawling around him, and wondering, dear God, just wondering. Something was going on out in the body dumps and sunken graves and green-stinking fields of carrion. How did he track it to its source and if and when he did, what the hell could he really do about it?

Colonel, now I know you don't like me because I'm a journalist but just listen for a minute, will you? The dead are rising out in No-Man's Land and something has to be done about it.

Creel almost started laughing at that one.

No, it wouldn't go over well.

The Tommies were suspecting things, hinting and intimating at the worst possible occurrences. Down in their hearts they knew something was wrong beyond the usual calamities of war. Maybe they would not put a name to it, but they knew. Some of them, anyway. But the officers? No, never, ever in a million years would they accept it. They didn't teach the old boys anything about the living dead at Sandhurst, it just wasn't cricket.

Creel stumbled through the mud, snaking through the trench system, eyes glazed, skin damp from the rain, heart beating with a low and distant rhythm, wilting beneath the pall of stark memory, sliding down deeper into himself, seeking a cool, smooth darkness that was his and his alone.

13

Battle Fatigue

Sometimes he would come awake at night gasping for air like a stranded fish and once the sweating and gasping were over with, he'd wonder what had been suffocating him, but he'd know: the war. After awhile in the trenches it was like all the sweet, pure breath was sucked from your lungs and you were subsisting on corpse-gas, marsh mist, and the smoke of burnt ordinance.

Awake and knowing sleep was beyond him, he'd make his way up to the fire trench and listen to the Tommies whispering, telling each other how they were certain they would die and they'd never see home again. He'd listen to their voices until they became a lulling soft murmur like ancient clocks ticking away into eternity and soon enough, those voices were rain and running water, clods of earth gently striking coffin lids which was the sound of time. As dawn neared, there were low voices, the rattle of equipment, the snap of a rain-soaked poncho, the slushy sounds of mud. Now and again, something like laughter or sobbing, and then deep silence winding away into emptiness. The wind would sing a final mournful song amongst the battlements and clay-spattered earthworks. Rats would scurry out beyond the sandbags. A lone dog would howl.

In the days following the Battle of Loos, Creel began to wonder—and not for the first time—about the state of his mind and more so, the state of *all* minds in that war. He was starting to think that there was some infectious, collective insanity making the rounds like a germ and he could not remember the last time he had spoken with anyone that was remotely ordinary.

The Tommies bothered him.

Their youth ground to ash, they contemplated their deaths like old men, hoping only that there would be something to bury. The relentless, dogged combat and deprivation and inhumanity and suffering of the trenches were deteriorating their minds into a stew of morbid dementia and pandemic melancholia. The good white meat of reason had been chewed away and what was left was something rancid that sought the earth and quiet entombment. So many of them had reached the stage where they were convinced that the only way to be a good soldier was to die in battle. And it was not some misguided heroism, but a sort of fatalism that each day survived only prolonged the pain and the sooner it was over with the sooner they would be out of the mud and filth of the trenches and even death was better than living like a rat in a hole.

With their wide white eyes and muddy faces, they would look upon Creel like he was some sort of exotic species, a mad thing that belonged in a cage, and ask the inevitable: "What in the Christ are you doing here? You could be home."

Creel would tell them that he had no home and a silent apartment in Kansas City didn't count because it depressed him. He hated being at the front and he hated being away from it. That was something they understood.

"No wife or little ones, mate?"

"None. One divorce. Can't hold a family together jumping around the world looking for that story I can't seem to find."

"How many wars for you now?"

"Thirteen," he'd tell them.

They wouldn't comment on that number as if acknowledging it would contaminate them with its poor luck. They'd just keep asking him why he was there and he'd tell them the truth: "I'm looking for something."

They'd ask what and he would not say.

What really *could* he say?

That he saw Flanders as a great poisonous flower and they were all trapped in its petals, waiting for it to close up, caught in the inevitable venomous darkness, waiting for the slow call of forever night? Even to him with the somewhat morose and macabre rhythms of his thoughts that sounded more than a little like some kind of psychological/metaphorical sinktrap, the result of an overtaxed mind and an overburdened imagination.

But that was how he saw it.

Death was *here*, in this place. Malignant, wasting, hungry death and it was a force far beyond anything as simple as the misfortunes of war. It was alive, elemental, discorporeal and sentient...and he could feel it and had felt it ever since he got to Flanders.

Like it has been waiting for me, he often thought in the heavy shades of night. *I've hounded it through battle after battle and now it's not running from me anymore, it's not hiding, it's just waiting in the darkness like an ivied graveyard angel, arms open to embrace me and draw me beyond the pale into a world of rustling shadows and nonexistence.*

And whenever his cynicism laughed at the very idea, he needed only take a tour of the countryside by day, chain-smoking and nail-biting, to see that it was not too far from the truth.

This was Death's place.

He did not know what Flanders was before it was scarred by trenchworks and gutted by shellholes, its viscera yanked inside out and covered in mud and sunken in stagnant rainwater, a great bog floating with carrion and peppered by bones...but he was pretty sure it had been a pretty place. Probably green and growing, fertile, old world European where you could smell the sweet flowers and count the yellow haymows at the horizon, listen to the creak of horse-driven farm wagons meandering up rutted dirt roads. Like something out of a pastoral landscape by Pissarro or Cezanne.

But now war had claimed it and forever changed its face from wonderland to wasteland. The countryside had been dotted with tiny farming villages—he knew that much because their ruins were everywhere—and he imagined they had been quaint little places once upon a time. But they would never be that way again. The hand of Death was absolute, it had cast a diabolical spell here, a sinister alchemy, an infection that rotted Flanders to its moldering bones. That could never be completely erased. When he looked around now and saw those villages like monuments standing in rubble, cold, blasted, and empty, surrounded by boneyards, mud swamps, refuse and the wrecked machinery of war, blown by a cold/hot thermal wind that stank of putrescence, sewage, and excrement...he was sick to his core.

For he could not get past the awful and somewhat monomaniacal idea that this was his private hell and it was being staged for his benefit.

Insane. Paranoid. Egostistical. Yet, it had now reached the point where he could not seem to remember a life before Flanders. Even when he tried to remember his mother, his father, his brother in Cleveland and his ex-wife in Boise, all he saw were the shattered faces of the war dead from his collection of mortuary photographs.

That's all there was.

And he feared it's all there ever would be.

Maybe I'm nothing but a maggot feeding on death like they always said, but it all leads here. It all leads to Flanders and what's happening here. The dead are rising and I'm going to find out why because that's my destiny.

One thing was certain: as he sought death, death sought him.

14
Shell-Shock

The fourth night following the Battle of Loos, Creel was in the support trench trying to catch a few winks in the shadow of the machine-gun blockhouse when German flares began to fill the sky. They burst yellow-green overhead, trailing sparks, drifting down on little parachutes, their flickering light turning the trenchworks into some surreal, expressionist tangle. Then the shells started coming down as the Hun worked their artillery and siege guns. While some covered their heads—Creel included—he saw many who just sat around, smoking, and staring off into the night watching the rounds coming in as sandbags disintegrated and huddled men vanished in thundering explosions and mud flew and the parapet crumbled, the air hissing with smoke and steam. He watched one young private looking up as a shell came down, greeting it, tracing its descent with his eyes, then there was eruption of debris and water and he was no more.

The barrage lasted another ninety minutes and when it was over Creel's ears were ringing, his gums sore from clenching his teeth, his hands throbbing from being balled into numb fists. It was amazing the things you would do as you waited to die, waited for the shell that would turn you into mulch. A few slugs of rum, a cigarette or two, and he began to relax somewhat though nobody in Flanders ever truly unwound.

For some time there was silence, only the sound of the wounded being evacuated, the dripping water, the air pungent with the stink of burnt cordite, hot metal, and burning canvas. A welcome odor that overpowered the stench of the trenches and the evil smells blowing in from No-Man's Land.

Creel drifted off.

Around three a.m., a noise cut through the night...something that might have been the tormented scream of a man or the agonized shrill howl of a dog. Creel came awake with Burke next to him and could not be sure. Only that it was eerie and it shocked him into silence as he listened to it rise up into a wild unearthly wailing then fade away.

Then there was the sound of rifles firing, men shouting and more than a few men screaming hysterically. Creel and Burke followed the sounds with a dozen other men down the communication trench and it came far from the rear where little sandbagged Elephant Shelters were being used as makeshift morgues for the dead from the barrage. It was sheer chaos as the Tommies either fought forward to get a look or fell back in waves after they had. Lights from lanterns and electric torches were jumping about, throwing wild shadows over the muddy ground.

That weird wailing sound rose up again and Creel could feel it right up his spine.

"*What the hell is it?*" he cried out.

"It's been feeding on them corpses!" one man said.

"Keep back!" shouted an officer and the men responded, pulling away as that wailing rose and fell, sounding at times very much like a piercing human scream and at others like a bestial roaring that fragmented into guttural cackling.

Burke tried to pull Creel away, but he shrugged him off. He had to see this...whatever it was. He just had to see it. He was drawn forward with a sort of magnetism.

"Jesus," Burke said when they got close enough.

Inside the shelter Creel could see a seething mass of motion, teeth flashing and eyes blazing. One of the officers had a Webley in his hand and he pumped three rounds into the thing and it snarled ferociously, then let go with that all-too human, high-pitched screaming that seemed to echo on and on as if there were a dozen creatures in there and not just one.

"Is...is that a dog?" Creel said under his breath, wishing like hell he'd brought his little camera with him.

Whatever it was—and he was making no rash guesses—it looked roughly dog*like* in appearance, like some massive hairless hound whose flesh was ghostly white and pulsating, almost vibrating with a jellied undulant motion. Yet, if it *was* a dog, then it was horribly distorted and grotesque, something made of mounded pallid flesh and twitching growths, a massive head rising up on a fleshy trunk, limbs seeming to splay out in every direction and Creel could not be sure that some of them did not have *fingers*.

All around it were mutilated corpses that it had been tearing apart in some manic feeding frenzy.

The stink of violated carrion was unmistakable...but a worse odor blew off the thing itself that was acrid and almost violent, like apples rotted to acidic cider.

A rifle squad came forward and just stood there, not sure what they were seeing or what they should do about it.

"WELL, BLOODY WELL SHOOT!" a sergeant-major called out.

The beast rose up on its back legs and it was taller than a man, some immense dog-thing snapping and growling and whining. In that moment, as the men opened up and slugs from the Enfields drilled into it, Creel saw more of it than he wanted to...in the muzzle flashes it was forever burned into his mind.

Darting back and forth on wrinkled accordion necks it had two jelly-fleshed, purple-veined heads with juicy, swollen eyes like plums gone to a pulp of decay and snarling maws set with spiked teeth which jutted from sagging gums at crazy angles. All of which was bad enough, but the thing that truly sickened him, that filled him with a crawling physical aversion, was the fact that the hairless heads of eight or ten pups were rising from its hide like tumorous growths. They were blind, almost fetal, but hideously alive and wildly animate, mouths opening and closing, a squeaky sort of mewling coming from them.

The sight of that put him down on his ass and he only vaguely remembered Burke pulling him away and the cry of the men and the reports of the Enfields and that sergeant-major shouting for everyone to get, "DOWN! DOWN!" as he pulled the pin on a Mill's Bomb and threw it at the thing. There was a thundering explosion and fiery bits of ejecta came drifting down along with smoking bits of the violated corpses.

The officers wanted the men to go back, but Creel got in there for a look before they stopped him. One of the Tommies trained a spotlight on it. The beast had pretty much been blasted into pieces, but enough of its hide remained in a single smoldering husk that he could see what he needed to see.

He couldn't say about all of it, but the heads of those pups were clearly sutured into place.

"A camera?" he called. "Does anybody have a camera?"

But none were forthcoming and that was because the sergeant-major was scattering the Tommies with an evil eye, daring them to challenge his might and authority.

"Out of there now!" he shouted as a thin young military surgeon came forward to look at the remains. "Let Dr. Hamilton through!"

And what struck Creel the most was that Hamilton did not seem surprised at what he was looking at. Shocked, yes; disgusted, certainly. But surprised? No, it was almost like he had expected this.

Later, back in the reserve trench—after Captain Sheers gave him a good dressing down for "interfering in military matters" of all things, promising him that he was done with the London Irish Rifles, thank you very much—he pulled Burke aside in the support trench. "You saw it same as I did and don't sit there and give me any of your goddamn Yorkshire stoicism," he said to him, his face inches away. "That thing is part of this. It did not happen by accident and you know it. That thing was fucking *stitched* together, Burke, and our Doctor Hamilton didn't even blink an eye about it."

Burke sighed. "And you want me to do what, mate?"

"I want you to help me figure this out, Old Shoe," Creel said, grinning almost maniacally. "That thing was no dog...good God, it *screamed like a woman*. It's part of the whole. All the weird things we've seen and heard about are part of something. Something that was *made* to happen."

"All right. How do we start?"

"We start by finding out about this lieutenant, this Doctor Hamilton. He's with the Canadians but his accent sounds American," Creel explained. "That's where we start. Because this guy, oh yes, he holds the keys to hell in his hands."

15

The Sleep of Reason

Tucked away in a little funk hole scraped into the side of the trench, just large enough to curl up in, Creel managed to drift off around five and the dreams came for him right away.

He saw the sun, buried behind layers of leaden clouds, extinguished like a match dropped in a puddle. It sought its grave and moist earth was thrown in after it and it was simply no more.

Then all across No-Man's Land, there was a stillness and a waiting; morbid seeking shapes drifting about with a lonesome whispering and a stifled, subterraneous breathing. For here it was always the witching hour and the grinning throng of tomb-shadows moved like an October breeze through a sullen churchyard with a sighing breath of rainy crypts. Their cadaverous moon-faces gave praise to the night and the rain and the human wreckage. They were formed of red casket velvet and white mannequin wax. They hid in shadowy pools of reeking water, the black blood of sunken graves, showing themselves only when there was movement and the beating of living hearts.

Creel moved with them, *as* them.

The legions of the dead.

They were aware, they were sentient, they were driven and relentless and unspeakably hungry. From the pestilent deeps of Flanders they moved, slinking and slithering through sewer-damps and flooded trenches like disease germs in clotted arteries. Throughout this night and many more there would be scratchings at parapets and whispers in the shadows, a clawing at the doors of ruined village houses. Fungous faces would be pressed to shuttered windows and crumbling fingers would scrape against casements. The dead would wake in flooded cellars and ooze down the throats of fire-blackened chimneys and expunge themselves from waterlogged shell-holes.

But they would come.

And every night there would be more.

And he would be one of them, never knowing or fathoming the stillborn depths of their decaying minds.

Together, they marched into the night.

When Creel woke up, a scream on his lips, three fat-bellied rats were gnawing on his boots.

16

The Workshop

When I finally caught up with West it was at the farmhouse and I wasted no time in taking him aside rather roughly and demanding some answers because it was far past the point where I wanted to listen to his sarcastic little denials and his cheeky morbid humor. Events were rapidly escalating out of control.

"You're in a blue mood today, aren't you?" he said.

"And I've got a damn good reason to be, Herbert. I've just come from Loos."

He wrinkled his nose. "Most unpleasant from what I've heard, hmm? The BEF advanced and were pushed back to where they started from."

"That's not what I'm talking about, Herbert. The LIR shot down one of your pets, that thing you had chained up in the corner," I said, pointing to where that abomination had been but was no more.

He gave me his typical little smile. "Hmm. Unfortunate. It seems to have escaped in the night. You know how dogs are."

"Herbert, please."

"Good God, you don't think I released it on purpose?"

It wouldn't have surprised me. "The point is, Herbert, that people are starting to ask questions. About that dog. About a great many other things. It's only a matter of time before they trace it here."

He held up a hand. "I have full and complete authorization from Colonel Wimberley to conduct research into advanced battlefield medicine."

"Enough, Herbert!" I said. "This has gone far enough! You apparently can't control these experiments of yours! It's time to destroy them! If the BEF traces things here, I don't even want to think of the reprisals."

"Destroy them? No, no, no, not yet. Not until I'm done, not until the tissue has properly fermented."

He was referring to that vat, of course, that he was freely feeding various bits of human anatomy daily. I did not like the constant low throbbing coming from that vat of hissing tissue which sounded very much like the steady beating of some huge fleshy heart or how those assorted parts in the glass vessels of bubbling serum seemed to respond with rhythmic contortions. It was not only obscene, but perverse, and, yes, evil. For the sinister, noxious atmosphere of West's workshop could not be denied and its source was simple enough to trace: the vat, that bubbling vat of nameless flesh.

West was in his usual disagreeable, argumentative mood. I put certain questions to him concerning certain stories circulating amongst the troops of animate dead things encountered out in No-Man's Land. Denial was all I got out of him. Sheer denial.

"Do you know anything about the orphanage?" I asked him, referring to the Catholic orphanage at St. Bru that had been devastated by a misdirected poison gas attack of the Hun using high-velocity, long-range shells. There had been no survivors. Some forty-three children died in that particular atrocity. I had not been involved in the reclamation of their poor little bodies, but heard it was horrendous as I could well imagine.

"St. Bru?" he said. "Of course. What of it?"

Such an exasperating man. I told him what of it. I put it to him with no due consideration to his feelings for I was sick of this cat-and-mouse. He denied everything and told me I was a superstitious old woman to believe any silly rot about walking dead children in No-Man's Land. But I would not let it rest there.

"Herbert!" I said, angered. "Did you or did you not disinter those children and give them injections of reagent?"

Now it was his turn for anger. "Listen to me, you simpering, gourd-rattling little peasant...I have no interest in children. Not now. Not ever. As far as I know, those little ones are still in their graves."

"Then how—"

"Tall tales, chimney-corner whispers, amusements from bored soldiers in the trenches."

Maybe I shouldn't have believed him for his sense of ethics was like some garment he donned only for convenience's sake. Yet, I honestly believed he was telling the truth and his stern gaze did not falter even for a moment. But I was not satisfied. One or two ghost stories told by the Tommies of scavenging undead children? Fine. But the stories had now reached critical levels and were being told by dozens and dozens of men. And I, yes, I had seen the corpses out in No-Man's Land. I had seen the gnawed bones, the tell-tale dentition of tiny teeth.

"The explosion, Herbert," I said. "Is it possible that when your other workshop was destroyed by the shelling that certain elements were released?"

He acted dumbfounded, but knew exactly what I meant. The barnlike edifice where his laboratory had formerly been located had been destroyed in a German barrage. That much was known. But was it conceivable that the vat of tissue he had germinating there...that its contents had been spread around the countryside in the explosion or even been thrown up into the air in fragments only to be carried back earthward by the incessant rains? For we both knew the uncanny, frightening reanimative properties of that tissue in its bubbling bath of reagent. I thought my hypothetical scenario was the tree that bore fruit, but West disagreed.

"Dissipated, it would have simply died. It was merely a colony of cells."

"And you can say," I put to him, "that the mutative properties of that tissue, it's inordinate, almost supernatural will to live could not be active at the cellular level?"

But he could not say that, only believed it to be "highly unlikely." Yet, I could see that it had not occurred to him because he was more than casually excited at the possibility as blasphemous as it was. I should say here that West was exceedingly nervous—his intellect was blazing, as always, but there was an undercurrent of dread and agitation beyond his usual frenetic excitability. Twice while I was there, he peered out the windows as if looking for something and no less than three times he turned to me and said, "Tell me...old friend...did you see anyone on your way up the road?"

I told him that I hadn't, yet he did not seem relieved.

Calmed somewhat by the fact that he had not deliberately resurrected any poor waifs, I relaxed somewhat even if he could not seem to sit still save for an occasional peep into his microscope. I brought a bottle of brandy and despite the mortuary spread around us, I forced him to drink with me for Michele LeCroix had accepted my proposal and we were to be married. West congratulated me, but I could see his mind was on other things—namely that awful vat and the unsettling sounds coming from it. I was certain at that point that whatever was coming to term in there had him scared to death.

17
Incoming

Sergeant Burke did a little snooping, something he was very good at, and learned that Dr. Hamilton was attached to the 1st Canadian Light Infantry, whose battle lines were only a few miles west of the 12th Middlesex. He was an American, as Creel had suspected, a lieutenant and quite a capable surgeon. Other than that, there was very little.

"There's got to be more," Creel said, somewhat exasperated.

"That's it, mate."

"Dammit. He's involved in this somehow and I'm going to find out how."

Burke sighed. "You're going to get your arse thrown out of the war. And if you don't care about that, think about me. I'll have to go back to the fighting and I'm not liking the idea."

Creel brooded for hours after that. He was too close. Right on the periphery of something that might be much bigger than even the war itself and he was not going to give up now. Though his relationship with Captain Croton was a little strained, maybe he could arrange a visit with the 1ˢᵗ Canadian, embed himself over there for a time because that's where he needed to be. That was the epicenter or damned near to it.

Burke was always warning him about going slow because he was already trying the patience of command, but he wasn't about to go slow. There was a time to hide and wait, a time to listen, and a time to spring and go for the throat and that particular time was now.

As he sat in the forward trench, lost in thought, watching the slugs inching out of the trench walls, listening to the frogs croaking out in flooded bomb craters, he tried vainly to find his cynicism, his detachment, his objectivity—these were the meat and blood of any journalist—but they were gone. They no longer existed. He was one great creeping mass of anxiety from his head to his feet.

Go ahead, boyo, track down this Dr. Hamilton. Let him open his dark chest of wonders and let you peer inside. Write it all down. Write the story that can never be published. But it's more than journalism now, it's more than war reporting...it's personal and you know it. Whatever's at the root of this madness, it's got your number.

And that number is about to be punched.

Sergeant Kirk came sloshing through the standing brown water and Creel nearly jumped out of his skin.

"Keep your head down," he said. "The Hun is about to come calling. I can feel it in my bones."

And Creel could too.

He could feel the tension building through the trenches like every man there was wired together, part of some machine of cycling dread. In the dugouts, on the firestep clutching rifles with almost religious devotion, huddled over meager dinners of cheese and Bully Beef, leaning up against sandbagged ramparts—all the faces were the same: bleached white, lips pulled into stern gray lines, eyes huge and almost neurotic in their intensity. The Tommies prayed, squeezed rosary beads in their fists, holding tight to good luck charms and fetishes, everything from rabbits' feet to a badly worn photograph of a wife or a cherished child, and—in some cases—the dingy brass button off the tunic of a mate who'd gone home or a favored spent shell casing that had saved a life or some nameless wooden effigy carved out of boredom and hope, smoothed into an unrecognizable shape by oily grasping fingers.

Creel was not immune to it.

He found himself gripping his field notebook, tensing fingers pressing into familiar grooves in the leather cover. He watched men going through the pre-battle rituals of survival—touching objects, holding their rifles a certain way, squatting in a particular stance, many of them humming beneath their breath or whistling a lost tune from childhood. These were all protections against evil, dismemberment, and death. Charms that would get them through one more battle and one more day and the stark horror of fatalism was apparent on the faces of any that had broken, however minutely or innocently, the sanctified steps of ritualization.

Night crept over the sandbags in black twisting worms of funeral crepe. Breathing was low, heartbeats high. Sweat broke on faces. Limbs trembled so badly they had to be held in place.

Sergeant Burke was next to him. "Hold tight, mate," he said. "We'll soldier through."

Good old Burke. Tough as nails. Made of the real stuff, as they said. Unlike himself whom he viewed more and more as some death-obsessed carrion crow picking away at the remains of lives, Burke was the real thing: a soldier, a hero, someone you could look up to, would be glad to call friend, the sort you'd be glad to give your daughter's hand to in marriage knowing that, in the end, he always did the right thing, the honorable thing. As he thought this, he felt Burke's hand take hold of his own and clasp it tightly in friendship. It was something the men did when the shelling got heavy—holding onto one another, fusing themselves together. But Creel had never been part of it. He was always alone...now Burke made him part of the chain and he felt a tear in his eye.

As darkness dimmed the sky and shadows crawled thickly, the German flares burst overhead, green and yellow, turning the trench system into some weird strobing shadowshow of stiff-legged figures as they drifted earthward, sputtering, on their little parachutes, revealing the jagged wounds in the earth and the insects that scuttled in them.

Then it began.

Shells came in with screaming blue-white velocities, dropping like autumn leaves and detonating the scarred countryside in vast, ear-shattering eruptions of pulverized earth and spraying black mud. Blazing shrapnel lit anything afire that was remotely flammable. Wood and fallen trees were blackened into charcoal sticks, water boiled to steam, sandbags glowed into blossoms of fire.

Creel saw lightning flash, heard thunder and felt earthquake. Smoke and fire and screaming and burning flesh. In the distance, the heavy guns popped like champagne corks, and every man in the trenches was listening intently, giving each and every round a personality all its own. Not just mindless projectiles, but death-dealing fingers of fate that were preordained to take certain lives and spare others. *Pop, pop, pop,* went the field guns and the men would think, worry, contemplate the unknown, the great mystery: *There...that one...that one sounds like the one for me, I know that sound, I heard it before, maybe that's what I heard when I died last time.* The sky rained shells and some detonated in the distance and some quite close, but all shrieking with their expulsions of shrapnel seeking flesh to macerate.

Crouched against the trench wall while men shouted and sobbed around him, Creel listened to the shells come as he always listened to them come, gripping Burke's hand ever tighter: whistling and screaming, buzzing like swarms of locusts...and others, fired from the heavy guns...came roaring like freight trains passing overhead. But the result was always the same—an eruption, flying shrapnel, a shockwave that would knock you flat and give you a concussion if you were close enough.

The shells kept coming and coming as if the Hun were intent on destroying the trenches themselves, erasing the battlescars of man's preoccupation with killing his own kind. They came in volleys that went on for thirty minutes or more then there was a shattered silence for maybe ten or fifteen and they started flying again.

When the trench wall blew apart, covering him in mud and dirt and sandbags, Creel crawled up through it like a mole seeking sunlight. All around him in the flickering glow of the German flares he could see that the trench system had been wiped out, reassembled. There was nothing but an irregular series of smoldering shell-holes all around him flanked by mountains of earth, sticks, rubble, and corpses. Men were crying out for stretcher bearers, but not many because most were either gone or buried alive.

He was still gripping Burke's hand...but Burke was no longer attached to it. He cried out and tossed the hand aside, almost hating himself for doing so.

The darkness was broken only by flaming wreckage or an occasional flare drifting overhead, the air thick with rolling plumes of smoke and a dust storm of dirt and grit and pulverized fragments that slowly rained earthward. There were cinders and soot everywhere. The entire landscape—what he could see of it—had been taken apart and rearranged and there was no way to tell where the rear was or where the Hun lines were or where to escape to.

Stunned, face black with ash and mud, Creel found he could not stand and when he did, he went right down to his knees. So he crawled over the earth, calling out for survivors in a dry, ragged voice that was barely above a whisper. A shadow stepped out of the gloom and he knew it was a German soldier, a big fellow in a shining steel helmet, rifle in hands, an enormous bayonet raised to strike. Then there was a single hollow report and the Hun fell to the earth and did not move. Another shape came out of the gloom and Creel called out to him, but was ignored. Whoever it was took the German's helmet and rifle and disappeared into the shadows.

Trophy hunter, he thought, *a goddamn trophy hunter of all things.*

He got to his knees, crawling again. The BEF artillery was answering in kind now, lobbing shells at the German positions. There was sporadic gunfire all around him, the sound of grenades going off, the occasional dull thump of a trench mortar. The Germans, he realized, had let loose with one barrage after the other and now raiding parties were moving into the sector. He saw the silhouettes of several men climbing atop a razorbacked hill that had not existed before the barrage.

He climbed to his feet again, still wobbly, but better. He stood there for a time, clearing his head, stumbling along a thread of earth that zigzagged haphazardly amongst a series of bomb craters. Then he tripped and fell into a shell-hole, emerging finally from muck and water. He heard a volley of machine-gun fire, felt rats crawling over him. His grasping fingers searched along the muddy wall and found he was in luck: a ladder. The crater must have been part of a trench before the barrage.

He crawled out, over the muddy pitted ground, scaling humped things that he soon realized were bodies. Then another flare passed overhead and he saw that he was in a field of corpses, hundreds of them spread in every direction. Not all were dead. Some were writhing on the ground calling for medics and stretcher bearers. He saw men without limbs. Men who were living trunks being worried by rats.

He kept moving, sickened, beaten, beyond hope.

"Hey, mate, over here," said a voice.

Creel crawled towards the form. He cradled the broken body in his arms and realized the man was dead, shattered by concussion. His head in Creel's hands, though intact, was almost liquid within, the skull nearly disintegrated. Everything inside moved with a slow gelatinous roll.

Crawling again.

Over corpses. Fragments of the same. Through muddy holes and pools of standing water, rats skittering around him, driven into panic by the bombardment. He came across a Tommy who was sitting upright, his back wedged up against a furrow of blackened earth. "Hallo, Captain," he said. "Bit of bitters tonight, ain't she?" His left leg was missing, his right arm nothing but a burnt fleshless mass. In his left hand he was holding his stomach and intestines. He kept talking as though Creel were not even there.

"Barmy bit of luck," he said as Creel moved off.

How long he crept through the nightscape he did not know, only that after what seemed hours, the war still murmuring around him from time to time, he began to see men coming through the moonlight. What appeared to be hundreds of them, gashed and broken, streaming blood from wounds. Their eyes were bulging. They were tearing at their throats. *Gassed. All of them gassed.* Yellow foam was gushing between their lips and he watched as they all began to fall, piling up atop one other, vomiting yellow slime from their mouths. Even in the pale moonlight, he could see that their faces were black as they gasped out their last breaths.

For not the first time, his writer's mind contemplated the possibility that he was in hell. For he'd been in lots of battles but never anything like this. Never anything that so completely took apart the earth and put it back together again like a puzzle missing half its pieces.

When he hadn't heard anything for a time, he crawled into a muddy furrow and let himself smoke, let his nerves calm, his heart find its rhythm. He was probably crawling in circles.

Better to wait. Listen. Make sense of things. An orderly retreat when the time came.

Sure, that was sensible military thinking.

He laid there for some time, the roaring of the guns in the distance now, the war having moved on to more fertile pickings.

Quiet.

Yes, it was suddenly unnaturally quiet. There was not a sound in any direction just that hushed weird stillness like a great switch had been thrown.

Creel had experienced it before, on many battlefields and in many wars.

Usually during the blackest hours of night, it would descend over the trenches and for a few shocking, gut-crawling moments you would wonder if you had died. If a shell had come screaming down on your position and blasted you to ropy fragments. They said you never heard the shell that got you and there was probably a truth buried in that one, but sometimes the silence was much worse than the shelling.

Out in No-Man's Land, beyond the perimeter and wire entanglements, just...nothing. No rats scavenging, no wild dog packs howling. No men moving. No rain falling. It was eerie, hushed, waiting. Like something hiding in the darkness making ready to spring and tear out your throat. And though it was soundless, that silence had a quality to it all its own. A bigness, a volume, a weight that you could feel crushing the wind from you second by second as it settled down like a stone slab over an open grave.

It never lasted for more than hour or so and oftentimes, much less, but while it did it was impossible not to feel it gathering around you. Impossible not to listen to it, to see if there was something out there, something hiding in that blank-faced murk...like maybe you might hear the soft thud of its heart or the sound of its breathing.

The bottom line was, for however long it lasted, he knew, senses became very finely attuned and your mind assured you it was hearing something that no ears could possibly detect: bodies decomposing, rats licking their fur, flies laying eggs, maggots bursting from the sweet-sickly pulp of carrion.

Creel was breathing hard now.

He hated this.

It was like all of Flanders was waiting for something, tensing, coiling itself into a tight silent ball.

Trembling, he lit another cigarette and the sound of his lighter echoed into the night with volume as if the very physics of the air was somehow...deranged, turned inside out.

Wait, just wait, boyo, because it's coming and you know it's coming. Something's about to happen. Get ready.

A perfectly white mist had gathered over the ground now, blown up, it seemed, from craters and shell-holes and jagged cuts. At first he thought with panic that it was gas, but gas was never that perfectly white, the color of bridal lace. About the time he finished his cigarette, he began to hear sounds out there in the desolation. Sounds like whispering voices.

Was it men like him sneaking about or—

He could hear feet in the muddy earth, splashing through puddles, pushed down, pulled free. Many, many feet and they were coming in his direction. Swallowing, a sudden heaviness in his chest, he felt a cool tingle at his spine and something like a current of electricity in his bones.

Closer now.

He did not see them, but he knew they were there. He smelled a stench of putrefaction that was warm and yeasty, but it could have come from anywhere out there, a dozen pockets of the unburied dead. It did not mean that...what was out there was not human. Yet—*yet*—he felt certain that what was coming to call was something other than lost soldiers creeping through the blasted remains of the trenches.

This was something else.

Something that was not evading, but...*hunting*.

He heard a sound, quite near, like someone breathing in through their nose with a quick wheezing intake of breath. The sound of someone sniffing like an animal, trying to scent prey, follow the spoor.

Creel felt himself go hot then cold all over. Drops of perspiration wetted his skin and a greasy sort of fear-nausea twisted in his belly.

Something was coming.

He would see it soon.

It was coming over the ridge.

And then he did see it and maybe he had been looking at it for some time, for there atop the ridge in a near-perfect band of moonlight was what he'd first taken to be a withered dead tree rooted in the earth...but it was moving and it looked, if anything, like some marionette: skeletal like a broken doll, twisted at the waist, head laid low against one shoulder sprouting hair like limp cobwebs, trailing limbs like living sticks.

It was sniffing the air.

"Where are you hiding?" it said, a woman's voice gone to a shrieking dry screech like iron scraped over concrete. *"I know you're there...I can smell you."*

Her face was bleached and bloodless, cratered and sunken like the dark side of the moon. He could see eyes that were a hot smoldering red scanning the landscape, fingers twitching, as she sniffed the air.

"Here," she said. *"I can smell him...he's here."*

All around her, figures rose up. A dozen then two dozen—wraiths, ghost-children whose faces were a luminous white in the moonlight like glowing paper lanterns. Moppets in ragged shrouds, rungs of gleaming bone jutting through, the buzzing of flies only slightly louder than their whispering voices.

"Find him!" the woman ordered.

They sank away into the mist like swimmers submerging, only they didn't vanish. They were down on their hands and knees, sniffing the earth like hounds, crawling down the ridge like spidery white ants on a hillside. Creel, seized up with a terror that was limitless, watched them coming, moving like lumbering insects, thick glottal noises coming from their throats.

Several passed quite near to him and it wasn't a matter of whether they would find him, but *when*. This was it. It all hung in the balance and he was painfully aware of the fact. To die by shellfire or a sniper's bullet was one thing, but to be taken down by these...these *children* was something else again. He would be rendered to the bone. They would suck his blood and marrow, swim in his viscera and bathe in the blood from torn arteries.

Out of desperation, he tried the simplest trick in the book. His hand found a stone that was perfectly smooth, perfectly worn, as if it had lay on a river bottom for many, many years. He felt its weight in his palm, hefting it. He tossed it over his shoulder with everything he had and heard it thump against something and then splash.

A dozen heads wreathed in flies popped up from the mist.

"There!" called the old witch on the ridge. *"There he is!"*

She joined the chase and passed within five feet of him. When they were all gone into the fog, he scampered away up the ridge and down the other side, running and stumbling and swimming across flooded shell-holes. He threw himself down and fell atop a waterlogged corpse that went to a gushing white slush beneath him. The stench was gassy and evil, but he did not dare cry out.

For far in the distance he heard the hag: *"Find him! Bring him to me! I want Creel! He's one of ours..."*

18

The Dugout

When Creel came awake there were hands on him. The hands of men. A shadowy face said, "Easy, mate. We found you out there. We brought you back. Quiet now. There's Hun patrols about."

The last thing he could remember were those creeping children, then running, hiding, dragging himself along on his belly, half out of his mind if not all the way. He must've went out cold. Something. He could not remember. Only a braying voice—

I want Creel! He's one of ours...

—he bolted upright, sweating, shaking, feverish. His teeth chattered and a canteen was pressed to his lips. Then a flask of rum. He calmed inch by inch, breathed, smoothed out the wrinkles and unsightly folds like he was an unmade bed. Even in the dimness he knew he was still with the 12th Middlesex, because that was Sergeant Kirk over near the gun slit in the dugout wall, scanning the terrain.

"How'd you get way out here, Creel?"

Burke...oh Jesus, Burke.

"I don't know. The barrage...everything was torn up...bodies everywhere...I didn't know which way was which."

"You're not alone," one of the Tommies said.

"Where is this place?"

"It's a dugout," Kirk said. "An old cavalry post the Hun overran last winter."

"How far are we from our lines?"

"Difficult to know," Kirk said. "I'm afraid the lines have been scrambled. My best guess is we're a few miles off."

There were two men with Kirk: Privates Jameson and Howard, both young, both scared, both looking like their mouths were filled with something they could not swallow down. It was near dawn and slowly the dugout began to fill with a soft bluish illumination. The dugout was more or less intact, though the far wall was crumbled as if it had taken a heavy shell. The rest was sandbagged, the brushwood roof heavily timbered. Rubble scattered across the floor, a few rat skeletons in the corner.

"Tonight," Kirk said. "After dark, we'll make our move. Until then we'd better sit tight."

By daylight, Creel peered out the doorway and what he could see was a gutted landscape that could have been anywhere in Flanders. He saw a line of deep-hewn trenches and sandbagged ramparts stretching around the dugout, some of it collapsed, most of it flooded. Beyond the trenchworks was just a flat expanse crated by shell-holes, a few stumps rising up, what looked like the surviving chimney of a stone house in the distance.

Not much else save for a few skeletons rising from the water and a stray skull that was perched atop a trenchknife sank into one of the sandbags like some sort of sentinel.

"We found two Hun last night," Howard said. "They was skinned. Right down to the muscle."

Sergeant Kirk shushed him, grumbling about horror stories and nonsense and the slow degradation of the British Army.

Creel had to wonder what other stories Howard knew. Or Jameson. Or Kirk. Because there was no way by this point they hadn't at least heard things if not necessarily seen them. It seemed unlikely that he himself could have had several encounters with walking dead things and they not a one.

But he had to ask himself: *Are you sure? Are you sure this isn't something more personal? That thing last night, it called you by name and you know it did. Don't bother pretending otherwise or deluding yourself by saying you were hallucinating. You know better. The dead know you. Maybe all these battlefields you been sneaking around in all these years, all the graveyards you've poked into...maybe they've laid claim to you...*

"You all right, Mr. Creel?" Jameson asked.

"Yeah." He wiped sweat from his face. "I'll be better when we get back to our lines."

"You and me both, mate."

Creel crept out into the trenches with Kirk to have a better look, but there was little to see but the gouged battlefield, a mass of barbwire clustered about a thicket of denuded trees. With Kirk's field glasses, he could see that a major operation had been fought here judging by the bomb craters and pitted earth, the spent shell casings in the mud.   Over in the thicket, amazingly, there were at least a dozen skeletons tangled up in the wire or tossed right up into the trees themselves, speared through limbs.   It was a ghastly, unnerving sight and one that Creel felt he would see for a long time to come.   When the wind picked up, a low moaning came from the skeleton forest, the sound of air blowing through hollow skulls and ribcages.   It sounded like someone blowing over a bottle...maybe dozens of them.

Everyone was hungry but there was no food to be had and precious little water.   So they waited.   And waited.   A light drizzle fell all morning and then, by two that afternoon, a heavy fog settled in thick as a tarp.   Just beyond the barbwire, the world was a surreal, gloomy place of gauzy mist and leaning, nebulous shapes.

Kirk did not like it.   "Too easy for a Hun raiding party to slip up on us."

He posted himself with Jameson outside, both of them with Enfield rifles but no grenades.   They stayed within visual contact and kept watch.

Creel heard his own voice speaking, talking about the barrage, about Burke.   When he had finished, he was sobbing. But it was out.   It had to come out.

"You got one of them cigarettes?" Howard said after a time.   When he got it lit and took a few calming drags, he stared at the wall, something old unwinding behind his eyes.   "I want to tell you something you'll never write about.   But I have to tell it before Kirk gets back.   He wouldn't like me talking of it."

"Go ahead," Creel said, burying the memory of Burke inside him.   "I'm listening."

Howard sighed.   "Last night, before we found you, mate, we found something else.   It was a tunnel.   We couldn't say whether it was one of ours or one of theirs but Sergeant Kirk got this idea that we should have a look in there, see if we could scavenge some weapons, maybe a few bombs.   Awful looking place it was, winding into the hillside like the barrow of a troll from one of them books me mam used to read to me as a boy. Well, in we went and it was a dank-smelling place, mud and water dripping from the roof.   The floor sort of mucky and wet. Kirk had hisself a little torch he'd taken off a Hun corpse, but he was using it sparingly as it was just about petered out.   So we move along in there and we can smell the dead, but the dead can't hurt you none, they says, better than the living far as that goes.

Pretty soon we're having trouble walking so Kirk lights his torch and, blimey, all about us is *bones*. A few corpses, too, all white and puffy, kind of spongy if you stepped on 'em. But the bones. Well, they was everywhere and it's not the sort of thing that a bloke likes to be looking at by the light of a flickering torch, now is it? Especially bones with tooth marks in 'em.

"Well, that torch, she gives up her ghost and I have to wonder if that ain't a good thing. Bloody hell, it's so dark you can't even see your feet or the nose on your own face. But Kirk wanted to push on, the bastard. So dark, so dark. Things was hanging from the roof on chains...husks, human husks. I saw them before the light died. All stripped down, eaten. Onward we goes deeper into it and it's like crawling down the throat of something hungry, something with teeth. I suppose it was...well, the *quality* of that dark which disturbed me clean to my roots, you see. There was something god-awful threatening to it that made my hackles rise and I figured the others felt it too, for about then we heard a funny sort of sound...a rustling, shifting sort of sound like we were in the lair of some sort of beast. We could hear it breathing with a rough, phlegmy sort of sound. Then...well, kind of a gnawing, crunching sort of sound like a big hound makes with a bone and being that there were only human bones and remains in there, well it don't leave much to the imagination, now does it?

"About that time, I figure, we hear these steps coming toward us and Kirk, he tells whoever it is to back off because we got weapons and we'll use them. *Retreat*, he tells us when those big slapping footsteps keep coming. *Get the hell out.* Kirk needs no more coaxing, see, he pulls his Webley pistol and fires off a few rounds. Well, about that time he screamed like a little boy seeing a ghostie coming out of a closet. Well, so happens, I looked back and wish to God I hadn't. In the muzzle flash of the Webley, I saw what he was shooting at...or part of it...it was big, Mr. Creel, much bigger than a man. It was naked, hairless, moving with a sort of side-to-side gait, something that wasn't any one thing but lots of different things all stitched together...different skins and shiny pelts and something like white blubber maybe...and a face. A blurry white sort of face. And eyes. Big yellow eyes. Well, that's it and I don't want to speak of it no more."

Creel did, of course, becoming very interested when Howard said it was *stitched* together, wondering what sort of feral horror it indeed was but Kirk came in with Jameson and from the looks on their faces, something had happened and it didn't look like something good.

"What—"

Kirk held a finger up, shushing him. His eyes were wild and stark and very close to lunacy. He had seen something and it was devastating. Jameson had a smile on his face that was stupid and mindless, like the painted grin of a wooden puppet. Nobody dared speak. They listened, they waited, they felt around with psychic fingers to make contact with what was out there. And by that point, Creel was certain it was not the enemy. A German patrol would have been welcome.

A sound.

At first he was not certain that he had even heard it: a subtle scratching sound. It could have been a rat, but the way Kirk sucked in a gasping breath, he knew it was not. He moved very slowly over towards the gun slit which gave him a pretty good view of the trench system before him. He saw nothing...but he could hear that scratching and that's when he knew.

Whatever was out there, it was circling around outside the sandbagged parapet, scratching for a way in like a hungry dog. The trenches themselves were over seven feet deep. You needed a scaling ladder to climb up and over the top. Outside the parapet, another deep ditch had been dug and this to make it that much more difficult for German raiders to make it over the wall. That ditch was slightly deeper, nearly eight feet in depth.

And that's what scared Creel at that moment, filled his throat with ice and made his scalp creep on his skull. For he could see just the very top of something, possibly a head, moving through the perimeter ditch. This was what had frightened Kirk and Jameson so badly and this was what wanted in: something large enough that an inch of its head could be seen above the sandbags.

An odor was coming into the dugout and it was an odor that Creel knew only too well. It was the rank, suppurating stench of infected wounds and gangrenous tissue, filthy battle dressings and bile. And maybe something beyond that—vomit and corruption and cesspools gassy with decay. It was the smell of the thing out there, something birthed in the ravaged, dead womb of battlefields and maggoty mass graves.

They could hear it raking splintered nails over the sandbags, patient, very patient, but anxious to get at them.

"What...what is it?" Howard finally whispered.

"A ghost," Jameson said in an airless voice.

Kirk licked his lips and kept licking them. "It...I saw it come out of the mist...something gray like a winding sheet...rustling..."

Creel was trembling now, as were the others, some defeated, hopelessly optimistic part of himself wishing it would just go away. His lips and tongue felt thick and ungainly and he didn't think he could speak to save his own miserable life.

And then he heard a voice, dry and scratching, filled with dirt: *"Creel,"* it said. *"Creel..."*

And he almost went out cold at the sound of it, his heart pounding so fiercely he thought it might explode. In his mind, he was seeing that thing out there, that graveyard horror that called him by name—death walking, death stalking—and it rinsed his face of color. There was a scream in his throat but he did not have the strength to let it fly. He tried to stand over near the gunslit and his blood went to his feet and he stumbled over, his fevered mind showing him exactly what was behind that shroud: a distorted death's-head with eyes like glowering moons, flesh that was acrawl with bloated black flies. Kirk caught him, held onto him, but there was little he could do to bring the blood back into him.

They gave him rum, rubbed some warmth into his face and finally his lips parted and he said, "It called my name."

Kirk and his two men looked at each other. "There was no voice," he said.

"None," Howard affirmed.

And that's when Creel knew it was in his head, only in his head, a very private thing, an invitation to a mass for the dead that only he was being summoned to.

"It got through," Jameson said, on the edge of hysteria.

Creel figured it would. Sooner or later. There were parts of the parapet that had been destroyed by shellfire and the thing had found one. They could hear it and it was no ghost: slopping forward through the trenches, casting a wake of brown dirty water before it. Closer, closer...

Sergeant Kirk led them out of the dugout and the mist pushed in from all sides, fuming and dank. The splashing sounds seemed to come from every direction, growing louder by the second. Creel could hear the pained rasp of breathing, that stench growing stronger. Finally, Kirk broke to the right and

Howard towed Creel behind him. As they made their escape he clearly saw an immense shrouded gray form emerging from the fog.

"*Creel,*" it said.

19

Entombment

The mist shaped itself into phantoms and drifting ghosts that followed Sergeant Kirk's retreating party as they pushed forward and away from the devastated cavalry post and what haunted it. The yellow-brown sucking mud came up to their knees and all around them were pools of standing water, shell-holes of bubbling muck, stumps and the masts of limbless trees. Nothing else but refuse and bones, a few corpses that had gone swollen and white in the rain, bursting with greasy gray toadstools. The mist blew around them in heavy blankets and fuming pockets.

Their boots and greatcoats were so heavy with mud that there were times when they literally could not go forward, but Kirk would not let them quit. After a time they found some higher ground, an island in the swamp of Flanders, and they took a few moments amongst the trees and wiry bushes to clean the mud off their boots.

Kirk, who had been judging position by what he could see of the sun—a hazy sinking disc at best—said, "We can't be far from our lines now. I'm surprised we're not right on top of the Hun. One should think they'd be thick out here."

Nobody commented on that. They smoked and breathed and stared about with glassy eyes set in pale, grime-slicked faces.

They had a short trip through the thicket and then into the battlefield again or what had once been one. More shell-holes, huge bomb craters, the remains of barbwire enclosures sinking into the earth, great bogs of stagnant fly-specked water floating with dead rats. But just beyond, duckboards rising in and out of the swamp. They were crisscrossed, zigzagging, a veritable maze stretching into the mist. There had been action here and not too long ago, for there were shallow pools of decomposing bodies, both men and mules, cordite cans, splintered trench supports, shell casings, sheet iron fragments, fallen trees, empty boots...refuse in every direction. They saw a few sandbagged posts, the bird-picked remains of soldiers who'd manned them.

They clambered onto the nearest duckboard and it was a relief to feel something solid beneath them. But the unsettling thing they all felt and felt deep was the almost unnatural silence. Not so much as a distant shelling or staccato burst of machine-gun fire, yet Kirk assured them they were moving south towards friendly forces.

They pushed forward, preying for some sign of life.

Then—

Out of the fog they began to see objects thrusting from the murk. They were tall and leaning, luminously white, some nothing but simple wooden crosses and others rising headboard-shaped gravestones.

"A bloody cemetery," Howard said. "Of all things."

"They were fighting in a graveyard...bloody hell," said Jameson.

"That fighting is long done," Kirk told them as they advanced, the duckboard sometimes sinking but never giving way completely beneath them.

They moved forward and Creel did not say a word. He could feel something around them, the same sort of feeling he'd had back at the cavalry post...and it was getting stronger. It moved up his spine like claws and settled into his belly in a thick dark mass.

"Look," Howard said.

There was a woman far to their left at the periphery of the mist. She was dressed in some ragged shift that was streaked with mud. Dark hair fell down one shoulder like a noose. Her face was gleaming white. She stood still as a statue, something sculpted, something incapable of movement. Then she opened her eyes and mouth and they were filled with a seeping blackness that was horrible to see.

"Keep going," Kirk said. "Bloody crazy woman."

But Creel knew better and so did the others.

The deeper they got into the cemetery the more profuse were the stones. They jutted from tangled stands of vegetation knotted with barbwire, from rank pools of water and ooze, rows upon rows of them, clustering and white and flecked with lichen, intersecting duckboard crossing amongst them. Creel heard splashing sounds too large to be rats. The noises seemed to coming from everywhere in the burial ground. And then they all began to see things in the mist, shivering white apparitions slowly weaving their way towards them.

As they moved ever forward, words beyond them now, it began to be hard to distinguish—out of the corner of one's eye—between the monuments and the *people* rising up behind them.

Creel saw children standing out there—pallid things, waterlogged and puffy, mouths opening and closing like those of suffocating fish.

Sergeant Kirk kept everyone moving until they were nearly running on the duckboard.

The sound of their boots echoed off into the still nothingness. Rifles were clenched in hands, stomachs in throats, hearts racing, minds spinning on the edge of madness. A bloated man who was quite naked and distended with gas stepped out of the fog and stared at them with sightless pockets of blood for eyes. Kirk went to his knees in a firing stance and put two rounds from his Enfield into the intruder. The first round made the bloated man flinch, the second made him pop like a balloon, nothing but white goo and clots of bloodless drainage on the duckboard.

They were everywhere now.

Puckered white heads were rising from flooded graves and looking at the men with eyes like black wormholes. Caskets bobbed to the surface of filthy ponds and gnarled hands reached from the mud. The dead were swimming like rats now, propelling themselves through the water and thick weeds with the side-to-side motion of snakes. They glided ever forward, ashen and pitted with holes, serpentine and sleek despite their disfigurements. The woman they had originally seen waited for them on the duckboard, black water running from her mouth and eyes, leaving trails dark as crude oil down her bleached face.

Kirk and Howard blew her off the duckboard with their rifles. The slugs made her seem to implode, to collapse into a tower of squirming pink-gray rottenness that struck the duckboard like an emptied pail of fish guts. Some of it was still moving.

The dead were swarming.

From every sunken hole and muddy ditch and slimy box, they rose and gave a slow, shambling chase, seeming to be in no hurry. They turned maggot-squirming faces the color of newly risen moons in the direction of their quarry and slowly, relentlessly, gave pursuit. They crowded the duckboards, swam through the water, clawed from the mud, emerged from the weeds and from beneath tombstones.

Creel followed behind the others, numb, used up, his mind sucked down into a narrow chasm. Then they were free of the cemetery and the duckboard was climbing a hill and they scampered up over it and saw a ruined, shelled village just before them.

And then Creel's mind began to work again and he knew that the dead weren't going to kill them. That had never been part of the plan. No, they were herding them into this place just as they had been compelled to do.

20

The Deserted Village

The village sat atop a low series of hills, a great junkyard of scattered rubble, broken walls, burned vehicles and upended carts lying amongst sandbagged gun pits, shattered roads and yawning ditches. The misty skyline was framed by roofless stone cottages, the high standing scaffolds of buildings and leaning chimneys. Weeds grew up from cracked cobbles and leaf-covered pools of water flooded cellars lacking houses to cover them.

Looks like a Medieval siege took place here, Creel thought. He looked around and was satisfied that this place was indeed of Medieval vintage. The mazelike winding streets, the great outer wall (now mostly smashed), the high towers, the houses and buildings crowding in upon one another...yes, certainly Medieval in design. A walled city. Defensible.

He tried to picture it intact and found that he could not; too many wars, too many battles, his mind was only able to sketch in somber grays and reaching darkness, destruction and desertion. Looking around, the city was some immense stripped skeleton of rising bones, femurs and ulnas and rib staves, split roofs like yawning skulls and a shrapnel-pitted church steeple like a reaching metacarpal.

Isn't it funny how it's always death with you? Or maybe it's not so funny at all, boyo. Even when you were a kid, you didn't care about dogs and cats...not unless they were found rotting in a ditch.

"This...I think this is Chadbourg," Kirk said to them as they stood amongst the crumbling wreckage.

Chadbourg was one of those places that changed hands a dozen times in the early days of the war. The Huns taking it, then getting tossed out by the British or Canadians, who themselves were forced out by successive attacks and concentrated shelling. There had been a few actions near the village in the past months, but only minor skirmishes.

"Chadbourg," Creel said. "That means we're well away from our own lines."

"Aye," Kirk said. "A bit west...probably quite near the Canadians, I'm thinking." He looked around, trying to get his bearings. "We'll have a rest here, I think."

Howard started shaking his head. "But those things—"

"Are not something we need worry about. Crazed, all of them. Broke free from an asylum, I shouldn't doubt."

That was so thin you could see through it, but it made Creel smile when he didn't think he had any smiles left. You had to hand it to Kirk; he just refused to give in. The living dead were crawling out of their graves and he was concerned with finding a place to lay up a bit before the march back to friendly forces. Creel almost burst out laughing at the very idea of it. *Well, the undead haven't lunched on us quite yet, have they? Let's have ourselves a nice brew-up. There's a good fellow.* He contained his laughter and mainly because it would have been hysterical and sounded more like a scream than anything else.

They moved up the main thoroughfare, the mist enclosing them from all sides, the ruins rising up around them in ghostly, vague shapes, shadows clustering in doorways, rats scurrying in dead-end alleys, ravens sitting atop the creaking signs of pubs and cafes that had fallen into themselves.

According to Kirk, Chadbourg had been abandoned over a year before when the troops starting moving in from either side. Yet, to walk through those streets, meandering amongst heaped rubble and broken stone and staved-in walls, there was a sense of decay that was thick, heavy, almost palpable with age. Shutters hung from empty windows by threads, collapsed doorways looked in on moist rancid darkness, stairways terminated in midair and crept below street level into flooded blackness. It stank the way a cemetery at Ypres had smelled, Creel remembered, after a vicious shelling by the Hun that churned up the ground, exhuming graves and rotting boxes, tossing skeletons into trees and atop roofs; a pestiferous, moldering stink of subterranean slime and leechfields.

Most of the houses and buildings were nothing but heaped debris, hills and ramparts of it, some so high you could not see over them and others filling streets so they were impassable.

When they did find a habitable structure, the roof was usually gone, nothing but splintered timbers overhead crisscrossed against the grim leaden sky.

Finally, they found a brick house with a half-timbered second story that was intact save the outside wall was scathed by machine-gun fire and the windows were broken out. It was cramped and damp-smelling inside, but there was some dust-laden furniture and even a grandfather clock with a bird's nest built into the face. Looking at it, Creel had to wonder how many times some aproned peasant woman, her back sore from churning butter, her hands white with flour, had looked at that clock face and waited for her men to come in from the fields, clumping boots dusted with wheat chaff.

Another world. Another existence. *This place will never know that peace and solid contentment again*, he thought. *It will never know tired backs settling into feather beds and old women sweeping children into dreamland with twice-told tales and kettles of soup steaming atop blackened stove gratings on Sunday afternoons.*

No. It will only know the cawing of crows, the scurrying of rats, the sound of leaves gathering and wind whipping through creviced walls, the spidersilk silence of gathering dust.

Filled with anguish and a bitter fatalism, he went to the window and looked out into the mist-choked streets. The breeze had picked up a bit and the fog blew along with rolling clouds of dust and fine debris.

"Nothing anywhere," Howard said after he returned from checking the rooms. "Not a scrap of food. Not a bleeding thing."

Creel found a lantern on a hook, half-filled with oil. "We'll have some light if we need it," he said.

Jameson started up the creaking stairs to the upper floor and stopped, grimy hand on the rail.

There was a sound from up there.

Like something dragged over a floor. Something heavy.

Standing there in his dirty greatcoat, dented steel helmet, and mud-caked trench boots, he looked like some little boy playing Army with his father's old uniform. His face was dirty, though unlined and impossibly smooth like it had been pressed. His eyes were huge and white and he looked like he belonged anywhere but where he was.

Just a sound, that's all it was, but it stopped everyone like they were standing in quick-set concrete.

The only thing alive about Creel at that moment was the cigarette in his lips: it was trembling. He felt a sharp stab of fear in his belly that kept cutting deeper, making a darkness that was toxic and oily spread through his vitals. It was not the fear of war. Of bullets and bombs and bayonets bisecting his stomach, nothing man-made. This was ancient. A formless, crawling terror that moved through him.

Jameson's voice, when it came, was dry as a crackling corn husk: "There's...there's something up there, Sarge."

Brilliant deduction, kid.

Kirk looked over to Creel and for the first time Creel saw that it was alive inside the man: fear and indecision. It was infesting him to the point that he was nearly unrecognizable. No more stiff upper lip or confident eyes or hard set to his mouth...no, his face was greasy with sweat and smudged with dirt like a chimney sweep. Eyes red-rimmed and bulging from their sockets, lips pressed tight to stop his teeth from chattering. Something had just given in him and he was now a dirty, hunched-over, chinless, scraggly trench rat, a middle-aged man who had no business in this war.

"We better go have a look, hadn't we?" Creel said.

Jameson and Howard nodded. Kirk did not move so Creel went over to him, patted him on the back and slid the Webley revolver from the sergeant's holster.

Poor guy had frozen right up.

He led them on a wild run through the living dead and did not bat an eye, and now...a simple noise from a shuttered room above was enough to suck the blood right out of him. It got like that sometimes in combat, Creel knew. You charged a trench and gored three enemy soldiers with your bayonet, you shot down another, skipped about on a merry lark avoiding machine-gun fire, bullets zipping around you, just so you could get close enough to toss a belt of Mill's bombs into a trench mortar emplacement. You did your duty and you didn't think twice about it. You made it through, got back with your mates...then you saw a bullet hole in your helmet that miraculously missed your skull and you fold up, start sobbing and can't seem to stop.

There's a breaking point to all.

His was last night when that living dead hag called his name and earlier today in the dugout when that...whatever *that* was...called his name again. Something broke loose inside and he was no good. Now he could feel the blood in his veins again and the wind in his lungs and he brushed past Jameson with a catty wink, looked back at Howard and the still immobile Sergeant Kirk. He did not feel betrayed by Kirk's momentary weakness. In fact, he felt stronger and his respect for the sergeant increased.

"Come on, son," he told Jameson, lighting the lantern, knowing this was what Burke would have done. "We'll soon sort this shit out."

Up the stairs then, feeling his strength abandoning him as nerves set in, as shadows pooled and lengthened, as things were heard scratching in the walls and others were sensed in the ganglia at his spine. A short, low corridor above. Two doorways. He knew even then which it would be. His fist sweating on the revolver, he kicked the nearest door open and a rolling wave of hot putrescence blew out at him and nearly put him to his knees.

"Gah," Jameson said. "That stink."

It was revolting and moist and cloying. It nearly made Creel stumble back down the stairs because he certainly did not want to look upon anything that smelled like that. Sucking in a shallow breath through his teeth, he stepped forward, holding the lantern high, night-black shadows swimming around him like eels.

What he saw made him step back because he was not really sure what it was he was looking at...just a swollen white mass spreading over the floor, a fermenting, yeasty excrescence.

It was a corpse.

Someone had died up here and instead of their remains crumbling away, they had *grown* in the damp shuttered darkness like a fleshy mushroom. He could see the basic outline of a skeleton—a grinning skull, a basket of rib staves, a pipe cleaner arm, a knee drawn up—all of it covered in a soft white pulp that had risen like bread dough turning the corpse into a great fruiting body that had ripened like a juicy peach, sprouting and budding and blossoming. Tendrils of that white decay had spread over the floor and grown right into the planks and up the walls like climbing vines in a cobwebby, lacey filigree that even hung from the ceiling in threads and ribbons.

It was disgusting to look at and worse to contemplate for given time, Creel thought, the creeping charnel rot would have invaded every last stick and board in the house until it all came down in a glistening fungoid mass.

"Who you suppose it was?" Jameson said, holding his nose.

Creel shrugged, staring at the oily gray toadstools that filled the eye sockets and sprung jaws in great clusters. "A peasant maybe. An injured soldier that crawled up here to die..."

"But we heard something move."

"Maybe it was that...*mass* weakening the timbers."

The words had barely left his mouth when the entire pulpy fungal mass shivered like jelly. Then it did it again. And Creel plainly saw a viscid wave pass through the thing like a breaker heading ashore in a sea of gelatin.

"Something in there," Jameson said.

Creel did not dare speak. For whatever it was, he was certain that it was somehow responding to their voices or the vibrations of the same. That wave shuddered to a rest in the lower regions of the corpse and from between the legs there was a wet, tearing sound as the membranes of soft rot were sheared.

Both Jameson and Creel saw it.

They saw that fleshy mound between the corpse's legs rip open and two tiny hands emerge that were waxy and gleaming, oddly boneless in their rubbery contortions.

Jameson let out a wild scream and just started shooting, he put three rounds into the mass where the rest of thing must have been and it stopped moving...those hands seemed to curl and wither, withdrawing back into the body cavity.

A *woman*, Creel thought with a madness scratching in his brain. *Died pregnant...only what was in her did not die, it gestated in moist putrid blackness, it came to term in her rotting womb, something inhuman, something unbelievable, and something somehow related to everything else that's going on.*

They came down the stairs, faces pasty and stomachs in throats, but they did not report on what they had seen and nobody asked for the war came to life again and they heard the distant *thump-thump-thump* of heavy guns sending out shells. They went shrieking over Chadbourg and a few hit nearby with resounding explosions that shook the earth. They were pretty close and Creel figured they landed out in the cemetery. Overhead, the shells were coming and going, the Canadians and the Hun exchanging pleasantries.

"We're right in the middle," Howard said.

The shells started landing inside the village, throwing rubble into the air, knocking down walls and opening immense craters in the narrow streets. A house across the way took a direct hit and was literally thrown up into the air, raining down as bricks and burning lathes and sticks and debris.

"We better get out of here," Kirk said.

As they crouched near the doorway two and then three shells hit around them, the shock waves sending them to the floor, plaster falling around them, nails ejected from walls. Outside there were clouds of dust competing with the mist and then all grew quiet.

For a moment, then two.

Then more shells were coming but they landed in the village with an almost gentle *pop, pop, pop*. Not high-explosive ordinance, these were shells of a different variety and everyone knew what they were just by the sounds.

"Gas," Kirk said. "Masks, everyone."

For the next twenty minutes one gas shell after another hit, the streets not only thick with fog and blowing dust, but vaporous clouds of phosgene and mustard gas. It all combined together into a heavy, consuming soup that brought visibility down to ten or twelve feet at best.

Creel had been at the Second Battle of Ypres when the gas shells were dropping all around them and men were dying in numbers. One enterprising medical officer in the trench told the men to urinate into their handkerchiefs and press them to their mouths, that the ammonia in their urine would neutralize the chlorine gas. Creel had tried like hell to pee, but nothing came out, his penis seeming to pull into itself like a snail seeking the safety of its shell. Another soldier pissed in his hankie for him and never was he so glad to press another man's urine to his lips.

But that was chlorine.

And he already knew from the smell that they were dealing with phosgene and mustard agents. The only thing that could be done was to keep the masks on and keep out of any concentrated clouds, for the mustard could burn right through cloth and continue burning into your flesh.

When Jameson made for the door, breathing hard beneath his mask, Sergeant Kirk pulled him back. "Let it dissipate," he said, his voice hollow and distant behind his trench mask.

They waited as the gas settled, four men in hot masks, staring around through bug-eyed ports, all riven with fear for gas was the one thing that terrified everyone.

"Somebody outside," Jameson said. "I saw them."

Creel began to feel that fear building in him. It was too soon for the Hun to arrive; they would wait until the gas had done its work before they came storming in. No, whoever it was, it certainly was not the Germans.

They all pressed in near the window, the shutters gone, the glass long broken out of it. And, yes, out in the billowing, blowing fog and gas they could see forms moving, dozens of them. They were staying within the periphery of mist, not showing themselves, just massing in numbers.

Creel heard a pounding.

Everyone went still, tense.

"The kitchen," Kirk said in a weak voice. "Somebody's knocking at the kitchen door...listen..."

The knocking came again: slow, relentless, almost mechanical in its complete lack of rhythm.

Creel, steeling himself, pulled the Webley pistol from his pocket, muttering, "I suppose...I suppose someone should see." Nobody volunteered to go with him and he was neither surprised at that nor disheartened. He moved away from them, keeping in a low crouch and he was not sure why. He went down the short corridor, feeling the insistent thud of his heartbeat at his temples. Sweat ran down his face inside the mask. Gently, easily, he pushed open the door and went in there, expecting the very worst and knowing he would not be disappointed. The door was heavy, wooden and latched.

The pounding went on.

The door trembled in its frame.

Through the broken window he saw them standing out there, ranks and ranks of them crowding in like flies: children. Probably the same ones that were haunting No-Man's Land. They pressed up to the missing window pane, dead things with faces that were almost phosphorescent in their whiteness, puckered and seamed like they'd been underwater a long time, wormholes drilled into them. Their eyes were red-rimmed, a glaring translucent silver. They were all smiling, schoolboys and schoolgirls, but those grins said nothing of happiness. They were crooked, tortured grimaces. They reached leathery hands towards the window, nails splintered and packed with black grave dirt.

"*Let us in,*" they said together, a whispering choir.

The door rattled as they pounded on it with more and more grave-cold fists and Creel stumbled away, a dreamlike sort of terror flooding through him like he was hallucinating, his mind unraveling one skein at a time.

Finally, he let out a choking gasp and fled for the others and that's when he heard the strangled screams. The dead children had flooded in and neither Sergeant Kirk nor his two riflemen got off a single shot. The children were like locusts, swarming, infesting, coming through the door and crawling through the window, more and more all the time, just as thick as graveworms in carrion.

Creel fell back, stunned.

He saw seven or eight of the little monsters take Howard down while another—a little girl in graying cerements—stripped off his gas mask, clutching his terrified face in her white little hands. Then she opened her mouth, yawning it wide and black like a manhole, and from the channel of her throat came a hissing yellow gas that enveloped Howard's face. He screamed, high and long, until his lungs began to come apart and his thrashing face began to blister and burst with spreading lesions and pitted ulcers. His face quite literally melted like tallow, running and streaming. They got Jameson the same way, breathing out their toxic breath of blister agents, phosgene, and deadly mustard gas.

As Creel heard the door in the kitchen come off its hinges and the undead children took notice of him, he broke for the stairs, taking one last look and seeing them dragging Kirk away by the legs. His mask was gone, his face hanging in blistered flaps. "*Help me,*" he wheezed. "*Dear God, help me...*"

But Creel couldn't help him; he was beyond help.

He raced up the stairs, breathing hard in his mask. Again, the two doorways before him in the dimness. He knew what one led to, but he was going for the other. As he paused before the room with the weird fruiting corpse in it, listening for the sounds of hell following, he heard something that sent fingers of panic threading through him.

In the room, behind that door...*movement.*

Not a subtle movement as before...no, this was a big sound, a *huge* sound that made him lose his balance, fumble against the wall so he did not go flat out. He felt a very real need to scream, but his tongue felt like it was slippery in his mouth, oily and sliding.

In the room, those sounds...

Like knotted roots being yanked up from stony soil.

Handfuls of them pulled from the earth.

That's what he was hearing along with sort of a moist shifting noise, a sort of slithering, and a dry hollow moaning. Then...footsteps, dull and dragging, something brushing the walls in there like vines rustling in the wind...a stench of vegetable decay and woodrot...

The door began to whisper open.

He saw a white pulpous hand reaching out of the darkness.

Then he was through the other door, throwing it shut behind him. As the children flooded up the stairs and that nameless germinating thing scratched at the door, he threw the shutters open and climbed out, trying to ease himself down the wall like a monkey and succeeding in dropping about twelve feet to a cobbled alley.

He saw two of the children right away coming out of the mist at him, hands held out to make contact. Their shrouds were but filthy shifts stained with grave-soil and grave-drainage, faces like those of grinning white clown-puppets, eyes the color of moonlight on water. They were filled with poison gases as if they had sucked them up like sponges....gas steamed out of them in wisps and slow-turning tendrils, rising from mouths, innumerable holes and crevices in their faces and flesh.

Creel did not hesitate for one moment.

He ran right through them knocking them aside, back into the fog where they seemed to dissolve and become part of it, two columns of corpse-gas.

He had no true idea where he was in the village and everything was crowded, compressed, debris laying in hills and mounds, huge craters filled with black water opening at his feet. Alone. He was alone now and he knew he was alone and the idea of that was something he did not dare contemplate. Not yet. Not here. He groped through the mist, edging along the bullet-pocked brick façades of buildings, staring up at blank windows looking down upon him, crawling over blasted, crumbling walls of stone, limping down narrow streets that were gray and misting.

And then—

For one moment, one that put him down on his knees, he saw something in the mist that could not see him. Just for a moment. It came out of the fog and was enshrouded by it just as quickly. A woman. A woman in a white bridal gown. She was feeling her way along a wall with outstretched fingers, looking for something and perhaps some*one*.

Creel just waited there silently until she passed.

He knew she hadn't heard him. In order to hear you needed ears and in order to have ears you needed a head and this woman had been missing that vital accoutrement. Just a wandering trunk.

Madness most certainly insinuating itself by this point, Creel came stumbling down a low hill, liking the sound of his muddy boots on the cobbles, the sound of rain dripping, the way the fog was a great hungry ghost trying to eat him—

And he screamed.

Screamed because it was there, waiting for him: the thing from the cavalry post. It still wore its tomb-filthy shroud, a great and graying winding sheet that covered its head in a loose hood and its outstretched arms in yards of worm-eaten graveyard cloth. Plumes of fog rose up around it, making it look like it was smoldering.

"Creel," it said in a voice of subterranean damps, "Creeeeeeellll—"

Then he was running again, slipping through the mist, hiding, waiting, rising to run again, knowing that those children were out there in numbers and that even if he managed to avoid them, he could never, ever avoid the shrouded thing...it would find him wherever he went.

He stumbled into an open square.

A dozen men trained rifles on him.

"Hold your fire," someone said. "He looks...almost human."

Creel dropped to his knees, shivering, holding himself, sobbing behind his gas mask.

He was taken inside a ruined building and soon, the gas dissipating sufficiently, all removed their masks. He found himself in the company of a reconnaissance patrol of the Canadian 1st Light Infantry.

A tall, handsome medical officer with stark, haunted eyes said, "You can return with us to the lines. My name is—"

"Hamilton," Creel said with something of sneer. "Doctor
to the dead."

21
The Corpse Factory

"You'll excuse my deceit, I hope," said Dr. Herbert West to me,
"but after you told me what was happening, I somehow lacked the
fortitude to confess to my crimes. I knew if I had admitted my foul
deeds you would have no longer helped me and I so dearly needed your
help...the reanimation of the dead is...is not a solitary pursuit. It is not
something one does alone by candle light.

"You see, old friend, I became somewhat fixated with the idea of
mass reanimation. I needed a group of cadavers that had all fallen at the
same time, sharing the exact or near-exact moment of death. It would be
a comparative study, you understand, wherein I would be able to
establish a certain modus operandi as to why certain animals rise up at a
certain time and others need more time for the reagent to regenerate
metabolic processes. So...when I heard about those children gassed
during the shelling of the orphanage at St. Bru...I could not help myself.
They were buried instantly in a common grave and it was there I went,
mere hours after their interment.

"I did not go alone. You will recall a certain Monsieur Cardoux
that I had become somewhat reliant upon in my researches? Cardoux
was the undertaker employed by the Army to bury not only our dead but
the Hun who had fallen within our perimeter. He was not well liked, as
you can recall, by either peasant or soldier. Both would turn away from
him in the street when they saw him coming with his boxy old hearse
towed by a single draft horse. The children of the villages...yes, they
would spit at him, throwing stones and shouting, "Allemands!
Allemands!" when they knew he had a berth filled with German corpses.
He was an odd sort, certainly, well known for his criminal dealings and
shady operations. I can see him even now—his dirty old coat, the red
scarf at his throat, the moth-eaten black satin top hat he wore so
proudly. His beady rodent's eyes, leering grin of yellow teeth. Yet...he
was of use to me and I had full authorization to use the Hun remains as
I so pleased.

"Well, it was to the cemetery at St. Bru that Monsieur Cardoux
and I went that very night, those unfortunate little waifs cold only a
matter of hours. Cardoux had been paid well, but as I saw him there,
skulking about the fresh graves with his shovel, a ghoulish figure to say

the least, I knew the matter before us was more than a matter of monetary compensation.

"Cardoux, you see, had something of an unsavory, unnatural fixation with the dead. I had seen it in his buzzard eyes many times, the carnal twist to his swollen pink lips. Do I dare even mention the shocking, nauseous activities it was rumored he partook of? The unholy grave-wares it was rumored his small stone cottage in the wood was decorated with? The grisly grinning death masks upon the walls so meticulously preserved and presented? The blasphemous trophies of mummified children frozen in gruesome poses of play? The grave-loot and charnel trinkets that he displayed with sardonic obsession? The locks of hair braided into funereal ropes that dangled from the ceiling? The revolting shelves of infant's skulls? The tanned heads and bone sculptures, the jeweled necklaces of teeth and the memento mori volumes bound in human skin? Yes, a thoroughly vile creature was our Monsieur Cardoux, graveworm, corpse-rat, a grinning, drooling deviant who—I later learned—shared his bed with that tiny, unspeakable golden-haired cadaver.

"Given time, oh yes, Cardoux would have been hanged by the peasants, perhaps his entrails would have been torn out with iron hooks and burned in the traditional way.

"But listen: to the cemetery at St. Bru we went, two skulking grave-robbers, resurrectionists in more than name, I assure you. The children, as I have said, were interred in a common grave. So beneath that pale harvest moon, cloaked by the crepuscular shadows of grotesque graveyard trees, we began to dig. Down into the black, moldering earth as the sepulchers and tomb-angels crowded about us. It was simple enough work. The boxes were four feet down. Deep enough to discourage the wild dog packs and tunneling graveyard rats, but not too deep for the weary workmen and their grim chore. We opened the communal grave and, one by one, we unearthed those small, pathetic plank boxes, scraping them free of dirt, flicking obscenely swollen earthworms aside. We opened each box and of the forty-seven cadavers within, only thirty-two were of use to me. We laid them out on the ground, single-file, moonlight washing their dead little faces an even boneyard white. Carefully then, Cardoux holding the lantern for me—and breathing quite hard, not out of exertion but some unnamable, abhorrent passion—I made the necessary incisions at the base of the skulls and injected each with a necessary concentration of the reagent.

"It took about thirty minutes.

"And thirty minutes later, there was still no reaction. I was encouraged by supple limbs and the pliability of muscles and tendons, but

I was unable to record any significant rise in metabolic temperature. I had given each a pre-measured dose that was less than used for an adult taking into account overall body mass. But nothing happened...or almost nothing. Some twenty minutes after I had injected the animals I noticed something not necessarily encouraging but certainly disturbing: their eyes were open. Every single last child had their eyes open and this after they had been gummed shut before the makeshift funeral. I examined each by the light of the lantern and those eyes were open, glistening like wet stones, almost brilliant and sparkling with vitality. Lips were pulled into pale smiles that were almost mocking.

"Yet...nothing was happening. It was almost as if they were playing possum, as insane as that sounds. Something about them unsettled me in ways I cannot describe. But it was a failure. Nothing more, nothing less.

"Cardoux kept staring into their faces, illuminating their grave-pallor with the lantern. 'Look at these little darlings, eh?' he said to me. 'Ah, it is as if they would wake at any time...can you not feel it?' I pretended I was unaware of his somewhat unwholesome attentions to certain handsome blonde girls, that macabre craven gleam in his eyes, the drool that hung from his lips. He volunteered to re-box them and re-inter them himself. 'A great surgeon and scientist such as yourself, Dr. West...he should not be bothered with such unpleasantries, eh? Let Cardoux take care of it while you run along. No, no, have no fear, my friend, for I will not be alone. My fine little darlings and sweet dumplings will keep me company far into the night...'

"I shouldn't have allowed it. I do not claim by any means, of course, to be of the utmost moral and ethical fiber where my work is concerned, but there are certain disagreeable things that sicken even I. Oh, I knew full the obscene attentions that Cardoux would impress upon those sleeping angelic forms...yet, thoroughly depressed and disheartened by what I considered another abysmal failure...I left him to it. And it was only several days later, after a marathon session of surgery at the aid station, that I knew I could not let the matter rest. I made inquiries of Monsieur Cardoux, but to my astonishment and ever-growing unease, he could not be located. I went so far as to contact Captain Fleming, the Corps Burial Officer—or, as the Tommies called him, the 'Body Snatcher', the 'Cold Meat Specialist'—but even our dour Captain could not help me. That's when I knew something had happened. Something horrible, yet, considering Cardoux's shall we say 'peculiarities', not unwarranted, hmm?

"It was through Fleming that I tracked down the grimy, crumbling hovel in the dark wood where Cardoux squatted when not involved in more funerary pursuits. It was just after sunset when I arrived alone and I found his tall, narrow, evil-looking peasant's hovel darkened, threaded in shadows of the blackest coffin silk. Repeated knockings upon the heavy, ivy-hung door brought no response. Finding the door unlocked, in I went. The stench of the charnel was immediate and I found it most repellent even with my nose which was somewhat jaded from the odiferous emanations of my laboratory and assorted battlefield litter.

"I immediately sought and found an oil lantern and there is no need to describe what I saw as I have already sketched that out for you. In the flickering orange-yellow light, shivering beneath the cold marble leering of his collection, shadows crawling about me like hell-spawned imps, each step revealed more unnamable, hideous sights in that museum of the catacomb. For everywhere was the blasphemous plundered tomb-loot and disinterred faces of the undertaker's ghoulish obsession. But it was not these things which made me perspire and chatter my teeth, but it was what I saw in the large high-timbered room amongst the moldering oblong boxes: the remains of Monsieur Cardoux, a mangled corpse riven throat to belly. But not alone, oh no. For crouched over him, their teeth sharpened upon his bones, were the children. They looked up at me with their vaulted eyes, grave-pallid faces pulling into sepulchral grins that are nearly indescribable. Bits of gore dropped from their mouths and I fled, dear friend, I burst from that house of horrors, a mad and gibbering thing. For, you see, they called me by name. They knew me."

This was the story told to me by West upon the morning of my wedding day. If it was intended as a gift, it was of the most dreadful variety. Yet, it certainly explained things and justified certain fears of mine. I now knew why he asked me if I had seen anyone on my trip out to his workshop; he was firmly convinced that the children were watching him, making no threatening overtures as of yet, but studying him intently for reasons he would not dare admit to me. But I knew it had something to do with a conspiracy of some sort directed against him by the dead risen by his hand.

It was but the first tragedy of that day I shall never forget.

At the chapel in Abbincour, I took the hand of my betrothed that day. If I could but capture the essence of Michele LeCroix standing there at the altar in her white bridal gown, the sun arcing through the stained glass windows and surrounding her in a halo of purity. But I cannot. Hers was a clean beauty, fresh, vibrant, and breathtaking as she stood there, tall and angular, looking upon me with her huge dark eyes, her olive skin contrasting the flawless white of her gown and lace. That is how I shall always see her. And that, you see, is in fact my *final image of her before that immense German shell came screaming through the air, landing just outside the church. It was fired—I later learned—by a gigantic siege gun, a 420mm Howitzer. The shell itself weighed well over 800 pounds. When it exploded, it took out the entire western wall of the chapel which had stood for some three centuries by that point. The wall literally vaporized, the chapel went to matchsticks, and all present save for a few were buried in an avalanche of rubble and debris, most mangled beyond recognition and crushed to pulp. I remember coming to as I was being dragged from the blazing, shattered husk of the church by West and Colonel Brunner. I fought free of them, completely out of mind, hearing the screams of the dying echoing in my ears, and I recall hearing Brunner say, "Dear God, man, don't go in there! Don't look at her!"*

But I did.

Coughing, eyes filled with dust, my uniform in rags, I crawled through the wreckage as what remained of the chapel threatened to fall. And there I found my Michele. Her dress was dirty, burnt in places, but nearly intact as was her body. But she had been cleanly decapitated by a falling timber, her head smashed beyond recognition.

In the days that followed, I was offered a sympathy leave but I refused. I buried myself in my work, volunteering for any hazardous duty that would take me closer to death and closer to my Michele. Weeks later, a thin and trembling specimen, I again met up with West.

Here is what he told me:

"As you know I had great success with the secretions of the reptilian embryonic tissue in the vat. By combining these in varying quantities with the reagent I achieved incredible results—the gassed children of the orphanage were but one of them. I found, to my amusement, that if I added certain animal parts to the tissue that it absorbed them, rendered them, made them part of the great hissing pulsating whole. That fascinated me. Whether it was the corpses of rats, dogs, or spare human limbs, all were assimilated. That mass of tissue was quickly becoming a colonial life form with its own specialized organic processes and metabolic peculiarities. A few excised cells grew at a fantastic rate under the microscope if given the appropriate nourishment.

"As you also know I had for some time been reanimating various body parts and had proved, I think, that there was some ethereal biophysical connection between divided anatomies of the same animal. Well, I soon discovered that parts of different animals would react to a common brain in the same way. And it was then that I formulated a very Frankensteinian hypothesis: would it be possible, I wondered, to

assemble a specimen from the raw materials of the grave and not just imbue each separate segment with life but bring into being an entire creature? The idea dominated my research for several months. I wasted no time in assembling my specimen piecemeal from the bodies of Hun that were brought to me on a regular basis. The Hun are large people and from the remains furnished me, I selected only those of the greatest stature, building my specimen piece by piece and fragment by fragment, a giant, a specimen of physical perfection.

"Perfection? Hardly. When my labors of dissection and engineering were at an end, I had put together an immense, grotesque monstrosity held together by profuse stitchwork and surgical stapling, a bulging mass of muscle, jutting bone, and artery. But I wasted no time. I applied my reagent to the limbs, the torso, various autonomic centers of the brain and spinal ganglia...all were a failure. Oh, I made certain limbs tremble and fingers wiggle, and once the specimen opened one bleary yellow eye and fixed me with a look of absolute loathing. But that was it. About the time I decided I would take the thing apart, it occurred to me that if the tissue in the vat could wield disparate remains into a colony, why could it not do the same to my creation? Unlike my crude attempts, the tissue would absorb, assimilate, and regenerate at the cellular level.

"Using a winch, for my specimen was incredible in stature and weight, I lowered it into the vat and let it 'cook' for nearly a week. And it was at this point that I heard the fleshy throbbing for the first time from the vile steel womb. It was, I knew, the gargantuan beat of a heart and why not? My specimen had several. I was improving upon nature, you see. You may recall visiting me and hearing it for yourself. It grew stronger by the day and then one night, yes, I heard the lid of the vat open and looked upon what came crawling out—it was an abomination, a sideshow grotesquerie, a gigantic, hulking mass of distorted anatomy from a dissection room that pulled itself in my direction, gaining its feet, and looking at me with a cold, fathomless hatred and something more—a deranged, icy intelligence. It was the embodiment of not only what I had made but of what lived in that vat. Its very life-force and, dear God, its dire ambition given form.

"Oh, how that walking carcass incited every scrap of tissue in my laboratory! Things in jars and tanks and vessels underwent violent contortions as if they were trying to break free to follow that horrendous being that inched ever closer to me...limbs trembled on shelves, heads began to scream, dissected animals thrashed post mortem. Hysterical, I ran from there and never returned. And as I did so, oh yes, I saw them: the children. Their corrupt grave odor belied their appearance. They were standing outside in the rain like servants of some dark, nameless resurrected god...and I think that's what they in fact were...and are."

This is what Herbert West told me, a confession to the obscenities his scientific mind had plummeted to. It was no worse than I suspected for in every case where West's methodical, somewhat perverse intellect was involved, there was tragedy and chaos and horrors beyond human comprehension. Who better knew that than I? But he had not confessed all. That I learned in due time. After the episode of Major Sir Eric Moreland Clapham-Lee, I should have known what he would do and in fact, did. But I was blissfully ignorant at that time and revelation did not come just then. No, not until my fate intersected that of the deserted village of Chadborg.

22

Morbid Anatomy

While the soldiers watched the street for enemy incursions, Dr. Hamilton took Creel into a back room and together they smoked and it took little prodding for Hamilton to tell him the story he so badly wanted to hear. It was a quick version of events because there was no time for much else.

"And you expect me to believe that?" Creel said, his cynicism alive again, spinning like a drill bit within him, hot, relentless, boring deeper into him as it sought truth not battlefield horror stories, but...truth.

This is the truth and you have to accept it. Truth couched in fiction and fiction couched in truth, raving, demented, full-blooded, surreal and hallucinatory, but the truth, he told himself. The whole nine yards, the scream-in-your-face truth.

"Whether you believe it is of absolutely no concern to me," Hamilton said, not miffed, not insulted exactly. He was beyond that. His eyes were the dismal, cheerless mirrors that reflected the war itself—graveyards, battlefields, and body dumps. And something more, something almost cabalistic and mystical lorded over by a pain that was without end.

And Creel, feeling all the horror and pain and madness of the past few months coming back at him, biting into his throat with teeth, began to curse him, to shout at him, to call him every rude, loud, boorish and ultimately meaningless name he could think of.

Hamilton said nothing.

His face was absolutely blank; he was untouchable.

The patrol moved out then and Creel tagged behind. Out of the rubble and twisted streets of wreckage and into the surrounding countryside which was ravaged, torn open, bleeding a sap of mud and brown stinking water. The fog still held and it was a grim world as the sun sank and the darkness crept up from hollows and ditches. The entire area around Chadbourg was a flooded trench system with staved-in bunkers, shattered stone and sandbag ramparts, collapsing dugouts and the remains of men, horses, ammunition wagons and mangled artillery pieces sunken into the earth.

Ten minutes after darkness found them, the world exploded with gunfire.

The darkness at either horizon was lit by flashing lights as heavy guns on both sides began to exchange salvos and the earth began to tremble as if from a distant quake. Shells were bursting and ammo dumps on both sides went up in great blazing pyres that painted the sky with guttering red light. The artillery officers were marching their salvos at each other's lines and soon enough the countryside surrounding Chadbourg was near to ground zero and shells were landing everywhere and men were being thrown down face-first in the mud.

"MAKE FOR THE TRENCHES!" someone cried. "TAKE COVER! TAKE COVER!"

Creel was knocked into a mud pool right atop two bodies in an advanced state of putrefaction. They were the only things that kept him from drowning in the slop. They were bloated like fleshy barrels and they *popped* when he fell on them, dissolving into a gray-white jelly beneath him as he madly scrambled to be free, hot gases of decay filling his head and making his eyes water. He fought free, pulling an entrenching tool from his belt and sinking it into firmer earth, pulling himself free of carrion.

The platoon was scattered as whiz-bangs and heavy shells erupted all around them, tearing men to pieces. The survivors leapfrogged from shell-hole to shell-hole, barely avoiding red-hot shrapnel that flew through the air in cutting arcs. Mud and dirt and water were thrown high above, coming back down again in rains of filth. The shellfire was stirring up the old battlefield, bringing up buried stenches of decomposed bodies and pockets of chlorine gas, a dozen pungent odors competing against the stink of cordite and burnt powder. Yellow and scarlet flares burst overhead, filling the mist with wavering shadows.

The Tommies made for the trenches and jumped into them with cries of horror, for the dirty water was deep with Hun corpses that went to a sludge of liquid putrefaction beneath their trench boots. They fought through the corpses and standing water as salvos of shells battered the earth around them.

By the time Creel managed to crawl over there, he saw rolling clouds of green and white smoke coming over the trenches in dense columns, mixing with the mist, forming a ghastly pall that swallowed everything, separating men but a few feet apart. It cleared somewhat after ten or fifteen minutes, but never went away entirely, just drifting around in fuming patches that hemmed the platoon quite neatly into their private hell.

"Something," a voice said, "something out there..."

Creel peered over the ruptured sandbags, digging his boots into the muddy trench wall. He had hoped to see a row of Hun helmets and fixed bayonets charging in their direction, but what he saw was something quite different.

Figures...forms...skeleton-shadowed apparitions rising up from the bubbling brown mud, from pools and lagoons and bogs of corpse-slime. In whole and in piece, Hun in rotted uniforms and Tommies with blank fish-white eyes and puckered holes for mouths, peasants with rotted faces of graveyard ooze, and the children, of course, ghost-faced, hollow-eyed, clouds of poison gas rising from their shriveled mouths like steam.

Creel saw them as he knew he would see them, ranks of them rising at every quarter. Like twisted, distorted things seen through a cracked window pane, they pulled themselves up in grim battalions, running with ochre-brown mud.

He saw a Tommy not ten feet away suddenly disappear in a flurry of reaching white hands that came from the trench walls and floor and the gurgling water that sluiced around his waist. Many of them were not attached to anything but limb shanks. He screamed as they tore at him, joints popping and ligaments snapping, rendering him to a dismembered flailing thing like themselves.

The Tommies were shooting, throwing grenades, hacking the dead apart with trench knives and bayonets and still their numbers swelled, more rising all the time like maggots—white and wriggling and voracious—abandoning graying meat for something sweeter.

The living dead came in waves of carrion washing ashore on a charnel beach of white gleaming bones, piling up into great ramparts of festering rot that were hideously alive, hideously animate, creeping and slithering, stumbling about on skeleton legs and pulling themselves forward on their bellies like corpse-rats.

As Creel screamed and fell into a black hole within himself, he saw hands crawling about like white bloated spiders. He saw hopping legs. Undulating torsos. Inching trunks. Things walking about with nothing above the waist...and still more fingers broke through the mud-scum and more tombstone faces floated to the surface of black pools.

The night became a surreal shadow-world backlit by blazing stumps and burning sandbags, described by rolling pockets of fog, punctuated by screams and gunfire and the occasional shell tossing earth up in fiery plumes like lava from volcanic cones.

He pulled himself up out the trenches as they were infested by the undead. He crab-crawled over the blasted earth, swimming across flooded bomb craters, navigating skeleton forests, picking his way through jawless skulls, jutting femurs and ulnas, yellowing ribcages and obscenely white lengths of vertebrae. Slicked with dirt and the slime of carrion, he found a dugout up above the water line and fell into it, landing on a heap of rubble that gave way and dropped him into a hollow filled with a few inches of rank water.

"Hello, mate," a voice said as he pulled himself free. "You'll give my best to Dr. West, won't you?"

In the flickering light of fires and descending flares, Creel saw a Tommy sitting there in a mildewed uniform. His face was like something braided from yellow, black, and vividly red ropes. Each alive, each horribly undulant. A slick green corpse-worm slid from his left eye socket and another from the cavity of his nose and then a dozen were coming out, splitting his face lengthwise and sideways, and the flesh was crumbling, dropping away in clots and loops, leaving something behind like a grinning fright mask feathered with strings of tissue. That grinning mask kept smiling until it burst apart in a wild, hysterical cackling that rolled into the night becoming part of the chaos that was breaking open in every conceivable direction.

Creel dragged himself from the dugout, moving over bones and through slime and ooze and mud. Then he fell into the muddy depths of the trench, sliding on his belly into the water like a seal. Clawing up walls of smooth moist clay, he saw a flapping gray shape above him and uttered a choking cry as his throat filled with a thick mass of terror he could not swallow away.

It was the thing from the cavalry post, the thing from Chadbourg...that malevolent shrouded graveyard angel.

Only it wasn't.

Just a scarecrow, he realized with a dry laugh in his throat. *Just a scarecrow.*

The shroud had been hung from a couple iron poles shoved into the earth that had been used as a framework for sandbags that were now blasted away. The thing had abandoned its winding sheet now. It was no longer hiding and Creel had the craziest feeling that it wanted him to know this, that there was something darkly symbolic in this offering of graying, slime-spattered cerements.

The shells were still coming intermittently, gouts of white and yellow smoke mixing in with the ground fog into a murky haze. The men of the 1st, those that were still alive, were firing and crying out. Creel was hearing other sounds, too, moist tearings and wet snappings, unpleasant sounds like boiled chicken peeled from bone.

And screaming.

"NO! NO! NO! PLEASE DON'T TOUCH ME! GET AWAY! OH DEAR GOD, GET AWAY—"

That scream tore through the night, raging and barely human, the sound of absolute animal fright and human despair. Then it cycled off into nothingness.

Another scream, somewhere off in the mist and shadows, terminated by a wet, meaty sort of sound like a cleaver sinking into a shank of beef. Then another. And another. And still another. Then Creel knew: whatever was out there, whatever was slaughtering the men, it was moving down the trench in his direction, killing anything that got in its way. Rifles fired. Revolvers. A grenade went off. But none of it could stem the black tide of whatever was rushing through the trenches and Creel had a pretty good idea what it was and what it wanted.

The water was up to his knees and he ran through it, slipping and sliding on the muck that covered the trench floor, tripping over buried things and losing his footing, falling, getting up, his mind gone white with panic.

"Oh...God...oh God," a soldier called out and Creel turned to see a figure coming out of the fog, limping, shambling, holding

itself upright by sheer force of will. In the light of the flares and flames, he could see that the soldier's face was a mask of bloody strings and ribbons like something had tried to tear it free from the bone beneath and only been partially successful. There were four ruts peeled from the left cheek to the right temple, the remaining eye just a red scarified pit.

"Run!" the soldier said with what life was left to him. "Run while you still can..."

And then something...a gigantic grotesque shape...came out of the fog and took hold of him and neatly tore him in half like he was nothing but a doll stuffed with rags, casting his remains aside and vaulting forward.

Creel ran, fell face first in that polluted water and came out of it, mad with fear, trying to claw his way up the trench wall, fingers digging into soft clay that oozed between his knuckles. Sobbing, he slid back into the water and shivered beneath the icy shadow of the thing that towered over him, the thing that exhaled a hot breath of gnawed corpses.

"Oh please..." he said.

"Creel," it said to him, reaching down with immense gnarled hands. "You're one of us..."

23
Catalyst

Make no mistake about it, we were torn apart in the flooded trenches outside Charbourg. Some men died gallantly in the shell-fire, but other men were reduced to whimpering things when they saw what our true enemy was out there, the walking dead that came slithering from their mephitic holes to rage a war of extermination against the living.

We were scattered in every direction and we did what we could, but men to each flank were dying. The Hun had buried their dead everywhere in the trenches—in the floor, in the walls, and that did not take into account all the other corpses in the mud. As I looked around for survivors, ducking every time a shell screamed overhead or erupted in a column of mud and black water, I did not—and could not—know what had reanimated so many. Certainly, West was responsible for some of it...but not this many. Even that megalomaniacal brain could not conceive of a mass resurrection on such a scale.

There was another factor.

A catalyst.

It was not until I found three soldiers who were putting up a fierce defense that I knew what that catalyst was. As the dead poured forward and the soldiers literally blasted them into fragments—some were so rotten and waterlogged from the mud holes and lakes of stagnant water that they burst apart—the earth began to tremble. The water boiled in the trenches. Sandbags collapsed and dugouts crumbled to rubble. A single limbless tree fell over.

The catalyst showed itself.

Not fifteen feet from us it burst from the muddy earth in a yellow, pink, and gray-white mass of surging corpse-jelly. It pushed itself up, hiding no more, a great pulsating, noisome coagulation of tissue in horrible, surging motion...it kept coming and coming, rising up into a great glistening wave of noxious flesh that was easily twenty feet high and twice that in volume.

The men screamed as it continued to rise from a great jagged cleft in the earth like a birth canal.

As sickened as I was, I did not scream.

I knew what it was, you see.

This was some great monstrous mutation formed out of West's vat of reptilian embryonic matter. When the Germans shelled the barn, West's original lab, completely destroying it...they had not destroyed what was in that vat. It had escaped and tunneled underground like a monstrous worm, breeding in the darkness, suckling itself upon corpse-fat, corpse-meat, and the rich marrow of thousands of bones sunken into the mud of Flanders. West had another vat, a larger one, germinating at his other workshop in the farmhouse—or had—but this massive organism was part of the original. I knew that without question.

As the men cried out, several going insane, I just waited for that blobby mass to fall over me and squeeze the life from me, make me part of its slithering immensity. But that did not happen. The Hun fired a devastating salvo at us—high-explosive rounds followed by incendiaries. They struck the creature, blasting it into fragments, into a pustulant rain of filth and hot drainage and spongy tissue that rained to earth and then went up in a massive fire storm as the incendiaries struck.

The soldiers were buried alive in mud and the creature's excrescence...I survived. I crawled out of the muck and somehow found my feet, blessing the Hun for intervention and begging only one last thing of them: that they would send but one more shell to end my wretched existence.

But that did not happen either.

I saw something coming out of the mist. It walked with jerking, mechanical motions, its arms held out before it. I knew what it was. It was dressed in a rotting bridal gown, holding out gray-skinned, black-veined hands for me. It had no head, but it knew where I was and it had been looking for me for some time. I could hear the rats that nested within, the buzzing of the insects that honeycombed that walking corpse.

I should have run, I should have done something.

But it was my Michele, resurrected—I like to believe—via the tissue that had burrowed below. She came for me and I waited for her with my trench knife in hand. Tears rolled down my cheeks and something inside me withered and went black. As she got closer I could see the rotting lace, the white of purity stained with corruption—mud and drainage and coffin-slime, a spreading furry fungi.

A stink of fetid graves in my face, she took hold of me and I allowed this last embrace. Somehow, someway, I heard her voice in my mind like the sound of tinkling bells:

I AM HERE.

I brought the trench knife down, crying, shrieking, laid open by savage, cruel memory. I brought it down and kept bringing it down, slashing her into a limbless, writhing thing at my feet that I stabbed and stabbed and stabbed and right before it stopped moving with its obscene graveyard gyrations, the voice again:

BUT I LOVE YOU

PLEASE

PLEASE HOLD ME

I slashed and cut until there was nothing but a reeking, pooling mass of putrescence at my feet and then fell back, struck mad, as carrion beetles came out of her in a black oily flood and rats crawled free and then her belly opened and spewed forth a slimy, shocking pink river of squirming fetal rats that I hacked to bits.

The trench knife still in my hand, splattered with my love's remains, I staggered off into the mist waiting for the shrapnel-kiss of a shell that never did come.

24

The Conqueror Worms

"Turn and face me, Creel," came the voice that was oddly eloquent like Death himself yet garbled as if spoken through a mouthful of suet. "Look upon me."

Creel did as he was told, kneeling there in the mud and slopping brown water, clay packed beneath his fingernails and dirty water running down his face. It was not a voice you could refuse. He looked and his throat filled with hot desert sand, a choking whirlpool of it. His lungs gasping, his eyes refusing to shut out the horror they took in.

The Angel Of Death—for it could be nothing else—was a huge, hulking, bulging mass of muscle, fleshy growths, and corded artery barely contained in a stretched, shining gray skin that was intersected by black suturing, a zigzagging, overlapping maze of it that held it together. It was manlike in form, but bulbous and mounded, its misshapen head bald on one side and sprouting with irregular tufts of long greasy black hair on the other, plated machine-like beneath by a jutting, distorted skull that was trying to burst free, the nose but a skullish cavity, one eye set much lower than the other, black and juicy like a tumor, the other yellow and bright and unbearably sentient.

It stood there breathing with a deathly rasp, its barrel-like chest rising and falling, ribs slats tearing through the skin, knobs of bone protruding from holes worn in the hide. It was like something put together from a dozen separate corpses, stapled and wired and catgut-threaded, a patchwork ghoul made from human hides and oily gray lizard skin and the bristling pelts of hogs. A mortuary crazy quilt. Even its face was an assemblage. Black stitching ran from the crown of its skull, down its forehead and nose and below the jawline. Suturing lines split off it, dividing the face into thirds, then fourths, and finally fifths...each offset and sucked in by hollows or pushed out by abnormal mounds of bone so that the effect was hideous...the blurred, subhuman face of something seen through a cloudy freakshow jar.

It reached down with one hand, fingers wired to the knuckles and hung with ropy strands of skin. It was immense and fleshy, disfigured, as it gripped Creel's own. And the feel of it...like being embraced by the cold guts of a dead fish...he could feel the squirming larval motion within.

"*You've hunted death your entire life,*" it said to him, swollen black lips peeling open from pockets of scar tissue and intricate stitching to reveal glossy yellow-gray teeth. "*Now death hunts you and has found you.*"

"Please..."

It reached in his bag, emptying his collection of mortuary photos over his head like pillow down.

"Mercy?" it breathed. "*At this juncture? Really, Creel. I expected more. I have cast aside my shroud to reveal my true* nature...maybe at this hour, you would do the same...show us the ghoul within...expose it so we may gloat upon its unbearable ugliness..."

"Dear God...just let me live," Creel sobbed. "Please just let me live..."

But the creature had no intention of that. It had been pursuing him for sometime now and this was the crossroads of their fates which had been twined together from the very first, from the moment Creel had stepped upon his first battlefield and seen his first ravaged corpse and taken his first photograph for his private morgue. *"You came to see and you came to know,"* it said to him. *"Now you will SEE and soon you will KNOW..."*

Then without hesitation, it released him, grasped a few strands of loose stitching at its chest and, like a child unthreading a bootlace, pulled itself open and unwound itself and Creel screamed as what was inside came flooding out in a slimy gushing river that covered him, enveloped him, drowning him in a steaming, wriggling sea of grave-maggots. They filled the trench, rising and bursting over the banks of sandbags and he fought in their depths like a swimmer going down for the last time. His fingers broke the surface of the squirming, noxious sea, but no more. They were at his eyes, in his ears, up his nostrils and pressing through the cleft at his ass. His mouth pulled open in a demented scream of violation and they flowed down his throat, filling him, gagging him, plummeting him into loathsome charnel depths, suffocating him on the death he had sought and finally made his own.

He sank beneath the carrion graveworm waters and the reanimated, carefully-sewn husk that had held the Angel of Death within collapsed like a balloon bled of air, just a collection of yellow bones and a shroud of skin that drifted to earth like a sheet blown from a line.

And from every quarter, the dead sank back into their holes, sunless, bleached faces closing their eyes for a final time and limbs going stiff and trunks dissolving into pools of maggoty rottenness and hot gassy putridity. Soon they were only carcasses, what was inside taking wing in great buzzing black clouds of corpse-flies seeking higher plains and fresher winds.

25
Breathing Out

As you may have guessed, I was the only survivor of the reconnaissance party to Charbourg. I wandered for hours seeking a peaceful oblivion that I never found. I remember little of it. I was told that a BEF raiding party of the 12th Middlesex found me and brought me back to the lines. After that, it's a feverish blur of aid stations and casualty wards. It was some weeks before I came to my senses and when I did, when I made a full recovery—or as near of a recovery as one could hope for after what I had seen—I was repatriated with my unit only to be brought before my commanding officers for court-martial proceedings.

West was there, too.

We were being held following evidence that was gathered at West's farmhouse, which we were told was of such a grisly, deplorable, and execrable nature, that there were those who wished us to be brought before a firing squad without trial. The farmhouse was burned to the ground along with what was still in there.

No matter.

After due consideration, command decided that the court records of the investigation would be sealed and we would be discharged, honorably, with the understanding that we would never utter a word of what we did or what we saw or other blasphemous, ungodly acts we had perpetrated.

Still, at West's side, I returned to private practice in Boston. I should have despised the man and I suppose I did, but there was a magnetism to his brilliance and soon we returned to our somewhat peculiar line of research skulking about midnight graveyards and moonlit burial grounds. For we had an appointment in the skull-toothed hollows of the valley of the dead and our work was not yet done...

THE END

MOOOAAARRRR

BOOKS FROM

Severed PRESS

WHITE FLAG OF THE DEAD

Joseph Talluto

Book 1 Surrender of the Living.

Millions died when the Enillo Virus swept the earth. Millions more were lost when the victims of the plague refused to stay dead, instead rising to slay and feed on those left alive. For survivors like John Talon and his son Jake, they are faced with a choice: Do they submit to the dead, raising the white flag of surrender? Or do they find the will to fight, to try and hang on to the last shreds or humanity?

Surrender of the Living is the first high octane instalment in the White Flag of the Dead series.

RESURRECTION
By Tim Curran
www.corpseking.com

The rain is falling and the dead
are rising. It began at an ultra-
secret government laboratory.
Experiments in limb
regeneration-an unspeakable
union of Medieval alchemy and
cutting edge genetics result in the
very germ of horror itself: a gene
trigger that will reanimate dead
tissue...any dead tissue. Now it's
loose. It's gone viral. It's in the
rain. And the rain has not
stopped falling for weeks. As the country floods and corpses float
in the streets, as cities are submerged, the evil dead are rising. And
they are hungry.

"I REALLY love this book...Curran is a wonderful storyteller
who really should be unleashed upon the general horror reading
public sooner rather than leter." – *DREAD CENTRAL*

Available at www.severedpress.com, Amazon and most online bookstores

THE DEVIL NEXT DOOR

Cannibalism. Murder. Rape. Absolute brutality. When civilizations ends...when the human race begins to revert to ancient, predatory savagery...when the world descends into a bloodthirsty hell...there is only survival. But for one man and one woman, survival means becoming something less than human. Something from the primeval dawn of the race.

"Shocking and brutal, The Devil Next Door will hit you like a baseball bat to the face. Curran seems to have it in for the world ... and he's ending it as horrifyingly as he can." - *Tim Lebbon, author of Bar None*

"The Devil Next Door is dynamite! Visceral, violent, and disturbing!." *Brian Keene, author of Castaways and Dark Hollow*

"The Devil Next Door is a horror fans delight...who love extreme horror fiction, and to those that just enjoy watching the world go to hell in a hand basket" – HORROR WORLD

Dead Bait

"If you don't already suffer from bathophobia and/or ichthyophobia, you probably will after reading this amazingly wonderful horrific collection of short stories about what lurks beneath the waters of the world" – *DREAD CENTRAL*

A husband hell-bent on revenge hunts a Wereshark...A Russian mail order bride with a fishy secret...Crabs with a collective consciousness...A vampire who transforms into a Candiru...Zombie piranha...Bait that will have you crawling out of your skin and more. Drawing on horror, humor with a helping of dark fantasy and a touch of deviance, these 19 contemporary stories pay homage to the monsters that lurk in the murky waters of our imaginations. *If you thought it was safe to go back in the water...Think Again!*

"Severed Press has the cojones to publish THE most outrageous, nasty and downright wonderfully disgusting horror that I've seen in quite a while." – *DREAD CENTRAL*

Available at www.severedpress.com, Amazon and most online bookstores

DEMONMACHY
Brant Danay

As the universe slowly dies, all demonkind is at war in a tournament of genocide. The prize? Nirvana. The Necrodelic, a death addict who smokes the flesh of his victims as a drug, is determined to win this afterlife for himself. His quest has taken him to the planet Grystiawa, and into a duel with a dream-devouring snake demon who is more than he seems. Grystiawa has also been chosen as the final battleground in the ancient spider-serpent wars. As armies of arachnid monstrosities and ophidian gladiators converge upon the planet, the Necrodelic is forced to choose sides in a cataclysmic combat that could well prove his demise. Beyond Grystiawa, a Siamese twin incubus and succubus, a brain-raping nightmare fetishist, a gargantuan insect queen, and an entire universe of genocidal demons are forming battle plans of their own. Observing the apocalyptic carnage all the while is Satan himself, watching voyeuristically from the very Hell in which all those who fail will be damned to eternal torment. Who will emerge victorious from this cosmic armageddon? And what awaits the victor beyond the blood-drenched end of time? The battle begins in Demonmachy. Twisting Satanic mythologies and Eastern religions into an ultraviolent grotesque nightmare, the Messiah of Death Saga will rip your eyeballs right out of your skull. Addicted to its psychedelic darkness, you'll immediately sew and screw and staple and weld them back into their sockets so you can read more. It's an intergalactic, interdimensional harrowing that you'll never forget...and may never recover from.

Available at www.severedpress.com, Amazon and most online bookstores

GREY DOGS
IAN SANDUSKY

WHEN GOD TURNS HIS BACK ON THE EARTH

Fires blaze out of control. Looters are run through with speeding lead. Children scream as their flesh is torn by broken teeth. Firearms insistently discharge in the night air. Over it all, the moans of the infected crowd out any pause for silence.

THE EPIDEMIC SHOWS NO MERCY

Men. Women. Fathers. Daughters. Wives. Brothers. All are susceptible, and the viral infection is a death sentence. One hundred percent communicable. One hundred percent untreatable. It's making people insane, turning them feral. *Zombies.* No end is in sight, and Carey Cardinal has run out of options.

ONE SHOT AT SEEING SUNRISE

Past lives, shadowed histories and long-kept secrets will emerge, making the twisted road ahead ever more difficult to navigate as Carey will discover a foe far more dangerous than the shattered grey dogs - himself.

Available at www.severedpress.com, Amazon and most online bookstores

ZOMBIE ZOOLOGY
Unnatural History:

Severed Press has assembled a truly original anthology of never before published stories of living dead beasts. Inside you will find tales of prehistoric creatures rising from the Bog, a survivalist taking on a troop of rotting baboons, a NASA experiment going Ape, A hunter going a Moose too far and many more undead creatures from Hell. The crawling, buzzing, flying abominations of mother nature have risen and they are hungry.

"Clever and engaging a reanimated rarity"
FANGORIA

"I loved this very unique anthology and highly recommend it"
Monster Librarian

The Official Zombie Handbook: Sean T Page

Since pre-history, the living dead have been among us, with documented outbreaks from ancient Babylon and Rome right up to the present day. But what if we were to suffer a zombie apocalypse in the UK today? Through meticulous research and field work, The Official Zombie Handbook (UK) is the only guide you need to make it through a major zombie outbreak in the UK, including: -Full analysis of the latest scientific information available on the zombie virus, the living dead creatures it creates and most importantly, how to take them down - UK style. Everything you need to implement a complete 90 Day Zombie Survival Plan for you and your family including home fortification, foraging for supplies and even surviving a ghoul siege. Detailed case studies and guidelines on how to battle the living dead, which weapons to use, where to hide out and how to survive in a country dominated by millions of bloodthirsty zombies. Packed with invaluable information, the genesis of this handbook was the realisation that our country is sleep walking towards a catastrophe - that is the day when an outbreak of zombies will reach critical mass and turn our green and pleasant land into a grey and shambling wasteland. Remember, don't become a cheap meat snack for the zombies!

BIOHAZARD

Tim Curran

The day after tomorrow: Nuclear fallout. Mutations. Deadly pandemics. Corpse wagons. Body pits. Empty cities. The human race trembling on the edge of extinction. Only the desperate survive. One of them is Rick Nash. But there is a price for survival: communion with a ravenous evil born from the furnace of radioactive waste. It demands sacrifice. Only it can keep Nash one step ahead of the nightmare that stalks him-a sentient, seething plague-entity that stalks its chosen prey: the last of the human race. To accept it is a living death. To defy it, a hell beyond imagining

THE GHOST TOUCHER

Gerald Rice

"Haven't you ever picked up your keys for no reason and realized you had nowhere to go?" Israel asked. "Or picked up a pen and didn't have anything to write?"

"No," Kelly said.

"Sure you have. Everybody has. It's like having déjà vu about déjà vu."

"What?"

"You know-you remember remembering you've done a thing before, but you only remember remembering it when you're remembering it?"

"So when I'm not remembering it, I forget it?"

"You got it."

"No. No, I don't."

In a world where ghosts are an accepted reality, Stout Roost, reality star and host of the Network's The Ghost Toucher reality series has vanished. But Israel, the spiritual detective they hire, doesn't exactly have a plan to find him. Kelly Greene, a customer service rep, is tapped to assist the detective, but he quickly realizes that as far as unconventional methods go, Israel's are insane. He informs Kelly there is an afterworld and it was already populated by pesty ghosts. They also hate humans because they eventually become ghosts and are seeking a 'clean' way to exterminate us all. The two learn finding Stout is the least of their worries as they are pursued through metro-Detroit by obsessive compulsive wannabe warriors, mutants who worship an insane deity, weapons from the other side and a mysterious, perpetually pregnant, augmentative woman with a gender complex.